Johanna Lindsey

Prisoner of My Desire

HarperLargePrint

An Imprint of HarperCollins*Publishers*

A mass-market edition of this book was published in 1991 by Avon Books, an imprint of HarperCollins Publishers.

HarperCollins books may be purchased for educational, business, or sales promotional use. For information please write: Special Markets Department, HarperCollins Publishers Inc., 10 East 53rd Street, New York, NY 10022.

FIRST HARPER LARGE PRINT EDITION

Printed on acid-free paper

Library of Congress Cataloging-in-Publication Data has been applied for.

ISBN 0-06-051864-2

02 03 04 05 06 WBC/RRD 10 9 8 7 6 5 4 3 2 1

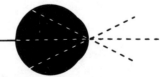

This Large Print Book carries the Seal of Approval of N.A.V.H.

Prisoner
of
My Desire

✵ I

The lady was small and fragile, but with the tall knight standing before her, her frailty was much more apparent. Her blond head reached no higher than his broad shoulders. And when his open palm cracked across her cheek, her thin body jerked to the side with the force of it. A blow like that would have easily sent her to the floor if she were not supported. But she was supported, by two of the knight's men-at-arms. They stood well behind her, her arms twisted just so to thrust her forward so they would not take a blow meant for her. This kept her upright when she might have buckled, kept her there to receive another blow, and still another.

Across the small chamber, Rowena Belleme watched. She also was being held fast by two men-at-arms, the same two who had dragged her into this chamber to witness her stepbrother's brutality. Blood trickled down the center of her chin from biting her lips to keep from screaming. Tears fell copiously over ashen cheeks. But she had not been struck herself. Like as not it would come to that if she did not give in to her stepbrother's demands after this demonstration of his seriousness, but while his patience held, he did not want to blacken her with bruises that would elicit comment at her wedding.

Gilbert d'Ambray had no such qualms regarding his stepmother, however. Lady Anne Belleme—nay, she was Anne d'Ambray now and once again a widow, now that Gilbert's father was dead—was of little use to him except as a hostage to Rowena's behavior. And there was not much that Rowena would not do for her mother. But what Gilbert wanted of her now . . .

Anne turned to look at her daughter. Her cheeks were blotched a fiery red with the imprints of Gilbert's heavy hand, yet she had shed not a tear, nor made a single sound. Her expression, so eloquent, wrung more tears from Rowena. It said plainly, **This has been done to me so often, 'tis naught. Ignore it, daughter. Do not give the cur what he wants.**

Rowena did not want to. Lord Godwine Lyons, the man Gilbert had found to marry her, was old enough to be her grandfather, in truth, her great-grandfather. And her mother had only confirmed the rumors she had heard of this old lord when

Gilbert had demanded that Anne convince Rowena to comply with his wishes.

"I know Lyons, and he is not for an heiress of Rowena's stature. Even if his age were not an issue, the man has scandals of perversion attached to his name. Never would I condone such a match."

"He is the only man willing to fight to regain her properties," Gilbert had pointed out.

"Properties your father lost through his greed."

"Nay, it is every man's right—"

"To encroach on his neighbor?" Anne cut in with a full measure of the contempt she felt for her stepson, which was not even a quarter of what she had felt for his brutish father. "To raid and make war without recourse? **To steal and force women into marriage before their husbands are even buried!** Such rights only came to men since that weakling Stephen was made king."

Gilbert had actually flushed, but more likely with anger than in embarrassment for what his father had done to Anne. In truth, he was a product of the times. He had been only a child of eight when Stephen had stolen the crown from Matilda after old King Henry died. The kingdom had split apart then, half the barons refusing to accept a woman as their ruler, the other half holding by their oaths to Matilda, and now her son Henry of Aquitaine. Hugo d'Ambray was one of the barons who had then sworn to Stephen, and so he had felt justified in killing Rowena's father, who was Henry's vassal, and then forcing Walter Belleme's widow to marry him, thereby gaining control of all of Walter's lands, which Rowena as his only child inherited, as well as Anne's dower lands. And neither Anne nor Rowena had any recourse for this injustice, certainly not from a king who had thrown the realm into anarchy.

Unlike his father, who had had a streak of malevolence to complement his brutishness, Gilbert was like most men of his day, respectful when necessary, churlish when not, and intent on filling his coffers with the fruits of other men's labors. But because he had lived seventeen years with anarchy, his policies were no different from any other baron's. Most of them might bemoan having such a weak king that the land was rife with lawlessness, but then most of them took advantage and contributed to that lawlessness.

Actually, in the three years that Gilbert had been Rowena's stepbrother, he had never said a harsh word to her, nor laid a hand to her in anger as his father had occasionally done. As a knight, Gilbert was well skilled and courageous. As a man, he was actually very handsome, with black hair and dark brown eyes that gave unease for their watchfulness. Until today, Rowena had hated him only because he was his father's son. For their own benefit and their petty wars with their neighbors, they had stripped her lands bare and taken everything of value that she and her mother had ever owned. They had broken the betrothal contract her father had made for her, keeping her unwed strictly for their own profit, so they could continue to draw what they could from her serfs' labors, and demand war service from her vassals each year.

But last year Hugo d'Ambray had thoughtlessly decided to take Dyrwood keep, which sat between one of Rowena's properties and one of his own. That was tantamount to stirring up a hornet's nest, for Dyrwood belonged to one of the greater warlords of the north shires, the Lord of Fulkhurst, who not only came to the aid of his vassal at Dyrwood, routing the besiegers and sending them back to their own borders, but then systematically set out to destroy the man who had dared try to steal from him.

Unfortunately, not only Hugo's properties became this warmonger's targets, but also those that Hugo had control of through wardship. And he found out how helpful a weak king was when Stephen refused to come to his aid, too busy with his own problems. But even though Hugo had been killed two months ago in this war that his greed had started, Fulkhurst was not satisfied. Gilbert was finding out that this particular warlord thrived on vengeance.

Gilbert had sued for peace and been refused, which had enraged him and made him determined to win back the d'Ambray lands at any cost. But the cost he had decided on was to sacrifice Rowena to the marriage bed of an old lecher. He had even told her it would not be for long, that he would soon have her back under his guardianship, for the man was two steps from the grave. But as long as she was wed to the old goat, Gilbert wanted to see a child come from the union. He had made that perfectly clear, for only in that way would he have her and her lands back, as well as Lyons' land and wealth through her child. Thusly he would obtain the resources to win back the d'Ambray properties that were now in Fulkhurst's hands.

'Twas a fine plan as far as Gilbert was concerned. It truly cost him nothing, but would gain him all that he sought—including, at long last, Rowena in his own bed. This above all else was at the heart of his plan, for he was halfway obsessed with the little flaxen-haired beauty who was his stepsister.

He had wanted her from the first day he had seen her, when she was only fifteen. But his father had refused to let him have her, pointing out that her value would be considerably decreased without her maidenhead, even though he had had no intention of marrying her off. But Hugo d'Ambray could not live forever, and Gilbert was intelligent enough to see that the damned maidenhead was not for him, and patient enough to wait until it was no longer an issue, bestowed on some future husband.

This was why Gilbert had treated her well, not wanting her to be aware of the streak of ruthlessness ingrained in him by his father. He wanted Rowena to want him as well when he finally took her to his bed. He wanted her enough that he would even have married her himself if there had been any profit in it. But since the d'Ambrays already controlled her lands, there was not. As soon as she conceived, he intended to have her, and to continue having her, even though he had every intention of marrying her off again for further gain at some future time. Getting rid of her husbands would be the easy part. Getting Rowena to develop a passion for him would not be so easy.

Unaccountably, to his way of thinking, wedding her to Lyons without her consent, which would be an easy thing to do, would set her against him. He did not see forcing her consent by beating her mother as a worse offense. Far from it. He was so used to seeing his father beat the Lady Anne, it was as if it were nothing. He did not take into consideration that Rowena, kept at Kemel keep these three years instead of with her mother at Ambray Castle, had not witnessed the same and so had grown indifferent to it, as he was. He was so certain that she would never hold ill usage of her mother against him that he was not very sure that his rough treatment of the Lady Anne would even work to sway Rowena. 'Twas merely the least of the things he could do to get her to agree to the marriage, and so had been the first he had sought to try when reasoning and pointing out the benefits had failed.

Gilbert's first mistake was in assuming that Rowena felt for her mother what he had felt for his, which was next to nothing. His second was in not expecting any kind of reaction from Rowena this soon, so he had not even looked toward her since he had begun striking her mother a few moments ago. But when he saw Anne look toward her daughter with such steady courage, he also glanced behind him, then stiffened in anger, seeing his mistakes clearly now. The girl did care for her mother, too much. Her large sapphire eyes were awash with tears. She was hurting herself to keep from begging him to stop, and that only because her mother had stated plainly that she did not condone the marriage to Lyons.

Better he had drugged her, married her to Lyons, and got even the bedding over with before she had regained consciousness, a fait accompli. Now those lovely blue eyes gazed on him with such loathing, he knew she would never desire him as he had hoped. So be it. He would still have her, and soon, but he was so enraged that it would not be as he had imagined it, his fingers closed into a fist and slammed into the side of Anne's head. She crumbled instantly, without a sound.

Rowena made the sound, a choked whimper, before she whispered, "Nay. No more."

He left the mother hanging between his men and moved to stand before the daughter. He still seethed over what his assumptions had cost him in personal gain. 'Twas there in his eyes, in his expression, and he lifted Rowena's face in his hand, forcing her to see it. But it was a measure of his feelings for her that his hand was not rough, even in his present anger. Unwittingly, he even gently wiped the tears away from one cheek.

His voice, however, was harsh in questioning, "Will you wed Lord Godwine?"

"I will."

"Will you do so with good cheer?"

Rowena stared at him blankly for a moment before she burst out, "You ask too much—"

"Nay. What will a smile cost you when it will ensure his speedy compliance with the marriage contract?"

"Is his compliance in doubt?"

"Nay, but there is no time to lose. Fulkhurst is now inactive, but only because he has just defeated Tures."

Rowena blanched at this information. She had known that two of her keeps near Dyrwood had been taken, one without even a fight, but Tures

Castle had been the largest of her father's properties, his stronghold, and was much farther north.
She had grown up in Tures. All that she knew of
love and happiness she had learned there, inside
those stone walls. Now an enemy warlord held it—
nay, enemies had held it these past three years, so
what difference to her, one or another? **She** certainly had not held it, nor did she ever expect to.
Even if Lord Godwine could win it back for her, it
would be hers in name only.

Gilbert mistook her expression and thought to
reassure her. "Do not despair, Rowena. Lyons has
become rich in bleeding his town merchants these
past twenty years that he has held Kirkburough.
The mercenaries his wealth will buy will quickly
defeat Fulkhurst and send him back to his own domain. You will have Tures back within the month."

Rowena did not answer. She had already been
told that the marriage contract had been worded to
her benefit; that her properties, once they were
won back, would be hers, not her husband's,
which meant nothing to her in this day and age
when law and justice were ignored, but would
mean everything if only Henry would come to
rule. Lyons no doubt thought to have full use of
her properties. Gilbert obviously thought to have
them back in his control, which to her mind meant
that if Lyons did not die soon enough of his old
age and ailments, Gilbert would help him along to

that end. But Gilbert wanted her to bear Lyons a child first. As she had done every day these past three years, Rowena shuddered and prayed for Henry of Aquitaine to win the throne of England. Her father had been Henry's vassal, and Rowena would swear herself to him quicker than she could blink. Then and only then might she escape Gilbert d'Ambray's control.

Instead of remarking what was in her mind, she asked Gilbert, "Does that mean my vassals will be brought to swear to me this time, or will they again be too busy fighting in your wars?"

Color stole into his cheeks. This was yet another way his father had ignored the letter of the law, for when the Belleme properties had changed ownership at her father's death, his nine vassals should have come to pay Rowena homage for the properties they now held through her, yet she had not seen one of those knights in these three years she had been kept isolated at one of Hugo's smaller keeps. Each time she had ever mentioned it, she had been fobbed off with excuses that her knights were besieged, or in the middle of a campaign, or some other such thing. Like as not her men thought her dead. That would have been the easiest way for Hugo to have gained their service without having to answer their concern for her welfare.

Gilbert said now in a hard tone that discouraged further comment, "Five of your vassals have died fighting Fulkhurst, and whether Sir Gerard lives or not is undetermined, as he had been made castellan of Tures. Likely that monster butchered him, as he has done to my own knights." He ended with a shrug that stated clearly he did not particularly care whether Gerard had been spared or not.

What color had returned to Rowena's cheeks left again. She did not question further, but only because she dreaded to know which knights still lived and which did not. Who should she blame for their deaths, Fulkhurst for striking the killing blow, or Gilbert and his father for gaining Fulkhurst's ire? God's mercy, when would this land be returned to peace?

Quietly, she asked Gilbert to have her released. At his nod to his men, she was immediately let go and started toward her mother. Gilbert's hand caught her arm and steered her instead toward the door.

She pulled away from him, but his hold was firm. "Let me go to her."

"Nay, her women will attend her anon."

"I have not seen her in three years, Gilbert," she reminded him, but should have known it would not make a difference.

"When you get yourself with Lyons' child to secure his lands will be soon enough for you to see her."

More manipulations and coercions. She could not be silent any longer, but released her feelings in a hate-filled hiss. "You are despicable, worse even than your father. At least he was honest in his cruelty!"

His hand tightened on her arm, the only indication that her words affected him. "I have only your best interests at—"

"Liar! I will do what you want, but if you tell me once more that I am to benefit by it, I will scream."

He did not argue with her. What he wanted to do was pull her into his arms and kiss her, for the fire of her fury stirred his desire for her even more than her beauty. But he did not dare even a kiss. Did she go to Lyons' bed without her maidenhead, he could repudiate her, thereby ending Gilbert's hope of getting his hands on the old lord's wealth.

So all he said was, "Then come, we ride for Kirkburough today. You will be wed tomorrow." And be in his own bed at the very first indication that she was safely breeding.

✣ 2

They arrived at Kirkburough just as the sun was setting. The gates of the town were still open, but it was to the keep overlooking the town that they rode. Rowena found it appropriate to see the high walls of this large fortress awash in a red glow, a portent reminder that she was entering hell.

Gilbert had wisely kept his own counsel during that twelve-mile journey, for Rowena had reached the point where she no longer cared what she said to him. Legally, he was her stepbrother and her guardian, and there was no one to decry that he was both of these by foul means. But if it were not for her mother, Rowena would have utterly balked and done anything to escape her present situation. She thought she might even be able to kill Gilbert, so much did she hate him after today. But she could not escape, for she had no doubt whatsoever that her mother would suffer horribly for it, and her mother had suffered enough at the hands of the d'Ambrays.

She understood more fully now why she and her mother had been separated immediately after they had been taken from Tures. If Rowena and Anne could have somehow escaped together, they could have found aid from one of the powerful magnates who were opposed to Stephen, as Walter Belleme had been. Likely Rowena would have had to marry then to protect herself from the d'Ambrays, but it could have been to a man of her choosing.

None of which mattered now. She was here, to be wed on the morrow. If only . . . God's mercy, how often she had thoughts that began so.

If only her father had not loved her so much, she could have been safely married at the tender age of fourteen, as most daughters were. Her betrothed was an honorable man. He would have waited to consummate the marriage until she was older and better capable of bearing children. But her father had not wanted to tempt that kind lord with her budding beauty, nor had he wanted to give her up so soon.

If only he had not ridden out himself to face d'Ambray's army, he might still be alive. Tures would have been besieged, but they could have escaped and gone to Henry's court, or even to one of the other lords who supported him.

If only the laws governing women were upheld, if only Henry were king . . . if only Gilbert would die. But 'twas too late even for that. She was in Lyons' keep, which put her effectively in Lyons' control, as if they were already wed. He would still marry her to have whatever it was he sought, whether Gilbert was there to force her into compliance or not.

Rowena was almost numb with despair as she mounted the stairs to the Great Hall. 'Twas immediately apparent that Gilbert had not spoken falsely of Lyons' worth. Just crossing the bailey, Rowena had counted nine household knights, and the towers and walls teemed with men-at-arms. There were more knights inside the hall, where tables were set for the evening meal with gold plates and fine linen. Even the walls displayed the lord's wealth in useless weapons of polished silver and gold, most encrusted with fine jewels.

Servants abounded, surely one or more to serve each guest, but in this Lyons did not waste his money. Their clothes were nearly rags, their bodies none too clean, their demeanor cowed to the point of trembling hands and haunted eyes, and no wonder. In the space of crossing the hall to the raised dais where Lyons sat like a king in state, Rowena saw three servants cuffed for no apparent reason, one struck so hard that he fell to the floor, only to be kicked twice where he lay unmoving so it could be determined if he was merely shirking his duties.

Rowena was so appalled by this that she stopped walking, making Gilbert jerk on her arm to get her moving again, but not before the knight who was kicking the downed man noticed her watching him and smiled at her. No shame, no contrition. He smiled.

It was a well-known fact that without any ladies present, men would behave nearly as beasts. But there were ladies present, wives of some of the household knights. Obviously, they had no effect on the men's behavior. This spoke clearly of the character of the lord of Kirkburough, for most men will do as their master does, in good or ill.

She had avoided looking toward the lord's table, putting off as long as possible what was to be her fate. But Gilbert stopped, telling her the moment was at hand. Even so, her first sight of Godwine Lyons of Kirkburough nearly made her cry out in horror. Gilbert's hand tightened on her arm, for she had taken an involuntary step backward.

'Twas worse than she could have imagined. The man wasn't just old, he looked like a corpse. His skin was a pasty white, and so deeply wrinkled there was not an inch anywhere to be seen that could be called smooth. What was left of his hair was white, except for one narrow streak of blond to attest to what the color had been. His body was so bent, he stood no taller than Rowena, who was only a few inches above five feet. His bright silk robe, trimmed at neck and sleeves with costly fur, merely made him look ridiculous.

The whites of his eyes were dark yellow. A white film covered the iron gray of one of his irises. He was almost blind. He had to come mere inches in front of Rowena to have a look at her, and she was assailed by his fetid breath, which nearly made her gag before he moved back. With crooked fingers, he pinched her cheek and cackled, revealing the only two teeth remaining in his mouth.

Gilbert was shouting the introductions, which told her the old man was also almost deaf. That was fortunate, because Rowena could not stop herself from swallowing her pride and begging.

"Please, Gilbert, do not do this to me. If you must marry me off, choose another, any other—"

"Be quiet," he hissed in her ear. "'Tis done, promises made."

Before he had her consent? "Promises can be broken," she told him.

"Nay; there is no other who would agree to all I ask."

What **he** asked for. For **his** benefit. She had lowered herself to plead with him for naught. She had even known it would be for naught. She would never beg again, not to him or any man, for only God had mercy. Men had only greed and lust.

She turned to look up at him, having to bend her head back, he was so near. And quietly, without emotion, she said, "Guard your back well, brother, ere my dagger finds it. The first chance I have, I mean to kill you for this."

"Do not speak foolishness," he replied, but uneasily, his eyes searching hers. And something in hers must have convinced him 'twas not an idle threat. He actually looked stricken when he cried out, "Rowena!"

She turned her back on him and summoned a servant to take her to whatever room had been prepared for her. If Gilbert or Lord Godwine had tried to stop her from leaving that hall, she probably would have shown them all a fine rendering of a madwoman. But neither did, and she had to stop on the darkened stairs that led up to the tower room where she was to pass the night, for her own tears, finally released, were blinding her.

❧ 3

Rowena woke with some disorientation, but it lasted only moments before she knew exactly where she was. When she had finally gotten to sleep she could not guess, but it had been long after midnight. Now she could almost feel her blood turning cold as dread seeped into her bones, keeping her immobile on the bed.

Some little light came through the high window in the tower room, but not much more than was had from the hearth and candles set about the small chamber. A long while passed before she wondered who had lit those candles and restoked the fire. And who, for that matter, had drawn her bed-curtain open? If Gilbert had dared . . .

"Do you mean to lie abed until 'tis time to face the priest?"

"Mildred?" Rowena gasped in surprise, recognizing that dear voice.

"Aye, my sweet one."

Rowena sat up and located the maid sitting on a chest that had not been there when she had first entered the room. Her own chest it was. And her own maid sitting on it.

Mildred had been her maid for as long as Rowena could remember, and before that, she had served Lady Anne. She was a small woman, smaller even than Rowena, though not small in girth. Quite round she was in that respect, for Mildred did indeed love to eat. Two score and five years in age, with gray streaking her brown hair, and warm brown eyes, she had been allowed to accompany Rowena into her isolation three years ago, the only kind thing Hugo d'Ambray had ever done for her.

"How came you to be here?" Rowena asked as she looked about the room to see if anyone else was there.

"When he came for you yestermorn, he left orders for all that you own to be packed up and brought here. Those churls thought to leave me behind, but I set them right on that notion."

"So sure he was that he would have my cooperation in this farce," Rowena said bitterly to herself.

"I saw that old man last eventide when I arrived. How could you agree to wed **that**?"

Rowena could feel the tears starting to gather in her eyes, but she fought them back. Her lower lip still trembled, however, when she said, "Gilbert was beating my mother. I doubt he would have stopped until I did agree."

"Oh, my lamb," Mildred cried, and came swiftly forward to gather Rowena into her arms. "I knew he was a monster, just like his sire. Those soft words of his never fooled me, each time he came sniffing 'round your skirts."

"God forgive me, but I hate him now. He has no thought for me in all this, only his own gain."

"Aye, that is true enough. Already they prepare for war here. 'Tis said this keep will be nigh empty come the new dawn. Every knight, and near a thousand men-at-arms, your new lord has committed to young Gilbert. And there is gold enough to hire thousands more. 'Twill not be long ere you have back all that Fulkhurst, that monster from the north, has reft from you."

"Not from me," Rowena snapped. "Think you Gilbert will ever give up my lands? He'll have them back, and when Lyons dies, he'll have me back as well, to marry off again the next time he finds himself in similar straits."

"So that is the way of it, is it?" Mildred asked indignantly.

"So he as much as admitted. But in the meantime, I am to get myself with child to secure Lyons' lands to Gilbert as well." Rowena gave a broken laugh. "Can a man so old still beget children, Mildred?"

The maid snorted. "So all men would like to think, but 'tis nigh impossible. Yet did I spend the eventide being regaled with stories of how this lord has tried to get himself another son to replace those who died in war. Four wives he has had in as many years, recent years, and that does not count the six he had in his youth."

"What happened to so many?"

"The early wives all died of one means or another, but the servants claim mostly by foul means. The recent wives he repudiated. All innocent maids they were, yet he claimed otherwise when they did not give him the hoped-for son as quickly as he expected. 'Tis all he wants from you, my sweet one."

"So if I do not give him a son, he is like to repudiate me within the year. No wonder Gilbert assured me I would not be married long."

"Nay, that old lord will not last even that long, do you ask me. Five years ago he should have been dead. Why he still lives can only be from a pact with the devil."

"Shush," Rowena hissed, crossing herself, yet she was inclined to agree. She herself had thought that he already looked like a corpse.

Mildred looked at her narrowly now. "Do you truly mean to wed Lord Godwine?"

"You say that as if I have a choice."

"Aye, you do. We could kill him instead."

Rowena scowled to have her hopes raised in one instant, then dashed in the next. "Think you I have not considered that? But if I ruin Gilbert's plans in that way, he might well beat my mother to death, he will be so furious with me. I am not prepared to take that chance."

"Nay, of course not," Mildred agreed. She bore as much love for the mother as she did for the daughter, and could not bear to think of either one suffering when she had certain skills with herbs to prevent it. "Then if it must be, it must be, but you need not share your body as well as your bed with that old lecher. He can be rendered incapable—"

Rowena waved that notion aside before it was completed. "Only blood on the sheets will satisfy Gilbert."

"It need not be yours."

Rowena had not thought of that. She need not suffer those wrinkled and twisted fingers, that fetid breath, the revulsion that was like to wither her soul? If only . . . She cringed inwardly. "If onlys" had never come to her aid, nor would they now.

"Lord Godwine might be ready for the grave, but that does not mean he is stupid. If he has no memory of consummating the marriage, is he not like to see the matter repeated the next morn?" She shuddered at the very thought. "I would rather suffer this horror in the dark of night than in the light of day, Mildred. I do not think I could bear watching him touch me, as well as feeling it."

"Very well, my sweet one. I will make a drink for you instead. 'Twill not put you to sleep, but 'tis the next best thing, for you will be so unaware of what goes on about you, you will not care what that old lecher does to you."

Rowena frowned. She wasn't sure she wanted to be totally senseless around Godwine Lyons. She was helpless enough in this situation; that would just make her more so. But which was better, not knowing, or merely not seeing?

"How long would your potion last?" she asked thoughtfully.

"A few hours. Long enough for him to do what he will do."

"And if he took it by mistake?"

"'Twould do him no harm. If he can perform, then he will. Merely will he not recall it."

Rowena groaned, dropping back on the bed. "Then again I must deal with him come the morn."

"Nay, why should there be a mistake? I will leave the potion in the nuptial chambers, already mixed in your wine. Yours will be poured and ready to drink, his will not. Merely do you drink it as soon as you arrive there. No matter who will be with you, no one would gainsay you that extra fortification for what you must endure."

"Then do it just so. Anything must be better than—"

Rowena broke off at the sound of a knock at her

door, but it was not Gilbert, as she had half expected. Servants came in, a great number of them,
with bath and water, with a tray of bread and
cheese to break her fast, with a wedding gown of
deepest cream. She was told Lord Godwine would
like her to wear it, if she had nothing appropriate.
She was also told, or actually overheard the maids'
whisperings, that his last two wives had also worn
that gown. How frugal of the man, to get so much
use out of it. This certainly showed how little he
cared for her feelings.

When one of the maids held the gown up for her
to better examine it, Rowena said, "Why not? His
other wives were fortunate enough to escape him.
It might bring me the same luck."

There was an appalling silence for a moment that
made Rowena realize she should have kept her
thoughts to herself. These servants were his after
all. But she had done no more than shock them
with her frankness, and soon there was a nervous
giggle, then another, and she found that they were
in wholehearted agreement with her, for all of
them hated the man who was to be her husband.

❧ 4

The day progressed, despite all hope that it would not, and just after Sext, Rowena was married to Lord Godwine Lyons of Kirkburough. Naught had happened to save her. Before witnesses, with man's blessing—she would like to think God withheld His—she was given over from the control of one man to another, her new husband. Feebleminded as he was, he had slept through the entire mass.

A feast had been prepared to last the rest of the day. Rowena sat beside her husband, watching him gum the slops he was forced to eat because of his lack of teeth. But graciously, or perversely, since he had noted she was not eating, he piled her own gold plate high. If she had tried to swallow anything, she was certain she would vomit.

Gilbert was in highest spirits. He had done what he had set out to do, so naught could sour him, not even her silence each time he spoke to her.

He sat on her other side, ate with gusto, downed

chalices of wine with even more gusto, and bragged endlessly of how he would now run Fulkhurst out of their shire, if he could not actually kill him, which was what he would prefer to do. And Mildred had spoken true. Gilbert was not even allowing Lyons' men to participate fully in the celebrations, to which there were many outspoken grumbles, but had them leaving the keep in groups of one hundred throughout the day. They were being sent to his own stronghold, to join his army there, which already had orders to march to Tures with the new dawn. He was not even going to wait until he could hire more men. He wanted Fulkhurst besieged at Tures before the warlord could slip away.

Rowena was not the least bit interested in his talk of war. She hated Gilbert enough now that she hoped he could not wrest Tures away from Fulkhurst, even though that would mean it would never be hers again. She no longer cared. Gilbert was as much a warmonger as Fulkhurst was. Heartily, she hoped they killed each other.

When the time came for the ladies to usher her off to the nuptial chamber, Rowena was so beset with dread, she was sure she was going to be sick. Her skin was as pasty white as her husband's, and her eyes hurt from fighting back tears all day.

There were no bawdy jests or crude advice, as was the custom at weddings. Looks of pity were all she received, and the women made fast work of preparing her and getting out of there. She was left in her thin shift. No one had suggested she remove it, not that she would have. Godwine was so blind he might not notice, and that would leave at least something between her skin and his.

As soon as she was alone, she slipped her bedrobe on and made haste to put out all the candles except those by the bed, which she could douse without leaving it. Then she headed for the table where she had already noticed the bottle of wine and two chalices, with only one filled. She hesitated in reaching for the drugged wine, however. The potion was to last only a few hours. What if her husband did not come to her for a few hours? Should she wait a while more? What she should have done was ask Mildred how long she must wait for the potion to take effect.

The door flew open without warning and Gilbert came swiftly forward, his dark eyes on the hand reaching for the chalice. "Nay, leave that," he ordered tersely, ready to stop her if she did not heed him. He carried his own bottle of wine and set it on the table. " 'Tis lucky I thought to wonder at your docility."

"What else can I be, when you hold my mother prisoner?"

He ignored her words, scowling down at the chalice of wine. "Did you mean to poison him?"

"Nay."

His scowl got darker as it turned on her. "Yourself, then?"

She let out a laugh, near hysterical, wishing she had the nerve. He grasped her shoulders and shook her.

"Answer!"

She shrugged off his hands. "If I would poison anyone, 'twould be you!" she hissed, angry enough to show him all that she was feeling in the look she gave him.

He looked flustered for a moment. And it occurred to her that he had actually been afraid that she might do herself harm.

He did not meet her eyes when he said, "You make too much of this." She was aware he referred to her marriage. "The sooner you get yourself with child, the sooner I will get rid of him for you."

"So you do mean to kill him?"

He did not answer, for he had left the door open, and they could hear the party approaching with the groom.

"Get yourself to the bed to await him." He gave her a little shove in that direction. "And behave yourself as befits a bride."

Rowena whirled around. "**You** aught await him there, as this marriage is your doing," she whispered furiously. "He is so blind, mayhap he will not notice the difference."

Gilbert actually grinned. "I am pleased to see you still have the spirit I ofttimes noticed. Indeed, 'tis wise of me not to trust you, so I will take these with me."

"These" were the bottle of wine and the filled chalice that had been standing on the table. Rowena had to bite her lip to keep from begging him to leave her the cup at least. But more determined would he be to take it if he knew how much she wanted it. Either way, 'twas lost to her.

With a dry sob, she ran for the bed, and had just covered herself when the groom arrived, carried in by the few remaining household knights who had yet to depart. Their crude laughter and jests ended at the sight of Rowena in the bed, and it was Gilbert who curtly ushered them out when he noticed them ogling her. In less than a minute, she was left alone with her husband.

He had been prepared for her. He wore a black bedrobe that made his skin look even whiter. The tie had come loose on the way to the bedchamber, and he did not bother to tighten it, but let it part completely with his first step forward. Rowena had closed her eyes briefly, but that image of his body would not leave her inner mind—legs whittled down to mere bone, ribs protruding, sunken belly, and that tiny thing between his legs. She had heard it called many things, all denoting some monstrous weapon, but that was no weapon to strike fear into her.

She almost laughed, but she was too close to tears. She began to pray silently, that she could bear this, that it would be over with quickly, that she would not be rendered mad when he was done with her.

"Well, where are you, my pretty?" he asked peevishly. "I am too old to go a'hunting."

"Here, my lord."

That he was still squinting off to the left told her he had not heard her, and she repeated herself in a near shout. That started him toward her, stumbling up the steps to reach the bed.

"Well? Well? What do you wait for?" he demanded in that same peevish tone, standing there on the top step, but making no effort to get into the bed. "Can you not see my warrior requires assistance ere he will stand at attention for you? Come and play with him, wife."

That tiny thing was supposed to be a warrior? Rowena made a sound of negation in her throat that he did not hear. He was chuckling to himself, his eyes not really on her, but staring beyond the bed with a dazed look in them.

"I would not take it amiss were you to kiss him, my pretty," he suggested, still chuckling.

Her hand flew to her mouth as the mere thought made her gag, the bile rising to her throat. Just barely she swallowed it back down. If he could have seen her expression, he would not be laughing. But he really was near blind as well as deaf. And she really was going to kill Gilbert for this.

"Well? Well?" he was demanding again. His eyes began searching the bed, but even standing right there, he still could not find her in it. "Where **are** you, you silly child? Must I needs call my man, John, to find you? You will meet him soon enough. If I do not have you breeding within the month, I will give you to John to have it done. I am too old to go through this again. You are the last, and I will have a son from you one way or another. What say you to that?"

Was he trying to shock her? Had she even heard him aright?

"What I say, my lord, is that you sound like a desperate man, unless—Do I understand you correctly? You would give me to this man John to get me with child if you cannot?"

"Aye, I would. I have a fondness for John. I would not mind calling his son my own. Better that than have my brother get what is mine, a man I despise more than any other."

"Why do you not just claim John as your own?"

"Do not be stupid, girl. No one would believe he is mine. But it will not be doubted that your child is mine."

Would it not? The man was worse than she had

thought. She was his wife, yet he meant to breed her just like his cows and pigs. If he could not see it done, he would let another, nay, **insist** another do it. Gilbert would not protest either, she realized, for he wanted the same end, a child.

God's mercy, did she really have to go through with this? He was so feeble and fleshless, she knew she could fight him off without half trying. But what would happen to her mother if she did? And he was her husband now. A husband was all-powerful. Her very life was now hers by his whim alone, for if he chose to take it, no one would bring him to task for it.

"Have I made a bad bargain here?" His voice rose with the possibility. "Come you here and ready me, wife, and do it now!"

That was a direct order, not to be gainsaid, but Rowena was positive she would faint if she had to touch him. "I cannot," she said, loud enough so she would not have to repeat it. "If you mean to take me, do so. I will not help you."

His face turned so furiously red, she was certain not one of his ten other wives had ever dared to refuse him. Would he have her beaten for doing so? 'Twas obvious he was not strong enough to beat her himself.

"You—you—"

He got no further than that. And it looked as if his eyes were about to pop out of his head. His color darkened still more. He swayed on the step, one of his hands pressed so hard to his chest, she thought his ribs might cave in. It was on the tip of her tongue to say something conciliatory, merely to calm him down, but before she could, he swayed backward, right off the steps without a sound.

She scrambled to the edge of the bed to look over the side. He was not moving. He lay there in the rushes, his hand still clutching his chest, his eyes still bulging. No breath moved his chest.

Rowena continued to stare at him. Dead? Could she be that lucky? A laugh bubbled up in her throat, but it came out in a soft wail. What would Gilbert do now? This was not her fault. Was it? If she had not refused . . . If it was her fault, she exonerated herself, feeling no guilt. How could she know a little defiance would kill the man?

But was he truly dead? She would not touch him to find out. Even now the thought of touching him was repugnant to her. But someone had to find out.

She leaped off the bed and ran for the door, then out into the hall—and right into Gilbert's arms.

"Aye, 'tis as I thought," he said with marked displeasure. "You intended all along to run away. But there will be none of that. You will go back in there and—"

"He is dead, Gilbert!" she blurted out.

His hands squeezed her arms painfully before he released one and dragged her back into the chamber with the other. He went right to the old man and bent to put his head to his chest. When he looked up at her, his expression was dark with fury.

"How did you do it?"

She stepped back from the blast of that accusation. "Nay, I touched him not, and there was only your wine in the room, which he did not drink. He was not even in the bed yet. He clutched his chest and fell off the bed steps."

Gilbert looked back at her husband, and must have believed her. He drew the black robe over Lord Godwine's body before he stood up and faced her.

After a moment's thought, he said, "Do not leave this room. Do not let anyone inside."

"What are you going to do?"

"Find you a suitable substitute. 'Tis imperative now that you start breeding this very night. Damn this black hair of mine, or I would do it."

Her eyes flared wide at the meaning of his last words as much as of his first. "Nay. I will not—"

"You will," he snarled, "if you wish ever to see your mother again—alive!"

Now it was stated plainly, what she had only suspected before, and she blanched, not doubting at all that he meant it. But the horror of what he intended . . . a substitute!

Desperately, she asked, "How can you even hope to perpetuate such a deception? The man is dead."

"No one need know that until a sufficient time has passed to see you breeding. When you are not directly attending to that, you will stay in this chamber—"

"With his corpse?" she gasped, taking still another step back.

"Nay, I will get rid of the body," he said impatiently. "When 'tis time to bury him, I will find another body to pass off as his. At any rate, he will be officially buried before his brother learns he is dead, and you will be for certain with child before the man arrives to try and wrest his due. But he will have naught. Godwine would have wanted it so."

That was likely true, but did that justify what Gilbert meant to do? And he sounded so confident in his new plan. But why not? Again, he had to do naught but sit back and wait while her body was sacrificed on this altar of deception. And this time her mother's life truly depended on her compliance.

❦ 5

They set upon him on his way out of the common bathing room at the inn. Five of them there were, dressed in the leather jerkins of men-at-arms, yet he doubted they were that. Thieves, more like. Lawlessness was prevalent in most towns that had a weak or absent overlord, or corrupt aldermen. And he did not know the town of Kirkburough, had never passed through it before. For all he knew, this could be another pocket of high villainy where all travelers and strangers were set upon and robbed, or tortured if they could not promise fat ransoms. To travel in Stephen's England alone or with a small escort was to risk penury as well as your life.

Truly, this had been an act of stupidity and conceit on his part, to come here with no more than his squire just because he wanted to beautify his appearance before he met his betrothed on the morrow. A bit of vanity, and look what it had wrought. Too long had he been confident in his reputation of swift retribution for any wrong done him, to keep offenders at bay. It had stood him in good stead for a goodly number of years, ever since he had turned his life toward vengeance. But for a reputation to do any good, it had to be known, and as he did not know this area, neither was he known here.

Warrick de Chaville could be forgiven his carelessness, though he would not forgive himself, for he was not a forgiving man. The town had looked peaceful and well ordered. He had a lot on his mind. He would soon be marrying for the third time, and he did not want this new wife to fear him as the other two had. He had much hope in the Lady Isabella. For nearly a year he had courted her when he could find the time, though that was not his way. Her father had given her to him at first asking, greatly desiring the match, yet Warrick had wanted Isabella's consent, and would not make contract for her until he had it. Now he had it, and he was eager to make her his.

Lady Isabella Malduit was not only a great beauty and much sought after, she was also soft-spoken, sweetly tempered, and had a charming sense of humor. Warrick wanted humor in his life. He wanted love and laughter, which had been absent since his family had been destroyed and naught but hate and bitterness had filled him. He had two daughters, but they were frivolous and self-centered creatures. He loved them, but he could not abide them for very long with their bickering and pettishness. He wanted a home life like the one he had known as a child, that would draw him home, rather than send him eagerly into war. And he wanted a son.

He did not ask for too much, no more than any man could expect. And the right wife could give it all to him. He had found her in Isabella. Already he was very fond of her. He hoped it would soon be more than that, though truthfully, he was not sure he was still capable of that kind of love after so many years of hate. But 'twas not necessary that he love his wife, only that she love him. None of which mattered if he was to die here this night.

He was not even properly armed. He had left his sword and armor in the room he had rented, where even now Geoffrey would be cleaning it. He had come down to the bathing room with no more than a dagger tucked in his belt. Now he did not even have his clothes, for he had left them with the attending servant to be washed. He wore only a large bath sheet, wrapped and tucked in at the waist, with the short dagger stuck under the edge of it at his belly.

Even though he was so defenseless, the five men surrounding him were hesitant at first to draw their swords, for Warrick de Chaville was no ordinary-sized man. At six feet and three, he stood a half head taller than the largest assailant, and more still than the other four. With his arms and chest bare, there was no doubt at the strength contained in his large body. But more than that, he looked mean. There was a hard ruthlessness in his face, as if he would enjoy killing for the mere sport of it. And the gray eyes that had marked him as their target were so coldly chilling, at least one man wanted to cross himself before he drew his sword.

But they did draw their swords. And the leader would have spoken, mayhap to make a demand instead of fighting, except Warrick was not a passive knight. He was aggressive in all things, and this was no exception. He clasped his dagger in hand and let out a war cry that very nearly shook the timbers. At the same instant he charged forward, slashing the man nearest him across his face. He had aimed for the throat, but the man's scream did him more good in putting fear into the others.

It became quickly apparent that either they were clumsy with their weapons or they were not trying to kill him. Well and good, that was their mistake. He wounded another, but then his blade began striking the steel of theirs. They had not meant to hurt him, but they did not intend to die either.

And then Geoffrey joined the fray with a less thunderous battle cry, having heard Warrick's. The lad was only ten and five, and not the squire

Warrick would have taken into any battle, for he deemed him not yet ready for that. He was skilled with a sword, yet his body was not fully developed, giving him not much weight behind his blows. He had more heart and will than anything else, but also the mistaken assumption that he could do exactly as his lord did. He charged, but without the powerful body behind it, no one stepped fearfully out of his way, and without his armor to protect him, he was gutted before he could even get in a full swing.

Warrick saw the look of disbelief and then horror that appeared on Geoffrey's young face as he bent over the sword buried in his middle and knew he would be dead in moments. The lad had been fostered in his household since he was seven. Only last year Warrick had taken him under his own wing, even though he already had several squires and did not need another. He had developed a fondness for this boy who had always been so eager to please, and now he let out a bellow of grief-filled rage just before he threw his dagger at the man who had killed Geoffrey. It struck true, buried to the hilt in his throat, and no sooner thrown than Warrick had snatched the sword right out of the hand of the man nearest him.

He did not get to use this better weapon, however. Another sword hilt smashed into his skull, and he fell slowly to the floor.

The two men who had been fortunate enough to stay out of his reach now stood over him panting. A full minute passed before they thought to sheathe their swords. One nudged Warrick with his boot, just to be sure he would not be rising. Blood appeared in the dark blond hair that was still wet from his bath, but he breathed. He was not dead and so was still of use.

"This man is no serf, as we were told to find," the one man said to the other. "The way he fought, he can only be a knight. Could you not tell the difference when you saw him enter the bathing room?"

"Nay, he was coated in travel dust. I merely noted he wore no armor, and he had the right color eyes as well as the blond hair Lord Gilbert insisted on. I considered it fortunate that I happened to see him at all."

"Gag him, then, and hope Lord Gilbert does not decide to speak to him."

"What difference? Half of Lord Godwine's knights are naught but churls. And we have found no other with both the right hair and the right eyes. What is he wanted for anyway?"

"That is not our concern, merely do we do as told. But did you have to hit him so hard? Now we must carry him."

The other snorted. "Better that than to deal with him awake again. When I first saw him, he did not seem so big as this. That boy, think you he was his son?"

"Mayhap, which means he will awake fighting again. Best to bind those hands and feet as well. Even Lord Gilbert might have trouble subduing this one."

❧ 6

Rowena had fallen asleep at the edge of the bed, staring at the spot on the floor where Lord God-wine had fallen. Gilbert had removed the body himself, then left her alone with the repeated admonishment to let no one in the room but him.

She would have liked to lock him out as well. If she had had a weapon, she might even have tried to kill him then, before he forced her to even more unspeakable acts. But she had no weapon. Nor could she run away without endangering her mother's life. She could not even say which was worse, wedding and bedding Lyons, or what Gilbert planned for her now. Nay, what could be worse to a girl only just eight and ten than bedding that lecherous old man?

She could feel not the least pity for his death, even though she might have been partwise responsible. He had likely murdered a goodly number of innocent women who had had the misfortune to be his wives, simply because he had tired of them or needed a new dowry to fill his coffers. She knew there were many unscrupulous men who did exactly that, and without the least guilt. But then she also knew there were different men, decent men, like her father. The whole world had not gone to hell, merely this small portion of it during this reign of anarchy.

It was still dark, the keep still silent, when Gilbert came back to wake her. Rowena could not guess at the time, though the exhaustion of her body and mind told her she had not slept long. But Gilbert's first words brought her wide awake.

"All is in readiness for you. My men were fortunate in their find. The hair and eye colors were what concerned me most, to be exactly those of your husband's, for that is what is first noticed on a babe, and those we have matched."

Blood rushed through Rowena, hot, then cold. Her stomach muscles tightened almost to cramps in her fear. He had really done it, found a man to throw her to, just as her husband would have done if she had not conceived soon enough for him. Two of a kind, they were, Lyons and Gilbert, even in their thinking. She would not be surprised if he had found the same man, this John whom her husband would have used. God's mercy, why would this nightmare not end?

"Make haste," he continued briskly as he pulled

her off the high bed. "There are many hours before dawn, yet you will need ample time with the man, to couple more than once to assure his seed is well planted."

"Why tell me?" Rowena snapped, trying to jerk her arm out of his hold as he rushed her toward the open door. "Give your vile instructions to the stud you have found."

"You will see," was all he said.

And she did see, almost immediately, for the man had been put in the small chamber directly across from hers. It contained a bed and two tall candle holders set on either side of it, but no other furnishings. It had been the room that her husband had used for his debaucheries with the female serfs under his rule, though Rowena did not know this. There were even chains attached to the wall above the bed, just out of sight below the mattress, though these were not used on the man, for he was too big. Gilbert had worried he might break those puny chains that had been made for females, and so had ordered long ones brought and strung under the bed, attaching wrist to ankle in this way so the prisoner could not move one limb without pulling on another.

All Rowena noticed was that the man was there, tied down to the bed, with no more than a large bath sheet draped over his bare loins. Tied down? Nay, she noticed now the iron cuffs at his wrists, which lay above his head. And two chains came out from under the bath sheet at the end of the bed to curve down under it. **Chained** down! He had to be chained down? And he was asleep—or senseless.

Understanding came easily enough, but all she could think to say was, "Why did you not just pay him to do the deed?"

Gilbert stood next to her at the end of the bed, still holding her arm. "Then he would take you. I give him to you to take instead, so you will not feel . . ."

He hesitated over the word long enough that she supplied it. "Raped?"

He flushed. "Nay. I merely thought to leave you to see to the matter in your own way. You would have given up your maidenhead this night either way."

She realized he felt he was doing her a favor. She did not see it as such, for in her mind, this was wrong. Tying the man down and forcing him to participate was even more wrong. But Gilbert saw things only one way, the way of gain and profit for himself. Without a child to inherit Godwine Lyons' estate, everything would go to Lyons' brother, including the large army of mercenaries that Gilbert desperately needed. Her stepbrother could make use of that army in the few weeks he meant to conceal Lyons' death, but a few weeks would not be enough to gain back all he had lost to Fulkhurst.

Damn that warmonger to hell, who was as bad

as, if not worse than, Gilbert. If not for him, she would not be forced to go through with this. If not for him, she would not have been forced to wed in the first place.

Having mentioned her maidenhead, Gilbert must have recalled that she was, in fact, merely a maiden. "Do you, ah, do you know what to do? If not, I will fetch someone to assist you. I would do so myself, but I do not think I can bear to . . ."

She looked at him in amazement when he did not finish speaking. "You yourself find this distasteful, yet you would still force me to do it?"

"It must be done," he replied, tight-lipped. "There is no other way to secure Kirkburough."

That he seemed now not to like it any better than she gave her hope. "You will lie about the old man's death," she reminded him. "You could lie about a child, too, long enough to use his armies."

"And when no child is produced of the lie? Nay, this is a rich fief, the town a large one. I will not lose it because of your squeamishness.

"You will do as I have commanded you, Rowena. I have put him close so no one will see you come here each night. During the day you may sleep, for I will put it about that Godwine has taken ill and you nurse him, as is only proper. The servants will be kept away except for your own maid, who I trust will do as you instruct—if you wish to keep her."

More threats? Mildred expendable, too? God, how she hated him!

"How long, Gilbert?"

He knew exactly what she asked. "Until you conceive. Do you find it so distasteful, I would suggest you avail yourself of his rod more than once each night. Aye, two and three times each night would not be difficult for this virile lout to manage, and would the sooner see the thing accomplished."

So the nightmare was not even to end with this night, but go on and on? And now it had become someone else's nightmare as well, this poor man whose misfortune it was to have gold hair and gray eyes.

"You mean to keep him like this the whole time?"

"You need not concern yourself with him," he answered carelessly. "He is no more than a serf, and will be disposed of when his usefulness is finished."

"A serf?" At first glance she had seen the man was large, but now she looked at his length again and could see his feet at the end of the bed, his head far up at the other end. "He is too big to be a serf. What have you done, Gilbert, stolen a freeman?"

"Nay, some lord's by-blow, mayhap, but no more than that," he said confidently. "If a lord had come to Kirkburough, he would have presented himself at the keep to pass the night at no cost to himself, not stayed in the town. Even a lowly, landless knight would have sought the companionship of his kind and come to the hall. A freeman he might be, however, but still no one of import, mayhap no more than a pilgrim."

"But you mean to kill him?"

The question caught her stepbrother off guard, and he snapped impatiently, "Do not be stupid. He cannot be left alive to lay claim to the child when we are done with him. No one would believe him, yet it might cause rumors, rumors that Godwine's brother would leap upon."

So even if she did exactly as Gilbert wanted, someone was still to die. That knowledge released the anger at the injustice of it all that her fear had been holding in abeyance.

"God rot you, Gilbert, and your cursed greed," she swore softly as she jerked her arm away from him. His surprised expression, as if he could not imagine what he had done wrong, was the breaking point for her, and her voice and fury rose to a shout. "Get out! I need no help to rape this man. But send Mildred to me, for I may need help to revive him. Little purpose he serves as he is."

It was her anger and bitterness that made her speak so, but those shouted words were what Warrick heard as he regained his senses. He did not open his eyes. He had been a man of war too long to give away such an advantage. But this time it availed him naught, for no more was said, and a moment later, a door was slammed shut.

Silence. He was alone for the moment, but that screeching female would likely be back soon if her words—nay, he could not credit those words. Females did not rape. How could they when they had not the proper parts? And she could not have meant him, in any case. A jest, then, from a crude wench. No more than that. But as long as he was alone . . .

He opened his eyes on a view of the ceiling. The room was well lit, the glow of candles on either side of him just discerned without his moving. He turned his head to find the door, and pain sliced through it. He stilled for a moment, closing his eyes—and became aware of things without seeing. He was lying in a soft bed. A gag pulled at his lips. He was as he had been when he was taken, without his clothes. That did not alarm him. There was no reason to dress him when he could do it himself once he was awake. The bed? Better than a dungeon, he supposed.

And then he felt the manacles on his wrists. He tried to move one and heard the chain rattle—and felt the tug and scrape on his ankle. God's blood, bound to himself, and with chain, not rope!

If it was ransom they wanted, then they knew who he was and were risking his vengeance, which was always swift. Thieves and outlaws, however, took anyone for whatever they could get. They did not care if they captured knight or merchant, lady or fishwife, and torture of one kind or another was swift to come if they did not get what they wanted. He had taken the keep of a robber baron once, and even he had been sickened by what he had found in the man's dungeon—bodies that had been slowly crushed under heavy stone, naked bodies hung by their thumbs with smoke-blackened skin, some with feet nearly burned off, all dead because they had simply been forgotten by their tormentors once he had laid siege to the keep. And this was no mean hut or forest floor, nor even the inn where he had been taken. Stone walls meant a keep. A petty lord, then, and just as bad as a petty thief.

Warrick opened his eyes again, ready to ignore the pain in his head to see what he could of his soft prison. He lifted his head and saw her there at the foot of his bed—and decided he had died, for that could only be one of God's angels, made perfect in the afterlife.

❧ 7

Rowena was still glaring at the door that had closed on Gilbert when she heard the chains creak and looked back at the man on the bed. His eyes were shut, he lay perfectly still, but she sensed instinctively that he was now awake. She had not looked at him closely before, had not seen him as much more than a male body, a large male body. He lay flat on his back without a pillow, while she stood several feet beyond a mattress that was as high as her waist. She still could not tell much about him from this position. Then his head lifted, his eyes riveted her to the spot, and she stood perfectly still, forgetting even to breathe.

The gray of his eyes was more silver, soft and luminous in his surprise. Even with the gag dividing his face, she could tell it was a handsome face, the features well defined and—arrogant. What made her think that? The broadness of his cheekbones? That hawklike nose? Mayhap that sharply squared jaw, thrust out more because of the gag. She had to be mistaken. Arrogance was a trait of noblemen. Arrogance in a serf would get his back whipped raw.

But this serf did not lower his eyes or look away in the presence of a lady. Bold he was, or still too surprised to recall his place. But what was she thinking? He could not tell she was a lady, when she wore her bedclothes. But then she realized he certainly could, for her white shift was of the finest linen, soft and nearly transparent, it was so thin. Her bedrobe was that rare velvet of the East, given her on her fourteenth birthday by her mother, sewn by her own hand.

A by-blow, then, as Gilbert had said, and apparently proud of it. And what did she even care what he was? She could not care—he was to die. But first she was to give him her maidenhead— oh, God! **How** could she? Fool, how could she not when her mother . . . ?

She wanted to sink down on the floor and cry. She had been raised gently, with love and care, the cruelty and harshness of life kept at bay. It was difficult for her to see her life now as real, because it was so alien to her. She was supposed to take this man, in truth, to rape him. How? In anger she had told Gilbert she needed no help, but she did, for she knew not the first thing about begetting children.

There was no longer surprise in his eyes. They were now—admiring. Was that good? Aye, 'twould be better for him did he not find her repulsive. She was glad of that at least. And he was nothing like her husband. He was young, clean, even handsome, his skin smooth, his body firm—nay, nothing at all like her husband. Even the gray of his eyes and the blond of his hair were different shades than Lyons' had been, the one lighter, the other darker.

She had the strangest feeling she could read his thoughts through his eyes, for she imagined a question there now. Had he been told why he was here? Nay, likely not, since he had been senseless until moments ago. And why would Gilbert bother, when the man had only to lie there and accept what was done to him? She was the one Gilbert had instructed, for she was the one who would be doing what must be done. But that question was there in his eyes . . .

It was left to her to tell him, and she could not even reassure him that he would be released when it was over. Her anger surfaced again, this time wholly for his sake. He had done naught to deserve this. He was an innocent, snared in a monster's plans. She would take his seed, but then Gilbert would take his life. Nay, she could not allow that. She would do the one, she had to for her mother's sake, but somehow she must prevent the other.

Somehow, she would help him escape when the time came, before she told Gilbert that his seed had taken, thereby ending the man's usefulness.

But she could not tell the man that. She would not give him false hope, in case she was unsuccessful in helping him. All she could do was try. And he did not need to know he was to die. There was no reason to tell him that. Let him think what he would, and why should he think that he would not be released when she was done with him?

Again he was communicating with her with his eyes, and again she understood him. He was dropping his eyes down toward his gag, then looking at her again. He wanted her to remove it so he could speak to her. That she would not do, for she did not think she could bear it if he begged her for his release, adding more heavily to her guilt. She **knew** what she must do was wrong, but what choice did she have? But to hear him beseech her—nay, she could not.

She shook her head slowly, and his own dropped back to the mattress so he no longer looked at her. If she did not know better, she would think she had been arrogantly dismissed, having denied him what he wanted. Like as not his neck was strained from being lifted so long. She came around to the side of the bed so he could see her without straining, but his eyes were closed now. He did not care that she stood there. Or mayhap he had not heard her approach in her bare feet.

She paused now that she could see him more clearly. His big body truly filled the bed. She thought he might even be taller than Gilbert, though she could not be certain, but he was surely much broader of chest. His arms were thick and long, and well corded with muscle from shoulder to wrist. His shoulders, neck, and chest were likewise thickly muscled, the sun-gilded skin taut, with no softness to speak of. Whatever he did to earn his keep, 'twas obvious he worked hard at it. A woodcutter, mayhap. One on her father's fief had been brawnier than any knight.

She realized she was staring, but she could not help herself. Strong he was, very strong, and she found herself being thankful to Gilbert, after all, that the man was tied down, then was ashamed of the thought. Yet this man could easily snap her in two with his bare hands, and 'twas better for her that those hands could not reach her.

"I am sorry," she began, wondering why she whispered when they were alone. " 'Tis better I do not hear what you have to say, but I can tell you why you are here."

His eyes opened again, his head turning slightly so he could stare at her. There was no question there now, no curiosity of any kind. Patience, she realized, was what he was displaying. He fully expected to have all his questions answered, but she was not as brave as that. She would tell him only what she had to and nothing more.

But now that it was time to do so, she could feel heat stealing up her neck into her cheeks. "I—I—you and I—we—we must—we must—"

The question was back in his eyes, and if he were not gagged, he would be shouting it. She could not blame him for losing his patience, but she could not say the word. She was too ashamed. She tried to remind herself that he was only a serf, and she had always been kind but firm with her servants, as her mother had taught her. But he was like no manservant she had ever ordered. And that arrogance—she could not get it out of her mind that he was more than a serf, and although that should make this no worse, it did.

And then she heard the scratch on the door and almost melted with relief that Mildred had finally come. She gave not another thought to the man on the bed, who had strained nearly every muscle in his body waiting for her to get to the point in her explanation. An explanation that was no longer forthcoming as he watched her rush from the room.

Warrick collapsed back and growled in frustration. Damn her. "We must"—what?! Why could she not just spit it out? But then he forced himself to relax. He could not blame her. She was a delicate thing, ethereal in her beauty, and she had not put him here.

He could not imagine for what reason she had been there, however, unless she had brought him food. He could see none left for him, but she could have set it on the floor. Yet she would not remove his gag, so how was he to eat it?

Questions without answers. Patience. Whatever was wanted of him would be demanded soon enough, and then he could think of revenge, for whoever had ordered his capture, whoever was responsible, would die. It was his vow, sworn to God many years ago when his soul had shriveled and died from the devastation of his losses, that no one would ever do him an ill again without paying for it in kind or worse. It was a vow he had kept for sixteen long years, half of his lifetime. It was a vow he would keep till the day he died.

The little wench intruded on his thoughts again, and he let her, for she was more pleasant by far than his dark musings. When he had first seen her, truly had he thought her an angel with her halo of golden hair glowing in the candlelight. All in white she was draped, and those flaxen curls cascading over both shoulders down to her hips.

Her sapphire eyes had dominated her small face, large and round and beguiling, hiding secrets, hiding thoughts—until he had seen that spark of anger. It had aroused his curiosity almost more than the reason for his being there. He had had the ridiculous desire to play the guardian to this angel, to smash and utterly destroy whatever was disturbing her.

He had wanted to ask her what caused her anger. He had tried to get her to remove his gag. Her refusal had surprised him, then annoyed him, enough that he had acted no better than a child in sulk, refusing to look at her again, refusing to acknowledge that she was even there. He thought now of what he had felt at the time and was amazed at himself. Truly, the wench had a strange effect on him.

But he had not been able to ignore her for long. In truth, he liked looking at her, she was so pleasing to the eye, and that she would tell him what he needed to know had been his excuse to look at her again. But he had been struck anew by her beauty at the closer range as she had stood beside the bed. Her alabaster skin was flawless, her lips lush, inviting, and to his chagrin, his loins had begun to heat.

He would have choked on his laughter if he'd given in to what he was feeling, but the gag that would have choked him had also kept him from seducing the wench to ride him while they were yet alone. But then bitterness reared its head to ask him, Why would she agree, when he was no more than a prisoner, and naked of his purse to offer her a coin? When he was released, he would see to the wench. When he was released, he would burn this place to the ground, so she would need another home. He would offer her his. He thought briefly of his bride, waiting for him even now, but that could not change his mind. He would still bring this wench to his home.

❧ 8

"So now you know," Rowena said dejectedly, having finished telling Mildred the whole sordid tale of her husband's death and her meeting with his substitute. "And Gilbert meant it, stated it plainly this time. Either I get myself with child, or he will kill my mother."

"Aye, I doubt not that he meant it. He is the devil's own son, that one. 'Tis fortunate he does not want to stand there and watch. Your husband would have, if he gave you to his own man, that John." Mildred sighed. "I suppose you must see it done, then."

Rowena wrung her hands. "I know, but—how?"

Mildred's eyes flared, closed briefly, then opened again, clearly filled with self-disgust. "I am that stupid, I am. How can you know how? Your husband would have taken what he wanted, with your having to do naught but lie there. But now you have to do it all on your own, and that lad in there not able to even direct you, with a gag in his mouth. And he is on his back, you say?"

"Flat on his back, and I doubt he can move at all, the chains are so tight."

Mildred sighed again. "I am trying to see it in my mind—I have never ridden a man, you understand. 'Tis not natural."

"Gilbert must think 'twill not be difficult, for he has left him bound so."

"I did not say it could not be done," Mildred said disagreeably.

This was a subject for kitchen wenches, not for her lady. Her cheeks were now as pink as Rowena's were pale. But that wretched d'Ambray would no doubt be back with the dawn to see for himself that the deed was done, so there was no help for it.

"Aye, all right, I have it now," she continued. "And I will speak plainly to get the telling over with quickly. You must straddle his hips, get his rod inside you, and then you ride it. There will be pain until your maidenhead breaks, but then it should not hurt so much. Just imagine yourself astride your palfrey at a canter. You bounce—nay, do not blush—you will likely adjust to this method as soon as you are seated. Just remember, that rod of his needs the movement to give up its seed, and you must provide that movement if he cannot. Just sitting on him once he is fully sheathed in you will not do it. Think you can do it now? Is there aught more that needs explaining?"

"Nay, I—nay."

Mildred hugged her then. "Treat this as any other chore, my sweet one. I would have other advice for you, easier to stomach, were he not a stranger and to remain a stranger. But remember that is all he is, that you will never have to see him again once the babe is well planted, so he does not merit your embarrassment."

But he had it, Rowena thought as she returned to the small room across the way, and the heat did not leave her cheeks again. His eyes were on her the second she opened the door, and he watched her approach the bed. Mere interest was all he showed this time, and she revealed nothing of her own turbulent thoughts.

A chore, like any other? Very well, she told herself. Just get it done.

She dropped her gaze to the bed, loath to watch him while she explained the horrid facts to him. "I must have a child, and it must be conceived immediately. You were chosen to aid me because your hair and eyes are the same as my husband's, for the child needs have the look of him. So we must copulate this night, and the next, and the next, until your seed bears fruit. I like this no better than you, but I have no choice—and neither do you."

His chains rattled, but she would not look toward those expressive eyes of his. Briskly, she took hold of the thick sheet covering him and flipped it to the end of the bed, where it slithered to the floor. She did not watch it fall. With a will of their own, her eyes were drawn to his manroot, and widened to their full roundness. There, truly, was the monstrous weapon she had heard tales of. It lay soft and still in a bed of golden curls.

A growl came out of his throat, making her start, her eyes flying up to his face. Expressive eyes he had, so expressive, and now they promised grim retribution if she did not desist. She took a step back, suddenly afraid. So much fury in an expression.

She had not bargained on this. Most men would not mind what she had to do. They spread their bastards far and wide, so what was one more to them? Nay, that was the attitude of nobles, not serfs. But male serfs took their pleasure where they could, too—only they rarely knew if a babe was theirs or not, for the maids they cavorted with were not constant—and they tended to marry if they were caught.

Did he think he would have to marry her? Or did he object to the way they would have to copulate, with her on the top, with her in control? Mildred had called it unnatural, so mayhap he thought so, too. Well, she could not help that. She could not help any of this.

"I am sorry you object, but that changes naught," she said now, her tone tinged with bitterness. "I still must do it. But I will be quick so you are not disturbed for long."

His eyes flared at her, as if she had said something incredibly stupid. She wished she could not read his thoughts so well. She wished he would make this easier for her, but why should he? He must feel as misused as she did. Well, she refused to look at him anymore. And she **would** get this done and over with.

So decided, she climbed up on the edge of the bed, but it suddenly shook so forcefully, she tumbled backward to land on the floor. She stared up at the ceiling, fighting for the breath that had been knocked out of her, wondering what had happened. But then she heard the chains settling down to silence and knew—and got mad.

Damn you! she wanted to rail at him, but all she did was get back on her feet and glare down at him. "I **will** copulate with you. Do you understand? I have to!"

She got back on the bed, ready for his violent thrashing this time, but less prepared to actually watch it. He **was** violent, and the power behind his bucking and twisting and writhing was terrifying to behold. His body strained beyond limits, seemed to grow in size. The entire bed bounced and moved across the floor. She lost her balance again, started to topple, but bent toward him just in time, so that she was thrown across his loins instead of to the floor.

He stilled instantly. She worried then that she might have hurt him, and lifted herself up to look under her. But his manroot still looked the same, so she could not tell if her belly had harmed it or not. But from that position she saw the blood coating his ankles. She glanced at his hands, and there, too, blood smeared over his wrists.

She hissed through her teeth at this evidence of his violence. "You stupid man. Why cause yourself pain over something you cannot prevent?"

He answered with another growl. But while he was still motionless, she swiftly threw her leg over his hips to straddle them and gave him a triumphant look. If he was going to buck now, it would be all to the good. But he did not. He just watched her with murder in his bright silver eyes.

Warrick had never been so furious in his life. She meant to steal a child from him, **his** child! If she succeeded he would kill her. Nay, that would be too quick. He would make her suffer the agonies of hell. But she could not succeed. What she intended enraged him, but it also left him cold, and the stupid wench did not even realize that, if that look of utter triumph she had given him was to be credited.

He watched her lift her shift just enough to bare her warmth and settle it against his loins. Perversely, it enraged him even more that she did not intend to remove her clothes. She could steal his child, but she would not show him her nakedness to do it. Well and good, she would learn soon enough that she was doomed to fail. To that end, he closed his eyes against the look of her, which was too lovely by half.

He fed on his anger. He seethed with it, his only desire to get his hands on her so he could beat her senseless. That she would **dare** do this to him! He recalled the words he had thought a jest, that she needed no help to rape him. For that alone he despised her. For that alone he could kill her, but she meant to steal from him as well, flesh of his flesh. The mere intent sealed her fate.

But she was a stupid wench to think it was even possible to rape a man. Had she kept her mouth shut and merely offered herself to him, she could have had what she sought. His flesh would have responded instantly to the invitation, as it had nearly done at the mere sight of her. But now he did not even have to fight to remain unmoved beneath her, for his killing rage continued to leave him soft and uninterested in her warm flesh.

She did not just sit there atop him and expect miracles. He could feel her fingers handling him, yet in a way that he had never been caressed by a female before. But when he became aware that she was trying to stuff his soft flesh inside her, his eyes opened incredulously. He saw that hers were closed now. She was biting her lower lip, and concentrating so deeply on what she was about, her features were scrunched together. He flinched when one of her nails poked him, but he realized she was not even aware she had done it.

He wondered how long she would continue to attempt the impossible. Not long. She finally released a sob of frustration, and without meeting his eyes again, she gave up her seat and nearly ran from the room in defeat.

Warrick felt such fierce satisfaction, he wanted to shout with it. To have thwarted her so easily, with no effort on his part. He had won. She had failed.

But she returned.

He had not thought she would. And her face was now flame-bright, but also filled with such a look of determination, he felt his first stirrings of wariness, and rightly so. She slowly shrugged off her bedrobe and let it drop to the floor. When she reached for the hem of her shift, he closed his eyes tight.

Her voice came softly to him. "You can fight me, sirrah, but I have it on good authority 'twill do you no good."

He would not have answered that even if he could, but he would like to cut the throat of whoever had just given her the courage to try again. He strained to hear if she approached. Her small hand lighting on his chest told him she had.

"You must have realized I am a virgin."

He did not know it, but the word had the desired effect on him, even though he did not believe it.

But so, too, did her hand, tracing a slow path down his chest to his belly. He expected his rage to distract him, but her voice continued to distract him instead.

"In my ignorance, I did not even know you were not ready for me—that you needed encouragement of a certain kind. I did not even know that this soft flesh of yours would change and grow to a hardness like the rest of you." She touched him, there, as she said it. "I find it hard to believe, for 'tis already large, yet did Mildred assure me 'tis so. I am eager to see this strange happening for myself."

Did she know that what she was saying was as stimulating as her touch? Damn her and her advisor to perdition! Sweat broke out on his brow. He would **not** succumb to this seduction.

"I am to kiss you and—and lick you, everywhere, even as a last resort—there. Mildred said you would have to be dead do you not respond if I kiss you there."

He was already responding. His mind screamed his rage, but his flesh was a betrayer of the worst sort, with a mind of its own, tantalized by her promise. He strained at his bonds. He went wild, trying to dislodge her hand. But she stood beside the bed, undisturbed by his thrashing, and her fingers closed around him, holding on tight. He stilled when he realized all he did was aid her.

"I would not have believed it did I not see it," she gasped.

There was awe in her voice. And she was petting him now, giving that worthless piece of flesh praise for obeying her instead of him. She did not even know he had not reached his full size, that he still fought with every particle of his being.

"I suppose now I need not kiss you."

Was that disappointment in her voice? Oh, God, he could not stand much more. What he had thought impossible was not. She **could** have what she wanted did she continue, and he had no hope that she would not continue.

When she climbed onto the bed, he thrashed again, but she grabbed hold of his hips and hung on. And he could **feel** her nakedness now as she hugged him, her breasts pressing against his skin, nearly at his groin. This, too, merely aided her, forcing more blood to rush to that traitor, so he stilled again, hoping he was not hard enough to penetrate her, praying she **was** a virgin so she would not know the difference and would still fail.

She crawled up him, still holding on tightly in case he tried to throw her off again. Warrick groaned at this further stimulation. And then she was seated, and he was hard enough that she only had to nudge him in the right direction.

Heat. Scalding heat and moisture. Why could she not be dry? Why could she not . . . ?

Her whimper went through him like a lance, even as he felt the cause of it. She was still trying to seat herself fully, but her maidenhead would not give, and she was progressing too slowly to do aught but cause herself pain. He felt a savage pleasure in that. So she was a virgin, and her own pain would defeat her where he could not.

To move now would truly aid her, so he remained deathly still. Yet she was so small and exquisitely tight, the urge was there, nigh overwhelming, to thrust deep into her. He killed it swiftly. He could not control that traitor, but he still controlled the rest of his body.

He heard another whimper, louder, and he opened his eyes to feed on her pain. Tears streaked her smooth cheeks. Her sapphire eyes, glassy with wetness, reflected that pain. But he had forgotten her nakedness.

She was a small woman, but she was generously formed, her breasts bountiful, her waist tiny. The spread of her hips over him, her splendid breasts bouncing with her soft panting, the feel of hot wetness squeezing only half of him—the sight of that part of him inside her . . . It was his undoing. He did not thrust. He did not have to. The blood rushed to swell him to his full, throbbing length, which pushed right through her maidenhead without either of them moving to help it.

She cried out as it happened, and her weight carried her down to sheathe him fully in her depths. Warrick ground his teeth against the gag in his mouth. His muscles strained, but he remained still otherwise. He fought now for impotence. He fought to ignore the powerful urges of his body. It was torture. He had never resisted anything so hard, never wanted anything so much that was so opposed to his will.

She moved on him, hesitantly at first, clumsily. She was still hurting, still crying, but still determined. Her breath, which was coming so hard, fanned his belly along with her hair, providing another caress, another torture. And he knew exactly when he lost the fight. He tried one last time to throw her off, welcoming the pain in his ankles and wrists, but she knew, **knew,** and she held fast to him. And then he no longer cared, was mindless in the throes of primal instinct, which took over completely to drain his seed with explosive, unbelievable relief. Damn her, **damn her!**

❧ 9

I am glad 'twas you.

Warrick would never forget those words, nor would he forgive them. He recalled them again and again in those next days while he lay chained to that bed.

She had collapsed onto his chest when it was over, her tears wetting his skin. She had found no pleasure in their coupling, but she had gotten what she wanted. And before she left him, she had touched his cheek and whispered, "I am glad 'twas you," and his hate had increased tenfold.

Her servant had come after that, to tend his wounds. The older woman had clucked her tongue over what he had done to himself, but she had also found the blood-encrusted lump on his head and cleaned that, too. He had let her. Devastated by his failure, he no longer cared just then what was done to him. Nor had it bothered him when the man came in still later to stare at the blood and seed still wet on his loins with an odd mixture of satisfaction and fury.

"She tells me you fought her. That is good, or I think I would kill you now for what you had of her."

The man had turned about and left after that, nor had Warrick seen him again. But those few words had given him a wealth of information. He knew now that he was not meant to leave here alive. They wanted no ransom from him. They wanted only the babe he might already have planted in the wench's belly. He also knew the man was jealous of him, that he would take pleasure in killing Warrick when his usefulness was at an end.

Still he did not care, not that next day, not about anything. He did not even feel the humiliation of having Mildred feed him, bathe him, and assist him to relieve himself right there in the bed. He did not even try to speak to her when his gag was removed for the feeding. His apathy was almost complete—until the wench came back.

Only then did he know it must be night again, for there were no windows in that small room to tell him of the passing hours. And only then did he come alive again, his fury driving him nigh mad. His thrashing loosed his bandages, embedding the iron manacles deeper into his still raw flesh.

But she was patient that second night. She did not try to touch him until he had worn himself out. And she avoided getting on the bed until he was nearly full ready for her.

Three times she visited him that second night, throughout the night, and three times the next, waking him if she needed to. Each time, perforce, took longer, with his body already sated, yet that did not stop her. She had him at her complete mercy. She examined him fully in the guise of caressing and stimulating him to readiness, everywhere, but mostly between his legs.

She was fascinated by his manroot, brought her face and breath close to it, yet never did she actually do as promised that first night, for 'twas unnecessary. The mere thought that she might affected him as if she had. And he could not prevent any of it, could not stop her, could not smite her with a look or put the fear back in her that she should feel. She used him, she drained him, she no longer displayed the least remorse. She had no mercy whatsoever.

Ah, God, how he wanted revenge on her. 'Twas all he thought about the third day, what he would do to her if he could just get his hands on her. And to think he had actually thought to give her a home when he had first seen her. Aye, he would give her a home, in his dungeon. But first he would pay her back in kind. Nay, first he must escape.

"Tell me her name."

'Twas the first time he had spoken to Mildred. She eyed him warily as she brought another spoonful of thick mutton stew to his lips.

"I think not. You do not need to know."

"My men will find me, Mistress. Do you want to live through the destruction I will wreck on this place, you will cooperate with me now."

She had the gall to snort at him. "You were alone when taken."

"Nay, I was with my squire Geoffrey. They killed him, did you know?"

Such coldness had entered his tone, Mildred was suddenly afraid of him, even though he was bound fast. Then she scoffed at herself and at him.

"A knight? Nay, they were sent for a villein. Think you they would not know the difference?"

He did not try to convince her otherwise. "My men were sent ahead. I was to join them the next morn. Think **you** they will just ride on without me?"

"Methinks you spin a fine tale, sirrah, but to what end?" she asked.

"Release me."

"Ah, fine tactics." She grinned at him. "But 'tis unnecessary to tell me lies. If I had the key to release you from these chains, I would not use it, not until my lady has what she needs of you."

She did not add that Rowena had already bidden her to find the key. But she had had no luck thus far, and she would not give him false hope any more than Rowena would.

The feeding had taken longer this time, because he would not be quiet. The extra time had given the red gag marks across his cheeks a chance to fade. She noticed this when she bent to tie a new gag in place, and the sight of him without those distracting marks gave her a distinct chill.

"God's mercy, you have a cruel look about you," she said more to herself than to him. "I did not see it ere now."

Warrick did not need to be told that. It was why his first wives had feared him. It was why his enemies feared him. It was why that cursed wench should have stayed away from him. It was mostly in his eyes, so expressive of his black thoughts, but also in the hard, bitter slant of his mouth, which rarely smiled. And his expression was particularly bitter now that he knew she would not aid him.

"You would do well to remember that—"

She stuffed the gag in his mouth to cut him off, saying indignantly, "It does you no good to threaten me, sirrah. I do my lady's bidding, not yours. 'Tis no wonder she is naught but aggrieved when she leaves you each night. 'Twould have done you no harm to have treated her gently when she had no choice in coming to you. But nay, you are as cruel inside as you are without."

He had sunk back into pure fury at those parting words. Was he supposed to feel pity for a woman who repeatedly raped him? Was he supposed to feel sympathy when the purpose was to steal a child from him? When she was glad, **glad** that 'twas he at her mercy instead of another? And why was that? Why would she be glad, when women feared him? It had been thus since his sixteenth year, when he had learned of all that was lost to him, his family, his home, naught left but his life and a betrothal contract that could not be broken. He had changed then, changed utterly, not just in character, but in appearance, for the darkness that had entered his soul had also been etched on his face.

Since then, he had never taken a woman to his bed who did not at first fear that he would hurt her in some manner. Even after a second or third time, they still did not trust him not to visit some cruelty upon them. His wives . . . such timid, meek creatures, they never did get over their fear of him, even though he had never given them cause to think he would be brutal with them. But they had both died many years ago. And they had lived with him during the years when he had lived and breathed for revenge, when his every thought was of destruction and killing—as it was now.

How could she be glad? Because he was bound fast and could not touch her? Because she knew he would be dead before the chains were removed from him, so she had naught to fear of him? That was a very real possibility, that he would be butchered right here in this bed, without a chance of defending himself, without a chance of obtaining the least retribution.

He did not fear death. There was a time when he had even courted it, when his life had been so empty and miserable he simply had not cared if he lived or died, and not much had improved since then. But he would regret the loss of this chance he now had to better his existence with Lady Isabella. Even more than that, however, he would regret being unable to avenge himself on these people for the ills that had been done to him here, much less for his death.

So it was to Warrick's utter amazement that Mildred came not with food the next day, but with a pile of clothes and the key to his shackles. And she came at her lady's behest, if her first words could be credited.

" 'Tis well I found the key, sirrah, for my lady wants you gone, and it must be now, whilst her brother is in the town hiring his mercenaries." She told him this while she removed his gag. "I will convince him your seed took root, but that does not mean he will not hunt you down."

"Brother?" Warrick remembered the man, and his jealousy. "I warrant not by blood."

"Nay, no blood betwixt them, thank the Holy Mother," she said, not looking at him, wasting no time in unlocking his shackles.

"And if my seed did not take? Will another take my place here in this cursed bed?"

"That need not concern you, sirrah."

"Then tell me why a child is needed. And **my** child? I deserve to know that at least."

Mildred was surprised, having assumed Rowena would have told him that, but she shrugged. "Why else? To secure this place. She wed Kirkburough's old lord, but he died the same day, the day you were taken. The child will be claimed as his."

Greed, aye, he should have known. And Kirkburough was a large fief, with the town included. He had seen the keep from the town. He had avoided it because he had not wanted to meet the lord and have to explain his presence in the area. His escort of thirty men would have been cause for alarm, even in the town, which was why he had sent them on ahead. All he had wanted was a bed and a bath, which any inn could supply. He had not counted on a greedy bride determined to keep what she had married for at any cost.

Mildred stepped out of his reach when the last chain dropped loudly to the floor. Warrick carefully lowered his arms, his muscles screaming after three days at that unnatural angle. He gritted his teeth against the pain. That, too, felt strange without the gag to bite on. But he did not wait for the pain in his shoulders to lessen before he reached for the clothes she had brought.

The tunic was made of the most inferior homespun he had ever seen, fit only for the meanest villein, and stunk to high heaven. But at least it fit him across the shoulders and arms, though it was lacking in length. So, too, were the coarse russet leggings, moth-eaten and frayed, and stopping well short of his ankles. The shoes were made of cloth, so at least they stretched to his size. The belt was a thin strip of leather.

He said naught about the deplorable clothes. Once dressed, he had only one thing on his mind.

"Where is she?"

"Nay." Mildred backed away to the door. "You try to hurt her, I will sound the alarm."

"I wouldst just speak with her."

"You lie, sirrah. 'Tis in your eyes. She bade me help you escape because she does not want your death on her conscience, but she never wants to see you again. Do you come back here, Lord Gilbert will kill you. 'Tis that simple. So take your life and go."

He stared at her for a long moment, his desire to get his hands on the wench who might or might not already carry his child warring with his desire for freedom. And he did not know how many he would have to fight if Mildred did cry for help. That settled it.

"Very well, but I will need a sword, my horse—"

"Are you mad?" she hissed. "You will go as you are, to draw no notice. The men who took you got rid of all that was yours, doubt it not. Now come. I will lead you to the postern gate. There is little time left."

He followed her, but he took note of everything

he saw as she led him out of the keep and through the bailey. He almost changed his mind about leaving when he saw how few men were about, other than servants. The defenses were strong, but there was no one there to man them.

No wonder the brother was off hiring men. Kirkburough could be taken in a day, and Warrick would be back in less than a sennight to prove it.

✿ 10

" 'Tis done."

"I know," Rowena said dispassionately as she turned away from the window. "I watched until he disappeared into yonder woods."

"I have a bad feeling about this," Mildred said uneasily. "We should have waited."

"Nay. Gilbert has already said he will not depart here until he is assured I have the babe. He intends to leave the siege of Tures in the hands of his knights, since they do not expect to make much progress in the early weeks, and he is not really needed there. Today was the first he has even stepped out of the hall, much less the keep. He might not again. And he watches everyone with a hawk's eye, to make sure no servants sneak up here. Think you he would not notice that huge lout leaving?"

"He sleeps—"

"And the keep is locked tight with his own men

set to guard at the doors. You **know** this was the best time, Mildred, like as not the only time to get that man out of here without Gilbert's knowing and setting off a hue and cry."

"But he did not serve his purpose," Mildred reminded her baldly.

Rowena shivered, though the chamber was not cold. "I—I could not do it again, even were he still here. I told you that last eventide. Not again."

"Aye, my lamb, I know 'twas hard—"

"Hard?" Rowena cut in with a harsh-sounding laugh. " 'Twas wrong, **so** wrong! And I can no longer commit a wrong to stop another from being committed. I had to at first, to show Gilbert I was doing as he demanded. But after I convinced him to stay away, convinced him his presence disturbed the man so much that I could not tempt him, I did not need to go back in there. Yet I did. I still obeyed Gilbert exactly, when if I had only stopped to think—"

"**Why** do you blame yourself?" Mildred demanded. "You did not even get any pleasure out of it, when **he** did."

"Nay, he did not. How could he have pleasure in what he hated? Mildred, he fought me every single time. He hurt himself to fight me. He hated it, hated me, and made sure I knew it. Those eyes—" She shivered again. "I could not have gone in there again. I could not force him again did my own life depend on it."

"But if your plan does not work?"

"It will. It must. Gilbert will not know he has escaped. He will think I still visit the man nightly. When I know if I have conceived or not, I will tell him that **I** let the man go. He will not punish me for it, for he will not risk the child. And the man's life or death is not that important to his plan. He said himself that no one would believe a serf did he lay claim to the child. That is the least of my worries."

"I am not so sure he **was** a serf," Mildred admitted with unease.

"You noticed his arrogance, too?"

"He claimed he had a squire who was killed when he was captured."

"God's mercy, another reason for him to despise me." Rowena sighed. "So he was a baseborn knight. Think you he will admit to anyone what was done to him here?"

"Nay, never," Mildred replied without a single doubt.

"Then we need not worry about him starting rumors—if there is a child. But whether there is or not, Gilbert will be told there is. He will leave then, off to fight that damn warmonger Fulkhurst—may they both kill each other. And as soon as he leaves, so will we. I still have all of my clothes, nigh worth a fortune, and we have a town right here where we can obtain a good price for all. We will hire our own men, collect my mother from

Ambray keep while Gilbert is busy at Tures, then make our way to France and Henry's court."

"Lord Gilbert will not be pleased to lose Kirkburough **and** you."

"Think you I care?" Rowena almost snarled in her bitterness. "After what he has done, 'tis my hope that he never finds pleasure in anything **ever** again."

Later that afternoon, Rowena seemed to get her wish, at least temporarily. Gilbert had not been long back from the town, where he had found no more than three men whom he deemed worthy of hiring and another four worth training, when a message came to him that turned him livid with rage. She was pleased to witness it from where she sat sewing by the hearth.

She had been allowed down to the Great Hall a few hours each day so that the people would grow used to her, and so she could assure anyone who asked that Lord Godwine was recovering but still too ill to leave his chamber, and still insistent that only she tend him. Gilbert had realized the necessity in this, and the necessity in claiming that Lyons was not so seriously ill that he could not do his duty to his new wife. When the time was right, Gilbert would merely claim that the lord had had a tragic relapse and died.

Now she watched her stepbrother turn purple, he was so furious, and curse and rant, sending nearly every servant running to vacate the hall. Her first thought was that he had somehow discovered that Lyons' substitute had escaped. But unless the man had stupidly got himself caught again, that could not be, for Gilbert had not gone abovestairs since the night it had all begun.

When he noticed her sitting there, his high color slowly receded. He appeared so thoughtful as he stared at her, too thoughtful—and calculating. She held her breath when he approached, suddenly horribly afraid that she was going to be forced into some new act that she would despise. But when she heard what he had to say, she would have laughed if she did not think he would slap her for it.

"I know not how he discovered that Kirkburough is now mine, but he must have, for Fulkhurst has followed me here. God curse him, the man is relentless!"

"I thought you said he was at Tures."

"He was. But he must have had warning that my army approached and escaped ere the siege began. And he must have gathered another army, for he comes with nigh five hundred men under his dragon's banner."

"If he raised another army, why did he not take it immediately to Tures to rout yours?"

"Do not be stupid, Rowena," Gilbert snapped impatiently. "Tures Castle was your father's stronghold. You know how defensible it is. Those men Fulkhurst left behind to guard it can hold it for him for weeks. There is no hurry for him to return to Tures, not when he has learned that I am here with naught but a handful of men. Does he capture me, he can make terms that will disperse my army."

"Or he can kill you."

He glared at her, but she was pleased to see his color recede even more to an unnatural paleness.

"Are you sure 'tis him?" she asked. "Tures is two days north of here."

"No one can mistake his colors, or that damn fire-breathing red dragon rampant on a black field. 'Tis him, and he will be without in less than an hour, so I must leave now."

"And I?"

"He will take this keep whether I am here or not. He knows 'tis mine, and he has sworn to take all that is mine for our trespass at Dyrwood. Curse him, why could he not be satisfied with my father's death?"

As that was said not to her, she did not try to answer. She could not understand vengefulness of that depth anyway. But she was not alarmed that the Lord of Fulkhurst was coming here, or that Gilbert meant to leave her behind to face him. Anything that thwarted Gilbert and his hateful plans would be well received by her.

"You will make terms with him for yourself," he

continued. "He will not harm you. Last year he captured another of my wards, Lady Avice, and only insisted she swear fealty to him. Do the same if he demands it, for it will not matter. I will be back here in three days' time with my army to defeat him. Aye, 'tis better done here than at Tures Castle, for Kirkburough can be easily surrounded. And I now have enough men to do so, three times as many as he. Do not fear, Rowena, I will have you back in my care shortly."

So said, he grabbed her and gave her a kiss that could in no wise be construed as brotherly. She was amazed. She was repulsed. She had not known he desired her until that moment.

ᣥ II

Rowena did not realize it until after Gilbert had gone, that she and her mother had been saved from his fury by his distraction. He was so set on his new course, with only Fulkhurst and defeating him on his mind, that he had forgotten about the man supposedly still chained upstairs. Were the man still there, she would have had a fine time explaining him to the invaders when they took over the keep.

Fortunately, that was not one of her worries. Nor did she give any thought to Gilbert's instructions, not at first, since she had had every intention of leaving the keep herself as soon as he had. But it took no time at all to discover that the despicable cur had taken every last remaining man-at-arms with him, as well as every last horse.

She had then thought briefly of taking herself off to the town to hide there, to leave the keep open with naught but the servants to greet Fulkhurst's army. But this was a man set on vengeance as well as on conquering, and such a man might well burn the town down in search of Gilbert—or the new lady of Kirkburough. Escaping into the woods as Lyons' substitute had done would not serve either. On foot, without money, she would not be able to rescue her mother before Gilbert discovered what she had done.

She was forced to follow Gilbert's instructions this time, because there was naught else she could do. But she would make no demands. She would wait and see what terms were offered and go on from there. It could not be known that the keep was completely defenseless. The portcullis was down, the gate closed. From without, Kirkburough looked a strong keep. She did not doubt that she could wrest favorable terms from the warlord for herself and the servants.

And once she had met Fulkhurst and taken his measure, mayhap she could appeal to him for help. If he was no worse than Gilbert, she would offer her wardship to him. Of course, he already had three of her properties in hand, and was not like to give them back. She would not mention them. She had others still in Gilbert's control—but Fulkhurst intended to take all that was in Gilbert's control anyway, for himself. God's mercy, she truly had naught to bargain with—nay, she could assist Fulkhurst. She knew Gilbert's plans, could warn of his return. But would the warmonger believe her?

Mildred had wanted to go with her to the gatehouse, but Rowena convinced her to stay in the hall and do what she could to calm the servants. She took four of the menservants with her, for she had not the strength to raise the portcullis by herself. But she had waited almost too long. Fulkhurst's army had arrived, was just beyond arrow range, and the sight of it, five hundred strong and armed for war, with nigh fifty mounted knights, sent the men she had brought with her into a panic.

They wanted only to run and hide, and she could not blame them when she felt the same. Yet she could not allow that, and her own fear added a coldness to her tone as she calmly explained that if they did not stay to help her, they would die; that either the enemy would kill them after crashing the gates open—or she would. The men stayed, though they cowered on the floor of the gatehouse, well away from the arrow slits.

Rowena watched, willing herself to calmness. So many knights. She had not expected that. And the red dragon breathing fire, aye, it flew on several pennants clearly seen, and many of the knights had it emblazoned on the trappings of their warhorses. It was indeed Fulkhurst, though she could not guess which of the mounted knights was him.

It did not take long before one man separated from the mass and rode up to the gate. He was not heavily mailed, not a knight, then. At least forty of the men-at-arms were also mounted, though not on the large destriers, and this was one of them.

He had a carrying voice. Rowena heard every word clearly, she just did not believe them. No terms, no assurances. Complete surrender or complete annihilation. She had ten minutes to decide.

There was naught to decide. Even if it were a bluff, which she doubted, she could not call it, for the men she had brought with her did not wait to hear her decision. They rushed to open the portcullis without her order to do so, and she could not stop them. All she could do now was go down to the bailey and wait for the army to enter.

The knights came in with swords drawn, but there was not a soul left in the bailey other than Rowena, who stood on the lower step of the keep. They did not seem surprised to find it so. And those sent to secure the walls did so quickly, without much caution or wariness that they would find aught to oppose them.

The remainder of the army approached Rowena, with three knights in the lead who dismounted first. Two had trappings so fine, they were likely both lords, though only one could be Fulkhurst, the other mayhap his vassal. Yet it was the third knight who walked slowly toward her, taller than the other two, sheathing his sword as he came. He did not take his eyes off her as he did this, eyes too shadowed for her to see clearly beneath his helmet.

She had chosen the wrong place to wait, with the sun behind them but shining directly on her. It lit her flaxen braids with golden sparkles, her alabaster skin to glowing whiteness, and made it difficult for her to tell anything about the man almost upon her, except that he was huge and fully armored. Even his mail coif was buckled over his lower chin, the helmet with wide nasal guard sitting low, both obscuring his features—except for the cruel slash that was his mouth.

She opened her mouth to give greeting, but only a gasp came out as his hands gripped her upper arms, so hard she thought the bones might crush. She closed her eyes against the pain, only to be shook once, sharply, to bring them open again.

"Your name?"

His voice was as cold as his mouth was cruel. Rowena did not know what to make of him. He must know she was lady here by her very dress, yet he was treating her like a field serf, and that terrified her.

"La-lady Rowena Bel—Lyons," she got out in a mere squeak.

"No longer lady. Henceforth you are my prisoner."

Rowena nearly sagged in relief. At least he did not mean to cut her down right there on the steps. And a prisoner was not so bad and was only temporary. Most of noble birth were given fine quarters for their confinement, and allowed all courtesies due their status. But what did he mean, no longer lady?

He still held her in that painful grip, waiting. For what? For her to argue against his making her a prisoner? Not with him, she would not. From what she had seen and heard thus far, he was worse than Gilbert. But what should she have expected of a man who reached for a league if you took a scant inch from him?

She was becoming unnerved, knowing that he stared at her, but she was too afraid to look up to confirm it. Finally he turned with her still in his grip, only it was to literally throw her into the mailed chest of one of the men who had come up behind him.

"Take the prisoner to Fulkhurst and install her in my dungeon. If she is not there when I arrive, there will be more than hell to pay."

The man behind her paled. Rowena did not see it. She was ashen herself, verily, near to fainting from those ominous words.

"Why?!" she cried, but Fulkhurst had already turned away to enter the keep.

🍀 12

Mildred found him in the chamber she had come to dread entering these past few days. The tall candles had burned out from Rowena's last visit to this room just before dawn, but he had found a new one and stuck it on the metal spike of the candlestand. His men were plundering the keep, taking all of value that they wanted. She could not imagine what he was doing here when a glance should have told him there was naught in this room save that bed.

She hesitated to speak. He merely stood there, staring down at the bed. He had removed his helmet, but his coif still covered his head. He was a very tall man. And those wide shoulders reminded her of . . .

"What do you want?"

She started, for he had not turned to notice her there at the door, nor had she made a single sound. And he still did not turn. Instead he bent down and dragged the long chains out from under the bed, and she watched, fascinated, as he slowly draped the two lengths around his neck like a layered necklace, the ends left hanging from his shoulders to his waist. She shivered, wondering why he would take the chains unless he meant to use them on someone.

"Answer!"

She jumped that time, and stammered, "They—they said you are the Lord of Fulkhurst."

"Aye."

"Please, what have you done with my lady? She has not returned—"

"Nor will she—ever."

He turned as he added that last word, and Mildred staggered back. "In God's mercy, not you!"

One corner of his mouth lifted in a menacing curve. "Why not me?"

Mildred thought about running. She thought about begging. She thought about her sweet Rowena in this man's hands, and she wanted to cry.

"Ah, God, do not hurt her!" she cried her horror aloud. "She had no choice—"

"Be quiet!" he roared. "Think you aught could excuse what she did to me? Her reasons matter not. By my sworn word, no one does me an ill without paying for it tenfold."

"But she is a lady—!"

"That she is a **woman** only saves her life! It does

not change her fate. Nor will you. So beseech me not on her behalf, or you may find the same fate for yourself."

Mildred held her tongue as Warrick passed her to enter the chamber across the way. But he knew she still hovered about the new doorway, wringing her hands, tears gathering and spilling from her soft brown eyes. He might be indebted to her, but if she made another entreaty for that flaxen-haired bitch, he would indeed send her to his dungeons as well. He did not give warnings twice.

The much larger chamber was fit for a lord with its costly, though meager, comforts, yet it held little of a personal nature to denote whose chamber it was. But Warrick knew. He flipped open the only chest there and the abundance of rich apparel within confirmed his thinking.

Still he asked, "Hers?"

Mildred found the voice lodged in her throat. "Aye."

"My daughters might make use of these."

He said it with such indifference, Mildred's fear dissipated and her anger rose, though she was not stupid enough to let him hear it. "That is all she has left."

He swung around to face her, and there was no lack of emotion in those baleful silver eyes, as there had been in his voice. "Nay, all she has left is the skin on her back, and what rags **I** choose to give her. Though I do not forget that I was allowed even less."

Indifference? she had thought. Nay, merely another revenge, those clothes, but likely the least of all he intended. And she could think of no way to aid Rowena when he did not want to hear that she had been as much a victim as he. Verily, Rowena's reasons would **not** matter to one such as he, who was not a serf, not a lowly knight, but a highborn lord. You simply did not do to a lord what they had done to him, and expect to live to tell of it.

Her fear returned, in abundance, but it still was not for herself. "You mean to kill her?"

"That pleasure would be too swift," he said coldly. "Nay, I will not kill her. She is my prisoner. She will never be ransomed, she will never leave Fulkhurst. She will be at my mercy until the day she dies."

"Do you have any?"

"For those who do me harm? Nay, Mistress, I do not." He glanced about the chamber again before he asked, "Did Lyons have relatives?"

Mildred was too sick at heart over his answer to wonder at his query. "Aye, a brother, I think."

"There will be naught but a blackened shell left for him," he said. "But then there will be naught left for her brother either."

Her eyes widened at his meaning. "You mean to burn the keep, too?"

" 'Twas all done for this place, was it not?"

She did not understand vengeance so all-encompassing, but it was true that everything Rowena had been forced to do had been for Kirkburough. Mayhap she could understand after all. She would not be sorry to see this place burn, and knew that Rowena would not be sorry either, to have Gilbert thwarted in that way.

"What of the servants you will leave homeless?"

He shrugged, as if it were no matter to him, but he said, "I do not burn the town—except for the inn," he added coldly. "The castlefolk can move to the town, or I will disperse them to my own lands, which would better their lot from the ragged look of them." And then he looked at her more intently, and at her fine woolen bliaut, and concluded, "You did not make your home here, did you?"

"I came here only three days ago, when my lady was brought here."

"Then you are free to return to your home."

Back to Gilbert's keep, which Fulkhurst was like to besiege in the near future? Or back to her true home at Tures, which he had already taken and Gilbert was determined to have back? Fine options, both to find her in the midst of war and destruction. But Mildred would not tell him that. If he did not know who Rowena was yet, or that her stepbrother was his avowed enemy, she would not be the one to tell him and thereby add to the vengeance he already sought.

"My home is lost," was all she finally said.

He frowned at her, and it sent a chill up her spine, for it only made him look more cruel. "As I repay those who do me ill, I also repay those who do me a service. You may make your home at Fulkhurst Castle if you so wish."

Where he had sent Rowena? Mildred had not expected that, could not credit this good fortune in the midst of total devastation.

But he saw her pleasure, understood it, and would have none of it. "Understand me, Mistress," he added sharply. "Do you go to Fulkhurst Castle, 'twill be to serve me and mine, not her. Never again will you serve her. If you cannot give me your loyalty—"

"I can," Mildred quickly assured him. "I will, and gladly."

"Will you?" he shot back skeptically, the doubt clear in those telling silver eyes. "That remains to be seen. But mayhap you will give me the name of her brother?"

The implications of that name swirled in Mildred's mind. Gilbert would not suffer for his knowing, any more than he would have if Fulkhurst ever found him, for he was already despised. 'Twas only Rowena who would suffer more for his knowing. He might even change his mind and kill her to have clear honors to her properties. Yet was he not like to learn Gilbert's name while he was here? Nay, the servants knew him only as Lord

Gilbert. And she doubted Fulkhurst would question every single man in the town.

"Why do you hesitate, Mistress?" he demanded. "Surely you know his name."

Mildred stiffened her back to meet his full rage. "Aye, but I will not give it. Though she hates him, he is now the only hope she has of being rescued from your 'mercy.' I will not aid her, but I will not aid you against her either. Do you ask that of me, then I must decline your offer."

He stared at her for a long moment before he said, "Why do you not fear me?"

"I do."

He grunted. "You hide it well."

He didn't react with rage, then, just with the typical male grouch which told her he accepted the circumstance, but was not the least satisfied with it. She found herself smiling at him, and wondering if he was not as cruel as he looked.

Warrick cared not for that smile, but he had no more questions for the woman, so he dismissed her to gather her things and to send one of his men to collect the clothes. Beatrix and Melisant could make use of them after the garments had been altered, for both girls were somewhat taller than the flaxen-haired wench. And he would enjoy having her see her possessions worn by others. Women set great store by their clothes. Aye, he would enjoy that—and a whole lot more.

He would have to find a suitable reward for Robert FitzJohn for his quick thinking in this misadventure. Sir Robert had been left in command of the men Warrick had brought to escort Isabella to Fulkhurst. Sixteen other of his household knights had also been in the troop, some older than Robert, yet Warrick had been impressed with the younger man's leadership during several skirmishes this past year and had only just promoted him to captain of the guard.

'Twas well done. When he had not met up with his men as expected, Robert had sent several back to Kirkburough town to see what had detained him. The innkeeper had claimed that Warrick had left as soon as the town gates had opened that morn, a lie that he would know the reason for ere the sun set. But Robert had had no reason to doubt the tale. Assuming Warrick was no longer in the town, he had begun a search of the countryside surrounding it. Yet the woods were thick and dense to the south, and thirty men could not cover much ground as quickly as Robert would have liked, and also have enough remaining on the road to meet Isabella when her party arrived.

Robert had then decided to send to the closest of Warrick's properties for help. This was Manns keep, held by his vassal Sir Felix Curbeil, and only a league and a half west of Kirkburough. In the meantime, Isabella had arrived and been rightly upset that Warrick had not been there to greet her, that he had, in fact, disappeared.

As it happened, another of his vassals had been visiting Sir Felix when Robert's messenger arrived, and Sir Brian had nigh two hundred men with him. So when Warrick had found his scattered men still in the area that morn, he had been told that Sir Felix and Sir Brian would be arriving within hours with their two small armies, with every intent of tearing Kirkburough apart if he still had not been found.

Warrick could not have been more surprised, or more delighted. He had thought to waste days in sending to Fulkhurst for more men, for Felix had already given him his forty days this year in the siege on two keeps belonging to his newest enemy, the Lord of Ambray. He would not have taxed Felix further, no matter his impatience, yet Felix had been glad to come. And Sir Brian simply loved to fight, the reason he always had a small army of mercenaries on hand. In fact, Warrick had only just sent Brian home this month to "see to his own," for the young lord had been in Warrick's service for nigh half a year and had given no signs of wanting to leave him.

The only thing that had not gone as he would have liked was that Lady Isabella had not waited, had camped no more than a day, then had departed the next with her small escort. He could not understand her reasoning in that. And she had left no message with Robert other than "I am going on." Verily, he did not want to chastise her before they were even wed, but he would not countenance such foolishness in a wife. He had left Robert in command. She should have stayed in his care.

But even that could not dampen his success, for the sight of Rowena Lyons standing in that bailey, alone, had filled him with a savage elation. He had her. As he had sworn to do, he had her in his power, and she would eternally regret that that was so.

Warrick left Kirkburough, but not before he had personally set a torch to the bed that had held him chained and helpless, and not before he had sent another twenty men to assure that his prisoner did not escape.

✺ 13

Rowena was in a daze for what remained of that awful day. She had been put on a horse, her wrists bound, the reins in another's control, so she did not need to concentrate on guiding the animal. And she did not take note of where they rode. Fulkhurst Castle was in the north. She knew that, and she knew she was being taken there with all speed. How she got there mattered not.

Her escort had begun with five men, though they were all of them knights, so less likely to be set upon by bands of thieves, if there were thieves in the area. However, a sixth knight caught up with them on the road with more specific orders from their lord.

Vaguely, Rowena heard that she was not to be spoken to other than to be given direction, that she was to receive no special treatment merely because she "appeared" to be a lady—which engendered much speculation—that she was not to be touched other than to be assisted on and off her mount, or to be tied thoroughly when she was not mounted. She did not care. She did not even think about it, still so shocked was she by what had happened.

They made camp that eve just off the road, and no sooner were the horses unsaddled and a fire begun than another twenty men arrived from the Lord of Fulkhurst. And by the look of their animals, they had ridden hard to reach them by dark.

Rowena's interest was finally stirred, only because she feared at first 'twas Fulkhurst who had come with so many, especially when she saw one man astride a destrier much taller than all the rest. But as they came closer to the light of the fire, she decided 'twas not him—unless he had removed his armor, for this dark-haired man wore only a tunic and woolen hose. But she had no way of knowing.

Though he was not dressed like the other knights, and there were nine in this new group, a squire took his horse off the same as the others. At least she assumed the other ten men were squires, since they were every one of them younger than she, and too finely garbed to be merely men-at-arms. But again she had no way of knowing. Too many talked at once for her to hear any distinct conversation from where she sat alone, with a tree at her back and the fire before her.

She had indeed been more firmly bound after she had been allowed to relieve herself, and that with a damn guard standing not five feet away. Her ankles now had a rope wrapped around them, so long a length it looped up nearly to her knees. Another rope, even longer, secured her waist to the tree trunk. And her hands had been retied at her back, so there was no way she could reach the cords at her feet. That she was extremely uncomfortable was of no concern to her guards, and in keeping with Fulkhurst's order of "no special treatment."

When the tall newcomer spared her only a curious glance, she felt immense relief. Not Fulkhurst, then, for that one would have given her more attention. And then she had it confirmed when she heard her original guard address him.

"He sent **you**, Sir Robert? I had not thought her such an important prisoner."

"Any prisoner is important to him, or he would not take them," Sir Robert replied.

"Forsooth," the other agreed. "Though I am relieved to give the responsibility of her over to you, when Lord Warrick made it imperative that she arrive safely in Fulkhurst. Know you what she has done to merit the dungeon?"

"He did not say, and 'tis not our concern."

But they were curious, all of them. Rowena could see it in their eyes when each of the newcomers looked at her, having heard the question, too. And if they did not know why she was being so harshly condemned, then she would not be finding out either any time soon. Their curiosity could not be as great as hers.

Mixed with their curiosity, however, she also noted admiring looks in some, which gave her naught but unease. Mayhap 'twas to her good, after all, that they had been ordered not to touch her, for she knew what could be done to female prisoners. One had been thrown in the dungeon for just a day at Gilbert's keep last year, merely as a light punishment, but the jailer had taken full use of the girl whilst she was in his care.

"Verily, Richard, are you quite sure she cannot get away?"

Sir Robert said this so dryly, Richard flushed. 'Twas the rope around her waist that Robert had noticed. The one binding her feet was hidden beneath her skirts and the single blanket that had been spread across her lap.

"You did not hear Lord Warrick's tone when he threw her at me," Richard said in his defense.

"Nay, but I am here with enough men to assure the prisoner is guarded at night as well as day. He said naught about denying her sleep."

Sir Robert came around the fire to untie the rope at her waist even as he spoke. He also retied her wrists in front of her again. Rowena thanked him when he had finished, but he gave no acknowledgment of having heard her, nor did he meet her eyes. And then she was forgotten by most of them as they ate what food had been carried with them, then settled down for the night.

One of the squires eventually brought her a crust of bread and a chunk of moldy cheese, with a bag of water. She had no appetite for the food, would likely be sick if she tried to eat it. But she was grateful for the water. She did not bother to say so, however. If they would not talk to her, why should she talk to them?

She wished she had not been brought to such a keen awareness of her predicament with Sir Robert's arrival. It had been much easier to deal with when her mind had refused to grasp all the implications.

She now knew his name, the man who was sending her to his dungeon. She had heard the name Warrick de Chaville earlier, but had not known the speaker had been talking about the Lord of Fulkhurst. His dungeon—God's mercy, a **dungeon**! It no longer lacked reality. A dungeon. And she would be there on the morrow at the rate they were traveling.

He must have known her, and that she was the rightful owner of three of the properties that had recently surrendered to him. Why else?—but how could he know? She had never met him, never even seen him before. But he could have simply heard that she was to wed Godwine Lyons, and she had given him her new name. Aye, why else would he want to put her away in a dungeon? People died in dungeons, from neglect, fouled food, or any number of other reasons. If she died, she could not make claim on her properties—and neither could Gilbert.

Ah, God, then it was not to be even temporary, her imprisonment. Fulkhurst wanted her to die, he just did not want to murder her with his own hands. She could see no difference, but he would.

She wished she were not an heiress. She wished she were a lowly serf with naught to her name that men would covet. Tures and all it entailed had brought her naught but grief since the d'Ambrays had decided to kill her father so they could have it.

Little did she sleep that night, but Rowena was not tired the next day. Her anxiety would not give her mind peace. And the day passed much too swiftly, as did the miles.

They arrived at Fulkhurst just as the sun was setting. The red glow on the castle walls so reminded Rowena of her first sight of Kirkburough that she was close to trembling. Had it only been four days ago that she thought she was entering hell? This, she knew, would be much worse—the home of the fire-breathing dragon of the north.

It was an impregnable fortress, a stronghold similar to Tures Castle. But whereas Tures just stretched toward the sky with a keep five stories high, Fulkhurst stretched and spread out over the land. An outer bailey had been added only in the past ten years, which was why the inner bailey was larger than normal. The walls of both baileys were massive in thickness and fronted by deep moats.

The larger outer bailey was almost like a town, it contained so many buildings, including a new hall under construction that would be only two floors in height. Arms practice was still done in the inner bailey, however, since it had so much yard space.

The stone keep was merely four stories high, though larger than the norm. But Rowena soon found that there was one other floor dug out beneath it. Reached through a trapdoor in the storage basement, the dungeon was another addition Lord Warrick had added to his castle.

The stairs led down to a small guardroom with stone walls and wooden floor that was presently empty. The only door was made of iron with an iron bar set across it. It led to a corridor no more than six feet long, with another iron door at the end, and two on either side. The cell at the end was the largest, though Rowena would not have guessed this, for it was only an eight-by-eight square. The floor was beaten earth, the walls well-set stone, the ceiling an iron grid similar to a portcullis, with the wooden floor of the basement seen above it.

This cell was entirely empty, without even an old rag to lie on. It was not exactly cold, for it was summer, but a draft seeped in through the floor-boards above. Rowena stared at this small, barren cell in the torchlight and willed herself not to cry.

Sir Robert himself had brought her to it. He said not a word as he removed the cords from her wrists, but he was frowning. When his eyes caught hers as he finished, she was sure he wanted to speak to her. But his lord's order held his tongue, for he was a man who followed orders down to the smallest detail.

But as he turned to leave, he growled at the man who held the torch. "Leave that and fetch the jailer so he can bring her a pallet and what other necessities are needful."

She had not realized until the door closed her in that awful cell that she might have been left in darkness. She was left in silence, however. Her ears strained to hear the parting footsteps, but the sound did not last long. Then there was the sound of rats scurrying across the floor above her.

❧ 14

Rowena knew she was in trouble when the jailer showed up with only two thin blankets for her to sleep on and a rusty tin of water. He was a heavy-set man in his middle years, with scraggly brown hair and watery eyes and a stink about his person that nearly gagged her. He had been surprised at first sight of her, amazed actually, but that did not last more than a moment, and then he did not even try to hide his delight that she was there. He was so pleased, he was close to laughing as he explained the routine he followed and that she would have to abide.

He would feed her only once a day, and she had already missed this day's meal, so she would have to wait until the next one. And if she wanted better than moldy bread and water, she would have to think of some way to pay him for it. Her fine bliaut might get her some butter and cheese for a fortnight, but after that . . . She was to relieve herself in the corner of the cell, and he might or might not get one of the stable lads to shovel it out once a week. There would be no water for bathing. He was not a lackey and he refused to haul buckets of water from the well, even though the wellhead was close by. She was to give him no complaints, or he might forget to feed her. If she wanted aught better, including another torch, she would have to pay for it.

Rowena managed to keep the horror from her expression during this recital. She knew what manner of payment he was anticipating. 'Twas there in his eyes, which returned repeatedly to her breasts and hips. She could say now that she would never, ever touch that stinking swine, but how would she feel a month from now? Even a sennight? She had not eaten last eventide, nor this day. Already she felt some weakness along with her hunger pangs. And no torch? Was she to be entombed in darkness permanently, looking eagerly toward this foul man's visits simply because he would carry a torch with him?

She could not have spoken if she tried, but he was not displeased by her silence. He even gave in to a chuckle, finally, when he left. As soon as the door closed, however, Rowena sat down on the blankets and cried. Her torch would last but a few more hours, and then . . . She did not mind the dark, truly, but she had never had to endure it without having the means to make light close to hand, and she had never had to endure it in a place like this, with rats nearby.

She was so sunk in misery she did not at first hear the loud argument coming from the guardroom. But it was a short argument, and the last of it, "Be gone!" she did hear clearly. Moments later, she cringed inwardly as her door was opened again. But 'twas not the jailer who came in with a brace of candles and set them down in the center of the cell. This man was a little older, and his surprise at his first sight of her lasted much longer. But then he looked around at what she had been given, and he swore foully.

"That whoreson, and I will wager he did not feed you either, did he?" Rowena blinked, then shook her head slowly. "Aye, 'tis as I thought, and him bewailing he wants the job. **Wants** it! He hates it, and well he should, but I can see now why he changed his mind about that. Such a tiny thing you are, and so pretty. It must be some heinous crime Lord Warrick thinks you guilty of, to put you here, but I am sure 'twill be straightened out once he comes."

Rowena just stared. She knew not what to make of this man and his tirade. He was certainly indignant about something, but she was not sure what.

He did not frighten her, however, as the other man had. Verily, there was such kindness in his light blue eyes, she almost started crying again.

He must have noticed, for he said gruffly, "Here now, none of that. 'Twill not be so bad, your stay with us. 'Tis a deplorable place to put a lady, but private for all that, and I will see what I can do about cheering it up for you."

Cheering up a dungeon? She could not help but smile at such an incongruous thought.

"Who are you?" she thought to ask.

"John Giffard I am called."

"Are you a jailer also, then?"

"Only when 'tis needful, which is not often. But I was just rousted from my fire to be told only I am to have the care of you. 'Tis late in coming, that order, though better late than not at all. That whoreson did not hurt you, did he?"

Which whoreson? she almost asked, but realized in time that he was speaking of the other jailer. "Nay, he did not touch me. But then, 'tis your lord's order that no one is to touch me, to assist me or otherwise, nor am I to be spoken to. Were you not told that you are not to speak to me?"

"Nay, no one said aught of that, nor would I mind it if 'twere said. I do as I will and always will, though I have a few stripes on my back that tried to convince me otherwise."

'Twas incredible, the anger she felt on his behalf. "**Who** whipped you?"

"Nay." He chuckled. "Never you mind. 'Twas long ago, and my own stubbornness the cause. Now, let me see what I can find for you at this late hour. The kitchen is like to be locked up tight by now, but I warrant there will be some fruit at least in the stores above."

He found her four plump apples freshly picked, which more than satisfied her hunger. But that was not all he found. He brought in a narrow wooden frame and a plump mattress heaped with warm bedding. He found an old, faded rug that covered nearly all the floor space. Another trip produced a crate to set her candles on, and a box with a supply of replacements so she need not deal with the darkness after all. There was a chamber pot, a bucket of water with cloths for washing up, and cold, fresh water to drink.

John Giffard was a godsend. He turned her dungeon cell into a room that was, if not pleasant, at least very comfortable. He brought her two large meals a day, food that was fit for the lord's table. He kept her well supplied with fresh water as well as bathwater. He brought her a needle and thread to keep her hands busy, and himself to keep her mind busy. He spent a great deal of time with her every day, gossiping about this and that, mostly nonsense. He simply loved to talk, and she loved to listen to him.

She knew she had Sir Robert to thank for John Giffard. He must have known what the other jailer was like, and also that this one had a good and kind heart. Robert had taken pity on her after all, though Warrick de Chaville was not like to thank him for it. But she would thank him if ever she had the chance.

The days turned into a week, then two, then three. When Rowena finally noticed that the time of her monthly flux had come and passed without flow, she sat down and laughed hysterically. Gilbert's plan had actually worked. That damn churl's seed had taken root with only three nights' trying. But Kirkburough was gone. From the road they had stopped to watch the smoke billow above the treetops as every wooden building and floor caught fire. There was naught left for a child to secure; a child conceived for only that purpose was useless now.

After the mad laughter came tears, a veritable flood of them mixed with self-pity. What had she done to deserve this ill fate? What would happen when Warrick de Chaville returned to Fulkhurst?

John Giffard would no doubt be taken from her, that was what, and all the comforts he had given her. That other jailer would return, or one like him. And would de Chaville even care that she was with child? Nay, he wanted her to die. She did not think that begging him at least for the child's life would work. He had not wanted Kirkburough. He had destroyed it, so he would not care about the child if she said it was Lyons' heir. But the child was hers, too, and his purpose in getting rid of her would be defeated if she left an heir to all that was hers.

She would not have to worry about giving birth in a dungeon. She would not be allowed to live that long—unless Fulkhurst did not return. And would not his war with Gilbert, who still had Lyons' army, keep him away for long? If she could just have the child before Fulkhurst even knew of it, she was sure she could convince John Giffard to find a home for it.

Rowena was not certain when the child became her first concern. It might have been conceived for the wrong purpose, might have lost its usefulness, but she considered none of that. It was hers. It did not even matter that its father was an overlarge lout who had hated her every touch. Its father . . .

She had too much time to think in that dungeon, and too often her memories dwelt on Lyons' substitute. She did not like that, but she seemed to have no control of it. If she closed her eyes, she could still see him stretched out before her, his body had been so memorable. She could still recall what it had made her feel like, the heady power in being able to control that body no matter how much he fought against it.

She had not lied when she had told him she was glad it was him. She had not enjoyed taking him, but after the original pain, it had not been unpleasant to touch him, or to taste him. He did not repulse her, did not make her gag with his clean smell. And he was very appealing to the eye—except for those silver eyes of his that hated her with such passion. But before she had first spoken to him, those eyes had been lovely, had made him very handsome despite the gag that had distorted his mouth.

She had not heard John approach until the door opened with its usual creak to draw her from her pensiveness. He was not wearing his usual pleasant smile and seemed disturbed about something. And then . . .

"Are you breeding, Lady Rowena?"

She stared at him in amazement. She had not been sick of a morn, as some women suffered, nor had her breasts enlarged the tiniest bit yet.

"How did you know?"

"Then you are?"

"Aye, but how—"

"I had not thought of it this soon, but my lord asked if you had had your—ah—woman's time yet, and I realized you had not asked me for extra—ah—cloths. Why did you not tell me?"

"I only just realized it myself. But what do you mean, your lord asked? When?"

"Just now."

Rowena lost what color she had maintained in that sunless room. "He has returned?"

"Aye, and I am to bring you to him now."

✣ 15

Rowena did not beg John not to take her to his lord. There would be no point to it. If he did not take her, someone else would come and get her. But she wanted to plead. All she could remember of Fulkhurst was his bigness and that slash of cruelty that was his mouth-and that icy coldness in his voice when he had sent her to his dungeon.

She barely noticed the Great Hall as she was led through it. 'Twas only the middle of the afternoon, so there were not so many people about, mainly servants busy at some task, a few soldiers, a few knights of no great stature.

It was to the lord's solar that she was taken, a large room beyond the hall. It was bright with sunlight streaming in through two deep-set window alcoves, one on each side of the hooded fireplace. The large bed was four-posted and finely curtained. It was set against the stone wall that divided the hall, so in winter it would have the added warmth of the great hearth in the hall heating the stones behind it.

There were other things to note, but Rowena was so arrested by the sight of what looked like a pile of chains in the center of the bed, she did not notice the man standing on the other side of the bed, not until he came around it.

His very height proclaimed him, if his fine black tunic and chausses did not—and his mouth, aye, that thin, cruelly shaped slash. It took her a moment more to see the dark blond hair, not quite brown with its golden sheen, and then the eyes, silver and blazing with emotion.

Her own eyes grew enormous, the single word "You" formed on her lips without sound, and then merciful blackness rose up to engulf her.

"Here now," John grunted as he caught her just before she hit the floor.

Warrick leaped forward to almost yank her out of the older man's arms. He carried her to the bed and laid her out on it. One of her small hands came to rest on the chain beside her. She would feel it when she awoke. He smiled.

"I cannot imagine what caused that, my lord," John said anxiously at his back. "She has been eating good."

Warrick did not take his eyes off the flaxen-haired wench. "So you did pamper her? She has no rat bites to scar that smooth skin?"

John's answer was a loud snort. Warrick knew his man. John was well known for his soft heart and gentleness with all creatures.

Warrick had been furious with himself after he had sent the order that John Giffard alone was to guard her. But he did not send another man to rescind it. He did not want her to suffer until he was there to make her suffer. And he did not want her small, delicate body shrunken with deprivation, not for what he planned. But mostly, he wanted no other man to touch her, at least not until he knew if she had been successful in her thievery. According to John, she had been.

"She is such a sweet, gentle lady, my lord. What did she do to warrant the dungeon?"

"Her crime was against me personally, so great I cannot speak of it."

"Surely not!"

"You have let that pretty face fool you, John. She is naught but a greedy wench who wouldst do aught, no matter how atrocious, to see her ends met. She possesses a stubborn core of determination worthy of a man. She—" He stopped, realizing he was saying more than was necessary. He did not need to explain his motives to any man. "I have stripped her of the title she gained in wedding Godwine Lyons, so call her lady no more. And you need not concern yourself with her further. She will not return to the dungeon—for now."

Warrick felt John's need to argue, though he did not look back at him to see it. The man would be wise not to overstep his bounds this once, and John must have sensed that, for he quietly left the solar without saying anything more.

Warrick continued to stare at his prisoner, not even minding that her faint was denying him his revenge. He could be patient now that the time was finally at hand, though he had not been patient until now. Yet he had stayed away apurpose, knowing full well that he could not be here without beginning the revenge he had decided on. Only that would not suit. He had to know first if the wench had been successful in her greedy scheme.

Now he knew, and that doubled her crime against him. If he had thought to spare her even a little, which he had not, her breeding settled the matter, and brought his fury back with a vengeance. She carried **his** child. **She had no right to it!**

He had known the very moment she recognized him, had seen the fear that had caused her to faint. He had gloried in that fear. He had not been sure if she had recognized him in Robert's borrowed armor in the bailey at Kirkburough. Now he knew she had not. But she did now. And mayhap by now she had learned what manner of man he was, had heard of his reputation for exacting utter destruction on anyone so unwise as to encroach on what was his. That he had never sought revenge on a woman before mattered not. He had only needed to decide what would be an appropriate retaliation for one of her sex, and he had had ample time to do that while he had searched for Isabella.

That had been a fruitless endeavor. When one of his messengers had returned to tell him that his future bride had not arrived at Fulkhurst, he had been thankful for a reason to delay his own arrival there. But searching for her had been an effort in frustration. There were simply too many different routes she could have taken along the way to Fulkhurst. Finally, he had left the matter of finding her to her father, who was certainly more upset by her disappearance than he was himself. And **that** had annoyed him, too, that it was more thoughts of this wench here that had plagued him the whole while, when he should have been concerned only with his missing bride.

She sighed, and Warrick's breath held, waiting, willing her to open those large sapphire eyes. Her lips were parted. He remembered the lushness of them, remembered the hot feel of them against his skin whenever she had had to work harder at coaxing his body's response. Her flaxen tresses were in two thick braids, one beneath her, the other curled across her breasts. He remembered those breasts, full and tempting, but never his to touch or taste, revealed to him only to inflame his senses, to aid in his defeat. He had them to touch now, and it was all he could do not to rip her gown open. But not yet. Not yet. She had to be fully aware of everything he did to her, just as he had been agonizingly aware of everything she had done to him.

She stretched, making a soft sound in her throat, then stilled, except for her hand. He watched the fingers of the hand that rested on the chains feel the cold iron links, watched the frown that creased her brow as she wondered what it was.

"A souvenir," he explained. "From Kirkburough."

Her eyes flew open, enormous eyes dominating her small oval face. She made another sound, as if she were strangling. Her fear was palpable, but it was too much, more like utter terror. He would be furious if she fainted again.

Rowena wished she could. God's mercy, no wonder she had spent these weeks in a dungeon. It had naught to do with her properties. She was going to die, but not by mere deprivation as she had thought. She remembered this man's hatred and knew he would probably torture her to death. She knew now why he had fought so violently against her rape of him. He was no villein to be in awe of her, but a powerful warlord, a man no one would dare treat as they had done. And Gilbert, that utter, utter fool, had not even known he had captured his worst enemy. Like as not Fulkhurst did not know who she was, either, or that it was **his** own worst enemy who had captured him.

A laugh bubbled up in her throat. She could not stop it. If she had not already lost her mind, she soon would. And he just stood there beside the bed, frowning down at her. Had she thought him handsome? A delusion. That mouth, those chilling eyes—he was a living nightmare, her nightmare, a man who defined cruelty with every line of his face.

She began to shake in reaction. He swore foully and brought his hand to her throat with firm pressure. Her eyes flared even wider.

"Do you faint again, I will beat you," he growled.

Was that supposed to reassure her? But he released her and moved away from the bed. In self-preservation she watched him, but he only went to the cold hearth and stood there staring down at it.

From behind, he was not a monster, just a man. His dark gold hair was not really curly, yet it curled at his neck. It looked soft, though she had never dared to bring her hand that close to his face to touch it. His body was still appealing to the eye. She had known he would be tall, just not this tall. And he held himself so taut with emotion now, the tunic pulled tight across his broad back and shoulders.

Minutes passed, then more minutes, and he did

not turn to look her way. Rowena stopped shaking and took several deep breaths. Her torture would not begin yet, not here in his solar. He had brought her here likely only to frighten her—and to gloat. The captive was now the captor.

"Have you calmed yourself, wench?"

Calm? Would she ever know that state again? But she nodded, then realized he could not see it, for he had not looked at her to speak.

"Aye."

"Though 'tis my right to do so, I do not mean to kill you."

Rowena had not realized she had held herself as stiffly as he until she sagged into the mattress with her relief. Under the circumstances, she would never have believed she could be so fortunate, nor would she have thought him to be merciful enough to tell her. He could have left her with her terror. He could have . . . but he was not finished.

"You will be punished. Doubt it not. But my retaliation will be in kind—like for like." He turned then to see her reaction, but he saw only incomprehension, so he explained. "As you and your brother intended to take my life if I had not escaped, yours now belongs to me, and I find it of little value. As I was treated, so will you be. You have had a reprieve only because I wanted to know first how great was your guilt, if you had succeeded in your theft. We both know that you have.

So as you took the child from my flesh, so will it be taken from you when it is born."

"No," she said quietly.

"No!?" he exploded incredulously.

"Possession is nine-tenths—"

"We do not speak of properties! 'Tis flesh of my flesh you stole!"

God's mercy, how had she dared defy him and tempt him to this level of rage? He was livid with it, a mere inch from coming after her and breaking her in two. But she could not let him include the child in his vengeance.

She continued softly, praying he would see reason. "I hold it, I will bear it, and I want it for itself, for no other reason than it will be mine."

"**Never** will that child be yours. You will be no more than a vessel to succor it till it is born."

He did not shout that, nay, he said it **too** coldly.

"Why do you want it?" she cried. "It will be no more than a bastard to you. Have you not enough of those to satisfy you?"

"What is mine is mine—just as you are now mine to do with as I will. Argue with me no more, wench, or you will immediately regret it."

That was a promise she could not ignore. She had pushed him too far, had dared much more than was wise at this point. She might know the man intimately, yet she knew him not at all. But time would tell, and she had time now. He had allowed her that, allowed her her life. The issue would definitely be raised again, however, for 'twas too important to her to let it be. But she could wait until she had more hope of winning.

She left his bed to stand beside it. She was surprised that she had even been put on it, as despised as she was. And he had every right to despise her. She wished she could not see his side of it, but she did. She wished he could see her side of it, but he would not. 'Twould not matter to him that she was sorry for what she had done, that she had not wanted to do it. She had still done it. Verily, she deserved whatever retribution he demanded. And to be fair, she did not deserve the child either, not if he considered it stolen from him, as he had said, only— she could not be fair where the child was concerned.

She was becoming tense again under his chilling regard, but finally he said with sneering contempt, "It should not surprise me that you lack intelligence, considering the plan you devised to keep Kirkbur—"

" 'Twas Gilbert's plan, not mine. He wanted it, not me."

"You still display naught but stupidity. **Never** interrupt me again, wench. And never mention to me again an excuse for what you did. Your Gilbert was not the one who came to me and forced me—"

He was too angry to finish. Rowena became alarmed once more as his skin darkened in hue.

"I am sorry!" she blurted out, knowing it was inadequate, yet knowing not what else to say.

"Sorry? You will be much sorrier, I promise you. But you may begin appeasing my outrage now. I hardly recognize you in clothes, wench. Remove them."

❧ 16

Rowena's breath had stopped completely. Her eyes closed in dread. Fulkhurst had said like for like. She had known that meant he would force her as she had forced him. And 'twould no more pleasant for her than it had been then, which was no more than it should be. But why would he choose this way to punish her when he hated her so, could not really want to touch her? But of course, the revenge was more important to him. Already she understood that about his nature. But to have to remove her clothes for him . . .

"If I must assist you . . ."

Another threat of she knew not what, but she did know she did not want to find out. "Nay, I will do it," she said in an abject whisper.

She turned around to untie her embroidered girdle, but in a few steps he was behind her, his hand gripping her shoulder painfully as he swung her back around. Whatever she had done wrong, his anger was high again. But he did not make her wonder why.

"You know I need the sight of you disrobing to wet my appetite. 'Tis why you stripped for me before. Whoever advised you, wench, advised you well. But know this. If I cannot accomplish what I intend through lack of interest in what you have to offer, **you** will have the blame for it. But you will not have another reprieve if that is what you think, because what I cannot do, I will bring in another to do—nay, ten others. I doubt you will disgust them as you do me."

Rowena met his eyes as he stepped back and wished to God she knew if he really meant that, or if it was just an idle threat. He looked cruel enough to do it. He looked angry enough to do it. But he wanted like for like, and watching her being raped by others would not be the same. Would it?

She dropped her girdle on the floor and reached quickly for the laces on the side of her bliaut. She could not take chances with him, not with such terrifying consequences. But she tried to remember Mildred's advice and could not recall a single thing. The chamber was too bright with daylight, her skin too hot with embarrassment, her fingers too clumsy. She **knew** she was not the least bit enticing.

Warrick's blood was already raging for her. Her fear was exciting him, that was all. Not that becoming flush to her cheeks. Not her virginlike demeanor. Certainly not the small though exquisitely curved body he remembered, and which was about to be revealed to him again. He realized, with chagrin, that he could not continue to watch her, or he would not be able to do all that he had planned to do.

With a silent oath, he moved to the other side of the bed and picked up the chain. He had meant to make her stretch it out beneath the bed and position it as he directed, just to increase her trepidation, but he did it himself now for the distraction. Only it did not take long, not as long as it was taking her to disrobe.

Her red outer gown was on the floor, her long-sleeved chemise on top of it. But she still wore a thin linen shift, though her fingers were gripping the hem, had been in the process of lifting it over her head, when she finally noticed what he was doing.

"Please, no," she pleaded, looking from the manacle still in his hand to his cold eyes. "I will not fight you. I swear it."

He did not even hesitate in his implacable reply. "It will be the same, exactly the same."

Rowena stared at the chains he had brought up on the outside of the posts at the end of the bed, positioned so the posts would prevent her from closing her legs. "That is not the same," she said.

"Allowances must be made for the differences in the gender of the body chained. My legs had no need to be open. Yours do."

She closed her eyes at the vivid mental picture his words evoked. Like for like. And she could not prevent it, could not even beg for mercy, for he had none. He was ruthlessly determined to do this to her, and it would be exactly as had been done to him.

"You are taking too long, wench," he warned softly. "Do not try my patience more."

She yanked the shift over her head and climbed swiftly to the center of the bed, anything to get this over with so this sick dread would leave her. She lay down before he ordered her to, but her body was as stiff as a board. She kept her eyes closed, tightly, only she could still hear him, and the sound of his steps took him to the bottom of the bed.

"Spread them." She groaned inwardly, but she did not dare to defy him. "Wider," he added, and she did that, too.

But she still gasped as his fingers went around her ankle to hold it until the cold iron was locked on. The manacle did not fit tightly as it had on him, the weight of the chain pulling it down to catch on her arch and heel. Her other foot was quickly done the same, but he uttered a curse when the chain did not extend far enough over the top of the bed to reach her wrists. It had been cut to his stretched length, which was much longer than hers.

" 'Twould seem another allowance must be made."

Disgruntlement was clear in his tone. Hope stirred, that he would now forgo the chains entirely. She should have known better, for he merely left her to come back with two strips of cloth that he bound to her wrists, then to the manacles. Like for like, so she had to hear the creak of the chain if she moved, as he had heard it; feel its weight dragging on her limbs as he had felt it.

She tested the bounds and experienced an overwhelming panic. My God, was this how he had felt? So helpless, so afraid? Nay, he had not felt fear, only rage. She wished she could bring that more powerful emotion forth to sustain her through this, but anger that he would do her thusly was the farthest thing from her mind just then. So it would not be exactly the same. She would not twist and fight to avoid his touch, would not try to smite him with her eyes or shake him from the bed. She could only hope these differences would not matter to him and make him angrier still.

Her eyes opened in surprise when the gag was shoved between her lips. She had forgotten about that, but he had not. He did not want to hear her entreaties any more than she had wanted to hear his, though their reasons were not the same. He was feeling no guilt, as she had felt. He was enacting vengeance. She had only tried to save her mother's life.

Satisfaction at her helplessness blazed from his eyes. She wished she had not seen it, or that he had removed his clothes before he fetched the gag. The evidence of his readiness, however, gave her small relief. She need suffer only **his** rape of her, then, not that enforced by many others while he watched. And she already knew what he would feel like inside her. She could bear it—she would have to.

"Are you virgin here, I wonder, as you were there?"

His hands came to her breasts to tell her of what he spoke, both hands, and his eyes went there, too, to watch what he did. Rowena stared only at his face so she could gauge the moment he finished toying with her. And that was all he was doing. There was no need to caress her and coax her to readiness as she had found it necessary to do to him. He was already in that condition. 'Twas unnecessary that she be. And she felt no more than the heat of his palms, and momentary surprise that his touch was gentle. She was simply too frightened to feel more than that.

He played long with her breasts, flicking at the soft nipples, squeezing and pulling on them by turns. But when he ended with a frown, Rowena thought she would die of fright. She did not know it was because he had been unable to make her nipples tighten in response to his caresses, not even a little, not even once. With that frown still terrifying her, he brought a hand between her legs and thrust his finger inside her.

She groaned at the sharp discomfort she felt. His frown got darker.

"So you would deny yourself the shame that was visited upon me? I think not, wench."

Another threat, but she was lost in the dark this time, nor could she ask him to explain. She had no idea what had so displeased him, or what shame he thought she was denying herself that he wanted her to know. She would have done aught that he wanted her to at that point, just to get that terrifying scowl off his face. But there was naught that she **could** do, chained to the bed.

She began to tremble, not as greatly as when she had thought she was about to die, but enough for him to notice and growl, "Close your eyes, damn you. You do well to fear me, but I will not have you reacting to my every frown, not now. I will do to you no more than you did to me, and you already know the way of it, so put your fear aside. I order it."

He was mad to think she could do that, no matter what reassurance he gave her. He was mad anyway,

for by his own words, he wanted her to fear him—
but not now. What difference when, for God's
mercy? But he had **ordered** it. Ah, God, how, **how**
could she comply?

She closed her eyes. He was right in that respect,
that she was reacting to the dissatisfaction clearly
written on his face. Not even the fear of being unable to anticipate what he would do next was as
bad as seeing those scowls. And what he did next
was as he had said, no more than she had done to
him. He began caressing her, not just her breasts,
but all over.

She stopped trying to reason why he was touching her when it was not necessary to his purpose.
His hands were soothing, and she welcomed his
touch as a means to appease him. Somehow, she
began to relax. She began to feel things other than
fear: the texture of his hands, callused yet gentle;
his warm breath whenever he leaned close; goose-
flesh when he neared a sensitive area.

She was so relaxed when his mouth came to her
breast that she felt only a moment's alarm that did
not last. Heat engulfed her then, and a sharp tingling that shriveled her nipple and sent a strange-
ness to the pit of her belly. She did not mind the
feeling. It reminded her of those not unpleasant
things she had felt at times when she had caressed
him. Had he felt them, too, at the time? Did he feel
them now?

His caresses became slightly rougher now that he had drawn a response from her that he wanted. She did not mind that either. In fact, unknowingly, she was arching into his touch, on her breasts, over her belly, as if she suddenly craved it. But when his hand drifted back toward the juncture of her legs, she stiffened again. Only he did not attempt to thrust his fingers inside her this time. He merely continued his caresses there, softly now, and he was touching on something hidden in that area that produced the most deliciously languorous feeling. She relaxed more, forgot why she was being done so, forgot who was doing it. The sensations were exquisite, coursing and commingling into that secret core of her.

She was not even aware of him moving over her, but when she felt his thick manroot sliding slowly yet easily into her warmth, her eyes flew open in surprise—and met his above her, so filled with male triumph that she inwardly cringed. He was leaning over her with the full length of his arms extended, so that the only place he touched her was where he filled her. She did not look down at their joined bodies. She could not take her eyes off his.

"Aye, now you know how it feels to have no control of a traitorous body," he almost purred in his satisfaction. "You made me want this, despite my fury, so I have made you want it, despite your fear." She shook her head frantically, but he only laughed and thrust more deeply into her. "Aye, deny it as I did, but the proof is the ease with which I entered, the wetness that surrounds me now. **That** is what I wanted, wench, to force you to readiness as you forced me. And the shame of being unable to deny me will be yours each time I take you."

The pleasure he felt in achieving his revenge was as hard for her to witness as his anger. Rowena closed her eyes once more against it, but that was a mistake. It let her feel the fullness of him deep inside her, which was no new experience, except before she had never been "readied" for him. The difference was beyond description, as day to night. Each slow plunge made her crave the next, harder, deeper, more . . . until she finally screamed against her gag as the full pleasure exploded and carried her beyond anything she could have imagined.

She was left limp and sated, and a while later, when thought returned, as shamed as he had wanted her to feel. It was inconceivable that she had found pleasure in that ordeal, pleasure at the hands of her enemy, a man who despised her with his every breath. And now she truly knew what he had felt, all of it, and hated him for showing her.

❧ 17

That first day in the lord's solar continued endlessly for Rowena, despite the fact that de Chaville
had left her the very moment he had finished with
her—just as she had always done with him. Of
course, she was to remain chained to the bed. Like
for like. And if he kept exactly true to what he had
endured at her hands, then he would not force her
again that day. Verily, she was surprised he had not
waited until the middle of the night to summon
her to him, for that was when Gilbert had taken
her to him that first time.

That first time . . . she had suffered terrible pain
in giving him her maidenhead, made worse because of her ignorance. To be fair, however, he had
caused himself pain each time he had fought her,
only—he had suffered none today. And she had received no pleasure in taking him, while he had received his man's pleasure each time. Yet in order
for him to rape her here, he would still receive his

man's pleasure, and there was naught fair in that. In fact, she resented it bitterly, that he would have his revenge **and** that pleasure.

Like for like. If he did keep true, she could expect to be chained to this bed for three nights, then to be released on the third morn. She could also expect him to force her three times the second night, and the third—if he could manage to do so without her caresses to coax him to it. If he could not manage it on his own . . . she refused to think of what he might do.

Hours passed with no sound to disturb her. Without realizing it had happened, she lost all feeling in her arms. 'Twas when she stretched that she noticed, and then the feeling rushed back with tingling discomfort. She carefully shook her arms periodically after that, and could only imagine what it would feel like after she had slept for long.

Sleep was a long way from coming, however. The chamber darkened with the approach of night, but she did not close her eyes. She had to relieve herself, but fought the feeling until it passed—and began to fret that she would shame herself on his bed if someone . . . Oh, God, she thought, he had never been released from his chains to relieve himself. Mildred had attended him, and when Rowena thought of how, her skin burned with mortification, and it had not even happened yet to her. But it had happened to him, another humiliation that he had suffered that she had not even been aware of.

Yet if she had considered it at the time, what could she have done to prevent it? Gilbert had not wanted anyone but her and Mildred to know of his presence in the keep, so she could not have sent a manservant to him to make it easier for him to bear.

'Twas almost as if he could read her mind, even through the thick stone walls, for the Lord of Fulkhurst returned then, and he had a maidservant with him, bearing a tray of food. He came directly to the foot of the bed. The woman stopped short as soon as she noticed Rowena, her dark eyes rounding in surprised horror. He had not even covered Rowena when he left her, while she had always drawn that bath sheet he had arrived with back over him before leaving him.

"Put that down, Enid, and go fetch what else is needed," he told the woman.

Enid did not hesitate and left in a great hurry. Her lord did not notice, for he was watching Rowena. She would not return his look, however, until he ran a finger along the side of her foot, his way of demanding her attention. So she gave it, but with all the hate he was forcing her to feel.

"Oh, ho, what is this? Finally do you show other than a faint heart?" He smiled, but 'twas not true humor, was no more than a further indication of the triumph he was still gloating over. "Notice your antipathy does not displease me. Nay, I welcome it."

She closed her eyes so he could not see the hatred

that pleased him, one small retaliation on her own part. He would not allow even that.

"Look at me," he ordered harshly, and when she immediately complied, he said, "That is better. Whenever you are in my presence, wench, you will look at me unless I tell you otherwise. Do not make me repeat it."

Another threat. He was so good at making them, without naming the consequences. This time she showed him how she felt about it with another baleful glare. Why not, when he **welcomed it?**

But he was off on a new subject, the one that had brought him there. "'Twould seem I needs make still another allowance because of your gender. You sent a female to attend me. I would have sent you a male, make no mistake, but I could think of no man I could trust to see to just your needs and not his own as well, when the sight of you as you are would stir any man to lust. So Enid will see to you, as she is used to tending the wounded and bedridden, and without carrying tales, for she lost her tongue long ago when another held Fulkhurst for a time."

His expression changed to the cruel visage she had seen earlier when he was in a high rage, the face of a man capable of committing any atrocity. Since she had done naught to cause it, she had to assume that it was that mention of Fulkhurst Castle being held by another. And she had thought only she and Gilbert had his enmity? She pitied that "other," if he or she were not already dead.

But his black look did not last; it returned to that smile that was not a true smile. "I find, however, that I will not be satisfied unless you have every humiliation that was mine. So I will lend you my own presence while Enid attends your needs, and as I have already warned you, you will keep your eyes on me. You will not try to ignore me or close your eyes against my presence. Do you understand?"

Rowena was too appalled even to nod, but she would have screamed invective at him if she could. And now she knew a further thing he had suffered, the frustration of being unable to answer back, with curse or otherwise.

Enid returned all too soon and began her new duties without being told. Rowena, cognizant of Warrick's threat, kept her eyes only on him where he leaned against the bedpost. But she did not see him. She concentrated on Enid instead, and on the brief glance she had had of her, picturing the servant in her mind. Despite her gray hair, the woman was not really old, mayhap only two score in years. She had a slightly crooked nose, but otherwise her features were fair, her skin smooth and unlined. And she had gentle hands that were swift and efficient, for which Rowena would be forever grateful.

The worst was finally over, but that violation of her privacy had been worse than the rape. At least with the rape, he had been naked, too, and with her sense of fairness, she felt she deserved it. But not this. Warrick, through his twisted logic, had given her two people to witness her shame, when he had had only one.

She tried to remember that he had suffered the same thing, the same feelings, and that was why he was forcing them on her. It made no difference. This she had not deserved. And the very moment her gag was removed, she cleared her vision of her self-induced blurring and told him what she thought of him, damn the consequences.

"You are the most despicable, cruel man alive, a thousand times worse than Gilbert!"

His answer was to tell the servant, "I do not care to listen to her, Enid, so keep the food in her mouth so she has no time to do aught but chew it."

"Bast—"

She nearly choked on the food, there was such a large spoonful of it shoved in her mouth. And before she had half finished chewing it, another took its place. Enid—had she thought she could be grateful to her?—obeyed her lord to the letter. And before Rowena had a chance to say another word, a new gag was being tied in place.

The servant was summarily dismissed after that. And Warrick left the foot of the bed to come to the side and lean over her. His face was almost handsome again, it was so without emotion.

"Stupid wench," he said blandly. "That was a clever trick, to distort your vision. But had you obeyed me, you would have seen that I lent only my presence, not my attention. Only now you have earned a punishment for your willfulness. Can you guess what it will be?"

His attention? Nay, more than that, for his hand went right to her loins, his fingers pushing painfully into her dry heat and staying there. Her lack of response did not bring a frown this time, however, for he had the memory of her earlier yielding to assure him that she could resist no longer than he.

Slowly, with supreme confidence, he began to undo the ties on his chausses with his free hand, while the other remained tightly pressed between her legs. And by his order she had to watch him do it.

"Fight it, little thief," he commanded softly. "Fight it as I did, and learn that the body cares naught about hate and rage and shame. It is but a simple vessel, with simple but powerful instincts, and one of the most basic is the age-old instinct to procreate."

His flesh sprang loose beneath his tunic, and by the bulge against the black cloth, she knew it was already full-grown. That very knowledge flooded her insides to wet his fingers and she groaned, knowing now what the moisture signified, though his triumphant laugh told her as well.

He did not touch her anywhere else, and he mounted her immediately to slide so easily into her body. This was a punishment, not part of his revenge, not part of his like for like, for he was not supposed to have forced her again until the morrow. Her body did not care. It was providing the means to avoid pain, welcoming the means to procreate, despite the fact that she had already fulfilled that basic instinct. But it was also welcoming another thing, and although she fought it this time, denied it with her whole will, screamed in rage against it, there was pleasure in the deep thrusts rocking her that could not be denied. And, God help her, Warrick was watching her when that pleasure culminated and burst into throbbing radiance, her total surrender to his mastery writ clearly for him to savor. But she was watching him this time, too, for the first time, and when the same pleasure took him, the cruel lines on his face vanished for an instant, showing her again the truly handsome man beneath the mask of hatred.

She did not want to see that, closed her eyes against it, and did not care if he killed her for it. All he did was collapse against her, his forehead to her pillow, his cheek against her temple, his labored breath ringing in her ears. Nor did he leave her as quickly as before.

When he did, his breath had returned to normal, and his mask was back in place. He made quick work of retying his laces, but with that done, he stared at her, letting his eyes rove down the length of her before coming back to her still flushed face, and his fingers trailed down the soft underside of her raised arm.

"Mayhap you will obey my commands more closely in the future—or mayhap not." And then his cruel lips curled to sneer contemptuously. "You will admit I never yielded as easily as you, wench. I wonder what the thought of how many times I will come to you in the next days does to you. And I will not wait upon the night, for I do not intend to lose sleep as you did. Are you in dread, little thief, or do you no longer find my revenge quite so distasteful?"

She would have spit in his face if she were not gagged. Her eyes told him so and he laughed.

"Excellent. I would not like to think you await my visits eagerly when I so detested yours, when all I thought about was getting my hands around this soft throat and squeezing the last breath from your little body."

That his hand came to that area now and squeezed did not cause Rowena alarm. He would never settle for anything as quick and final as her death when he was so cruel and merciless. But he saw her lack of fear, and his hand moved down to squeeze her breast instead of her throat.

"Think you you know me, do you?" he bit out, clearly displeased with her now. "Think again, wench, for you will **never** know me well enough to guess what I am capable of, never know what demons have shaped me and made me into what I am. Best you pray I find revenge against you satisfying, for if it palls, you may well wish for death."

If he thought merely to frighten her with those words, he was diabolically ingenious.

❧ 18

When Rowena thought of Warrick de Chaville coming to her again, she would begin to tremble, so she did not think of it. But he came.

She was not even awake when he came the next morn, the darkness of the night only just receding. But when she finally became aware of him, she was also aware that he had already coaxed her body to receive him. And he made quick work of it, so quick that she was almost more bitter about having her sleep disturbed than about having her body invaded, for the one was over and done with before she felt much of anything, but as exhausted as she was, she still could not get back to sleep after he left her.

Enid came not long after, but Warrick did not come with the servant this time. And Rowena was in no mood for the sympathetic looks she was receiving from the older woman, yet she again found herself grateful to her. She had not even known

her shoulders were aching from the forced restraint until Enid started to massage the area, and
although it was not necessary that she do so, she
thoroughly washed the smell of that monster from
Rowena's skin.

But he came again at midday. And he came again
at dusk. Rowena's only compensation was that he
had had to work hard to caress that shameful moisture from her the third time. And so it went the
next day also, except the third time that day, the
last time she should have to suffer his body into
hers, was the worst of them all.

The man was not interested in merely preparing
her to receive him, he was after something else,
and she would not be surprised if it was to drive
her mad. He touched her long after he knew she
was ready for him, caressed her more than she
could bear. He stirred lust in her until she would
have begged him to take her, but all she could do
was take what he gave, a new knowledge of her
own body, a knowledge of her weakness of spirit
as well as flesh. The bastard made her want him.
And he knew it. 'Twas his final triumph.

The only thing that sustained Rowena was her
certainty that she would be released on the third
morn, to satisfy his like for like. Yet she dreaded
what further revenge he had planned for her, for
she did not think for a minute that he would be
satisfied merely with what he had already done. He

had said her life now belonged to him in payment for Gilbert's intention of killing him, and that he placed little value on it. He had said she was now his to do with as he would.

Nay, he would not let her go as she had him—at least not until the child was born. If he meant to keep it, and keep her from it, then he would have to let her go—or merely send her to another of his properties. She still could not let that happen, though she knew not what she could do about it now, when she did not even know what the next day would bring.

It brought Enid with the key to her chains. Rowena had expected Warrick to come himself so he could tell her what further humiliations were to be hers. Enid, of course, could tell her naught. But she had brought food that Rowena was able to feed herself, and she had brought clothes.

The clothes gave Rowena her first suspicions of what was now to be her lot. Her own clothes had long since been taken away, but these new ones were nowise like them. The chemise and outer bliaut were both homespun wool in a drab dun, not overly coarse, but naught that could be considered of a fine quality. They were clothes for a castle servant, the bliaut shorter than any lady would wear it, new, clean, and now Rowena's. For a girdle there was a strip of braided leather. Thick woolen hose were included, as well as plain cloth shoes, but no soft braies or shift for underwear. She was to be naked under these garments, likely as one more humiliating reminder of her changed circumstance.

And she was to leave the lord's chamber.

As soon as Rowena had worked the stiffness out of her arms, and dressed and rebraided her hair, Enid beckoned her to follow. The woman could not tell her what was to be done with her, but she obviously knew where Rowena was to go. And no sooner had they entered the Great Hall than she felt the stare that drew her eyes to the lord's table.

Warrick sat there, a sunbeam slanting through one of the high windows giving bright gold highlights to his dark blond head. Though the hour had long since passed for breaking his fast, a trencher and a tankard of ale still sat before him. He stared at her without expression, just stared, which made her recall the last time he had seen her, naked on his bed.

But that was over, she reminded herself. She could endure anything else that he intended for her—as long as that was over. However, he did not summon her to him. He had no intention of giving her warning of what was to come. So be it. It could not be so bad if he did not want to witness her horror upon learning of it.

A movement behind him caught her eye before she continued on. She glanced toward the hearth to see a group of women sitting there, all stopped in what they had been doing and staring avidly at her. She had not noticed them sooner because the brightness at the lord's table did not extend back to the hearth. In fact, the sunbeam was so bright, all around it seemed almost in shadow. But her eyes adjusted now and noted that most of the women were ladies, several of them very young. And the two youngest were frowning at her, frowns so similar . . .

God's mercy, Warrick had daughters nigh fullgrown! They did not closely resemble him, except for those frowns that marked them clearly de Chavilles. Then he must have a wife, too. Nay, what lady wife would give up her solar so her husband could rape another woman in it? Then again, any wife of Warrick de Chaville's would have no say in whatever he did, whether he kept mistresses or raped women in his bed. And Rowena could only pity a woman with such a husband as he.

And then she gasped as one of the women stood up from her stool so Rowena could see her clearly. Mildred! How was it possible?

Joy burst in Rowena's breast, lit up her face, and she took a step forward. Mildred turned away from her to look toward Warrick, then sat back down, hidden again by the women sitting in front of her. Without a word? Without even an expression of greeting? Rowena did not understand. But then her gaze came back to Warrick to see his smile, and she did understand. In some way this was another revenge on his part. Could he have somehow turned Mildred completely against her? Nay, she did not think that possible, but obviously Mildred was not to talk to her.

The anger burst on her as swiftly as the joy of a moment ago. She had already been disturbed that she was to be allowed naught up her skirts but stockings and skin, already suspicious of the next step of Warrick's plot to break her, but this, to deny her the woman who was like a second mother to her? She forgot her tenuous position, forgot that he could throw her back in his dungeon, beat her, kill her.

She ignored Enid's hand pulling on hers and marched up the raised dais to the front of his table until she stood across from him. He did no more than raise his brows in question, as if he could not see that she was enraged.

She leaned forward to hiss for only his hearing, "You can deny me every last thing that I hold dear, but I can and will pray every day for the rest of my life that you rot in hell, Warrick."

He gave her that cruel smile that she was coming to know so well. "Am I supposed to fear for a soul that is already damned, wench? And I did not give you leave to be so familiar in your address."

She leaned back, incredulous. She had just

cursed him to everlasting hell, and he was only concerned with her use of his first name? She was seething, and he continued to merely smile at her?

"I beg your pardon," she sneered. "What I should have called you was bastard."

He stood up so fast, he startled the anger out of her. And before she even thought to run, he leaned completely across the table to grab her wrist.

Rowena gasped, his hold was so tight, but all she heard him say was, "My lord."

"What?"

"You did not end that statement with the proper address due me. Say 'my lord.' "

He was not going to kill her for calling him bastard? "But you are not my lord."

"I am now, wench, and henceforth I will hear you say so—often. And I will hear you say it now."

She would rather cut out her tongue. He must have seen that in her stubborn expression, because he jerked her close to warn in a soft but menacing tone, "You will say it, or I will have a whip fetched and mete out the standard punishment due for such insolence."

'Twas no bluff. He had said it, so he would do it, whether he wanted to do it or not. A man such as he did not give idle threats. And she liked it better when she did not know the consequences.

But she waited several pounding heartbeats before she gritted out, "My lord."

He released her immediately. She rubbed her wrist while he sat back down, his expression no different from what it had been before she had challenged him—and lost. But this time his look was deceiving, for he was in fact annoyed that the first thing she had done upon her release was to castigate him, when after the past three days she should have been too intimidated to don any mantle of noble outrage.

"Mayhap you are not as bereft in wisdom as you are in intelligence," he said in response to her capitulation, but then added in a growl, "Get you from my sight ere I take exception to what you **did** call me."

Rowena needed no further prompting, did not even spare him a parting glare. She hurried over to Enid, who was waiting anxiously below the dais, and followed her out of the hall and down one floor to the kitchen.

The kitchen could usually be found in a separate building out in the bailey, but it was becoming popular in recent years to have the kitchen moved right into the keep, particularly in areas that received a great deal of rain and foul weather. Fulkhurst's kitchen was one such new addition, having taken the large area where the castle garrison used to be quartered.

There were at least twenty people busy at different tasks in the large room. Preparation of the evening meal was already under way. A huge fire pit was being stoked under a roasting side of beef. Cooks surrounded a long table where vegetables were being peeled, pastries made, meat chopped. The wardrober was doling out spices. Two men-at-arms were eating a hasty meal standing up while a pretty maid flirted with them. A dairymaid was cuffed for spilling a bit of milk from her bucket when she tripped over one of several dogs under-foot. She in turn kicked the dog, which only yelped, but did not relinquish its seat near the butcher's block. A scullion was washing out tankards from the morning meal. The baker was sliding new loaves into his oven. Two hefty serfs were coming up from the basement with heavy sacks of grain.

Because of the room's size, it was not oppressively hot, but it was exceedingly warm and smoky with so many fires going and so many wall sconces burning. Rowena took it all in with dread. The steward was there, just leaving the clerk's office up on a higher level above a store area. But it was not to him that Enid took her. It was to the large woman who had cuffed the dairymaid. Blond, florid-faced, and quite tall for a woman, at slightly over five and a half feet, she was not a serf but a freewoman, and wife to the head cook.

"So yer the other one from Kirkburough," Mary Blouet said as she looked Rowena over from head to foot, as just about everyone else in the room was also doing, though not so openly as Mary. " 'Twas rumored it were a lady kept in the dungeon, but yer being sent to me puts the lie to that right quickly. Ye will call me Mistress Blouet, and give me no airs or back talk. I have had right well enough of that from that haughty Mildred, and her having the lord's favor, I cannot give her the back of my hand. But ye be not so favored, are ye, wench?"

"Indeed," Rowena replied, unable to keep the dejection from her tone, "I am so ill-favored, 'tis my lot to be eternally punished."

"Punished?" Mary frowned. "Nay, not unless it be needful. Well, come along, then. I have to make my rounds, or naught will ever get done, not with the lazy sluts I have in my charge. I will explain yer duties on the way."

Rowena was surprised. "I am not to work in the kitchen, then?"

"Here?" Mary laughed with genuine humor. "They have enough hands down here to not need more, and my husband does not like my wenches in his domain. He cannot abide laziness in his workers, whereas I am cursed with naught else, and can find no cure for it, not when that bitch Celia belittles my authority the moment my back be turned. And she gets away with it because she be Lord Warrick's favorite slut, and everyone knows it. How I wish . . ."

The thought was left unfinished as Mary mounted the stairs back to the Great Hall. Rowena dragged her feet, dreading another encounter with Warrick, but he was no longer in the hall. Not as many ladies remained by the hearth either. And there was no sign of Mildred.

"I have no say over the ladies' maids," Mary said when she noticed the direction Rowena was looking toward. "But yer not so lucky as that Mildred was, to be getting such an easy job as that."

"Has Mildred been here long?"

"Nay, she came with the lord. Why? Do ye know her?"

"Aye."

"Well, stay away from her. There be levels of hierarchy amongst the castlefolk here as in any keep, and her having the care of the lord's daughters puts her higher up even than the other ladies' maids, which be all higher than ye. But yer higher than those kitchen lackeys, so stay away from them, too. Ye will have enough wenches to choose yer friends from that be under my care, but do ye take my advice, ye will not make that Celia one of them."

Rowena was not interested in "that Celia," even if she was Warrick's favorite. She was more concerned with her own predicament. She knew she was to be one of Mary's "wenches," but she had yet to be told what that entailed.

Her shock over her new servant status was only

mild, for she had already suspected that her fate would be something of that nature by the clothes she had been given. And one of the first things Warrick had said to her, back in Kirkburough, was that she was lady no longer. The irony was that she could remember wishing for this very thing, that she were no more than a lowly serf with naught to her name that could be coveted and fought over. Verily, she would have to be more careful of her damn wishing in future.

Warrick could not, however, make her a true servant, for she was nobly born and raised, and that could not be taken from her, no matter how much he might wish it. But he could have her treated like a servant, had already ordered it so, and there was naught she could do about it, for she was, in truth, a prisoner at his mercy. Yet when it occurred to her that he could have had her sent back to the dungeon instead, and without the kindly John Giffard's protection, she had to consider herself lucky, more than lucky. A servant had free movement, went about almost unnoticed. A servant could escape.

❧ 19

"This be where ye will spend most of yer time," Mary said as she opened the door to the weaving room on the floor above the Great Hall.

Three women immediately dashed from the window where they had been watching the men practice arms in the exercise yard. But they did not quite resume their seats before Mary noticed. And she could not help but notice the spindle with thread attached that rolled across the floor to disappear under her skirts. One of the women had quickly tried to continue spinning with it, but had dropped it instead.

Rowena took in the small room while Mary glowered at her workers. There was a basket full of spindles with stone whorls, enough to spin a great amount of thread if there were more women to do it, but there were only these eight. Larger baskets of newly treated wool lined the walls, ready for spinning into thread. There were six large looms, and another stack of smaller hand looms in the corner, but only three of the large ones were presently threaded, and only one had woven cloth nearing completion. The single window gave ample light, so at least there would not be the problem of candle smoke staining the newly made cloth.

Mary finally got around to blasting the women with her displeasure. "Wasting time again, are ye?" she admonished sternly. "Ye will finish what yer due for the day, or there will be no dinner for the lot of ye. And if I find ye idle one more time this week, ye will find yerselves demoted to the laundry. There be others than ye with nimble fingers, if I have to bring them up from the village."

So saying, she slammed the door shut again, surprising Rowena into saying, "I thought I was to work here."

"Aye, ye are, but there be enough for ye to do the rest of this day, for ye not to start weaving and spinning now, and sharing in the punishment of those lazy wenches."

Rowena could not agree more after what she had already suffered, and in gratitude, she informed Mary, "I know how to produce a fine thread, though it takes longer with a double spinning, and I am capable of instructing the weavers to get a better-quality cloth, fine enough for the ladies of the castle."

She had had little opportunity to direct servants in the past three years, other than those who served only her. But she had been ten and five when her life changed so drastically, and her mother had already taught her all that she needed to know in the running of a castle. And anything that she could direct to be done, she could do herself, for how could she direct properly unless she knew exactly what needed doing? Yet there were some things she could do better than others.

Having gained Mary's complete interest, she continued. "But my talents would be wasted in this area, for I am better skilled with a needle."

"So my lord must have thought, for he has also ordered ye to have the care of his clothes, and the making of new ones for him, though we have better than the spun wool for that. But ye can teach others to get a finer weave, ye say?"

Rowena was still flushing over what she considered a further punishment, to be forced to handle **his** clothes, so she only nodded stiffly. But Mary did not notice her high color in the dimly lit corridor; she was merely surprised.

"Did ye have the care of the weavers at Kirkburough?" she asked.

"Nay, I was not there long."

"Well, I would not take it amiss did ye do a little instructing of my wenches whilst ye do yer own weaving, but 'tis not what I was ordered to have ye do, and ye will have little enough spare time with all ye have to do." And then she turned to leave, adding only, "When ye finish for the day, ye can return here to sleep with the others."

Rowena pictured that small room with so little cleared floor space and asked, "**All** of them sleep in there?"

"Nay, only three. The other five are as sluttish as Celia. They all have men they sneak off to at night." Mary stopped at the top of the stairwell to pin Rowena with narrowed eyes. "Yer not of that bent, are ye?"

Rowena knew that people had seen her enter the lord's solar three days ago, and others had seen her leave it this morn. Though Mary did not seem to know that, she was bound to hear of it eventually. If Rowena was to be under Mary's care **and** discipline, as it seemed, she did not want to make enemies of the woman by leaving her to be surprised later by facts that Rowena could make clear to her now. And Mary did not seem to be a mean woman, just a beleaguered one. Mayhap she could even help Rowena, if she could gain her sympathy.

"I would be immensely grateful, Mistress Blouet, if you could keep **all** men away from me, but—there is a thing you should know, if your lord did not tell you. He kept me in his solar these last three days—chained to his bed."

"Nay, he would never!" Mary said indignantly. "Why do ye lie?"

The last thing Rowena expected was to hear someone staunchly defend that cruel, vengeful man. Was it possible Mary had no idea what kind of man he really was?

"Enid knows 'tis so, and I doubt your lord would deny it, for he had reasons to punish me so. I tell you only so you do not wonder if he singles me out for further punishment, for 'tis not likely he is through having his vengeance on me."

Mary still looked skeptical, though she allowed, "Aye, likely not, for yer other duties, now I think on it, can be seen as a punishment if they be not to yer liking. Ye are also to serve Lord Warrick at table for all meals, see to the cleaning of his chamber with only Enid's help, and attend him at his bath, which Celia is likely to take umbrage at, for 'twas previously her duty, and one she relished."

Rowena felt sick to her stomach. And she had thought at least the worst was over, that being demoted to servant class would be the end of it?

"There is one other thing you should know. I am with child, and Lord Warrick knows 'tis his."

"And he gives ye more work than any other serf here? Nay, I cannot believe that either."

"Why would I lie when the proof will begin to show in a few months' time?"

"Then he does not know of it," Mary insisted.

"No other has ever touched me, Mistress Blouet. The child is his and he even means to—to take it from me."

Mary gasped. "Now ye go too far in yer accusations, girl. If it be true yer breeding, likely my lord will find ye a husband, so say no more about it to me. Now come along. Ye have the cleaning of the solar to do the rest of this day, for it has been neglected these . . . last . . . three—"

Mary did not finish what, in truth, supported one of Rowena's claims. She pursed her lips tightly and headed down the stairwell.

Rowena did not follow immediately, feeling overcome with a new dread that Mary had unwittingly given her. Warrick **could** marry her off, and to a serf, to the meanest villein. **Please, God, do not let that occur to him**.

❧ Rowena hated entering that solar again, but found it was not nearly so oppressive when she was not lying bound in the bed. Getting anywhere near that bed was out of the question, though. She would rather scrub the floor on her hands and knees, and did, while Enid saw to changing the bedding, dusting, and general tidying. Rowena would have taken the rugs out for a beating, too, but Enid shook her head. They had laundry to see to today instead, Enid the linens, Rowena **his** clothing. She was told this by having the clothes dumped in her arms and Enid, with her own arms full, beckoning her to follow.

Rowena had washed clothes only once before in

her life, though she knew well enough how it was done. 'Twas not a pleasant chore. The sheets could merely be soaked in a wooden trough with a solution of wood ashes and caustic soap, then pounded, rinsed, and hung out to dry. The servants' coarse woolen clothing could be done the same, but not so the lord's fine clothes. These had to be boiled and washed by hand with a milder soap, then boiled again and rinsed not once but three times before they could be hung.

With the great cauldrons of water in the washhouse constantly boiling, the wilting steam, the milder though still abrasive soap reddening her delicate skin, Rowena decided this still was not the worst of her chores, especially since the other laundresses were all friendly, and some even came to help her once Enid left. Nay, she had not gotten to the worst chore yet, but hopefully the Lord of Fulkhurst was not a fastidious man to demand a bath more than once a week, and mayhap she would have a few days' grace before she had to deal with **that** duty.

When she returned to the hall, it was to find the trestle tables for the evening meal already set up. Warrick was not present yet, but the lord's table was beginning to fill with those privileged to eat there: his daughters, several of his knights, the steward, who was also a knight, and a lady past the middle years who was tutor to the daughters in the household arts.

One of the knights there was Sir Robert, and Rowena made haste to the kitchen to see what needed carrying to the lord's table, hoping she would have a chance to speak privately with him before Warrick arrived. She had not forgotten the knight's help in assigning her John Giffard, or her promise to thank him for it. And it would not hurt to cultivate his friendship, for help given once might be gained again, and she would need all she could get to escape this place.

But when she returned with her first tray of meats, Warrick was in his seat, and his eyes lit on her the moment she entered the hall, nor did they leave her until she was gone from sight. She did not see this, she felt it, for she refused to look at him again after that first glance. But there was something so unnerving about his regard, she did not mistake it.

She was amazed to find Warrick waiting for her at the top of the stairs when she came up with her second tray. And his expression definitely boded ill for her.

"Did I not warn you to watch me when in my presence?" he demanded.

"I—I forgot," she lied.

That only half appeased him. "Will you forget again?"

"Nay."

"Nay, what?"

"My lord," she gritted out.

That appeased him. "Mayhap you need something to remind you of who you belong to now," he said in a thoughtful tone, just before his hand reached for her breast.

Rowena jumped back so quickly, her action took her into the stairwell, where she lost her footing. Warrick grabbed for her, but it happened too fast and he could not catch her in time. She did not scream. She felt an instant of relief to have her misery ended in this way, before regret filled her mind. But this feeling, too, was too brief to provoke a scream, for she fell no more than two steps, right onto the manservant coming up behind her with another tray of food.

Both trays hit the stone steps with a clatter as the man reached out to keep himself from falling. It was fortunate he did not grab her, however, or she might have experienced a painful wrenching, for Warrick hauled her off the man about as quickly as she had crashed into him. Nor did he release her at the top of the stairs until he had shaken her hard at least twice.

"**Never** try to avoid my touch again, wench, or worse will happen to you than a tumble down the stairs. Now clean up the mess you caused, and you will do so quickly, because I will not eat until you fill my trencher yourself—and I am hungry."

In other words, she could expect his anger to mount with each passing minute that he had to wait while she cleaned the stairs? 'Twas no wonder her hands were trembling before she finished.

❧ 20

Rowena was furious over the anxiety Warrick had caused her, for when she finally got back to the hall with a new tray of food, it was to find him picking on what was already available on the table, and so deep in discussion with his steward that he likely had not given her another thought. But he did still insist she fill his trencher, merely pointing to what foods he wanted. And he also insisted she remain there to refill his tankard with ale, though a young page stood behind his chair with a pitcher of the brew to do just that. And all the while she had to keep her eyes on him.

Rowena was furious about that, too. She did not **like** to look at him and see his every nuance of expression, to know exactly when his thoughts turned to her. But she knew this was just another form of revenge, his forcing her to watch his cruel visage, just as serving him at table was. Both were calculated to drive home the fact that she was still at his utter mercy, and he still had none.

When he was almost finished with his meal, he beckoned her forward with a wave of his hand without even looking to see if she noticed. She would have been in trouble if she had not, and knew then that he was also testing her to see how well she obeyed him, though he obviously expected full compliance. That, too, made her furious, that he was so arrogantly **sure** she would do everything she was told to do. Did no one ever defy him? Did no one ever deliberately provoke his anger? A stupid thought, since even when he was not frowning, he was frightening. And no matter how angry he made her, she did not have the nerve to tempt a beating or other added punishment—not yet.

"I require a bath this eve," he told her when he sensed her presence at his side. He still did not look up at her. "Go and see to it."

Rowena closed her eyes briefly in regret that she would not be granted a reprieve from that after all. She heard one of the daughters giggle, then a stern admonishment from the lady tutor, and felt herself blushing. Everyone there would have had to be blind not to notice how Warrick's attention returned to her throughout the meal. And anytime a lord singled out one of his female servants for his notice, she was almost guaranteed to end up in his bed—or so they would all think. That was not the rule in her case, for she had already suffered that unpleasant experience.

But they did not know that she was being punished, rather than favored.

She left the hall quickly, just to get away from those cold silver eyes. She found Mary in the kitchen having dinner with her husband, and was reminded that she had not eaten yet herself. But when was she supposed to have time to eat, with all the duties that had been given to her? Obviously not today—but then, today was an exception, with three days' cleaning to do, and she had started late—and he could not want a bath **every** night.

Mary merely explained how Rowena was to see to her present chore herself, while she continued to stuff succulent pieces of roasted partridge in her mouth, and Rowena's belly rumbled in complaint at being allowed only the scent of food. She learned she was not expected to carry in the large tub that was stored in the small antechamber outside the solar, where Warrick's squires slept, for in the summer he bathed in there. Nor did she have to lug in the many buckets of water, and was shown which menservants had that duty so she would be able to command them herself next time. She was told where to find the bath cloths and soap that were only for the lord's use. She was warned the lord liked his bath very warm, but not very hot, and that the temperature would be her responsibility, and was worth a slap if she got it wrong. Another worry she could have done with-

out but should have expected, for most knights reacted violently to the smallest discomfort, and woe
betide whoever was closest to them when they did.

It was maddening to have to cross the length of
that hall again just to reach the solar. But Warrick
seemed not to notice her this time. And although
she glanced at him every few steps she took, to
comply with his unreasonable order to watch him
always, she could not be expected to stare at him as
she walked and not run into something. Could she?

She assumed not, for she was not called to ac-
count for watching her own step, and once in the
antechamber outside the solar—she came face-to-
face with Celia.

She knew exactly who the young woman was
by her vivid beauty, and by the pure hatred blazing from her green eyes. She wore both her bliaut
and her chemise cut low to show off her ample
breasts, and her wild mane of copper curls gave
her an untamed sensuality that any man would
find challenging. The yellowing teeth were barely
noticeable, but the overwhelming scent of roses
was almost gagging. The woman was obviously
under the mistaken impression, as were a great
many nobles, that sweet perfumes could mask un-
cleanliness.

Celia did not mince words, but went right to the
attack. "I know ye—you were in the dungeon.
What did you do to get out of that punishment and

be so favored? Did you spread your legs for him?
Did you get on your knees and—"

"Take your filthy mouth and get out, Celia!"

Green eyes flared incredulously. "Ye—you dare
speak so to me? Me?!"

Just what Rowena needed, a fight over a man she
despised. It was almost laughable. And to be
thought favored? To be envied her hateful duties?
God's mercy, what next? But the arrogant attitude
of the woman was annoying, reminding Rowena of
what Mary Blouet had said of her. Celia had obviously let her position as the lord's favorite go to her
head, giving her a haughty condescension that was
inappropriate in a servant. And she **was** just a servant, no matter that she was trying to better her
speech so as not to sound like one. **But so are
you—for now**, Rowena reminded herself. **So what
right do you have to take exception at another
servant's audacity?**

That realization, unfortunately, did not keep the
sarcasm from her tone when she answered. "I believe I can speak to you as I please, Celia. Am I not
the one presently **favored?**"

That got her a slap that was wholly unantici-
pated, and a vicious rejoinder. "Not for long,
bitch. Remember that when he gets tired of yer
pale, skinny body, for I will be making ye sorry
then that ye thought to take my place."

Rowena was too stunned to say a word as Celia

flounced out the door. She had never been slapped before, never in her life, and 'twas definitely not pleasant. But she supposed that was one other thing she would have to get used to here, for what recourse did she have, particularly if the abuse came from Mistress Blouet, who had the care and discipline of her, or Warrick himself? But from another servant? Nay, she did not have to take that—only from that particular servant, she still had no recourse. She could just imagine Warrick's reaction if she tried to slap his "favorite" back. And Celia **knew** that. 'Twas why she got away with her appalling behavior.

The menservants began arriving with the water. Rowena went to fetch the bath cloths and soap from the appropriate chest in the solar. But she brought an extra washing cloth to dip in the cold water and place on her cheek. It relieved some of the heat, and the red mark was partially faded by the time Warrick sauntered in.

He looked first at the tub with steam slowly rising from it. It had taken every bucket of hot water to warm all the cold that had been dumped in when she was not watching, leaving her only cold water to rinse him with. She had been about to order more hot when he arrived, but his presence put the thought right out of her mind, especially when his eyes glanced at her and narrowed on her cheek.

He came right to her then and lifted her chin. "Who hit you?" he demanded.

"No one."

"You lie, wench. What did you do to cause Mistress Blouet displeasure with you already?"

Why did he immediately assume **she** had to be at fault? She ought to tell him the truth, except the slap was no more than she deserved for slipping down to Celia's level. But she knew full well he would do naught if he knew 'twas his precious Celia, and for some reason that hurt more than the slap had.

So she lied, and found it quite satisfying to do so in this particular instance. "I merely tripped, because I could not watch my step in the hall for being ordered to watch you." And he had not been observing her to know better.

His scowl, for once, did not frighten her. "Stupid, wench. Must you be taught common sense along with your duties?"

"If I am allowed to watch where I walk when you are present, you must tell me so. I do not wish to disobey you."

"Do you not?" he growled at her meek answer and let go of her. "Then we will see just how well you wish to obey. Undress me."

She had expected that, but color still flooded into her face, so both cheeks were now equally red. And he just stood there towering over her with his hands relaxed at his sides. He was not going to help at all. She hated this, hated getting anywhere near him, but he knew that. This **was** just another part of his revenge, after all, treating her no better than a serf—nay, more like his personal slave.

She made quick work of disrobing him, not even trying to conceal her resentment. That humorless smile she hated came to his lips, so she avoided looking at his face. But that left only his body to look at—which she had never found fault with and still did not.

He did not even bend down so she could remove his tunic, forcing her to get closer to him to shove it up his chest and shoulders, then pull upward instead of down. She gasped as her breasts accidentally brushed against his chest, then gasped again as her nipples immediately tingled into hardness. She yanked so hard then that she fell back several steps when the tunic finally came off in her hands.

He laughed at her glowering expression—at least she hoped that was all he laughed at. He could not know the reaction her body had just had to his, could he? And how could that happen at all when she despised him? It made no sense to her.

She did not want to approach him again. There were his chausses and boots yet to be got rid of, but she could not do it, not that. Her breasts were tingling again with just the thought. God's mercy, what was wrong with her?

He waited patiently, but when she made no move toward him, he said, "Finish." She slowly shook her head, watching as one of his brows rose in question. "You would prefer to be chained to my bed again?"

She leaped forward, nearly colliding with him in her rush. She heard his laugh and gritted her teeth. So he would hold that over her head now, too, would he? He was utterly despicable, beyond—

"On your knees, I think."

She dropped to her knees without even thinking about this new order, and was faced with the thick bulge beneath his chausses. Color came hot into her cheeks again, and her fingers trembled now as she reached up to untie his laces to free that vengeful weapon of his.

" 'Tis quite satisfying, seeing you in that humbled position—like a pet at my feet," he continued in a casual tone. "Mayhap I will have you serve me at table just so."

In front of everyone? "Please." The word was torn from her with a groan.

His hand came to the top of her head—just as if she were no more than a pet dog panting for attention at his feet—and pushed back until she was looking up at him. "Will you hesitate again in your duty?"

"Nay, I will not."

He said no more, leaving her in an agony of

doubt that her answer had satisfied him. She was on her knees now because she had dared refuse to finish, a punishment swift and humiliating. Was that not enough?

She pulled the braies and chausses down his legs, but avoided looking at what sprang forth by bending over to see to his boots. When she finished, he still just stood there, so she stared at his bare feet, a defiance, but not an exact disobedience, for were his feet not part of him?

"Verily do you test my patience," he said when she continued to just stare at his feet.

But he did not press the issue this time, and she watched his feet move away and then disappear into the tub. She sighed in relief. But she was forgetting what else "attending him at his bath" signified. He reminded her.

"What do you wait for now, wench? Come and wash my back and hair."

'Twas part of "attending" him. She knew that. And at least he was not insisting she wash all of him. But she did not want to get close to his naked body again, when just the thought of it was making her feel warm and mushy inside, which in turn sparked her temper.

She fetched the washing cloth, soaked and soaped it, but before she touched him with it, she demanded, "Why does your wife not tend to this?"

"I have no wife."

"But you have two daughters."

"And I had two wives, both long dead. Yet I would have had another—" He suddenly grabbed her bliaut to pull her close and growled, "I was to meet her, but I was otherwise detained, so she rode on and is now missing. Know you where I was, wench, that I could not meet my bride as intended?" She was afraid to answer. He did not wait for her to. "I was chained to a bed for **your** pleasure."

God's mercy, he had this, too, to blame her for? "Not my pleasure," she whispered.

He let go of her with a slight shove. "Best you pray Lady Isabella **is** found and not dead."

Another dire warning with unknown consequences. She wondered if the lady was not lost, but had taken the opportunity to flee a marriage to this man. Rowena certainly would have if given half a chance.

The subject had angered him. She could feel it in the tautness of his back as she quickly scrubbed it now. So she was not truly surprised, when she handed him the cloth to finish, that he did not take it. She had earned another punishment for getting him riled.

"I find I have overtaxed myself this day, so you may wash me, wench—everywhere. And best you remove your clothes to do it so they do not get wet."

Damn him to perdition. **Why** did he have to take

revenge for the tiniest little things? He was the devil's spawn, to be this cruel.

But Rowena did as instructed, whipping off her chemise and bliaut together, ripping several laces in her haste. Then she immediately slipped the sleeveless bliaut back on before he noticed that she was, in fact, defying him again in solving the problem of getting wet in her own way.

And when she came around to kneel by his side and began soaping his chest, and he saw what she had done, it did surprise him. She held her breath, wondering if she would now have her first slap from him. But when he did naught, she finally glanced at his face—and found him smiling, a genuine smile that restored his handsomeness. Her own expression mirrored her amazement, and that caused him to burst into laughter.

Rowena sat back on her heels, chagrined. The last thing she cared to do was **amuse** the monster. But she was not getting **anything** that **she** wanted today.

When he was merely smiling again, he said, "Come, finish ere the water grows cold."

She did, but the washing of that large male body was pure torture, could be described as naught else. It made her heart pound to do it, her pulses race, and her pointed nipples became almost painful, prodding against the scratchy wool of her bliaut. Washing him was just too reminiscent of the times she had forced him to readiness, too similar to caressing him. And his manroot had grazed against her arm enough times that she knew it was fair to bursting before she got around to washing it, too.

Her face was on fire. His was still strikingly handsome, for he was still grinning, amused by her discomfort. She did not even care about that now, because her face was not the only thing heated. She had the sudden, mad urge to crawl into that tub with him.

She leaped to her feet instead and began soaping his hair. But she did it too vigorously, with too much soap that drifted down into his eyes.

"Enough, wench," he complained. "Rinse it now."

Rowena reached for the bucket, relieved that she was almost finished—and remembered there was no hot water left. "You will have to wait—"

"Nay, do it now."

"But—my lord, the water is—"

"**Now**, blast you!"

Her lips pinched together. Well, he asked for it, did he not? With a good deal of pleasure, she dumped the icy well water over his head.

She heard him suck in his breath, along with the water streaming down his face, which then caused him to choke and sputter. Her moment of pleasure turned to alarm. He was going to beat her now, even though 'twas not her fault. He did not leap from the tub, but she still backed slowly toward the door as he wiped the water from his face—until his hands lowered and those silver eyes pinned her to the spot.

"I—I tried to tell you there was no warm water left—my lord."

"So you did. Were my eyes not stinging, I might have listened."

She stiffened. "So you will blame me anyway? Had you asked, I could have told you I had never bathed anyone ere this, knew not the way of—"

"Be quiet!"

He was definitely annoyed, but it did not look as if he was going to get up and beat her, so she offered, "What will you wear now? I will fetch it."

"There is no need. I have missed my own bed and intend to go straight to it."

"Then—may I be excused—my lord?"

The hesitation she kept giving his address was deliberate, and the look he gave her said he knew it, which was possibly why he answered, "Nay, you will dry me first," but that was more likely her punishment for the cold water. Only he stood up as he said it, and standing far away from him, she could not help but see too much of his body.

She started to shake her head, to refuse again to obey him, but he asked first, "Are you pleased with what your ministrations have wrought?"

"Nay!" she said emphatically.

"You always were before," he reminded her.

His voice was too husky. God's mercy, was he going to try to seduce her into wanting him? If so, 'twould likely only be to then dismiss her and send for his Celia. He had had his like for like. He could not want her again. Nay, all he wanted was more revenge.

"I—I like rape no more than you did," she told him miserably. "I have told you how sorry I am for what was done to you. When will your revenge end?"

"When it no longer infuriates me to look at you. When every offense has been satisfied. When I have killed your brother for my squire's death. When I lose interest, wench, and not before . . . mayhap never."

❧ 21

Rowena lay on her uncomfortable bed on the floor of the weaving room, wide awake. She had put her chemise back on before bedding down. The coarse wool might be scratchy, but the even rougher woolen pallet was much worse, and so the chemise offered her some little ease. She was getting no other kind, not from her thoughts, not from her belly—and not from the disquieting feelings Lord **Vengeance** had stirred up in her.

She did not understand those feelings. She did not want Warrick de Chaville. She could not want a man she hated. Yet many times these past days he **had** made her want him, despite her hate, and her body had remembered that tonight and responded, once again, not as she wished it to.

And he had been so angry after being reminded of all the reasons he wanted revenge against her. He had contained it well, however. It had only been seen in his expressive eyes. But that was enough to make Rowena tremble. And he liked her fear. 'Twas almost enough to pacify him—almost.

Her feet had felt wooden when she approached him with the soft drying cloth. And his cold voice had not relieved her any.

"On your knees again," he had ordered. "And take care, wench, that you do not miss a single drop of moisture. Do I catch a chill because of your negligence, I **will** beat you for it."

He had said that as if his other threats of beatings had lacked substance. She doubted that, but was concerned only with **this** threat. And in self-defense, she forced herself to dry him slowly, to make sure she left no patch of skin even a little bit damp.

'Twas an experience she did not ever want to repeat. Her fearful trembling had turned to another kind. And he knew. He watched her like a hawk, so he could not help but see the effect he was having on her. Of course, the effect she was having on him was even more obvious, was staring her right in the face, and her fascination with his manroot returned. Against her will, she even caressed it as she dried it.

That was when he had snapped at her to get out. She had been surprised, but had not waited around for him to repeat the order. She had run out of there, and straight up the stairs near his solar that led to the women's quarters, which included the sewing and weaving rooms.

The latter had been dark and empty then, for the hour had still been early, the other women down in the hall. Rowena should have just calmed herself some, then gone back down to get something to eat. Instead she had fetched a torch from the corridor to light a few candles in the room, made her pallet, put her chemise back on, and gone to bed.

Getting to sleep was another matter. She was still awake when four of the weavers came in together, spoke quietly amongst themselves for a few minutes, then all drifted off to sleep without the least difficulty. She was still awake when the noisy rumbles from her belly joined the soft sounds of the others' sleeping. She was still awake when the door opened again sometime after matins, and a huge shape stood there, silhouetted against the light behind it.

She knew who it was. She had even somehow suspected he would come, even while she had imagined him relieving himself with Celia. Unless—did he think his Celia was here? Was it his favorite he had come for, and not her?

But 'twas Rowena he faced when he said, "Come."

She did not doubt now that he spoke to her, even though his face was no more than a black shadow. None of the other women stirred, but Rowena did not move either, except to shake her head.

He put out his hand and repeated that single word, and she was assailed with memories of his hands on her, of the incredible pleasure his body had recently forced on hers—and she shook her head again, violently. She did **not** want that pleasure again, not from him.

He had more words to say to her denial, quietly, for only her ears. "You are having the same difficulty as I, or you would not be still awake. I for one do not mean to suffer it any longer. Come now, or I will carry you from here."

She dreaded the scene that that would cause, which was guaranteed to wake the others, but still she did not move, so he added, "Your screams will not matter. Have you not realized that yet?"

She had a little more dignity than that. But since she **was** likely to scream if he touched her, she got up and followed him out of the room—but no further than the empty corridor. He walked on, fully expecting her to follow him. When he finally realized she was not behind him, he came back, though he was not angry—at least not yet. His brow was merely lifted in question.

"Do you require assistance?"

His nonchalance was infuriating. "I am not going with you," she told him baldly, stiffly. "You had your revenge on me in that way. To force me again would not be like for like."

"Did I say you would **only** have like for like, wench? After today you should know better. However I choose to exact retribution from you, so it will be done." And then he shrugged, just before that humorless smile came to his lips. "But this has naught to do with that. Merely has it occurred to me that you truly are no more than a serf now, and so bound to Fulkhurst as any other serf. This means you can do naught without my permission, and like any other serf, you owe me my due. This also means that, as with any other **female** serf, if I decide to toss your skirts and avail myself of what lies between your legs at any time, in any place, that is my privilege. So if I tell you to get yourself to my bed, you will make haste to do so. Is this clear to you?"

"Aye, but—"

"Aye, what?"

"My lord," she snapped.

"You are a slow learner. But then, little better can be expected of one so stupid as you."

"I am **not** stupid—my lord."

"Are you not? You do not think it was stupid of you to try and steal a child from me?"

"Not stupid," she confessed, "just very wrong— but I had no choice."

"No one held a knife at your throat," he said harshly.

She had been warned not to offer excuses. He was now angry, and not like to listen to them even if she dared try to make him understand. But she could not let pass what he had kept her from saying after his damning recital of her present position, even if it made him angrier.

"You know as well as I that I am no serf, **Lord** Warrick. If I were, I would no doubt agree with all you have said, and might even feel differently about a—a summons from you in the middle of the night. But calling me serf does not make it so, does not change feelings, does not let me accept what you term 'privilege.'"

"You are fond of telling me you had no choice. Think you that you have a choice in this?"

"Then you will have to chain me again," she assured him, "for I will never come willing to your bed."

He laughed cruelly at her confidence. "Those chains were for your benefit, wench, not mine. I would prefer it do you fight me, for I do not want your willingness. Nay, I want your hate, and your shame when you finally succumb. Mayhap I will even make you beg this time—for what you do not want."

She paled at those words, though he did not see it in the dim light. But she could remember clearly the last time in his bed, when he had played with her and made her so wild, she had thought she would beg him to take her if she were not gagged. And that would be more humiliating than all the rest combined. But she had been chained then and unable to prevent all of those intimate caresses.

Unchained, she would fight, so he would be unable to bring her to that pitch of need again—nay, he could not make her beg him. Never.

Armed with that conviction, she was about to make the foolish mistake of telling him it was impossible, which was the surest way to make him prove otherwise, when her belly broke the silence first with a loud rumble. Even **that** embarrassed her, particularly when his eyes dropped to stare at the offending noisemaker.

"When did you last eat?" he demanded.

"This morn."

"Why? You had ample time—"

"Not before your bath, I did not, and after, I—I just wanted to hide and lick my wounds."

"You will not blame me for a missed meal, wench, nor will you miss another. I care not if you starve yourself, but you will have to wait until you no longer have my child to succor in your belly. You have little enough meat on your bones now. Do you miss another meal, I will beat you."

She was beginning to wonder about that threat. He sounded as if he meant it, looked as if he meant it, but he said it too frequently for it to generate much fear anymore.

"I have no intention of starving myself to escape your vengeance."

"Good, because you will find there is no escape, not for you. Now come—"

"I am going back to my own bed."

"You are coming with me—and did I not warn you about interrupting me?"

"You did, but since you do not subscribe to that rule yourself, I did not think you would want to be thought a hypocrite as well as a monster."

That humorless smile was back. Actually, that smile was much more intimidating than his threats, because it had so far presaged most of his punishments.

He took a step forward. She took one back.

"You would not think to run from me, would you, wench?" he taunted.

Her chin went up. "Aye, why not? You mean to punish me anyway." **And I cannot help but be quicker than you, you overgrown lout.**

Before he took the step that would bring him within arm's reach of her, she bolted past him toward the circular stairs at the end of the corridor. If she could just reach the hall, there would be countless places to hide, even among the servants sleeping there. But 'twas the storage area in the basement that she had in mind.

She raced down the stairs two at a time. She heard his curse behind her, heard the rasp of her own breath—heard the scrape of steel at the bottom of the steps. She came to a skidding halt. The man blocking her way held a candle in one hand, a sword in the other. He was no older than she, but at least a hand taller.

Rowena did not have a chance to figure out a way around that sword or the young man holding it. She was lifted off the floor from behind, and Warrick commanded, "Put that away, Bernard, and go and wake the cook." But the moment the boy left to do as bidden, the hard voice turned softly menacing to whisper by her ear, "If you had not earned a punishment before, wench, you have now—but first I will feed you."

✖ 22

The kitchen was an eerie place without its blazing fire pit and many torches to chase away the shadows. The resident rat-catcher hissed in complaint before streaking off to hide behind the well. The cook was mumbling about missed sleep; Bernard was holding his candle high so the cook could see what he was doing. Rowena was still cradled in Warrick's arms. Each time she moved the slightest bit, he interpreted it as an attempt to escape and tightened his arms around her.

When he finally set her down on a stool before the table, a fine array of food was spread out for her to choose from, all cold, but still tempting to an empty belly. The half loaf of bread would have served as a trencher on the morrow, but just now it was still soft, as was the butter to spread on it. There was a thick slice of roasted beef, jellied veal hocks, and a chunk of mackerel spiced with mint and parsley, minus the sorrel sauce it had been served with earlier. A wedge of cheese, spiced pears, and an apple tart rounded off the meal, along with a tankard of ale.

"Were there no partridges left?" Warrick asked the cook as Rowena started eating.

"One, my lord, but Lady Beatrix has requested it be served her in the morn—"

Warrick interrupted to order, "Fetch it. My daughter can eat whatever is prepared on the morrow, as will the rest of us. This wench is starving now."

Rowena could not believe what she was hearing. Did he not realize he would be making another enemy for her? You did not take from the daughter of the house to give to a servant. To a guest, certainly, but not a servant. And the cook would have to deal with the angry Beatrix on the morrow, so there was another enemy for her—and he was husband to Mary Blouet, who had the care of her.

"This is more food than I can eat," Rowena quickly assured them. "I do not need—"

"You need variety," Warrick insisted.

"But I do not like partridge," she lied.

"You do not feed only yourself," he shot back.

That reminder made her face go hot with embarrassment, especially since it had the other two men looking at her differently, as if Warrick's strange behavior was now quite understandable. That she was with child was likely to become common knowledge at this rate. Coupled with the undue amount of attention Warrick was giving her, 'twould not be hard for anyone to guess who the father was. Did he not mind? Nay, why should he, when he intended to keep the child himself.

That reminder had Rowena glaring at him. "The babe **and** I do not like partridge, nor will **we** eat it."

He stared at her for a moment more before he conceded in a grouchy tone, "Very well," then turned back to the relieved cook to add, "But she should have wine instead of ale, I think, and none of that soured brew. Fetch a bottle of that sweet wine I sent from Tures."

Rowena stiffened. So did the cook, saying, "I will have to wake the butler to get the key, my lord."

"Then do so."

Rowena had just avoided the acquisition of two new enemies in giving up one of her favorite foods. She was not going to get another in the form of the butler by accepting her own wine, which she would likely choke on because it **was** hers. 'Twas cruel to offer her a sample of what she had lost, but this was one cruelty she could not even place on Warrick, for he did not know she was the Lady of Tures.

She stopped the cook on the way to the stairs. "That will not be necessary, Master Blouet. Wine makes me ill just now," she lied again. "So I could not drink it."

The cook turned back hopefully to get confirmation from his lord, but Warrick was now frowning down at Rowena. " 'Tis strange that only what will inconvenience others is what you cannot stomach just now," he remarked to her.

"That is not so," she insisted.

"Is it not?" he replied doubtfully, then with a cold edge added, "And never counter my command again, wench. Did Master Blouet obey you instead of me, he would receive ten lashes for it."

Having heard that, the poor cook was now racing up the stairs to wake the butler. Rowena stopped eating, bringing her hands to her lap so Warrick would know he was ruining her appetite.

"You are contemptible in your spite." Bernard drew in a sharp breath at her effrontery, but she still asked, "What will you do with the wine? For I will **not** drink it."

"I will have it delivered to my solar for my own use—as you will be delivered there as soon as you are finished with that meal—unless you are finished now . . ." Rowena reached for the food so fast, that humorless smile came to Warrick's lips. "Bernard?"

Bernard did not need to be told. "Aye, my lord, as soon as she is finished," the boy assured him.

Warrick put a finger under her chin, which was moving vigorously with her chewing. "Do not stuff yourself, wench, and do not be long, else I will have to return here to see what delays you, and I would not like that."

So saying, he left her alone with the squire and the food. Rowena chewed more slowly now, but anxiety was beginning to knot her stomach. He was going to rape her again. He as much as promised he would.

Mayhap she ought to fight the boy instead of Warrick, then run off and hide. Bernard was bigger than she, though not fully grown, so she would certainly have a better chance of winning free from him than from his master. But would that not get the squire punished? And if Warrick came looking for her, would he not wake others to help in the search? Inconsiderate wretch, of course he would. He did not care that his castlefolk worked hard all day and needed their sleep. She should not care either, but she did not want the whole of Fulkhurst mad at her, when there was not a single soul there who would protect her from their retaliating abuse.

"Best you hurry, Mistress," Bernard said from behind her. "His mood does not include patience for waiting long."

She did not look back to answer, "So he has to come and fetch me again. Think you I care? Either way I have to deal with his anger." And his little punishments . . .

She wondered what would be her humiliation this time for defying him outside the weaving room, for running from him, for annoying him here. The begging he had mentioned? Worse? Nay, what could be worse than begging for pleasure from a man she despised?

"You are a perverse woman, not to be grateful for his generosity."

Rowena choked on the beef she was chewing. When the coughing spasms eased, she turned around to glare at the young man who had made that outrageous statement.

"What generosity?" she demanded.

"He feeds you after the kitchen has been locked for the night. Never has it been opened before. Master Blouet would not even dare were he starving."

'Twas a standard rule in most castles. Too much pilferage would ensue otherwise. But Rowena was not impressed.

"He feeds his child, not me," she scoffed.

"He would not open the kitchen for his daughters," the boy scoffed back.

"You know naught!" she snapped impatiently. "The man hates me."

"When he desires you instead of another? When he debated for hours whether to wake you, though his need was great? When he even carried you so you would not catch a chill in your bare feet?"

She could have shot down each of those statements with ease, but she was blushing crimson over his mention of Warrick's need, which she knew she had caused at his bath. She had assumed he would send for Celia. Why had he not? **Because with you he gets revenge** and **his need seen to**. But why wait so long? Because, in truth, he could not bear to touch her, any more than she could bear to touch—nay, she was lying to herself. She had never really minded touching that finely made body when she had him in her power. And tonight, she had actually become aroused from touching him, while he had not touched her back. But she minded that! She minded his effect on her!

"Does it not matter that I want none of his attention?" she asked as if the boy could be made to understand and change his view.

All he replied was, "As I said, you are perverse."

"And you are ignorant and biased! Your lord is a cruel, vengeful—"

"Nay!" Bernard cried, upset himself now. "He is good and benevolent to those who serve him. He is only swift in retribution with his enemies."

"And I am one of those enemies," she whispered, turning her back on him.

She stared at the food she no longer desired, and heard Bernard say behind her, "His enemy? A woman? What could you have done to earn his enmity?"

Only rape him and steal his child. But that was a crime so appalling in her own mind, she would never willingly admit it to anyone. Warrick would likely change his mind and murder her if she did, because at least half his hate must come from the fact that such could have been done to **him**, so powerful a lord.

So she did not answer the question, saying dejectedly instead, "Do you mean to take me to him, do so. I am finished here."

The cook returned with the butler then, and hurried over to her. "You did not care for leftovers, girl?"

" 'Twas excellent fare, Master Blouet, merely have I had my fill. And I will be sure to eat at normal times henceforth so you are not disturbed again."

He waved that aside. "The babe must have nourishment. I will see that you have extra portions at your meals."

"Nay, you need not—"

"Lord Warrick would have it so."

And whatever Lord Warrick would have, so it would be done.

Rowena ground her teeth together and headed out of the kitchen. But before she reached the stone steps, she was picked up from behind, just like before. Only she did not feel secure in these arms. She felt as if she was about to fall.

"Put me **down**, Bernard. I am perfectly capable—"

"Perverse," he huffed to himself as he trudged

up the stairs. "She would rather catch her death so that I will be flayed alive. Utterly perverse."

" 'Tis more like I will break my neck when you drop me, you fool."

" 'Tis chivalrous to assist all women—but next time wear shoes, Mistress."

He was complaining? Rowena would have boxed his ears if she did not think he would drop her in startlement. God save her from aspiring knights.

"There," he said at last, and set her quickly on her feet. "The wooden floor is not so cold. I needs catch my breath, but you may go on."

She could, could she? Rowena decided to be as perverse as he had called her.

"How would you know how cold the floor is when your feet are not bare? My toes are freezing. You will have to carry me after all."

He was standing there laboring for every breath. The dark hall stretched long before them, with only a torch at the far end to light the narrow path through the sleeping bodies of the servants.

Bernard looked at her in horror. "Ah—mayhap you could wear my shoes instead?"

"Mayhap I will return to my own bed."

His horror magnified. "You cannot do that!"

"Watch me, sirrah."

She turned and started down the path, but no more than five seconds had passed before she was picked up again. Now Bernard was angry, and it came out in biting scorn.

"Your ladylike airs do not become you, Mistress. Think you the lord's favor elevates you to that status? It does not, and best you remember that."

His words stung, prompting a thoughtless reply. "I do not need elevation to a status already mine. 'Tis your **good and benevolent** lord who would make me other than what I am, which is Lady of—" Her common sense returned before she blurted out "Tures." "Kirkburough," she amended. "Which he did recently destroy."

"You lie, wench."

"And you sound like your master, lout," she retorted. "Verily, the only thing I lied about was the freezing of my toes. Now put me down!"

He did, half dropping her as the strength in his arms gave out. But little good it did her, for they had reached the antechamber to the solar, and the door to the inner chamber stood open—and promptly filled with the presence of her nemesis, drawn by her raised voice.

"What ails you?" Warrick asked his squire, for the boy was truly wheezing now.

Rowena answered before Bernard could. "He thought to mimic you and carry me, but found he must grow some ere he starts acting the barbarian in forcing women to his will."

The double gibe was not lost on either male. Bernard flushed with angry color. Warrick smiled, that chilling smile she hated.

"So my new serf has claws, does she?" he remarked. "I will have to see what I can do about plucking them. Come inside, Rowena."

She did not move an inch, horrified by what she had just done. What had made her think she could taunt and insult him without paying for it? But as long as she was damned anyway . . .

"I—I am through accepting punishments that have naught to do with—" She cast a glance at Bernard before ending with, "What lies between us. Do you want me in there, you will have to drag me in. I told you, I do not go willingly."

It would have been nice if Bernard were not blocking the only exit from there, but he was, and so there was nowhere to run to when Warrick accepted her challenge and came to get her. And although she tried with every bit of strength she possessed to remove her wrist from the clamp of his fingers, she was summarily dragged into his solar, where he slammed the door closed behind them. Nor did he stop until he had reached his bed and shoved her down on it.

Then slowly, with a good deal of obvious pleasure, he lowered his body over hers until she was left with the sure knowledge that she could not budge him.

"You see now how little it matters, your unwillingness?" he taunted.

"I hate you."

"The feeling is returned wholeheartedly, and I

assure you I am much better at it than you could ever be." He was wearing his cruel smile, so she had little doubt about that either.

Suddenly she felt like crying. A few tears even gathered to brighten her eyes to a jewellike radiance.

He noticed and studied them thoughtfully for a moment before he said, "You would not be thinking to make this easy for me, would you? Where is the fight you promised me?"

"You take too much pleasure in my hate and my resistance. I would prefer not to give you any pleasure at all."

"Selfish, wench," he chided, though there was suddenly real humor in his eyes. "So you think to lie there like a dead thing and hope I will grow bored and let you go?"

She had yet to meet this particular mood of his and said warily, "Now that you mention it . . ."

He laughed, confounding her, and laughed even more when he saw her confusion. Then his hand came to her cheek, so gentle, and his thumb rubbed slowly, tantalizingly, over her full lower lip.

"What am I to do with you?"

The question did not seem to be for her, actually, merely was he wondering it aloud. But she answered him anyway. "Let me go."

"Nay, never that," he said softly as his eyes dropped to her lips. "You were virgin in more than one area. What about these, too?"

There was warmth now in his eyes and smile that made him so handsome she was nearly mesmerized. And then his lips touched hers.

She had seen it coming, had been prepared to resist, but she was unprepared for the unexpected involvement of the rest of her that she had no control of. His tongue licked at her lips, and she felt sensations in her belly. His tongue slipped between her teeth to caress her own, and she felt heat in her loins.

'Twas true that no lover's lips had ever shown her the way of kissing. What Gilbert had done just before he left her to Warrick's mercy was naught like this. That kiss had been brief, hard, and repugnant to her. This one was soft, unending, and she wished she were not being made to know the difference. There should have been no difference. But she could not deny this was another thing about her enemy that she did not mind.

"As I thought, another virgin terrain to explore," he said, and seemed pleased by it. "You must have been locked away until I found you."

Words seemed to be the only defense he would allow her. She used them now as a desperate measure, for she realized that she would have herself to fight as much as him if this continued.

"You did not find me, you were found **for** me. Remember that, and that you do not really want to do this. Let me go, Warrick."

His answer was to kiss her again, a kiss not so gentle this time, but still not the least bit repulsive. In fact, she was caught up in the passion of it so quickly, she forgot the taunt she had just used to avoid it.

He did not. He was as angry with her as she had hoped he would be, merely was the result not what she had wanted. Nor did she become aware of it until much later, when she heard his whispered command, "Beg me," and she had reached the point of such frustrating need—that she did.

❧ 23

Warrick was in a bemused state of utter repletion and disgruntlement. Neither feeling sat well with him at the moment, but neither would leave him alone. The one made him wish he could deny the other, but he could not, for burying himself deep inside that flaxen-haired witch had been unbelievably satisfying. Of course, obtaining revenge against her had made it so good. Such immense pleasure could not be for any other reason.

But he should not have experienced that at all, for he had had no intention of touching her again after she had been released from her chains. He had meant to continue plaguing her, certainly, and heaping shame on her. He still meant to, for he had not allowed her to live without paying a price for it, and he wanted her constantly reminded of that.

But tonight had shown him that he was a fool to think he could shame her by having her perform intimate services and not pay a price for it himself.

He could have if she had continued to feel only shame—but she had become aroused instead, though she tried so hard not to show it, and her wanting him had sent him over the edge. Still, he had resisted her siren's call and sent her away. Yet she had continued to prey on his mind—and body.

That should have enraged him, that she could still make him want her so powerfully. Verily, it did infuriate him, for 'twas no different from his lack of control when she had had him in her power. And he **had** fought the overwhelming urge to go and fetch her back to him tonight. But once it had occurred to him that her very status now gave him all the excuse he needed to have her again, he lost the fight.

He leaned over to look at her now. She was pretending sleep, hoping to avoid any further attention from him. He smiled to himself. He had not expected to find her so amusing. Her spirit, her attempts to defy him, were ridiculously funny. Most of the time she truly feared him, but at other times she was too angry to, and he found he enjoyed her anger much more than her fear, which made not much sense to him.

Nor did her daring in deliberately trying to prick his anger make much sense, considering the seriousness of her position. He had not bothered to undress her or himself, merely tossing her skirt up as he had warned her he could do.

But he had also told her he did not want her willingness, yet hearing her beg him to take her had
been sweet indeed, appeasing the anger she had
sought.

Her skirt was still hiked up to her hips. He
brought his hand to rest on her bare flank and
watched her hold her breath. But she did not open
her eyes, still pretending sleep. Another little defiance he chose to let pass for the moment.

His mood was certainly strange, despising her for
what she had done to him, but enjoying too much
having her in his power. And this urge to touch her
when he was well sated—that increased his disgruntlement.

He removed his hand from her with a frown, deciding that her presence had to be responsible for
his strange mood. At least that he could rectify,
and right quickly.

"Be gone, wench. My use of you does not include sharing my bed more than I already have. I
did not like sleeping on a hard pallet these last
three nights."

"I am overcome with sympathy," she retorted as
she rolled off the mattress to the floor and headed
straight for the door.

Her sarcasm was too blatant to amuse him. "Remember my soft bed when you sleep on your own
hard pallet," he called after her.

She turned to give him a tight little smile.

"Your bed has already been forgotten—except for me to know a stone slab would be preferable to it."

"Such was not your attitude when you were begging me to take you."

Her face went scarlet at the reminder. Good. That would teach her to be a little wiser in her taunts. But he forgot about that the moment he noticed her bare feet.

"Come back here, Rowena." Her face went from red to white, making him snap, "I am in no mood to carry you back to your bed because you were forgetful in bringing your shoes along."

"**Me** forgetful? I had had no intention of leaving the weaving room. You wake me in the middle of the night and expect me to be fully dressed?"

"You were not sleeping. But regardless, now you must sleep here after all, until I can have your shoes fetched in the morn."

"I will not catch cold, I swear I will not."

"Do you mean to stand there and argue with me, wench?" he demanded.

She lowered her head. "No," she said so softly he barely heard.

"Then get you back in this bed now."

He said no more while she came forward at a snail's pace, tempting his patience, his temper, his good intentions. But by the time she had reached the bed, he was annoyed enough to add, "Remove that chemise first. I do not care to be chafed by it do I roll toward you in my sleep."

Her head snapped up to show him she was not cowed, as he had thought. She had been trying to hide her fury from him. She gave up the pretense now to yank the chemise over her head and throw it to the floor. That demonstration of pique was merely amusing. The redness on her skin from the coarse wool was what kept him annoyed.

Damned delicate skin. He had just made one exception by permitting her to share his bed to safeguard her health, and here was another he felt compelled to make for her.

He did not like having his revenge undermined by incidentals, but still he made a mental note to tell Enid to fetch the soft linen shift that Rowena had come with, mayhap her own chemise, too, when she brought the shoes in the morn. But this had best be the last allowance that must be made because of her size, gender, or softness, or the wench would begin to think he was not serious in his dislike of her.

To ensure that she did not think so now, he let his eyes roam over her nakedness and said, "'Tis pleasant indeed, teaching you your place."

"Which is beneath your feet?" she snapped.

He began to remove his own clothes, but spared her a brittle smile before replying. "If I so wish it. Now get under the covers. I do not care to hear another word from you this night." Or see any more of that luscious body she did not even attempt to shield from him now.

For once she quickly did as bidden, but when he joined her moments later after dousing the candles, and turned toward her merely to find a comfortable position, she cried out, "I cannot endure your touch again. I will go mad!"

He was tempted to disprove those words. Instead he said, "Be quiet. I am too tired to force you again—no matter how much you might beg for it." But perversely, he now put an arm around her and drew her into the curve of his body.

"I will not be able to sleep like this," she gritted out.

"Best you hope I can, wench, or 'twill not matter how tired I am." She became so still she did not even breathe. He laughed and hugged her closer. "Do I want you again, your silly antics will not prevent it, so go to sleep ere I change my mind."

She breathed again and said no more. Warrick **was** tired, but not so tired that he did not appreciate the warm body pressed to his. There was a benefit to her softness after all, and he realized he could get used to it if he was not careful.

❧ 24

God was merciful the next morning in allowing Rowena to wake to an empty chamber. She did not know how she was going to endure facing Warrick in the bright light of day after last night, but at least she had a temporary reprieve—but not from the memories.

She groaned as they assailed her, and buried her head beneath the pillow. She had been so sure she could resist begging Warrick, but with his fingers and lips tormenting her, with her blood soaring ever faster with need, the words he had wanted to hear had tumbled from her lips. And she had not cared then, had cared for naught but the exquisite pleasure he had withheld until she did as he wanted. The mortification and self-loathing had come after, but would last for much longer—most like forever. And she still could not bear the thought of facing him and seeing his gloating expression.

She would die, burn up with the shame of it, and he would laugh. Her weakness meant naught to him; his own triumph was everything. Aye, he would laugh, and she would hate him more than ever . . .

"Unbury yourself, wench, and put these on."

Rowena gasped and swung around to find Warrick standing beside the bed with her shift and chemise in his hands, as well as the bliaut and shoes she had left in the weaving room. He was frowning at her—and had more to say in his brusque tone.

"Think you you can laze abed as you are likely accustomed, simply because I found some little pleasure in you yestereve? Nay, your status does not change, nor do your duties, which you have thus far neglected this morn. However, as I have already eaten, you need not serve at the high table until the evening meal, so go and break your fast now and attend to your other duties."

He left before she could come up with a suitable scathing reply. Laze abed indeed. As if she would, especially in **his** bed.

And then it dawned on her that she had faced him and survived it. He was not going to gloat about her shame? He was not even going to mention it other than that he had found some **little** pleasure in her? Verily, she did not understand him at all. He had passed up the perfect opportunity for further humiliation.

She glanced at the clothes left on the bed, and her confusion increased. She knew **why** she had been given servants' clothes—so she would be constantly reminded by their roughness of her new status. Yet here were her own undergarments back in softest linen to protect her skin. She would still have to wear the servant's outer gown, but she would no longer be chafed raw by it.

She stared in bemusement at the door through which Warrick had departed. This cruel man refused to let her go hungry, refused to let her get chilled, albeit his concern in those matters was for the babe she carried. But now he refused to let her skin become abraded by the clothes **he** had insisted she wear, and that was not for the child. That was only for her. Cruel? Aye, certainly he was—but mayhap not to the core.

Nay, what was she thinking? There was no kindness in Warrick de Chaville, not even a little. No doubt he had some ulterior motive in giving her back her underclothes that she just could not see yet, but was like to cause her embarrassment somehow. The hateful man. Did he have naught better to do than plot ways to plague her?

She dressed quickly, sighing with pleasure at the familiar comfort of her thin white shift and the snug-fitting red chemise that covered her ankles as was proper—for a lady, anyway. The coarse dun bliaut no longer touched her skin at all, but she found she would have a problem keeping it up on her shoulders, now that she had her smooth chemise under it instead of the rough wool that had at least kept the loose garment in place.

Regardless, she felt so much better wearing at least something of her own that she was almost smiling when she entered the hall, and did smile when she saw that Warrick was not there to unnerve her with those chilling silver eyes. She looked for Mildred at the hearth, but only Warrick's daughters were there with their tutor, learning new stitches. She did not spare them another glance, so did not notice how they watched her all the way to the kitchen stairs, with looks almost as baleful as their father's.

"Pay her no mind, my dears," Lady Roberta admonished. "A lady does not deign to notice women of her sort."

"But she passed the night in his solar," thirteen-year-old Melisant pointed out. "Celia never passed the whole night with him."

"Celia is hardly pleasant company with her haughty airs," Beatrix said with a disdainful sniff.

Beatrix was the older daughter at ten and four, if you did not count the bastard, Emma, whom their father never even asked after, and whom neither legitimate daughter acknowledged as sister. Melisant was the prettier of the two, with her light blond hair and gray eyes, which had just enough blue in them to make them not so cold as her father's. Beatrix had brown hair and eyes herself, and cheekbones too narrow. She would have been passing fair if her expression were not always so pinched and disapproving. But then, it was a well-known fact that Warrick had been betrothed to her mother at a young age, and her mother had been a plain-looking woman. Whereas Warrick had picked Melisant's mother himself for her comeliness.

Beatrix did not hold this too much against her younger sister. She was older, after all, and her father's heir. Melisant would have her mother's dower property, but Beatrix would have all the rest—as long as there was no male heir. Which was why Beatrix had lived in dread of the Lady Isabella's coming, and had silently rejoiced to hear the maid was now missing, possibly dead. It had taken Warrick so long to find her when he had decided 'twas time for another wife, and longer still to make contract for her. And he was so busy with his wars and increasing his property, which would be Beatrix's property, that he would not have time to look for another wife.

But she did not like the rumors she was hearing about the new servant. Twice now it had been whispered to her that the wench was breeding, and that the babe was likely Warrick's. That was not alarming in itself, for Warrick would never wed a lowly serf, and a serf's bastard would never inherit Fulkhurst, even were it a male child. But the other rumor she had heard, that the wench was not truly a serf, but a lady born who had merely earned Warrick's enmity—that put a different face on it.

She did not believe it. Even her father, who was utterly ruthless to his enemies, would not treat a lady so. But if it **was** true, and the girl gave Warrick a son, he might be induced to wed her.

Beatrix knew he wanted a male heir. Everyone knew it. But she could not bear it if it came to pass, not now, after she had lived her whole life with the expectation of having it all. She **wanted** it all, needed it. She did not have Melisant's prettiness. Only the promise of Fulkhurst would get her the husband she wanted.

"There she is again," Melisant said as Rowena appeared in the hall with Enid in tow this time. "I wonder from where she got that pretty red chemise."

"Spoils Father no doubt gave her," Beatrix replied with narrowed eyes. "I think I will summon her and—"

"You will **not**, young lady," the tutor scolded sternly, fully aware of how spiteful her charge could be. "Do you make trouble for your lord's leman, the trouble is like to come back to you. Remember that for when you have a husband."

Beatrix glared at the old woman, but did not argue. She had found it easier just to ignore Lady Roberta's sage advice and then do as she pleased when the pious old fool was not around.

❧ 25

With the thorough cleaning done yesterday, Rowena and Enid finished early in the solar, so it was well before noon when Rowena climbed the stairs to the weaving room. But she nearly jumped out of her skin when one of the doors she had to pass to get there opened and she was yanked inside.

"'Tis about time you came along," a voice grumbled, though with unmistakable affection.

"Mildred!"

"Aye, and spending my whole morn up here just waiting for you to leave the weaving room. How did I miss you that you are coming from below?"

Rowena was too busy hugging the older woman to say anything for a moment, but then the words flowed out of her. "How do you come to be at Fulkhurst? Has Warrick sought revenge against you, too? I am so **glad** you are here, Mildred, but not if you are being abused by that monster. But I thought never to see you again and—"

"Shush, my sweet one," Mildred soothed, and led Rowena to sit on a stool amidst baskets of sewing materials. "How can I answer if you do not pause for breath so I can? And why did you not answer my own question? I was told you would be sleeping in the weaving room."

Mildred took the stool next to her, but Rowena did not look at her when she said, "I slept below yestereve."

From the bright pink tingeing Rowena's cheeks, Mildred was wise enough not to ask where. All she said was, "I am not surprised."

Rowena's head snapped up. "You are not? **Why** are you not? It shocked me that he would want to—to . . . He had already had his revenge in that way."

"Did he?"

"Aye, exactly like for like. All that was done to him he did to me—and now more."

"Then it has been so terrible?"

"Worse than terrible."

"All of it?"

Rowena frowned at that particular question. "What do you fish for?"

Mildred shrugged. "Like for like, my lamb, means you would experience the same pleasure he had at your hands. Did you?" Rowena's cheeks got pinker. "I see that you did. But 'tis to be expected when you have such a fine-looking—"

"**Cruel**-looking—"

"—man who knows what he is about."

"The **only** thing Warrick de Chaville is about, Mildred, is making me pay for Gilbert's greed. Now what do you here? I feared you would be left in Kirkburough's ruins, with no way to return even to Tures."

"No one was left in the ruins. Lord Warrick did not burn the town except for the inn where he was captured, but even so, he offered all at the keep new homes on his own properties did they want them. For myself, he felt he owed me for his release, even though I had told him I did only your bidding."

"I know how he does not like to hear excuses, **will** not hear them."

"Aye, I thought he would kill me did I say another word about it, so angry was he at the mere mention of your innocence. But he offered me a home here at Fulkhurst if I would give him my loyalty henceforth—forsaking you. 'Twas the only way I could follow you here, so I accepted gladly. Only he has forbidden me to speak to you."

Rowena sighed. "So I guessed. He would not want me to have comfort in your presence, though just knowing you are near is a comfort to me."

Mildred squeezed her hand. "Do not despair, my lamb. I do not think he is as mean-spirited as he would like us to think. I have heard much about the events that have shaped him into the man he is today, and I hesitate to admit this to you, but I find myself feeling sorry for him."

"Sorry for him?" Rowena said incredulously. "Did he bash you on the head, Mildred, ere he brought you here?"

Mildred chuckled. "Nay, he dragged me about the countryside with his army in search of his missing betrothed, but I swear he thought little of Lady Isabella the while he looked for her. Never did he seem disappointed when each place he inquired at turned out to have no word of her passing. But you should have seen him when the messenger who came from Fulkhurst each day was even a little late in arriving. Lord Warrick would send out dozens of men to find him, and when the newsbearer did arrive, woe betide him if he had no word from John Giffard."

Rowena stiffened upon hearing that name. "John? But I thought he was only the jailer here. What news could Warrick want from him?"

Mildred gave her a look that said plainly, Do not play dense. "What else?"

"But Warrick did not know John had the care of me in the dungeon."

"How could he not know when he ordered it?"

"**He** did? But I thought Sir Robert . . ."

Rowena paused as the implications of what Mildred had said occurred to her. Warrick had put her in his dungeon not to suffer, then—other than with her own imaginings? Those imaginings had been terrible, true, but her cell had been like a palace compared to what it would have been like without

John as her keeper. Could Warrick not know how kindhearted John was? Nay, John's goodness was writ all over him, sensed at a glance. To know him was to know he would never hurt a soul.

Suddenly she cried out almost painfully, "I do not understand! Why would he assure I was well cared for **before** he knew I carried his child?"

Mildred's brown eyes flared wide. "So it happened, and in only those few days of trying? Are you ailing with it? I have some fine remedies for that, and for the swelling that might come later."

Rowena dismissed Mildred's offer impatiently. "Nay, no symptoms other than the most obvious of missing my monthly time."

"Aye, so it was with your mother, going blithely about her duties as if she were not—"

"Mildred, I do not want to discuss babies when Warrick means to take mine from me."

Mildred frowned thoughtfully before asking, "Did he say he would?"

"Would I say it had he not? He claims he will take the babe from me when it is born, as I—as I took it from him. Like for like."

"Do you want it?"

"Of **course** I want it. 'Tis mine!"

"And his," Mildred pointed out calmly.

"But he did not want the making of it."

"Neither did you."

"But he wants it now only to hurt me. That is no reason to keep a child."

"Aye, and mayhap he will realize that ere long. 'Tis much too soon to worry about what he plans eight months from now. Like as not you will be gone from here before then. Or have you not thought of escape yet?"

Rowena snorted. "Certainly I have. Do you tell me how I might accomplish it when both baileys have gate guards on constant duty, then I will leave this very day."

Mildred grinned. " 'Twill not be **that** easy. But mayhap Lord Gilbert will help when he learns where you are. Surely he must know by now that 'twas the Lord of Fulkhurst who destroyed Kirkburough keep. I am surprised he has not brought his army here already."

Rowena gasped. "Do not even think it! I would rather stay here and suffer Warrick's every little cruelty than be back in Gilbert's control."

"Now **that** I find interesting. Your stepbrother would merely marry you off again, while—"

"One decrepit old husband was enough for me, Mildred. And Gilbert . . . before he left Kirkburough, he kissed me, and 'twas in no way brotherly."

"Ah, so he finally showed his craving, did he? And there would be more of that if he had you back, for there is naught to stop him now from taking you to his bed, particularly while you carry the heir he wanted for Kirkburough. But then, he is a very handsome man. Mayhap you would not mind."

"Mildred!"

"So you would mind? Well, then, 'tis fortunate that you find yourself unable to leave here for the while. 'Tis the safest place you could be to keep Lord Gilbert from getting you back again."

That was possibly true, but Rowena wished Mildred did not make it sound as if she ought to thank Warrick for making her his prisoner **and** his unwilling leman. Mildred was not giving this subject the gravity it deserved. In fact, she seemed not the least bit concerned over Rowena's plight.

"Why do I sense you are not worried about any of this, Mildred? Think you Warrick is finished having his revenge against me? I assure you he is not. To him I am a thief, and although he did not cut off my hands for it, he means to inflict his little cruelties on me each day I am under his roof."

"Ah, but I wonder how long his animosity would last did you develop a fondness for him and let him know it. Not long, I warrant."

"Now I know he bashed your head, and so hard you do not even remember it."

Mildred laughed. "Nay, my lamb. Merely have I had more opportunity to observe him unawares than you, and I do not think him so very cruel. A cruel man would have had you tortured to death and watched every minute of it. Lord Warrick has instead given you back like for like."

"He denies my status, has declared me a serf."

"He was thought one by us and treated just so," Mildred reminded her. "But do you ask me, the man is obsessed with you, and for reasons other than revenge. He wants the revenge, surely. 'Tis his nature now to have it. But mayhap it does not sit well with him in this instance. You are a woman after all, and all of his enemies thus far have been men. He **knows** how to deal with them. With you he does not."

"These speculations do not help me, Mildred," Rowena said irritably.

"Then you have not thought of using a woman's weapons against him, have you?"

"What weapons?"

"Your beauty. His lust. Then even marriage will be an option, with the child as an added inducement."

"He would never—!"

"Aye, he **could** be brought to it, if he wants you badly enough. And you can make him want you that much. You could even make him love you if you did but try."

Love? What would Warrick be like with that tender emotion fixed in his heart? Would he be as fierce in love as he was in hate? Nay, what was wrong with her? To even think of it was absurd.

But Mildred had not finished. "Most ladies loathe the marriage bed, and small wonder if they are wed to rutting louts who use them only for

breeding, while taking their own pleasures elsewhere. But you already know what the marriage
bed would be like with this lord. And for a husband, you would be hard pressed to find one as
well matched to you in estate, who is also young, a
power to reckon with, virile—as you can attest—
and not too ugly."

"He is not ugly," Rowena protested without
thinking. "He is even very handsome when . . .
he . . . smiles." She glowered then to realize she
had just said something in that man's favor. "You
have gone mad, Mildred, and these notions are
pure fancy. Warrick wants naught from me but
the babe I stole from him and my eternal atone-
ment for that theft. The man despises the very
sight of me."

"More like the very sight of you stirs his lust,
and **that** is what he despises just now. But you miss
my point. I did not say the idea of marriage would
come easily to him, only that 'tis possible to bring
him 'round to thinking of it. First you must rid
him of his animosity toward you, and that will take
effort on your part."

"**That** would take a miracle."

"Nay, merely set him to thinking of other things
than what was done to him. Confound him. Do not
do what he expects. Deliberately entice him. If he
can be made to think you want him, despite his
treatment of you thus far, all the better. That

would completely baffle him, and he will spend more time wondering about it than thinking up those little cruelties you mentioned. Are you willing to try?"

"I can foresee only making a fool of myself should I do so. Methinks you have deluded yourself with wishful thinking, Mildred."

"And if I have not? Do you like the treatment you get from him now?"

Rowena recalled last night with a shudder, the shame of being made to beg—the unwanted pleasure that begging had gotten her. "Nay," she said in a whisper.

"Then use your weapons to change it. Show him the maid you were before the d'Ambrays' coming. Your winsome ways were nigh impossible to resist, as any man who knew you then can attest."

"I do not think I would know how to be that carefree, happy girl again."

Mildred leaned over to give her a brief, sympathetic hug. "I know, my sweet one. A pretense is all that is necessary. Can you manage that?"

"Possibly."

"Then will you try?"

"I needs think on this first. I am not sure I want more of Warrick's attention than I already have."

"That is not like to change either way."

Rowena's chin rose stubbornly. "And I am not sure either that I want to stop hating him."

Mildred chuckled. "Then do not. Merely keep him from being aware of your true feelings. He is the one who wears his moods on his face, not you, so that should not be hard for you. But be aware that once he changes and begins to court your favor, you may become as caught up in the game as he and find yourself other than hating him."

The thought of Warrick de Chaville courting her was so ridiculous, Rowena did not bother to argue against the likelihood of it ever happening, or of her feeling differently than she did now. Besides, she was heartily sick of the subject, and so changed it.

"How is it we have this room to ourselves, Mildred? 'Tis the sewing room, is it not?"

"Aye, but I sent the women off to experiment with a new dye."

Rowena laughed at Mildred's mischievous look. "Not that awful green we made last year?"

"Exactly. But I did not tell them 'twas awful. I told them to expect a most beautiful shade, so they would be long in trying to create it. Later I will confess I forgot to mention the addition of yellow, which brightened the shade to that leaf green we ended with."

"Have you the direction of the sewing women, then, that you can order them?"

"Nay, but the castlefolk are wary of me in my new position as maid to both of the lord's daughters. They know not the extent of my authority, and so do my bidding without question."

"And how do you like serving his daughters?"

Mildred snorted. "Two more haughty, self-centered bitches you never met. 'Twas no favor Lord Warrick did me with that position, but to be fair, I doubt he knows how truly spoiled his daughters are. They brag readily enough that he is never here to correct them, and you and I know why that is so."

"Aye, his damn war with Gilbert and heaven knows who else. Has aught been said of when he will leave again?"

"Do not sound so hopeful, my lamb. He needs be present for you to work your wiles on him to better your own lot. Does he leave soon, your load will not be lightened the while he is gone."

"Nay, 'twould be cut in half. I could easily live with that."

"And what if he thinks to stick you back in the dungeon instead, to assure you will still be his prisoner when he returns?"

That was a distinct possibility, and without the guarantee that she would have John Giffard again as a guard. But the alternative, to actually try and entice that man . . . she did not care to think on it yet, **could** not.

She stood up in agitation, saying, "Best I leave ere we are found out and both punished."

Mildred protested. "This is the women's floor. He is not likely to come up—"

"He did last eventide," Rowena cut in as she headed for the door. But there she stopped, and it was a moment before she turned to ask with a thoughtful frown, "What did you mean, 'tis his nature now to have revenge?"

"Have you heard naught about what occurred here sixteen years ago?"

"Warrick made mention of another holding Fulkhurst long ago. Is that what you speak of?"

"Aye. Lord Warrick was not here at the time, was fostered with another lord, or he would no doubt be as dead as his family."

"Was it a siege?"

"Nay, treachery. As I was told, a baron, Sir Edward Bainart by name, coveted Fulkhurst, as well as the Lady Elisabeth, Warrick's mother. Bainart called himself friend to the family, his desires unknown to them, and during one of his visits, he acted to have what he wanted. He waited until all slept, then sent his own small band of men to dispatch the Fulkhurst men-at-arms and any servants who thought to interfere. He then sneaked into the solar and murdered Warrick's father in his own bed, with the Lady Elisabeth as witness. The stupid man thought she would be too afeared to give him trouble after that, but he had not counted on how much she had loved her husband. She reviled him most foully before his men, enraging him so that he gave her to them, all of them; and, ignorant churls that they were, they killed her through their rough handling. Warrick's two sisters, one younger than he, one older, thought the same fate would be theirs and jumped off the parapet together, the one dying instantly, the other broken of body, but lingering nigh a week in horrible pain ere she died, too."

Rowena knew now wherein Mildred found sympathy for Warrick. "I wish you had not told me this."

"'Tis wisest to know your enemy, and a simple question can bring a wealth of information when you are in a room full of gossiping women. Lord Warrick was only six and ten when the news reached him that Fulkhurst was in the hands of another, his family all dead. 'Twas another six months ere he learned the full details, and twice during that time attempts were made on his own life. He was, after all, still heir to Fulkhurst, though without the aid of king or an army of his own to win it back. Bainart knew this and so dismissed Warrick as a threat. He did not know of Warrick's one remaining resource, a betrothal made in his youth and still in effect. He was too young to do aught about it then, but the very day he was knighted, he rode straightaway to claim his bride, and with her dower lands to supply men, and additional aid from her father—"

"He won back Fulkhurst?"

"Aye."

"And killed Bainart?"

"With his own hands. But that was not enough. His inability to act immediately to avenge his family had allowed his hate to fester for those two years. Fulkhurst had declined in prosperity because many of the servants had been maimed or killed under Bainart's rule. What Warrick had won back was a sorry estate."

"And so Bainart's other properties became targets," Rowena guessed.

"Exactly. It took three years, but in the end, all of Bainart's holdings were added to Fulkhurst, doubling it in size. Lord Warrick lost his first wife and took another during that time, with an eye to increasing his resources in the second marriage, but with a more comely maid than his first wife had been."

"Had he new enemies by then, that he needed an even larger army?"

"Nay, but he had made a vow that no one would ever do him an ill again without paying for it tenfold. 'Tis a vow he has kept ever since, and it has earned him a reputation of swift retribution for all trespasses. 'Tis a vow that has involved him in one war after another, year after year, for he will not let the slightest offense pass."

" 'Tis what finally turned him into the cruel monster he is today," Rowena remarked bitterly.

"Nay, how he is today is how he was from the day he learned of the destruction of his whole family. 'Twas his grief and despair that changed him from the boy he was to the man he is. They say there is no comparison between the two, that the boy was kind, loving, full of mischief and the joyous exuberance of youth."

"And the man is cold, heartless—"

"But now you know why, and I doubt not that if he changed once, he can change again."

"Or not."

"Where is the optimism of your own youth?"

"Destroyed at the hands of the d'Ambrays."

"Then nurture it back to life, my lamb, for you have an opportunity here to secure your own future—and heal a man who has lived too long with demons from his past. A worthy endeavor do you ask me."

"I did not ask you," Rowena said with growing annoyance. "You can feel sorry for him, but you are not the recipient of his current enmity. Do you ask **me**, he and his demons deserve each other."

"Will you let your own tragedies turn you as hard and unforgiving as he?"

"Now you contradict yourself to badger me, by admitting he **is** hard and unforgiving. Leave go, Mildred. I said I would think about it."

"Very well." Mildred sighed, but added tenaciously, "You do not feel just a little sorry for him now?"

"Not even a little," Rowena said stubbornly—and wished it were not a lie.

26

"Welcome, Sheldon!" Warrick exclaimed and clasped his old friend in a bear hug. "It has been too long since you came for a visit."

"Likely because you crack my ribs each time I do," Sheldon grunted.

"Liar," Warrick shot back, but with a laugh, for Sheldon was not as wide as he was, but was as tall—and in full armor.

Sheldon de Vere had been the eldest son of the household where Warrick had been fostered, and Warrick had been his squire for four years. That there was only some five years difference in their ages had made them friends as well. Sheldon was merely thirty-seven now, but his beard and straggly, long brown hair were prematurely salted with gray, a trait common to the men of his family. It did not detract from his handsomeness, but it did cause strange stares from folk seeing him for the first time.

"Come, seat yourself and let your squire remove some of that heavy mail," Warrick continued as he led the way to the hearth. Then he called to a passing servant. "Emma, order refreshment for my guest." The girl turned to do as told, but after a moment Warrick called again. "And fetch the new wench to serve it."

Sheldon watched the lithesome girl delegate the first order to another, then move toward the stairs to the women's quarters. "You still treat her like a servant?" he remarked after she had gone from sight.

"She is a servant."

"She is also your daughter."

Warrick frowned at that bald statement. "That cannot be proven. God's blood, I bedded her mother but once in my fifteenth year, when you had given me leave to come home for a short visit. 'Tis unlikely—"

"Why do you make excuses for it not to be so," Sheldon interrupted, "when you have only to look at her to know she is your get? She is the only one of your girls who actually does look like you."

Warrick slumped down in his chair by the hearth, his frown darkening. "I had no knowledge of the girl until she was nigh full-grown. Her mother was so afeared of me, she kept her hidden in the village during my infrequent stays here, and my servants are so circumspect, none would mention her existence to me. Even you have never mentioned her to me ere now."

Sheldon flushed, for that was true enough.

"Did you acknowledge her as yours when you did finally notice her?"

Warrick snorted. "When I first noticed her, my friend, all I saw was a comely wench I might like to sample in a few years and I told her so, whereby she promptly explained, with a good deal of affronted heat, that I could not because she was my daughter. Verily, I have never felt like such a fool, because I did not see it, because I did not know it."

Sheldon laughed. "Embarrassment like that is not easy to forget."

"Indeed, nor have I. I would as soon she continued to hide herself when I am home, but now she does not."

"But did you acknowledge her?"

"Nay. I told you it cannot be proven she is mine, or do you forget that my father yet lived when she was conceived? She could as easily be his get."

"You believe that no more than I. Your father was much too devoted to your mother to find any interest at all in the castle wenches."

Warrick could not deny that, and his frown turned into a scowl. "Mayhap I welcomed you too hastily, old friend. Why do you badger me about the girl?"

Sheldon sighed. "I should have said so to begin

with. My second son, Richard, would like to have her to wife."

Warrick stared at him for a long moment before he burst out laughing. "His wife? What jest is this?"

"No jest. I doubt you care to note it, but you have made yourself a power to reckon with. An alliance with your house is coveted by more powerful lords than I, or are you not barraged frequently with requests for your girls?"

"Aye, too many for me to have the time to consider. But I have two legitimate daughters, either of whom I would gladly give to Richard."

Sheldon grimaced. "No offense, Warrick, but Richard has threatened to move to France do I come back with a betrothal to either of those two. He wants no other than Emma, and I would be glad of the match myself."

"But she is no more than a serf!" Warrick burst out.

"Not if you acknowledge her as yours."

Warrick was back to scowling. "'Twould be a disservice to your family. She has not the deportment or manners of a lady. She would shame—"

"She can be taught all that needs knowing."

"By who?" Warrick snorted. "Did I ask Lady Roberta to include my bastard in her teachings, she would laugh in my face, or more like leave affronted. 'Tis not done, Sheldon."

His friend sighed again. "She should have been taught long ago, but as you say, you knew not of her existence. And I have no lady wife to take her in hand either. What, then, do I tell my Richard, who has his heart set on her? Is she really so lacking in all graces?"

Warrick did not hear the question. Emma had returned to the hall, and right behind her was Rowena. And the sight of the flaxen-haired wench sent all thoughts of Sheldon's problem out of his mind. She did not look his way, but his eyes followed her until she disappeared down the kitchen stairwell.

Memories of last eventide returned and caused him to stir uncomfortably in his chair; then he realized that Sheldon was staring at him.

"What?"

Sheldon raised a brow at the surly tone. "I asked if you would object if I found a lady willing to instruct Emma. Doubtless 'twill not be easy to find such a lady, yet would I need your permission ere I make the effort."

But Warrick was not looking at him, and all he said was, "What?" again, though with less heat.

"Warrick, what the devil ails you, that you are so distracted?"

Rowena had reentered the hall with a tray laden with refreshment. **She** ailed him, that cursed wench. He could not look at her without being reminded of all she had done to him, and he could not recall that without feeling the heat stir in his loins. Fury and desire clashed and warred in him once again, and it was getting harder for fury to win the battle.

"Do you require aught else, my lord?"

She had set the tray on a table between the two chairs and now stood there with her hands folded and her eyes demurely lowered—to Warrick's feet. He had dressed her in servants' clothes, yet in no way had she ever appeared the serf. Even standing there waiting to serve him, she held herself with all the regal grace of a queen. 'Twas more than annoying, those ladylike airs, but the thought suddenly made him smile, for it occurred to him that he had someone right here who could instruct Emma in all she would need to know, and he did not have to ask her to do it, he need only order it done.

Just then, he ordered, "Go you and inform Mistress Blouet to prepare a chamber for my guest."

"I see I no longer need my last question answered," Sheldon said as soon as she left. "Is she the lady you had locked in your dungeon?"

Warrick was surprised. "How did you come to know about that?"

"I came to Fulkhurst a fortnight ago, expecting to meet your bride. Did no one tell you?"

"Nay, 'twas not mentioned. But how did you hear of Rowena?"

"Considering the large escort that brought her and installed her in your dungeon, 'twas all your people were talking about. Speculation was rife, as I recall, as to whether she was indeed a lady or not. Is she?"

"The question wouldst be better put, 'Was she?' She was. She is not now."

"How so?"

"Because she is my prisoner, without rights and without concessions. As I do not care to hang her, or flay the skin from her back, or otherwise maim her, I have instead punished her with the loss of her previous status. I have made her my serf."

"What did she do?"

"I do not care to speak of her crime. Suffice it to say, she is lucky I did not kill her."

Sheldon said naught for several moments, possibly because Warrick's tone had turned too defensive. "It must have been grievous indeed." But then he shrugged, not all that interested, since his own problem had yet to be solved. "About Emma?"

"Do you leave the matter to me. As it happens, my new serf is capable of teaching the girl, if she **can** be taught. Let us see if the iron can be wrought into silver ere we speak more of it."

❧ 27

No sooner had Rowena returned to the weaving room than Celia showed up there, sauntering in with a superior-than-thou expression and a tight little smile that warned Rowena she was not going to like hearing what the girl had to say. Indeed, she did not.

"Get you to the East tower, wench. A bath has been sent there for Sir Sheldon's use, and you are to assist him."

Celia's diction was much improved, Rowena noted, when she was not upset. Gloating and delighted were what she was just now, while Rowena felt as if the floor had fallen out beneath her feet.

"Did Mary send you with that order?"

"Nay, Warrick did." Celia smirked. "And best you hurry. Sir Sheldon has already been shown to the chamber. And mark you, wench, he is not merely a guest, but a good friend of your lord. Warrick would not like it were his friend not pleased with your service."

A couple of the women snickered at that. Rowena merely got up and left the room. She was angry at Warrick for this new humiliation he would force on her, but even more angry at herself for beginning to think seriously about the suggestions Mildred had made earlier. Any man who could send her to another man's bed—and she did not mistake Celia's taunting warning any more than the other women had—was not worth seducing, even if it might better her lot to try it.

She was surprised, too. When the girl Emma had summoned her, she had expected to receive what she had missed that morn, utter shame over her behavior yestereve in his bed. Yet when she had stood before him, Warrick still had not mentioned last eventide, though it had been there in his eyes as he stared at her, full memory of it. Instead he had as much as given her to another man with his blessing.

Verily, this could be seen as another punishment, yet she could not think what she had done to merit it. She had not even hesitated over calling him her lord. She had not delayed in coming when summoned. Had Warrick reached a point, then, where he did not need a reason to punish her, where good behavior would avail her naught? If so, why should she bother to do as bidden? **Because there are worse punishments than attending a stranger at his bath.**

Attending that stranger in his bed was out of the

question, however, no matter if it was Warrick's wish that she do so, no matter what was done to her for refusing. The stranger would have to rape her, and he was not likely to do that. A knight might take a field wench without a thought, but he would not abuse his host's servant in that way— not without his host's permission. But there was the rub. Had Warrick told this Sir Sheldon that he could have her?

Mixed in with the anger was hurt that aught not to be there, but dread took over both emotions the closer she got to the East tower chamber, until she was nigh sick with it. Yet there was a core of stubbornness in her that would not let her run and hide instead.

The door to the chamber was open. A young squire was just leaving the room with Sir Sheldon's heavy armor. Steam rose from the tub that had been set in the center of the room. Buckets of cold water had been left to temper the hot. And Sir Sheldon stood next to the tub, rubbing the back of his neck as if it pained him. It took him a moment to notice her standing just inside the door. When he did, his surprise became quickly evident.

"**You** are to assist me, lady?"

Lady? So he knew. Warrick had told him about her and **then** sent her here, making it all the worse for her. Damn that monster and his diabolical methods of revenge.

She lowered her head and gritted out, "I am ordered here by Lord Warrick."

"I would not have thought—" he began, but ended with a slight flush. "I am grateful."

That single word put a new light on what she had to do and took the shame out of it. Were she lady of this castle and married, she would not think twice about assisting an honored guest. Her mother had frequently done so, and did the guest require more than a bath, he would be sent a willing light-skirt of whom every castle had its share. Granted, virginal ladies were not expected to assist at a bath, but Rowena was not exactly virginal any longer. 'Twould be best to treat this as any other chore and see first if Sir Sheldon made any untoward advances before she condemned him.

With that settled in her mind, Rowena moved forward to help the man out of his tunic, which was already half unlaced. She was still slightly nervous, so thought to make small conversation to distract herself.

"Did you travel far, Sir Sheldon?"

"Nay, not overly."

"I was told you are a good friend to Lord Warrick. You have known him long, then, have you?"

"Aye, he was my squire."

"Yours?"

He grinned down at her. "Why does that surprise you? Thought you he came to knighthood without the training?"

She grinned back at his gentle teasing. She had barely noticed this man in the hall, her attention so set on Warrick, but on closer inspection, Sheldon was not nearly as old as he had seemed at first glance. Verily, he seemed not much older than Warrick.

"So you knew him ere he turned so—" To call the man's friend what she would like to would not be very wise, so she settled for "Hard?" But that word made Sheldon burst into laughter.

"You do not know him very well, damosel, if all you can call him is hard. Most women call him terrifying."

Rowena flushed. "I do not claim to know him at all, yet does he not frighten me—much."

He laughed again, a deep, rich sound. She yanked hard on his chausses to show him she did not appreciate it.

"What do you here, wench?"

Rowena gasped at the sound of **that** voice and looked toward the doorway whence it had come. Warrick filled the opening that she had not thought to close and put the lie to her last words, for he looked terrifying indeed in his present anger, of which she could not begin to guess the cause.

"You ordered me here, my lord," she dared to remind him, but that just made him look angrier.

"Nay, I did not, nor would I have. Your duties are exact, wench. Do they increase or decrease, I will tell you so myself. Now get you to my solar and await me there."

She was hot-cheeked with indignation, but she did not care to argue with him in front of his friend. She left without another word to either man, but had gone not even halfway down the stairs before Warrick caught up with her, roughly yanking her about and shoving her up against the stone wall. The arrow slit that gave light to the stairwell was blocked by his wide back, so she could not see clearly just how angry he still was. His voice told her, however.

"Explain to me why I should not punish you for being where you do not belong!"

"I thought 'twas a punishment, my being sent to him. Now you tell me I am to be punished for doing as I was bidden? If you dare—"

He shook her once. "You were **not** bidden to come here. If you speak that lie again, so help me, I will not order you beaten, I will do it myself!"

Rowena swallowed the retort she would have made. The man was simply too angry, and beginning to seriously frighten her with it.

She made her tone soft and placating. "I know not what to tell you but the truth. I was told I was to assist Sir Sheldon at his bath, and that 'twas by your order."

"**Who** told you?"

"Celia."

"She would not dare."

"Mistress Blouet can tell you how much Celia dares, if you do but ask her. And the other weavers all heard her send me here, not just to assist your friend, but to please him in whatever way he required." She winced as his hands bit more into her arms. "Do not take my word for it, my lord. The other women will vouch for what I say—" She paused, her stomach turning with dread as a thought occurred to her. "Unless Celia has bidden them to lie. Mistress Blouet says they do all follow her lead and—"

"Did he touch you?"

Rowena blinked at the new subject, which could not help but prod her bitterness and release it. "Nay, but what matters if he did? A servant has little say in these things. You told me so yourself."

"You have no say in what **I** do to you, wench, but no one else is to touch you."

As if to prove it, his hand went to her thick braid to hold her head still and his mouth closed over hers. 'Twas an angry kiss, punishing and claiming at once. She did not like it. She liked even less that her loins heated, preparing her for his further invasion.

But he did not intend to take her there in the stairwell. He ended the kiss, but she was still pressed to him. And his hand tightened in her hair as he demanded, "Would you have **pleased** him did he ask?"

She did not even think to goad him with a lie. "Nay, I would have refused, and did that not work, I would have fought him." She felt the tension leave his body, and the hand in her hair loosened its grip. **Then** she goaded him. "But little good it would have done me without weapon to hand, which I am not allowed."

"Nor will you be allowed one," he growled, angry again.

She did not heed his anger this time because she felt too much of the same emotion herself. "Then what is to stop any man from raping me, when you dress me as a serf and when female serfs are considered fair game? Even your men-at-arms would not hesitate—" She stopped when she saw his grin.

"My interest in you has been noted and understood. No man here would dare to touch you. Nay, wench, you still will find yourself bedded only by me—but then, you are coming not to mind that overmuch. You protest, but not for long."

She knocked away his hand, which had moved to caress her cheek. "I hate it, as much as I hate you!"

But **that** only made him laugh, infuriating her so that she pushed away from him and ran the rest of the way down the stairs. He let her go, but the thought that he **could** have stopped her if he wanted only increased her fury.

All the power was his. He had control over her body, control over her emotions, control over everything she did. She could not even get angry without his leave, for he knew well enough how to frighten the anger out of her.

'Twas intolerable, such utter domination, and she could bear it no more. She had accepted it as her due for what had been done to him, but she had been punished more than enough for that, and still had the worse punishment before her, the taking of her child. Well, she was done with meekly accepting her lot. If Mildred's suggestions could shift some of the power, to give her even a little sway over that insufferable man, then she would try them.

❧ 28

Warrick had not noticed before how many of his men watched Rowena just as he did, but the moment she entered the hall, many eyes besides his were on her. He did not like that at all. In fact, he so disliked it that he did the unthinkable and called for complete attention to himself for no reason other than to show his displeasure.

His men knew him well. They did not mistake what had displeased him. But ironically, he was even more annoyed that they **did** understand and did not look toward the girl again. His action smacked of jealousy, which was absurd. God's blood, she was no more than his prisoner. Yet . . . yet what he had felt just now was no different from what he had felt earlier when he had found her with Sheldon—nay, that had been more powerful. Utter rage had consumed him to see her kneeling at his friend's feet, in the process of disrobing him.

"You did not like the shape of your tankard?"

Sheldon asked as he took the seat next to Warrick at the lord's table.

"How so?"

But Warrick looked at the vessel in his hand and saw that the soft metal had collapsed under his grip. He threw it away angrily and called for another, which a page quickly supplied, along with the ale to fill it. **She** should have been there already to do it. What the devil was keeping her in the kitchen? But then she appeared with a large platter of meats, and he schooled his features to conceal his rioting emotions.

"You must do better than that if you do not want her to know how she affects you," his friend warned, trying unsuccessfully to hide his amusement. "You are wound so tight—"

"Go to hell, Sheldon."

The older man laughed, but said no more, leaning to his left to speak with Beatrix, with whom he was to share a trencher. Warrick did try to relax, only it was impossible. The closer Rowena came to the table, the more he tensed, as if expecting a blow. And it did seem as if he received one when he saw her smile at him.

"What will you have, my lord?" she asked pleasantly as she set the platter down in front of him. "A sampling of each?"

He did not even look down at the meats she was offering. "Have I made things too easy for you, wench?"

"Nay, my lord."

"Then why do you smile at me?"

The smile vanished instantly. "I forget myself. What is it you require? A frown? Indifference? Mayhap fear? You need only say—"

"Be quiet!" he grumbled and waved her off.

Rowena could feel his eyes boring into her back as she hurried from the hall, and it was all she could do not to laugh before she was out of his sight. Lord Vengeance was going to be easier to confound than even Mildred had thought. With no more than a smile, she had soured his mood and received no punishment for it. She wondered if she could force herself to touch him next, without being bidden to. 'Twas not something she wanted to do, but she had made the decision and so could not cavil over the means.

"So ye heard, did ye?"

Rowena started and looked around until she spotted Mary Blouet. She knew not what Mary referred to, but 'twas unwise for her to look so pleased with herself where others could note it.

"Heard what?"

"That the high-and-haughty Celia got sent away to Dyrwood keep. I know not how ye did it, wench, but ye be having my thanks for it."

Rowena could not speak for a moment, she was so incredulous. "He actually sent her away?"

"Aye, and good riddance, I say. But why do ye look so surprised?"

"But I did naught that would—I mean, I only told him she gave me an order in his name. I did not know she lied, and he was angry, but I . . . he actually sent her away?"

Mary chuckled. "Did I not say so? And what ye did be more than anyone else wouldst dare. I should have warned him myself of the advantages she took of her position, but a man is funny about such things. Like as not the bearer of tales gets the brunt of his displeasure."

Rowena tamped down the pleasure she was starting to feel, reminding herself that what Celia had done was outrageous and deserving of some kind of discipline. Warrick certainly had not done it for her sake. He had merely been made aware that Celia had overstepped herself, and he had acted swiftly to punish her for it. After all, the man thrived on meting out punishments. Why should his favorite leman be excluded from them?

Rowena hurried back to the hall with another platter of food, her plan to baffle and subtly seduce her tormentor forgotten for the moment. She noted, however, that his mood had taken a turn for the worse. There was that risk, of course, that instead of merely confusing the man and making him wonder about her, he would get angry instead. The frown that followed her to the table now said he was definitely angry about something.

She hesitated to get near him when he looked

so forbidding, but there was no help for it. Her duty was to serve him his food, not merely set it before him.

"Does aught tempt you here, my lord?"

Rowena did not realize the implication of that innocent question until she saw the fire leap into Warrick's eyes. She flushed. She had not meant to be deliberately provocative, yet so she had sounded. And to her amazement, his frown turned into a grin, not of that cruel humor she abhorred, but of genuine male amusement.

"Come you here, wench, and we shall see what if aught will tempt me."

Sir Sheldon guffawed beside him, as did a few other knights within hearing. Rowena's flush turned to hot flames. But she did not hesitate this time. She hurried around the table and came up to stand beside his chair—and found herself pulled onto his lap.

'Twas the perfect opportunity to further her seduction of him—if she could forget that they were the center of attention. But she could not forget that there were other nobles present, including ladies, including Warrick's young daughters, and all she wanted to do was crawl into a hole and hide for the next decade. Verily, if she were given even a little of the respect her true status was due, Warrick would never have treated her so before his entire assemblage. But she was classed as a lowly serf, beneath the notice of ladies, defenseless against lustful innuendos as well as lustful assaults—at least by the Lord of Fulkhurst.

"What think you, wench, will tempt my palate?" he continued to tease her. "Do you select it and we shall see."

A reprieve? She could fill his trencher and be gone?

She wasted no time in leaning forward to reach the nearest platter—and felt Warrick's hand come to her leg, then press between her thighs. She sat back so fast, her head cracked his chin. They both winced, but then he chuckled.

"Think you none of the viands will tempt me, then?"

Rowena groaned inwardly. There was no way she could win this game he had instigated, but she did not think he would simply let her leave his lap did she try. If she could bear his touch for a few moments, he might grow tired of the game and recall that he was sitting here to eat, not to amuse himself with his newest plaything.

She leaned forward to try and fill his trencher again. But his other hand groped beneath her skirts until he found a bare thigh, and she felt a wave of heat that had naught to do with embarrassment. Suddenly she was horrified that he might be able to bring her to the state he had last eventide, right there with hundreds of eyes avidly watching.

Pride be damned, she curled toward him and whispered at his neck, "Please."

"Truly do I like that word on your lips," he replied, a wealth of satisfaction in his tone.

'Twas a blatant reminder, at long last, of the begging that had so shamed her, but at the moment she was not embarrassed by it. She was too embarrassed by what he was doing now.

But he had more to say. "Mayhap now you will tell me what caused you to smile before?"

Rowena's eyes flared wide. Was all this because she had perplexed him with that damn smile? Did he have to get even for being confounded by her? The thought infuriated her, and anger made her forget her embarrassment, forget even that other ears than his would hear her answer.

Answer him she did, with another smile, waiting only until he took a swallow of his ale. "I was merely thinking of your display of jealousy this noontide, my lord."

He choked, his response coming out as a wheezing rasp. "Jealousy!"

She leaned back so he could see that she gave his reply thoughtful consideration. "Mayhap possessiveness would more aptly describe it. I understand now that you feel I am only yours to use and abuse, that no other should have that privilege."

Warrick scowled at Sheldon, whose shoulders were shaking in mirth, evidently because he had heard those words. Then Warrick turned his scowl on Rowena, and she had no more than a moment to wish she had not chosen so public a place to get a little even with him.

"I make certain that you are kept available to see to my own whims, and you see this as possessiveness?" he growled low. " 'Twould not bother me to throw you to my men and watch as they have you—as long as I am not in the mood to have you myself. Need I prove this to you?"

'Twas one of those threats that, by merely saying it, he would be forced to carry out did she not make immediate amends. Her anger increased, but that did not stop her from throwing her arms around his neck and squeezing tight.

"Do not, I beseech you," she said by his ear, then softer, her lips touching his earlobe, "I want only to share **your** bed, know only **your** touch."

She felt a shiver run through him just before he pushed her off his lap. She noticed his flush as she straightened; then her eyes collided with his and she felt seared by their molten heat.

"Get you below and have your meal, then come to my chamber."

"You want a bath, my lord?"

"I want to find you in my bed, wench, where we will ascertain if you bespoke the truth."

❧ 29

Rowena was never going to live it down. She was certain the whispers about that awful scene in the hall would follow her until the end of her days, across shires, across countries, wherever she went—if she ever left Fulkhurst. But what did Lord Vengeance care? No one would be whispering about him. 'Twas naught for a nobleman to make sport with one of his serfs in his own hall. Who would gainsay him, after all?

She abhorred the thought of returning to face her most recent shame. 'Twas deplorable that there was no way to reach Warrick's solar from the kitchen, without passing through the full length of the hall. But when Rowena returned after her long-drawn-out meal, there were no whispers about her that she could tell. In truth, the men did not look her way at all, and those women who did happen to notice her glanced quickly away.

Had she been wallowing in mortification for

naught, then? she wondered in confusion. Or had no one noticed her sitting on Warrick's lap except those at his table? But she was ignored from that direction also, except by Warrick. He watched her now, but in a distracted manner, since he was deep in discussion with his friend, Sheldon.

She was perplexed, and liked it not. **He** was the one who was supposed to be confounded, not she. But there was an easy enough way to find out if something unusual had happened in the short time she had been belowstairs, something that made the women, even those lazy weavers who had disdained her instruction that afternoon, seem almost fearful now when they saw her.

She saw the young girl, Emma, who had come to fetch her when Sir Sheldon had arrived, and stopped by her table. Only vaguely did she note that the girl sat alone.

"Emma, may I presume upon your good nature to ask what has occurred here that I missed when I went below?"

"Naught has happened since the fine entertainment you gave us."

"I see," Rowena replied stiffly and turned to leave, disappointed, since the girl had seemed friendly earlier.

But Emma caught her hand to quickly assure her, "Nay, lady, I meant no insult. 'Tis just strange to see the dreadful dragon behave like a normal man."

Dreadful dragon? How aptly put, but Rowena was more concerned with what she had just been called herself, as she realized how much worse it would be to be treated like a serf by Warrick if others knew she was not.

"Why do you call me lady?"

Emma shrugged. "You cannot hide what you are in serf's wool. Your manner speaks more clearly than words, lady, though your words speak just as clearly of noble breeding."

"You speak just as clearly," Rowena pointed out, relieved that Emma was only guessing.

Emma grinned. "I do but mimic—though better than Celia, I warrant."

Rowena could not help laughing. "Aye, much better than she. But tell me, if naught occurred, why do the women seem, well, almost fearful?"

"When they look at you?" At Rowena's nod, Emma's grin got wider. "They have heard what happened to Celia and think it was at your behest."

"But I never—"

"I did not think so, but they do. They are also in awe of you that you do not fear the dragon even in his darkest moods."

"Certainly I fear him. He holds my life in his hands."

"Nay, he is no killer of women. But even Celia hid from him when he was angry, and everyone here could see how angry he was—and then you made him laugh. 'Tis a rare thing, to hear him laugh."

For some unaccountable reason, Rowena felt a sadness upon hearing that, but she quickly shook it off. 'Twas naught to her if the man had little enjoyment out of life. She had had little enough herself these past years.

Though she would rather have stayed and talked, feeling she might have a friend in Emma, she left the girl, too conscious of Warrick's order to appear in his chamber—nay, in his bed. And now that her embarrassment had worn off, she had that order to deal with and the nervousness it was already generating in her.

Verily, she had him set up ripely for her seduction, or rather, he had set himself up for it with his ribald teasing earlier at the table. She need not even be subtle about it now. The only thing that could thwart her plan was if he thought she was motivated by fear, rather than by actual desire for him. She would have to appear in no way fearful. But the thought of seducing him and the actual act of seducing him were in no wise the same, and her nervousness was so close to fear, it was indistinguishable to her.

And what if 'twas all for naught, if her overtures made no difference in his treatment of her? Mildred was certain it would be otherwise, but

Rowena was less so. And yet . . . he had been stirred to lust by a mere few words, and it had drastically changed his mood—not his treatment of her, but definitely his humor. She would just have to wait and see what further advances on her part would do.

Rowena entered the inner solar and had no more than glanced at the bed, which she had no intention of waiting in for Warrick, when he closed the door behind her. She swung around with a start. He had to have followed her as soon as she passed his table, yet he had still seemed deep in conversation. And then she noted the heat still in his eyes and she understood.

The man wanted her right now, wanted her badly. He had not been willing to wait any longer. The thought gave her a heady sense of power. 'Twould make what she would do and say so much easier. But it also, to her chagrin, stirred her own senses to arousal.

He stood there in front of the door, staring at her while he slowly unclasped his mantle. He was wearing a rich brown tunic embroidered at hem and neck in gold. The color suited his dark gold hair, grown long since his confinement at Kirkburough, to where it now reached his wide shoulders. He was not frowning, so the handsomeness of his features was there to see and disturb her senses.

Rowena found it difficult to look at him when he

was like this, normal, not the cruel monster she knew he could be. Since shyness was appropriate on her part after what she had said to him in the hall, she took refuge in it and lowered her eyes.

"Come here, Rowena."

She did not hesitate to approach him, but she would not meet his eyes again. Those expressive eyes did things to her that she could not control.

"So you want to share my bed?"

"Aye."

"Why?"

God's mercy, could he not take her at her word? Why? She had not thought there would be an interrogation, and could not think now with him so close.

"Why does any woman want to share a man's bed?" she countered lamely.

"Because mine is softer than yours."

Her eyes shot up to clash with his. The bastard. He doubted her, was going to make her work to convince him. She had not wanted to seduce him in the first place. She would be damned if she would grovel to do it.

"That is true," she said stiffly. "Yet I do not get much sleep in yours. Mayhap mine is preferable after all."

She turned away angrily, but he caught her arm and yanked her hard against his chest. And then his mouth was showing her what she had made him feel, passion blistering hot, consuming. She clung to him as her limbs got weaker, clung to him because she could do naught else. And he was relentless in his assault, determined to make her feel what he felt, and God's mercy, she did.

She nearly crumbled to the floor when he released her. He did not notice. He had moved away from her, his body taut with agitation. He sat down on his bed, running both hands so hard through his hair that Rowena winced in empathy for his scalp. But when his eyes lit on her again, she groaned inwardly. He wore his cruelest look now, the one she dreaded.

"Do you still maintain you want me, wench?"

If she said aye, he was going to make her suffer for it, she knew it, read it in his eyes. But if she said nay, he was likely to try and prove her a liar, and just now, with the taste of him still on her lips, she was not sure if a nay would be the truth. Either way she was going to lose—or win. But winning was going to cost her more of her pride, for 'twas a two-edged sword, her plan. She knew now that she was going to bleed a little from her part in it.

He waited patiently, giving her ample time to take the coward's path. She stiffened her resolve. She would see it through, whatever the cost.

"I still want you, my lord."

He did not answer for a moment. 'Twas almost as if he could not. And then his voice came out in a husky rasp. "I require proof. Show me."

She had expected no less. She walked toward him slowly, unlacing her bliaut on the way. This she pulled over her head as she stopped within reach of him. The chemise she unlaced more slowly. In truth, she was mesmerized watching him watch her undress, for everything he felt was there for her to see, and that sense of power was back, giving her a boldness she would not have otherwise dared.

She let the chemise drop to the floor, leaving only her shift, stockings, and shoes. To untie a shoe, she did not bend over, but put her foot up on the bed next to Warrick's thigh. 'Twas wantonly brazen, deliberately so, and it was his undoing. He groaned. His arm reached out to wrap around her bottom and pull her forward. She landed hard against him, her knees sliding on either side of his hips, her back bent awkwardly as he pressed his face into the soft mounds of her breasts.

'Twas an arousing embrace. It also struck a tender cord in her, for he did naught else, just held her like that for a time. She wrapped her own arms around his head, not sure anymore if she was playing a part or acting of her own accord, for it felt right to hold him like that.

And then he tilted his head back and told her "Kiss me."

She did, placing her hands on his cheeks, a kiss void of passion, sweetly innocent—for all of the three seconds it took him to participate. His lips nudged hers open, his tongue licking the insides before thrusting deep into her mouth. For the first time she thrust back tentatively with her tongue and felt the thrill of aggression, then was overwhelmed by the passion her small response unleashed in him.

He dropped back on the bed, taking her with him, his mouth devouring hers now. But he quickly rolled over, pressing the hard bulge of his manroot between her legs, and her pulses leaped, her insides rolled, her heart slammed out of beat. Her fingers had worked their way into his hair and were gripping great handfuls. She needed that anchor, for her rioting senses were leaving her control.

She groaned when he left her, but it was only to straddle her thighs, and that to whisk the shift from her body, naked now before him. His eyes burned her, then his hands, bringing gasp after gasp as they slid slowly up her belly to cup her breasts. One he held captured for his mouth as he bent over to roll the tender bud on his tongue before he tried to draw the whole plump mound into his mouth.

She lost her breath with the next gasp, was unaware that she arched toward him, that she held his head in a viselike grip, unconsciously demanding more.

She actually cried out in protest when he stopped

to lean back again. But he displayed no triumphant smile upon hearing it. His need was too great, leaving no room for petty revenge just now.

His breath came hard. His eyes would not leave her as he attempted to shed his clothing. The rich tunic was ripped in its removal. Rowena sat up to help, but her fingers trembled so, she only succeeded in knotting the laces on his chausses, and those were ripped, too, when he took over the task. And then his manroot was there between them, inflamed, velvet steel, and it seemed the most natural thing in the world for her to wrap her hand around it.

He sucked in his breath before he groaned, "Nay," and took her hand in his and held it to the bed. She whimpered at the restraint, but his mouth came down to take the sound, then his body came down to spread her thighs, and she cared about naught except the heat about to enter her. Her free hand she brought to his lower back, as far as she could reach, to urge him on. But he was holding himself back, and that hand found itself imprisoned also as he fought for control—only she could not wait any longer.

"Now—please, Warrick, now!" she begged, this time without his command, and this time with immediate compliance.

He plunged. She melted around him. He thrust hard and fast. She screamed in her climax, reached before him, continuing after him, so intense she nearly fainted.

She was floating in languid contentment when she heard him say a while later, "I wonder if I will ever have you at my leisure, wench, or will you always provoke me to such madness?"

Rowena merely smiled.

❦ 30

Warrick was still there when Rowena awoke the next morn, still lying beside her in his big bed, but not still asleep. She had the feeling he had been watching her for some time without her knowing it, and the thought disturbed her, for he looked too serious by half this morn.

"You should have awakened me, my lord, and sent me about my duties."

"Should I? Why, when one of your duties now, by your own behest, is right where you are?"

The blush spread across her cheeks with exceptional speed. "Does that mean I am to ignore my other duties?"

"Ah," he said, as if in sudden understanding. "Now do we have a motive for why you sought my bed."

"I did not—the labors that presently fill my day do not overtax me—as yet."

"As yet?" He frowned, until his gaze dropped to

her belly, and then those silver eyes were like shards of ice. And yet his voice continued mild, deceptively so. "I see. Once again you prove yourself incredibly stupid to remind me of the child you stole from me. But then, this is just another motive that can be attributed to your sudden passion for me, is it not? Or do you tell me now that you had no thought to bargain with me for the babe?"

"I want it. I cannot deny that."

"Enough to spread your legs for me whenever I say?"

How could she have forgotten his cruelty, or how much she hated it, when that was what she was trying to end? Obviously, what passed between them during the night had changed him not a whit, which was a crushing realization—but she was forgetting that he did not believe she really wanted him, and that was why he was taunting her now. And she could think of no further way to convince him, be it lie or not.

It made her angry, suddenly, to have failed so completely. Why could the man not simply accept what she offered? Why did he have to search for hidden motives?

And his damn question—well, she was just angry enough to spread her legs wide beneath the cover, just wide enough for him to notice, and taunt him back. "Come, then, Sir Dragon, and breathe your fire on me."

His frown turned black as sin. "I want a reason, wench, and I want it now."

She began heatedly, glaring right back at him. "You are cruel in all your demands, vengeful in all your motives, yet when you touch me, you are naught but gentle." She was amazed that the words were coming to her after all, and so she quickly amended her tone, adding uncertainty to it, and a blush for good measure. "I did not want to admit it to myself, certainly not to you, but I find I—I crave your touch."

God's mercy, but she was getting good at lying. And his expression changed. She could tell that he **wanted** to believe her, and that—that put a tightness in her throat that was distinctly unpleasant.

"Were you so hot for my body, you would not wait this long to tempt it into pleasuring you again. Must I needs teach you the ploys of a whore?"

The insult did not touch her this time, for she recognized it for what it was, an attempt to fight the temptation to believe her. Did he think no woman could want him without an ulterior motive? She recalled Emma's words that the women were awed that she did not fear him. And Mildred had said that for half his life he had been the hard, vengeful man he was today. Was that all he expected then, fear? And what woman could truly want him if she feared him?

She spared a moment to wonder why she did

not fear him anymore, before she put her hand to the center of his chest to push him down from his half-leaning position. "Mayhap you will have to teach me, my Lord Warrick," she said softly, now leaning over him. "I have some little advice to go by, yet I am sure I could benefit from more."

Her hand slipped under the cover and she found to her amazement that he had not been immune to their close proximity. Neither had she. Nor was she immune to touching him. It should have been difficult. She should have had to force herself. But it was easy, too easy—she liked doing it. So did he. His eyes closed. His breathing quickened. And 'twas not long before she was flat on her back again, with his mouth fastened on hers, and his hands paying her back in kind for the sweet torment she had just brought him.

But before he got around to giving Rowena what she now desperately wanted, Bernard walked into the chamber unannounced, as was his habit. The poor boy went up in flames of embarrassment when he saw that Warrick would not appreciate being disturbed, and to give him credit, he did try to leave without disturbing the occupied occupants of the bed. But Warrick was too much a man of war and quick responses not to have heard the intrusion.

He lifted his head to snarl, "What?"

And Bernard could only stammer, "Father . . . here . . . with bride."

Rowena heard the message in confusion. Since Warrick's father was supposedly dead, the squire might mean his own father, or one of Warrick's two fathers-in-law. But that word "bride" half succeeded in blunting her aroused senses.

Warrick, however, suffered no bewilderment over the cryptic message. "Are they only approaching Fulkhurst, or have they already arrived?"

The calmness of that question gave the boy back his own composure. "They are within the hall, my lord, and are desirous of your presence. Do I tell them—?"

"Tell them naught. I will be there in a moment to make them welcome."

Rowena gathered from that answer that Warrick was not going to finish what they had started, and her body was screaming in protest. Her face, however, was utterly void of expression when he turned his attention back to her. His was not. He looked frustrated, chagrined, and after he studied her for a moment, resigned.

"Lord Reinard's timing leaves much to be desired." He sighed and rolled away from her.

She found she wanted to grab him back to her. That word "bride" was now giving her a distinct chill. But she did naught to let him know how disturbed she suddenly was.

'Twas safe, however, for her to ask, "Is Lord Reinard one of your fathers-by-marriage?"

"Soon-to-be."

There it was, her worst fear confirmed. Gone now was her opportunity to gentle this man. With his betrothed arrived, he would no longer dally with Rowena. And soon a wife would share this bed with him. What, then, would he do with his prisoner? Put her back in his dungeon? Make her serve both him and his new bride?

"So your betrothed is found," she said tonelessly as she watched him rummage through a chest for clothes, something splendid, no doubt, for his precious Lady Isabella. "At least that is one crime no longer set at my door."

He gave her a sharp look. "Do not count yourself free of blame yet, wench, until I learn what, exactly, has kept her missing these many weeks."

She said naught to that. She did not care what the lady's excuse was; she only knew that she wished Isabella had not been found. And that was a disturbing realization, for she should not care either way.

Warrick was ignoring her again, his mind on his waiting guests. Rowena could not ignore him as easily, though her mind was likewise on his guests. But even as her worry increased about how this new situation would affect her, her eyes were fastened to Warrick's splendid nakedness, the long bare flanks so thickly muscled, the tight curve of his buttocks, the muscles bunching and rippling on his broad back with his movements. Strength and power in every hard line, and . . . beauty, aye, there was beauty in such stark masculinity. In no wise could she deny it, nor the need still coursing through her to feel that splendid body pressed tightly to hers.

He turned slightly before he bent to put on his braies, and she saw that the same need was still prevalent in him also, though he was ignoring it just as he was ignoring her—at least that was what she thought until her eyes drifted up again to find that he had caught her in her blatant scrutiny of him.

He came back to the bed then and, without a word, caught her behind the neck and drew her toward him until his mouth was grinding hard against hers. Her heart thudded with relief, but before she could get her arms even halfway around him to urge him back into the bed, he released her. His visage was a terrible mixture of desire and anger just then, anger, no doubt, because she was tempting him to ignore his precious Isabella. Obviously the temptation was not quite enough.

In that she was not entirely correct.

"Stay exactly as you are, wench," he ordered harshly. "I will return ere the fire dies from those sapphire eyes, and we will see if you can fulfill the promise in them."

He did not see the blush creep up her cheeks as he turned away to finish dressing with haste. She was **not** supposed to be as easy to read as he was, but obviously this once she had hidden naught from him. It made her feel more vulnerable than she had at any other time with this man. It was one thing for her to admit to herself that she could want him, **did** want him, at least right then. It was something else again to let him see it for himself without her lies to convince him of it. Lies? Mayhap earlier when she had been in control of herself, some of her actions and words had been lies, but they were not lies now.

He left the room without looking toward her again. Vaguely she noted that he had yanked on a bare minimum of clothing, none designed to impress a long-awaited bride. In fact, she thought smugly, he looked quite sloppy and harried, and with his emotions still on the angry side, the cruel lines of his face were well in place. He would be lucky if his lady bride did not take one look at him and burst into tears.

The thought made Rowena smile, but only for a moment. Then her anxieties returned with a vengeance. No matter how Isabella reacted to Warrick, she was still here to wed him. A bride's fear was the last thing that could stop a wedding from taking place, so it **would** happen, and that meant Rowena's situation **would** change, and no matter how she looked at it, she did not see her own lot improving with the change.

She might still inflame Warrick's lust, but he would now have a wife to slake it on, leaving only his subtle cruelties and little revenges for Rowena. Without the intimate contact that his lust had brought so far, she would have no hope of altering his treatment of her. Verily, it would only get worse.

She had been ordered to stay in his bed, but she could not. She got up, dressed quickly, then paced the floor in her agitation, awaiting his return. But he did not come back as soon as his parting words had predicted. And whatever desires he had stirred to life in her were long since cooled.

She finally curled up on the hard bench of the window embrasure to do her fretting. 'Twas not long before she drew the definite conclusion that it would behoove her to reevaluate the possibility of escape—mayhap during the excitement of the wedding.

Warrick returned suddenly without warning, only he was not alone. The woman who followed on his heels was tall and richly gowned—and pale as new parchment. She was hauntingly lovely in her paleness, with her raven hair and dark green eyes. She was also terribly nervous about something, though there was a resigned, determined look to her.

Rowena noted this with wide eyes. She could not understand why Warrick had brought the lady here, when if Rowena had followed his orders she would still be lying naked in his bed. He could not have forgotten that, could he? Nay, he looked toward the bed first, and when he found it empty, his eyes searched until he located Rowena tucked deep in the embrasure.

She saw immediately that he wanted something of her. She sensed it the same way as before, when he had been chained in front of her and she had felt she could read his thoughts. But she could not grasp what it was that he wanted this time, until she heard what Isabella began saying.

The woman was afraid, aye, and with reason. What she was confessing to Warrick's hard back was why she did not love him. And now Rowena knew exactly what he wanted of her. He wanted to show Isabella that what she was telling him mattered not at all to him, but just to say so would not suffice. Rowena was not sure if 'twas only his pride he wanted to protect, or if he also wanted to relieve the lady's anxieties. Either way, he obviously had hoped he would find Rowena where he had left her, a position that would have spoken more clearly than words.

She was not sure why she wanted to aid him or even how she could, but she stood up to reveal herself to the other woman. That, unfortunately, was not enough. Isabella was too deeply into her explanation to care that a servant was present. She was trying earnestly to make Warrick listen to her, while he would not even turn around to face her, but continued to watch Rowena instead.

Rowena approached them both, but she stopped before Warrick, telling him without words that he could make use of her presence however he chose. What he chose to do was face Isabella now with Rowena behind his back, but he put his hand behind him until she took it, then drew her closer until she actually leaned against his back. What this tableau would appear like to Isabella, if she deigned to notice, was Rowena shyly hiding behind Warrick, with him trying to reassure her without actually drawing attention to her.

Mayhap it was a bit too subtle for Isabella, for she had not even paused in her lengthy explanation of how she and someone named Miles Fergant had loved each other since childhood. Rowena could have been invisible for all the notice she was getting. Better to have just brazenly returned to Warrick's bed, mayhap even stripped off her clothes again. She smiled to herself at the absurd thought, then almost laughed aloud when it occurred to her that Isabella still might not have noticed that—but Warrick certainly would have.

The moment of whimsy put her in a mischievous state of mind that she had not experienced in a goodly number of years. She considered wrapping her arms around Warrick's waist from behind. Nay, too bold. She slipped her hand out of his instead, saw his back tense, but he relaxed when he felt her hands settle on his sides, just above his hips. Her fingers were not actually noticeable, but she was no longer even thinking about giving Isabella something to see. 'Twas Warrick she felt like teasing now, and tease him she did, running her hands slowly up his sides, feeling him stiffen, then try to stop her movement by pressing his arms tight to his sides. She merely worked her fingers loose and moved them down to his hips.

She almost burst out laughing when she heard him suck in his breath. But when she brought one hand back to pat his buttock, he startled her by swinging around and pinning her with a look that for once she could not read. She gave him an owl-eyed look of innocence in return, which brought the tiniest curve to his lips before he recalled himself and glared a warning at her. She was supposed to be aiding him in dealing with Isabella's confession, not distracting him from listening to it.

And then they both noticed the sudden silence behind them, just before Isabella asked impatiently, "Warrick, who is that woman?"

He turned back around. Rowena stuck just her head around his wide shoulder.

"She is my prisoner," was all Warrick offered in answer.

"Lady Rowena of Kirkburough," Rowena added

at about the same instant, well aware that he would not have, and aware too that he would not like it that she did.

She was right. The rejoinder he came back with made her flinch.

"Lady **before** she became my prisoner. Now she is the wench who will bear my next bastard."

Rowena sank her teeth into the back of his arm—hard—to thank him for that unnecessary disclosure. He moved not a muscle to acknowledge he had even felt it.

"I see," Isabella said coolly.

"Do you finally? Good. Mayhap now you will explain why you found it necessary to follow me in here with this tale of childhood lovers when I expressly told you in the hall that I was not interested in hearing it. Think you that your love is a requisite of our marriage?"

The brutal coldness in his tone made Isabella pale even more. Rowena, behind him again, winced and felt a moment's pity for the other woman.

"I—I had hoped to make you understand," Isabella said miserably.

"Indeed do I understand. You love me not. I care not. Love does not happen to be what I require of you."

"Nay, Warrick, you do not understand at all. I cannot wed you now. I—I am already wed to Miles."

A long silence followed. Rowena was shocked. She could not begin to imagine what Warrick must feel.

His voice, however, was amazingly mild when he finally asked, "Then what do you here, with your father, who seems to think he brought you here for a wedding?"

Rowena stepped to Warrick's side, too curious now to miss a word of this. The lady was wringing her hands, but Rowena was surprised to see that Warrick did not seem to be as disturbed by this news as he should be.

"When my father found me in London, Miles was sent to York on the king's business, so not with me. I—I could not tell Father the truth. He had forbade me to see Miles again after he had refused his suit. He wanted you for a son-by-marriage. No one else would do."

"Lady, I cared not for your father's approval to wed you. 'Twas your consent I asked for, and you gave it."

"I was forced to give it. For the same reason, I could not tell my father I had wed with the king's blessing. Miles is Stephen's man. I have given up much to have him, but he is all I want. But my father, he would kill me if he knew what I had done."

"Think you that you have less to fear of me?"

Rowena was sure the woman was going to faint, so horrified did she become at that question. Rowena could have kicked Warrick herself for deliberately frightening Isabella. And she did not doubt 'twas deliberate. She knew him well enough now, and was too familiar herself with his ways of quick retaliation. Isabella, obviously, was not.

Seeing someone else being the recipient of Warrick's enmity was strange. Even stranger was her desire to defuse his anger for his own sake.

"You will like his dungeon, Lady Isabella," she said into the tense silence. " 'Tis really quite comfortable."

Warrick looked at her as if she had gone mad. But Isabella just stared at her blankly, not understanding what Rowena was implying.

"Well, you **are** going to toss her in your dungeon, are you not, my lord?" she continued. "Is that not where you put all females while you wait to see if they are—"

"Rowena," he began warningly.

She gave him a sweet smile. "Aye, my lord?"

Whatever he would have said would not come out while she was smiling at him like that. He made a sound of exasperation instead, but when he glanced at Isabella again, his expression was not as dark.

"So you hied yourself to London to wed your sweetheart?" he said to Isabella. "Tell me, my lady, was this your plan when you journeyed to me, or did it precipitate when I was delayed in meeting you?"

Rowena held her breath, praying the woman's

answer was not going to add another mark to her own list of transgressions. She was not that lucky.

"Miles had joined my escort that noontide. I had not seen him for months. I had been without hope. But when you were not there with your men, it did seem fortuitous—I mean—Miles and I, we saw it as our only—"

Isabella finally stopped, flushing furiously, but added after a moment, "I am sorry, Warrick, truly. I did not mean to deceive you, but my father was so desirous of a marriage to you."

It was uncalled-for, outrageous, but Rowena simply could not resist interjecting, " 'Tis too bad he could not wed Warrick himself."

She regretted the impulsive remark immediately. Levity was misplaced with such a serious subject. Warrick could not appreciate it and would be enraged with her. Isabella must think her crazy. And then Warrick burst into laughter. His eyes caught Rowena's surprised look and he laughed even harder. 'Twas Isabella who did not appreciate it.

"How dare you make light of this?" she demanded of Rowena. "My father is still like to kill me when he—"

"Not if Warrick breaks your betrothal contract," Rowena pointed out.

Warrick stopped laughing at that suggestion. "God's blood, 'twould start a war. Better she gets the beating she rightly deserves and I assure Lord Reinard I am not aggrieved over the loss of her."

"That does not relieve her plight," Rowena reminded him.

"Do you imagine, wench, that her difficulty is now a concern to me?"

Rowena ignored that. "The alliance was good enough for you, my lord. Are your daughters spoken for, that one of them could not form the alliance in your stead—if the family has unwed sons?"

Warrick shook his head at her in bemusement.

"Get you gone about your duties, Rowena, ere you think to promise away my castle as well. This matter does not concern you—except for your own indirect part in it—which I am not like to forget."

"Ah." She sighed, unimpressed with the warning. "I see I am due for more of the dragon's fire—"

"Go!" he cut in, but his expression was not daunting. In fact, it was just short of breaking into a grin.

She smiled at him for good measure and heard Isabella say before she closed the door on them, " 'Twas an excellent suggestion she made, Warrick."

"I am not surprised you wouldst think so, lady, as it solves your dilemma nicely. It does not, however, get me the son I desired."

Rowena did not wait around to hear the lady renew her apologies. But she left wondering about the sex of the babe she carried. A son would be nice for a firstborn, but a son was what Warrick wanted. The question was, would a son gain her an offer of marriage, or guarantee her losing her first-born child?

❧ 31

Warrick was not sure what complexity the wench was perpetrating on him, but he had already drawn the conclusion that he did not mind it. What Rowena hoped to gain with her strange behavior he could not guess. Not that it mattered. What he had planned for her would not change—well, mayhap only slightly, for he no longer had any desire to make her suffer. Her puckish wit was also a pleasant surprise. As solemn and determined as she had been at Kirkburough, he would not have expected a playful side to her.

Kirkburough—'twas not her town, nor would it be now. But for the first time, he wondered who Rowena was and where she had come from.

"Have you spoken to the lady yet about Emma?"

Warrick turned from watching his men testing their skills against Sheldon's knights on the training field. For a moment he had no idea what his friend referred to—until he saw whom Sheldon was staring at. Rowena was crossing the bailey to the washhouse, her arms piled high with linens. So easily was she noticeable, her long braid glittering in the sunlight, her bright red chemise only visible at her neck, arms, and feet, but such a contrast to the drab dun bliaut she wore. In no conceivable way did she look like the servants around her. 'Twas almost ridiculous to call her so, yet he would continue to do so, regardless of how others saw her—or called her.

He was chagrined, however, that he had completely forgotten the new task he had agreed to give her. Obviously, when she was near him, his thoughts gravitated in only one direction.

"With Isabella's coming and going, there was no opportunity—"

"Say no more," Sheldon interrupted what was in truth a lame excuse. "'Tis appalling the treatment you have had from that family, and young Miles, the boy must be mad to think he could steal your bride and not die for it. 'Tis a shame. I know his father and—"

"God's blood, Sheldon, do not put deeds to my hand that have not entered my head."

Sheldon stared at him so incredulously, Warrick flushed to the roots of his hair. "You cannot mean to actually let the boy live after the ill he has done you. You? Are you feeling quite well, Warrick?"

Warrick was scowling before Sheldon finished,

because his friend was absolutely serious in his concern. "I am in no wise addled, damn it. Merely do I not care overmuch that the lady is lost to me. The alliance stands, since I have now promised Beatrix in my stead. Lord Reinard is as satisfied as I with the end result. Verily, what have I lost but the lady herself, who was already bespoke in her feelings, so would no doubt have turned shrewish on me. In truth, I must thank Miles Fergant for his daring."

Again Sheldon just stared, prompting Warrick to growl, "How is your arm, my friend? Grown as rusty as mine has these past weeks?"

Sheldon finally laughed. "Do I dare refuse such a pleasantly expressed offer?"

"I would not recommend it."

"Then have at me," Sheldon said, drawing his sword. "Just do not suddenly forget that you are forgiving the Fergant whelp. The last time you substituted me for one of your enemies, I did not rise from my bed for a fortnight."

Warrick cocked a brow as he drew his own sword. "That bedridden time lengthens each time you make mention of it. Is it sympathy you seek, or a light practice?"

"The day you give anyone a light practice—"

Sheldon did not finish as he met Warrick's first swing. The clang of their blades joined the others on the field, but soon only the two rang out as their men quit their own sport to watch. Rowena watched through the open door of the laundry, ignoring the bedding she had brought there to wash. Near the inner gate, a messenger who had just arrived was now reluctant to deliver the challenge he carried, when he was directed toward the two seasoned knights hacking at each other in what appeared mortal combat.

High on the castle ramparts, Beatrix also watched her father, hoping he would trip or err in his offense, thereby making a fool of himself. She was so furious with him, she had already slapped two servants and caused her beloved Melisant to cry.

'Twas the horrid disappointment in having his betrothed arrive when Beatrix had begun to think Isabella never would, and expecting the worst, a wedding within days, only to be told a few hours later that her father was not to wed, that **she** was instead—and into **that** family. The Malduits might have been good enough for her father, but **she** could have aspired to a more lofty title, more power, more wealth, an earl at the very least. But nay, she was to have a stripling of a boy, only just knighted, who could not hope to inherit for many a year. She would not even have her own castle, but was expected to live with her father-by-marriage. 'Twas intolerable, and all because **he** decreed it so. She would, **must** make him sorry for it. That he would dare do this to her . . .

Warrick sat up slowly, his pride more bruised than his arse. Sheldon stood over him laughing, and with good reason. Never in Warrick's life had he been taken so unawares, like a squire with his first wooden sword in hand. Damn that flaxen-haired wench and her eye-drawing red chemise, not to mention that delectable body it covered. He had no more than caught that flash of red out of the corner of his eye, just enough to be drawn into looking further—just enough for Sheldon to knock him off his feet as their blades connected low, the unprepared-for impact sending him backward, flat on the ground. And now she stood there, having stopped across the yard to stare at his ignoble position on the ground, looking as if she might be concerned, when 'twas more like she was fighting not to laugh, as Sheldon was doing.

"You realize, do you not," Sheldon said, "that my prowess in downing the dragon will travel—"

"Go to hell," Warrick grunted as he rose to his feet, but added with a tight smile, "Or better yet, do you care to try that again?"

Sheldon backed up, still grinning. "No fool stands before you, friend. I will take my laurels and quit whilst—"

"A messenger, my lord," Warrick's bailiff interrupted at that point.

Warrick turned impatiently to the messenger, noting that he was too clean to have traveled very far. He took the rolled parchment handed to him without the least change in expression to indicate that he recognized the seal.

The messenger waited to repeat the words that he had set to memory, but the Lord of Fulkhurst had no need of them, as he was reading the missive himself—or pretending to, the man thought, smirking to himself. He assumed this since the lord was not reacting properly to his master's words of challenge. He was no longer nervous either, after witnessing the Lord of Fulkhurst's clumsiness on the field. The feared dragon of the north obviously depended on his men to win his battles for him.

The messenger was less sure of that opinion when Warrick met his gaze directly with the most chilling gray eyes he had ever encountered. The renowned dragon had a cruel look about him, too, damned if he did not.

"If your lord is so eager to die, I will oblige him, but at my leisure. You will have my full answer anon." And with a wave Warrick dismissed the man.

Sheldon barely waited for the man to turn away before he asked with lifted brow, "Is it anyone I know whom you mean to dispatch?"

"You do not know him, but you have certainly heard of him. 'Tis d'Ambray, and with a new change in tactics. He now requests we meet at Gilly Field two days hence to end the war between us with individual combat."

Sheldon whistled through his teeth. "The man

must be as lacking in wits as his father was, to think you would not know Gilly Field is a ripe setting for trickery. I had heard the same challenge was issued to Walter Belleme, the old Lord of Tures. But when Belleme rode out to accept, he was ambushed and murdered. 'Twas how the d'Ambrays gained Tures and all it entails."

"I am aware of that," Warrick replied. "And I have taken that prize from his collection. I had even entertained the thought of letting him have the peace he sued for—after Ambray Castle is lost to him."

"So that is your next campaign, his own stronghold?"

"Aye, but obviously I delayed too long in the taking, giving him ample time to consider treachery as an alternative."

"Mayhap, though you must admit, Warrick, that you are **not** an easy foe to stop once you set out to destroy an enemy. 'Tis well known that no one prods the dragon without getting burned. It has made more than one man consider murder instead of fair means to defeat you, especially when Stephen will not lift a hand against you."

"Why should he? Half my enemies are his enemies, and he delights that I rid him of them without cost to him."

"True," Sheldon agreed, then asked curiously, "Were you serious, that you would not have destroyed d'Ambray completely?"

Warrick shrugged, looking again toward the spot where Rowena had stood, but was now gone. "Mayhap I am growing tired of constant war. Too many things have been neglected in the pursuit of it. My daughters have lacked proper guidance, my lands are barely known to me. God's blood, I traveled warily across Seaxdale to reach Tures and did not even know 'twas my own fief. And I have neglected the getting of a son—"

"Oh, aye, and you are so old that 'tis nearly too late to—"

"Go to hell, Sheldon."

The older man chuckled before his expression turned serious again. "I am sorry about Isabella. I know you were pleased in your choice of her."

Warrick waved that aside. "Verily, I should be furious with the lady, and with her father for forcing her into deceit when he knew her heart was well set on another. But instead I feel almost—relief—to have it ended, particularly since 'tis plain that she would not have suited me as well as I had thought."

"And mayhap you have someone else in mind already to replace her?"

It took a moment for Warrick to realize whom Sheldon referred to, but then he scowled. "Nay, you are mistaken. Never would I honor that little witch with—"

"Aye, you would—if she gives you the son you desire."

A picture of Rowena with a babe in her arms came to Warrick's mind and filled him with such longing he was shaken by it. But the precepts he had lived by for half his life had refused to let anyone escape retribution after doing him a harm, much less benefit in the end.

He shook his head adamantly. " 'Tis inconceivable that—"

But Sheldon held up a hand, interrupting yet again. "Speak not words that you will then feel forced to adhere to." And before Warrick did so anyway, he added, "I will see you anon, my friend."

Warrick stared after Sheldon with his darkest scowl yet. There had been times when he had regretted that his manner kept him almost friendless, except for Sheldon, who had known him from before his tragedies and understood what drove him. Then there were times when he was quite certain 'twas better to be friendless—like now.

✖❧ 32

Warrick was not in one of his better moods when he entered the hall late that afternoon. And there was Emma to remind him that he had not yet seen to the matter of her transformation. He called her to him now as he headed for the empty hearth area. There were only two chairs amongst the many stools, reserved only for him and his guests, or for his daughters. That he motioned Emma into one of them as he took the other brought a wary look to her face, and made him realize that she did not consider herself a member of his family any more than he had ever thought of her as such.

That he thought of it now did not bother him unduly. Bastards were a fact of life, and very few ever rose above the stigma of their births or the serfdom of their mothers, unless they had a royal sire—or no legitimate siblings.

Emma was, as far as he knew, his only bastard, if he did not count the one growing in Rowena's belly. Though she must be nigh six and ten, he had only known of her existence these past few years. Possibly he would have done better by her if he had given her more thought, but he had rarely been home since she had come to his attention, and rarely had he had other than war on his mind— until now.

He stared at her, noting what Sheldon had so easily seen, that she was indeed more like him than either of his other two daughters. There was strength in her face and bearing which the other two lacked. Even her eyes and hair were exactly the shades that his were, except whereas his eyes could be coldly chilling and most times were, hers held a warmth that lent a certain beauty to her face.

He noted also that she did not fidget under his direct regard. Had he stared at Melisant this long without speaking, she would have burst into tears. Beatrix would have started volunteering excuses for whatever she had recently done wrong, without waiting to hear an accusation made. Emma just quietly sat there and stared back at him, though she was nowise at ease. Courage, then, that he had not expected. Mayhap she would do well for young Richard after all.

Warrick did not think to ease lightly into the subject. His first words to her were, "Sheldon de Vere has a son who wants you."

"Is it Richard you speak of?"

He nodded. "Had you knowledge of his intent?"

"None."

"But I take it you have had some converse with him, else he would not have asked specifically for you."

"He has sought me out each time he comes here with his father."

"To steal kisses, no doubt." Warrick snorted. "Are you still a virgin, girl?"

Her cheeks pinkened, though her gaze remained locked to his, and her lips turned down at the corners. "No man here will even look at me, for fear of you."

Warrick grinned at her chagrin. "I am pleased to hear it. Richard will no doubt be even more pleased. But before I agree to give you to him, you will have much to learn so you will not bring shame to his family."

She stared at him incredulously. "You intend to have me **taught** the ways of a whore?"

He frowned. "What have I said that could lead you to think so?"

"You say he wants me and you intend to give me to him. If not as his leman, then what?"

Warrick's lips turned down in disgust, but at himself. "I suppose I cannot fault you for thinking so. But 'tis his wife you will be, **if** you can be taught the ways of a lady."

"Wife?" She merely mouthed the word without

sound, her surprise was so great. But when the implications of that word fully sank in, her face lit up with a radiant joy, her smile nigh blinding. "To Sir Richard?"

"If—" he started to reiterate, but she would have none of that.

"There is no if, my lord. Whatever needs be learned I **will** learn. Doubt it not."

For the first time in his life, Warrick felt pride in one of his children, something he had not expected to know until he had a son. Her determination he did not doubt. Her capability, however, remained to be seen.

But for her sake, he wanted her to succeed. To that end, he was now reluctant to order Rowena to the task of teaching her. Rowena's current behavior might not speak of held grudges, yet was there much that he had done to her that she might still resent. He had done naught that had not been deserved, yet the way a woman's mind worked was not to be trusted. The possibility **was** there that she might teach Emma incorrectly just to get even with him.

"Lady Roberta wouldst be the likely choice," he remarked thoughtfully, but before he could state why she would not be acceptable, Emma did.

"She would not do it," Emma said, some of the radiant glow leaving her face. "She despises me, and—and I am not so sure she knows aught more than stitchery. 'Tis all she finds important—"

Warrick's chuckle cut her off. "There is much to be said for a fine stitch, but I mention the lady as the likely choice only in that she is already employed in that capacity, and so 'twould be ideal— yet do I agree that she would object to teaching you. As an alternative, I believe Rowena can help you in this area do you ask her."

"But she has so many duties now—"

She did not finish because he was frowning again, and he was frowning because he had not realized he had overburdened the wench. Rowena had said nay, that she was not being overtaxed in her labors—yet. But had she lied to him? What did he know of servants and what was considered a normal workload? He had never had the directing of anyone other than his men. But now that he thought of it, even Mistress Blouet had looked at him strangely when he had mentioned everything that he wanted Rowena to do. All he had considered at the time was to give her tasks that he felt she would object to, because they were as near to wifely duties as he could think of. Putting her in the weaving room had merely been an afterthought so it would not appear that she served only him.

"Her other duties will be lightened to give her ample time to devote to you—if she agrees to the task."

"I will be most grateful for her help, but should you not be the one to approach her on this matter, rather than I?"

Warrick grunted. "She would not do me any favors, Emma, and for me to insist—suffice it to say, you are like to get more from her in asking than I would get for you in ordering her to teach you." It occurred to him, finally, that his daughter had not once questioned his choice of tutor, and he asked, "You knew she was a lady?"

'Twas Emma's turn to frown with her correction. "But she still is. 'Tis not something you can take from her merely because you—" She blushed, amending, "I am sorry, my lord. Was no one to guess? We have wondered why you treat her so, but 'tis your affair."

The censure in her tone had him nearly growling. "Exactly—my affair and not to be questioned, so wonder about it no more."

But he knew before he finished speaking that 'twas guilt that had struck a sour note in him. God's blood, now Rowena even made him feel guilt, when he had, in truth, been more lenient with her than she deserved. When he thought of what he **could** have demanded of her—her very life! Nay, he would not feel guilty over his treatment of her.

To speak of the devil, Rowena came up from the kitchen just then, drawing his attention instantly with that damn red chemise, which he promised himself he was going to burn one of these days. She noticed him almost immediately as well, only she then turned swiftly about to return whence she came. Running from him now, was she? Aye, mayhap she felt she ought to after the foolishness she had instigated that morn with Isabella.

But now that he had seen her, he knew he could no longer concentrate on Emma, so he dismissed her with the admonishment to wait until after he was gone on the morrow to make her request of Rowena. Thusly he would not have to order Rowena's duties lessened; they would be so with his absence. And hopefully when he returned from killing d'Ambray, she would have developed a routine of working with Emma that he could then allow to continue.

No sooner had Emma left than Rowena reappeared and headed toward him with a pitcher of ale in one hand and a tankard to receive it in the other. She was managing to surprise him again with her willingness to serve him without being summoned to. Or did she feel she needed to do some amends-making? Aye, 'twas likely that, and rightly so. God's blood, the wench had bitten him without a thought to how he would react. And it had been no small nibble either. The muscle that she had sunk her teeth into was still sore. Her daring—he admired, damned if he did not. But she was not to know that. She . . .

. . . came to a sudden halt halfway to the hearth, her attention gone elsewhere. Warrick turned to see what had distracted her, but 'twas no more than Beatrix entering the hall with a servant in tow. Yet when he looked at Rowena again, she appeared stricken for a moment, then resigned; then even that she shook off. He glanced at Beatrix again, frowning, unable to see what had caused Rowena to react that way. And then he noticed the cerulean-blue bliaut his daughter was wearing, a gown much too fancy for one of such tender years, nor what he was accustomed to seeing her wear. 'Twas deeply cut in front, designed mayhap to display a special chemise underneath, though the chemise Beatrix wore with it was unremarkable, obviously not a match to the outer gown.

He made the connection, but wished he had not. The bliaut was Rowena's, cut down to fit the smaller frame of his daughter. But where was the pleasure he had thought he would feel when he had first decided to give Rowena's clothes away to trample her pride and self-worth? He was uncomfortable with what he did feel instead. The gesture had worked. She was actually hurt to see her clothes on another. And now he had the urge to rip the gown off Beatrix and hand it back to Rowena—which, of course, he could not do.

Devil be damned, he liked not these things she made him feel. More guilt now, and 'twas becoming annoying that such an unfamiliar feeling was getting in the way of what had been a perfectly plotted revenge. Which was why he snapped at Rowena when she finally reached him.

"I am sorely displeased with you, wench."

Her eyes flared slightly before she replied briskly, "So I can see, my lord. You wear your emotions most eloquently as usual."

His scowl got a little darker as he pointed out, "Yet you do not tremble before me."

She shrugged, setting the ale down on the table next to him instead of offering it, as she'd intended. "You point out frequently how stupid I am."

"Or very clever," he said sourly.

She laughed at that. "As you wish, my lord. I am adaptable."

"We shall see how adaptable you are after we discuss your most recent transgressions of the morn. Mayhap you thought I wouldst forget your behavior before the Lady Isabella. You **bit** me, wench."

Rowena made a valiant effort to conceal her grin, but failed. "Did I?"

"You know very well you did. You also disobeyed me."

That had a more serious sound to it, so she quipped, "And a good thing, too. **You** might have wanted the lady to find me in your bed, but I would have been quite embarrassed by it."

"That matters not—"

"I see," she cut in stiffly, her amusement gone completely. "Then I am to assume that humiliation is no longer to be used as a means to punish me, merely will it be mine now to experience at any time."

"Do not put words—"

She stopped him yet again. "Nay. I understand perfectly."

She whipped around to leave him, but he caught her long single braid as it swung past his face. He pulled it slowly until she was forced to bend over, their heads nearly touching.

"Indignation is misplaced in a serf," he said in soft warning. "Did you forget you are my serf?"

She waited a half-breath before she whispered back, "Never would I forget that I am yours, my lord."

Her sapphire eyes held such sensual promise as they met his that, coupled with her words, Warrick's manhood warmed and swelled in full appreciation. He wondered if she did it apurpose—or if she even knew what effect she had on him. Were they alone, she would find out quickly enough.

He released her braid, needing distance between them before he made a fool of himself by carrying her straightaway to his bed. But she did not move back as he expected, and her fingers lightly touched the back of his hand in what was clearly a caress.

"May I ask a boon, my lord?"

He stiffened, recalling how Celia had always

waited until he was so hot to have her that he could deny her naught. Even so, he said, "Ask."

She leaned even closer to whisper by his ear, "You have made it my duty, but what I want is to explore your body at my leisure—as I did before. Will you lie down for me without chains to bind you and let me touch you as I would like?"

Words failed him. Of all the things she could have asked for, including her release, never would he have thought her request would be to pleasure him. He was going to make a fool of himself after all, because he wanted her so badly now, he was about to explode with it.

He started to stand, but her hand came to his shoulder and she added, "Forsooth, I did not mean now, but later, when you decide you want me again."

"Wench, think you you can say such to me and I can then wait to—"

"I was not trying to lure you to your bed," she quickly assured him.

"Were you not?"

A soft blush rose to her cheeks. "I had thought— this eventide, when 'tis dark and—" She did not finish.

Warrick, so ready to bury himself inside her that he could barely stand it, understood her dilemma, though he wished he did not. "I forget at times that you were a virgin. Just now I would have it otherwise, but— Go, wench, and do not let me see you again ere the sun sets—but then you had best be waiting in my chamber for me. Only do not expect your boon until I have had you at least once, more like twice. Verily, I may not give you rest until the morn."

Her slight blush had turned bright scarlet before he finished. She gave a short nod in answer and hurried away. Her absence, however, did not cool his ardor, and his discomfort began to infuriate him.

Damn the wench, what was it about her that caused him to react with such extremes of emotion? From his first consuming fury that demanded revenge to this raging lust he was in the grips of now. And then there was this sudden mellowing of his need for absolute retribution, with young Fergant, even with the Lord of Ambray, who had earned his vengeance for nigh two years now. Had it been gradually occurring, or was it, too, a result of the profound effect Rowena was having on him?

Verily, it seemed she occupied his thoughts now to the exclusion of all else. And he could not even say it was because she, too, had earned his complete ire, since he no longer thought of revenge when he thought of her. Even d'Ambray's challenge was of little interest to him now, whereas a month ago he would have leaped at the opportunity to meet his enemy face-to-face. He would ride out on the morrow to do so, but he saw it now as more of a bother.

It occurred to him suddenly that he **was** riding out on the morrow, not to return for a goodly number of days—not to see her for that long.

He left the hall in the direction Rowena had taken. She could have her boon later, aye, he would insist upon it. But he could think of no conceivable reason why he should have to wait until the sun set for what he wanted. She might need the dark to become bold with him, but he preferred the light when he was buried inside her, so he could watch every nuance of her expression when she reached her pleasure beneath him.

❧ 33

He was gone, but Rowena had not been thrown back in the dungeon as she had feared. She had not even been roused from his bed to attend her duties this morn, but had been allowed to wake on her own—to the empty chamber.

Warrick had bid her good-bye, however, at the crack of dawn. She remembered that, just barely, remembered being swept up into his arms, pressed tightly to his mail-clad chest, and kissed tenderly. Tenderly? Aye, she was not mistaken in that, for her lips had been sore, were still sore, yet that kiss had not hurt. But she had fallen back to sleep almost immediately after she had been lowered back to his bed, the exhaustion of the night she had spent with him too much to pique her interest in his leaving or aught else.

Now that she was awake, she wondered about that kiss, so different from all those she had accepted—and given—throughout the long night.

Her swollen lips could attest there had not been much tenderness in those other kisses. Not that she minded. The pleasures she had received far outweighed the little discomforts she was left with. And now that she thought of it, she also wondered why Warrick had been so insatiable. Surely not because she had brazenly spoken aloud what she would like to do with his body. And yet—and yet he had found her not long after she had left him in the hall yesterday afternoon and had dragged her to his chamber, where he had shown her the—consequences—of teasing him like that.

He had been so hot to have her that it had happened only moments after they reached his bed. There had been some discomfort when he plunged into her, but so arousing did she find his unbridled passion for her that she was moist by the second thrust, and as mindless as he by the third. After that he made love to her more leisurely, but with no less ardor. And it was lovemaking, for he gave more of himself than he took, without once mentioning what stood between them.

At one point they both realized they were hungry for something aside from each other, and he went himself to wake the cook. But 'twas unnecessary, for someone had left a tray of food in the antechamber for them, as well as a full bath. They availed themselves of both, though the food was as cold as the water by then. That they had so lost track of time . . .

But the night was not over, and Rowena had not forgotten what had started this odyssey of sensual indulgence. Neither had Warrick. But only after he was confident that 'twould take a miracle to stir his manhood to life again did he grant her original request. Yet the man was mistaken in what he was capable of, for he had been unable to lie still for her for very long.

Twice he had tried, and each time when his control finally broke he was like a wild man in his possession of her. She had started at his neck with her mouth, working slowly to his shoulders, down those thick arms, across to his chest. She had wanted to lick every inch of his body, but she had not got much lower than his belly ere he would push her back on the bed and drive into her. 'Twas not until he was nigh exhausted that she finally had her way with him, and even now she blushed to remember her boldness—and the sounds of pleasure she had wrung from him.

It seemed like a dream now, how he had been with her, so different from how he usually was. Not once had he shown his cruel side. And she was amazed, now that she remembered, how often she had made him laugh. It had been a night she was not likely to ever forget.

What she did not know, and was not going to find

out now with him gone, was if his new behavior and treatment of her was the hoped-for result of her seduction of him, or if it was only temporary. He was going to be away less than a sennight, he had told her, but just now that seemed an infinitely long time to wait to learn if she really had succeeded with Mildred's plan. Of course, even if it had worked, this separation just might undo it, so she would have to start over again.

Rowena sighed as she got up and dressed. She was being impatient, she knew, especially when it was, in truth, unrealistic to assume that she might have actually tamed the dragon this soon. One night did not make a changed man. And one little reminder of why he had sought revenge against her would bring the fire-breather back. But she **had** made progress. There was no denying that. And she could not deny either that seducing Warrick de Chaville was not the hardship she had thought it would be. Nay, 'twas most definitely a pleasure.

She did not realize how late it was until she entered the hall and saw none of the morning sunbeams that usually winked in from the high windows. The large room was almost deserted as well, except for a few servants. Mildred was one, and hurried to intercept Rowena on the way to the kitchen.

Rowena was surprised enough to ask, "Is it safe, then, with him gone, for us to be seen talking?"

"His order be damned," Mildred replied. "What I have learned cannot wait for a private moment. But why do you not seem distressed at his leaving?"

Rowena grinned. "Behold, this is not the dungeon."

"Nay, I do not refer to that, but to where Lord Warrick has gone. Can it be you do not know?"

"Know what, Mildred? Warrick told me only that he would be gone a short while, not why he must leave." Rowena began to frown. "It cannot be to make war, not in so short a time."

"Nay, not war, but a battle nonetheless. Gilbert has challenged him, and Warrick rides now to meet him—face-to-face."

Rowena paled. "God's mercy, one of them will die."

Mildred blinked, startled that **that** should be a concern. "Certainly," she said impatiently. "But first they will recognize each other."

Rowena barely heard, for she could not get the picture out of her mind of how large Gilbert was, how well skilled with a sword, and how Warrick would fight fairly, but Gilbert likely would not. Nausea churned in her belly as the picture became Warrick . . . lying on the ground . . . with blood . . .

She was shoved forcefully into the chair by the hearth, with no knowledge of having walked there. Mildred's hand was cool on her hot cheek.

"What ails you, my lamb?" the older woman was asking anxiously. "Is it the babe?"

Rowena looked up with utter despair in her eyes. "I do not want him to die."

"Ah," Mildred said knowingly. She sat down on the stool beside Rowena and continued briskly. "And why should he? He left here anticipating and prepared for a trap. 'Twill not likely even come to a fight—at least not between the two of them. But I thought you would be more worried about Warrick realizing who you really are. Once he gets a good look at Gilbert, he will recognize him as one of his captors at Kirkburough, and he will make the connection. Does that no longer concern you?"

"Not for the same reason. I know now that he will not kill me—at least not for my properties," she added with a smile that was more sickly than wry. " 'Tis his rage I fear if he thinks I deceived him with my silence, which in truth I did. For that I could end up back in his dungeon."

Mildred's smile was even more sickly. "Sooner than you think, my sweet one."

Rowena frowned. "How so?"

Mildred glanced behind her first to make sure they were still alone. "The Lady Beatrix has been throwing tantrums since she was informed she must wed into the Malduit family. She is utterly furious with Warrick, and if the man has taught his daughters aught, 'tis the satisfaction of revenge. She means to make her father sorry for giving her

to a mere boy she does not deem worthy of her—
and she means to do it through you."

Rowena's eyes widened. "Me? But—does she
have authority, then, with Warrick gone?"

"Some, not all, but she is too clever to depend on
that. I overheard her plotting last eventide with
her sister, and 'tis clever indeed what she intends.
She does not know what your crime against Warrick was to make you prisoner here, no one does,
but ironically, she plans to say 'twas thievery, that
Warrick told her so."

Rowena closed her eyes against full understanding. "She is going to say I stole from her."

"Aye, and her most valuable trinket, a pearl
necklace given her by Warrick. Melisant will support her, to say that you were the last one seen outside their room ere it was found missing. Beatrix
will then demand a search of the weaving room, as
well as Warrick's chamber, and whilst there, she
will pull the necklace out of its supposed hiding
place, confirming your guilt."

"And she will not even have to insist I be put in
the dungeon. 'Twill be done no matter what, until
Warrick's return, and he is like to believe her tale. So
often he called me a little thief. He will be forced to
punish me, severely—mayhap a whipping or—"

"**That** is not your worry, my lamb. What will be
done to you ere he returns is how Beatrix hopes to
hurt him."

Rowena frowned. "But John Giffard—"

"Is not here. There is another jailer, a man not so nice who they say takes pleasure in abusing those given into his charge."

Rowena paled. "I—I have met him."

"That still is not all. Beatrix intends to suggest that you should be questioned to find out what else you might have stolen. Do you know how prisoners are questioned by this man?"

"Torture?"

"Aye. That little bitch hopes you will be so scarred and—and used that Warrick will not want you back in his bed, but more than that, that you will lose the babe you carry. **That** is how she thinks to hurt him, because she knows—all know—how much he wants a son, even a bastard."

"I am going to be sick."

"I do not blame you," Mildred said sympathetically.

"Nay, **really** sick." And Rowena ran to the garderobe.

Mildred was waiting with a cool wet cloth when she emerged. Rowena accepted it gratefully, then asked, "How long do I have ere this trap is sprung on me?"

"Until Beatrix readies herself for the evening meal. That will be her excuse to want to wear the necklace—and find it missing. But you will be safely gone ere then. I have already prepared you a sack with food and clothing, some of yours but more servant's garb also, which you will need to wear in order to leave. I hid the sack in the ale-house, and was just about to see what was keeping you so long—"

"I overslept."

"Ah, then 'twas working, our plan?"

"**Your** plan, but aye, it did seem to be—" Rowena laughed joylessly. "Not that it matters now."

"Nay, this matter will right itself with Warrick's return. And you need not go far. There is a woods a league east of here, big enough to hide a whole army. Stay near the edges, and I will send Warrick to find you once I make him understand why 'twas necessary that you go."

"Can you not come with me instead, Mildred?"

"I would be noticed missing too soon, which might draw attention to your own absence, which should not be otherwise noted until the accusations are made. You will have a better chance do you go alone, and I needs be here to assure Warrick hears the truth ere Beatrix offers her lies."

"You forget he does not listen to excuses—least-wise not from us," Rowena said in a small voice. "If I must go, better I not return. Tures is not so very far from here—"

"'Tis a good three or four days on foot!" Mildred exclaimed.

"But my people there will help me, or hide me

until I can figure out a way to rescue my mother from Ambray Castle."

"Rowena, you **cannot** think to travel that far alone on foot. Trust in Warrick. Given time, he will do right by you I feel it."

Rowena shook her head. "I have not your confidence. And now that I think of it, I do not want a man who breeds such vicious children to have aught to do with the raising of my child."

"Fault him for his negligence, but remember that neither of those girls had mothers to guide them, whereas you—"

"Mildred, there is no time to debate this issue now," Rowena cut in impatiently. "Tell me only how I am to get outside the gates."

That Mildred was annoyed to leave the subject unfinished was obvious by her sour expression. "There is only one guard at the postern gate. You will slip through whilst I distract him. But if you are determined to escape for good, then wait in the woods a day—nay, best make it two days, until the furor dies down. I will join you then."

Rowena hugged her in relief. "Thank you."

"Thank me **after** you have to listen to me telling you all the way to Tures how foolish I think you," Mildred grumbled.

✿ 34

The woods were not a welcoming haven for a woman alone, not when every little sound was an imagined thief or murderer about to pounce on her. The sky had clouded over with the threat of rain ere the sun set, so there was no moon to mark the passing of time, but time crawled for Rowena. Hours passed while she tried to sleep and could not, her only consolation that it did not rain.

She felt no sense of exhilaration for having made good her escape. The ground was too hard for comfort, even with her serf's woolens spread out for a thin pallet, and she was cold. She had changed into her own clothes as an act of defiance, one that would not last past the morn, when she would have to don her serf's garb again for what little protection it afforded. The bright yellow bliaut and scarlet mantle that she wrapped herself in gave her back a sense of herself, which had been shaken by the Lord of Fulkhurst's intimidations.

Fulkhurst . . . she wished she dared wait for his return, but she had none of Mildred's certainty where he was concerned. He might not be as cruel as she had first thought him to be, but he was still capable of brutal retaliations and judgments, and she doubted not that if he believed she had stolen that twice-damned necklace, the fact that she was sharing his bed **and** carrying his child would not stop him from meting out the same punishment he would give anyone else found guilty of the crime.

There was the chance that he might believe her if she was given the opportunity to declare her innocence. But 'twas a slim possibility considering what he knew about her—naught much good, thanks to Gilbert—and she was not willing to risk a whipping or worse just so his daughter could have her revenge against him.

She discovered she had a few vengeful thoughts herself for that young lady for forcing her out into a lawless countryside. Ladies never, ever left their homes without armed escort to accompany them. Most often even female serfs were given a guard or two if they were sent out on errands. But here she was completely alone, with only the small dagger she had found in Mildred's sack to protect her. Mildred had included another of her fine bliauts, which Rowena could sell to buy escort if she could reach a town, but 'twas a big word, "if," and any number of unpleasant things could happen to her in the meantime, especially once she left the concealment of the woods.

When she thought of some of those unpleasant things, she found how easy it was to hope that Beatrix de Chaville received some just reward for what she had instigated. If Rowena should die ere she reached an end to this misadventure, mayhap she could come back and haunt Beatrix . . . aye, now **that** would be a just reward, eternal revenge. Warrick would love the idea.

The thought put a smile on her lips that was still there when she finally drifted to sleep moments later. But the noises of the woods still gave her no peace, waking her again and again in what little was left of the night, until she opened her eyes to the dim light of a lavender dawn—and a man standing over her.

She sat up so fast, pain stabbed at her temples. But 'twas no dream. The legs were still there next to her, and the sound of horses that had woken her. She turned to see other men dismounting near her, nigh a dozen who would be within reach of her in moments.

She did not wait to learn who they were. After her nerve-racking night, Rowena panicked, grabbing the dagger she had stashed at her waist and slashing wildly at the legs next to her. The man howled, but 'twas cut off as one of his companions leaped toward him and clapped a hand over his mouth. Rowena did not see this; she had shot to her feet and was running deeper into the woods, where their horses could not quickly follow. But **they** could, and did, three of them giving chase, laughing for the sport of it, which frightened her more than anything else. She **knew** what happened when men chased women through field or woods. They ended wanting a reward for their effort.

They were gaining on her. She could hear it over the violence of her heartbeat, now pounding in her ears. They were encumbered by armor, which she could hear clanking, but she had her long skirts to hamper her, and could not manage to grasp them with her one free hand to lift out of the way. She kept trying, for 'twould be the worse luck if the damn skirts tripped her up. Then they did, her toe catching in the hem of her chemise enough to throw her off-balance.

Her dagger fell from her hand as she braced herself for the fall, but she merely stumbled a few steps, then regained her footing. There was no thought to retrieving the weapon, however, and with both hands free now, she was able to yank her skirts out of the way. But the advantage was too late gained because one man was close enough behind her that he took the chance to dive at her. Had she seen him do it, she could have jumped out of his reach, for 'twas mere inches that undid her. He grasped only the very edge of her mantle ere he hit the ground face first, but that was enough to jerk her to an abrupt halt and right off her feet to land hard on her backside. Had the mantle been clasped at her throat instead of around her shoulders, she would likely have broken her neck. As it was, for the first few seconds she was sure she had broken her spine, so painful was her landing. And before she realized that she **could** move, 'twas too late to do so.

The other two men had arrived, panting, one stopping in front of her, one at her side. And the one behind her was getting to his knees, so angry at the smarting from his own fall that he jerked again on the mantle still in his hand.

Rowena fell back the rest of the way, her head hitting the ground. But she was not so dazed that she could not kick at the man in front of her as he bent toward her, nor did she forget to scream. This she did shrilly, and it changed their minds about what they might have done with her first. Their concern now was to end the noise she was making, and they nearly collided with one another in their haste to reach and cover her mouth. She bit one hand, threw aside another, but then a third slapped her, and was about to do it again when that arm was caught and held by one of the others.

"Wait, I know her."

"You are daft, man. How can you—?"

"God's truth, she is our lady."

This was said with a great deal of surprise, but Rowena felt even more. **Their** lady? She thought of Tures, but she did not recognize the faces leaning over her—then she did remember one and groaned inwardly. She even had it confirmed by a fourth visage looking down at her, and an incredulous voice she had hoped never to hear again.

"Rowena?"

He did not expect an answer. He had come upon the scene as she was being struck, and as the memory of that intruded on his surprise, his fist knocked back one of the three still crowded 'round her head. Then her stepbrother was lifting her up and holding her so tightly to his chest she could barely breathe.

"How came you to be here?"

The question broke through her thoughts, which were a jumble of fear mixed with annoyance. If someone had to find her, **why** did it have to be Gilbert? And she knew not what to tell him, except naught of what had truly happened to her in the month since she had last seen him.

But she could tell him one truth, and did. "I was held prisoner at Fulkhurst Castle, but was finally able to escape—"

"**He** had you? I have been mad with grief, when all this time **he** had you?" He had shoved her back as he questioned her, but now he crushed her again to say with a trace of the genuine regret he had felt, "I thought you dead. There was no one at Kirkburough to tell me what Fulkhurst had done with you."

That he was serious in his concern made Rowena feel strange considering how much she hated him. "I am not surprised," she answered carefully. "He had sent me straightaway to his dungeon ere the servants at Kirkburough came out of hiding to witness it."

"His **dungeon!**" Gilbert roared in his amazement. His men hissed at him to be less vocal, but he merely glared at them, then brought that glare down to Rowena. "The man must be mad. Did you not tell him who you were?"

She glared back at him for his stupidity. "You would have had me confess all when you know he means to destroy you and all you hold? He had already taken properties of mine because **you** held them. Think you he would not have murdered me to take the rest from you in so easy a way? So I told him naught other than what he assumed, that I was Lady of Kirkburough." Then she lied to support his original assumption that Warrick had come to Kirkburough for him. "He sent me to his dungeon because he was so furious that **you** were not there for him to kill."

Gilbert actually looked guilty, then confirmed it by saying, "I am sorry, Rowena. I did not think he would harm you, or I would not have left you there, but I was not thinking clearly that day."

When did he ever think clearly, or without greed uppermost in his mind? she wanted to ask, but he was leading her back the way she had come, and so she asked instead, "What do you here, Gilbert? You cannot think to lay siege to his strongest castle."

"Nay, not that, yet will I have control of it by nightfall."

She stopped, only to be dragged along again when he did not. "How?"

"I sent him a challenge. If he is not stupid, he will have suspected a trap and so taken most of his men with him." Now he stopped to demand excitedly, "Can you confirm this? Know you how many men he took with him?"

"I did not see him leave," she replied crossly, "nor did I have time to count how many were left behind when I was leaving myself."

He was disappointed, and so continued on, dragging her behind him again. "No matter," he finally said. "He **would** take most of his men. Why would he leave them behind when, as you pointed out, Fulkhurst is his strongest castle, capable of holding an army at bay with just a handful of men?"

"Then how do you think to take it?"

He turned his head to grin at her. "With a handful of men."

"Ah, of course. So stupid of me to ask."

He jerked on her arm to show he did not like her sarcastic tone. "I had planned to approach at dusk for shelter."

"They have a village they will direct you to," she predicted.

"Nay, not when I am on Stephen's business, with a message bearing his seal to prove it."

"Are you?"

"What?"

"On the king's business?"

"Of course not," he replied impatiently. "But the message is genuine. I had the good fortune to find it, since 'twas a message going nowhere with the bearer dead."

"Did **you** kill him?"

He stopped once again to snarl at her. "Why must you put every black deed at my door?"

"Nay, only what you are capable of," she shot back.

He scowled at her. "What matters how I came by it? 'Twill gain me entrance to Fulkhurst. Or mayhap I will return an escaped prisoner instead," he added nastily.

She wished he would. She would give warning to those inside the castle no matter what it cost her, as long as it thwarted Gilbert's plans.

He must have thought he had managed to subdue her with his threat, for she said no more until they reached the other men who had been left with the horses. She recognized a few of them from Kirkburough, Lyons' knights, men who should rightfully be serving Godwine's brother now, not Gilbert.

Rowena became very still when she realized that. God's mercy, did they even know? Or were they following Gilbert blindly, under the mistaken belief that he had some claim to Kirkburough through Rowena simply because Lyons had ordered them to fight for Gilbert's cause ere he died? They must know Lyons was dead, for Gilbert said he had returned to Kirkburough after the keep had been destroyed. Was the marriage contract binding them, then? But that contract had been voided when Lyons failed to consummate the marriage. And no one knew that except her, Gilbert, and Mildred—and Warrick. Gilbert certainly would not have told them. More like he had hinted that a child had been conceived . . .

She wondered why he had not asked about that yet, but suddenly she knew. Gilbert still had what he wanted, what he had gained through her marriage—Lyons' army. And he was about to strike a brutal blow against Warrick, the capture of his stronghold as well as his daughters. Gilbert was about to win the war between them, and **she** had given him the means to do it. Because he had been able to act so quickly, Kirkburough no longer mattered, so neither did a child to hold it.

Warrick . . . he would be devastated. He would be crazed with rage. And Gilbert would be able to demand any terms for the release of his daughters—including his life.

She had to do something. She should not care

what befell Warrick, but she remembered his laughter, his passion, and that tender kiss in parting; and, damn him, she did care—leastwise, she did not want to see him die. Nor did she want to see Gilbert win this war of theirs.

She wanted to blurt out to Lyons' men that they did not belong here, that the contract that had put them here was never valid. But did she do so, Gilbert would beat her senseless; she doubted it not. He might even kill her in his anger, and little good she could do then. But what **could** she do? Warn the castle, or convince Lyons' men, without Gilbert knowing, that they did not belong here? Verily, she needed to do both, for even if Gilbert were reduced to only his own men, he still might try to take Fulkhurst while it was so undermanned.

The man she had cut, as well as one other, had left the area, likely to return to their camp. Rowena waited until Gilbert was watching her to glance over those men remaining.

"Is this your army, then?" she asked innocently. "I thought my marriage had gained you much more."

He could not really fault her for that observation, though he did not like it. "Do not be foolish. My army is concealed deeper in these woods. Two hours after dark, they will move toward the castle to await my signal that the gates have been opened."

"That is **if** you can get inside. I still think you will be turned away. They will be cautious without their lord in residence. Likely he warned them, too, to watch for trickery, since 'twas **you** who lured him out with your ruse of challenge, and he trusts you not. Fulkhurst is a smart man."

"Are you trying to annoy me?"

"Certainly. Think you I have forgotten what you forced me to do?"

"Be quiet!" he hissed, dragging her away from the others' hearing to hiss again, "If you remember so much, remember also that I hold your mother still."

'Twas unnecessary to say more. Rowena nodded, feeling a depression settle on her shoulders. What had made her think she could do aught to prevent the disaster Gilbert was set on creating? With her he always won in the end, always knew just what to say to take the fight out of her, leaving her utterly defeated.

❧ 35

The sun made only a brief appearance that morn ere it was swallowed up by the bank of gray clouds that had been threatening rain since yesterday. Rowena wished it would rain in torrents. Why not? She was already feeling so miserable she was sick to her stomach with it. Why should the men guarding her not feel some of that misery in discomfort?

Only six sat around her, appearing relaxed and unconcerned. Gilbert had gone with two others to a vantage point where he could watch the comings and goings of the castle. He had not actually ordered those men remaining to guard her. They saw her now as **their** lady, so 'twas now their **duty** to protect her, which excluded letting her just leave on her own. But leaving now would not suit her new purpose, which was to prevent Gilbert from capturing Fulkhurst.

He had left her so few options with his threat. Unless Gilbert died himself, her mother would pay for whatever Rowena could accomplish to thwart Gilbert's plan—unless she could do something without his suspecting her of the doing. But what could be done so indirectly?

Of course, she could cut off the head of the snake herself and hope the body would then slither away. But if she **could** manage to kill Gilbert, one of his own men was likely to cut her down for it, and she could not see herself as being **that** self-sacrificing, not for a man who wanted only revenge against her.

She could tell Gilbert that Warrick was the man he had held at Kirkburough. That might make him so enraged he would do something foolish, mayhap even want to challenge Warrick in truth, mayhap even ride after him to do so . . . She was dreaming. Gilbert would never put himself at risk, not knowing the size of the army Warrick had taken with him, not certain his own was bigger. She wished **she** knew how big was his army. There had been many men at Kirkburough, but she knew Gilbert had counted on hiring many more with Lyons' wealth. Had he had a chance yet to do so?

There was one hope that she held fast to, that Gilbert would begin to worry about the predictions she had cast about what would happen when he tried to enter the castle. If only a few doubts would arise, there was the rest of this day for them to magnify. He could, in fact, end up convincing himself that his original plan was doomed to fail. Then he would remember the gibe he had made at her, and think seriously about using her after all to gain entrance. She would then have time to give warning, for in his telling her when his army would approach, she knew he did not mean to take the gate as soon as he entered the castle. She would likely be taken straightaway to the dungeon, but that would benefit her in separating herself from Gilbert, so she could confess who he was without his knowing 'twas she who betrayed him.

Aye, he would use her if he began to be plagued with doubts, and he would do so without suspecting that she would want to help the man who had imprisoned her. He knew she hated him, but he would think she hated Warrick more.

She began to feel better—until she remembered what awaited her in Fulkhurst's dungeon. Had Beatrix enacted her farce ere she knew Rowena had escaped? If not, then she might not have made her accusations, might have decided 'twould serve no purpose with Rowena gone. And the capture of Warrick's worst enemy might stay her hand as well, especially if Rowena was ultimately responsible for his capture. She might not even be put in the dungeon. They might even be grateful to her—nay, she was dreaming again. But at the very least, it might make that damn jailer think twice about abusing her—until after Warrick returned and passed judgment for her escape. But if she was going to be greeted with that charge of theft . . .

There was not a thing she could do about that, she realized. Whatever awaited her inside the castle she would have to face, **if** Gilbert decided to use her. But she was now not so eager to be used. And she began to look at the men around her again, wondering once more if there was not something she was overlooking, something that she could say to turn them away from Gilbert's command, without their confronting him about it and thereby exposing her to his rage—and his retaliation.

Of the six men left behind with her, only two she was certain were from Kirkburough, though all could be. But surely not all. Surely Gilbert would want more men he knew to be loyal to him at his back when he took the gate, than not. If she could just talk to one of the Kirkburough knights, without Gilbert's men hearing . . .

When one of them made mention of a meal, Rowena realized she was starving. But she ignored the food in her own sack and got up casually to move away from the group. She assumed they would share what they had with her, and hoped one of the two she wanted to speak to would bring it. But as usual, her luck would have it otherwise. The man who offered her some cold venison and stale bread she did not know, and the simple expedient of asking his name got her the additional information that he was from Ambray.

She thanked him but refused his offering, claiming she was not hungry, though her belly raged at her for the lie. Then she waited until they had finished eating and were relaxed again, then waited a while more, praying Gilbert would not return for a meal himself. He did not. And finally she looked directly at one of the Kirkburough men and confessed that she was hungry after all.

He jumped up to fetch her food from his own stores, and after she thanked him, she quickly remarked, "I am surprised that you have involved yourself in this cause that is not your own and is doomed to fail." Then she hazarded a guess. "And you do it without pay."

He did not deny it, saying, "I am sworn to Kirkburough, and Lord Gilbert—"

"Has no claim there, nor do I," she got out ere she lost her nerve. She then feigned surprise. "But surely you knew that. Without issue from my union with Lord Godwine, his brother inherits all. **He** is now Lord of Kirkburough and is no doubt there now and wondering what has become of his brother's retainers, men he will certainly have need of for the rebuilding of his keep. Verily, I do not understand why men prefer war and death to building, but obviously you must, or you would not be here instead of there."

He said naught for a moment. In truth, he seemed incapable of speech. Then he gave her a frown that was worthy of Warrick himself.

"Why do you tell me this, lady?"

That she had been reminded of Warrick gave her an answer. "I do not want to die, but my step-brother will not listen to me. He is obsessed with killing Fulkhurst, and no wonder, for Fulkhurst has sworn to destroy him. But Gilbert does not know the man as I have come to know him as his prisoner. You will take his castle easily, aye, but you will never leave it alive, nor will I, for Gilbert will drag me back in there as well."

"You make no sense, lady. We will have hostages, the man's own daughters."

"Think you that will matter to such a ruthless warlord? That is what I cannot make Gilbert understand, why he will not listen to me. His plan would work—against any other lord. But this lord has no care for his daughters or anyone else. He will sacrifice them, as well as his people, without any regrets. He will besiege his own castle, but no terms will be offered, no surrender accepted. All that man cares about is getting revenge against anyone who dares trespass against him."

"What if you are wrong?"

"What if I am right, sirrah?" 'Twas not easy keeping exasperation from her tone. "Have you been promised so much that you will take the risk?"

"You expect **me** to turn your brother from his goal?" he asked, aghast.

She was getting nowhere, and the others were starting to look their way, wondering what they were speaking of. Why did the man have to be so stalwart and dense? A coward was what she needed.

"Gilbert will not listen to you either, when all you can tell him is that **I** warned you. Like as not he will clout you for your trouble." Then she sighed, as if in resignation. "I am sorry. I should not have spoken my fears to you, but I thought mayhap you might save yourself and any friends you might have at the other camp, since this is not your war, nor do you even belong here. I thought to ask you to take me with you if you are smart enough to leave, but now I realize you cannot help me. Gilbert's men would stop you. Mayhap I can still convince him to send me to Ambray ere he enters the castle. Aye, I will do that."

She turned her back on him, praying he would say naught to the others, at least not to Gilbert's men. When she dared to glance around again, she saw him talking only to the other Kirkburough knight—in earnest.

Had she finally earned one small piece of luck? If those two would make excuse to return to the other camp, warn the Kirkburough men there, mayhap the army might actually disperse. If it happened soon enough, Gilbert would have warning of it and might give up his plan. He would rant and rave, and call the deserters cowards who knew only how to bully town merchants, but what could he do about it? He **knew** he had no right to use Lyons' army. She would remind him of that if necessary—nay, she could not do that, or he would look to her for the reason they had departed.

She would confess instead that she had innocently referred to Fulkhurst as the dragon of the north, and that the man she spoke to had turned white as a shroud. She would then demand to know if Gilbert had not warned his men that Fulkhurst was the renowned dragon, that they had obviously heard of him as far south as Kirkburough, but had not made the connection ere then. She **would** be at fault, but innocently, so Gilbert would not blame her **too** much—she hoped.

At any rate, he would not chase after those men if he were convinced they were cowards and would not now fight for him. He would have to come up with some other scheme to gain another army, and unfortunately, he had her again to do it. As soon as he realized that, he would not be so mad. But as soon as he realized it, she would be more heavily guarded. God's mercy, was there no way out of this dilemma for herself?

But the man she had spoken to did not try to leave any time soon. She began to think he was too brave for his own good when one of the men who had gone with Gilbert returned to warn that several patrols had been sent out from the castle, likely to search for Rowena. She was inclined to agree. Whether she was runaway serf or escaped prisoner, the castle guards were obligated to find her or face Warrick's wrath. But their search was not to Gilbert's liking, for it put his plan in danger.

A man was to go and warn the other camp just in case the searchers went that deeply into the woods. If the army was sighted, they were to capture the men, for at no cost were tales of their presence to return to the castle. Both the Kirkburough men volunteered to go, then suggested they ride together in case they came upon one of the patrols.

'Twas all Rowena could do to keep from smiling.

✿ 36

The afternoon dragged by with nerve-racking slowness. Rowena went through countless imaginings of what was going to happen, but the fact remained that unless the other camp was in the next shire, one of Gilbert's men should have returned ere now to report that the Kirkburough men were departing—unless they were not departing.

That was, of course, possible. The two men who left here might not have bothered to stop to save their comrades from "certain death," but merely decided to save themselves. Or she could have misconstrued their eagerness to leave with wishful thinking. For that matter, the man she spoke to might not have said aught of her tale to his friend. Their earnest talk could have been about something else entirely, her tale discounted since it came from a frightened woman.

She must have been mad to think a few words

from her would panic a large army of men—nay, she had not hoped to panic them, merely to point out that they did not belong in this war, would not get paid for participating, and would be better served by returning to their rightful lord. Fat lot of good it had done her.

With rain still threatening, it had been impossible to tell when dusk was approaching. Suddenly 'twas just there, and so was Gilbert, riding pell-mell through the trees in his excitement, bringing his poor horse to a painful stop. He did not seem to notice that the number of men he had left behind had decreased, but mayhap he did not intend to use them all anyway. After all, the more men who rode with him, the less chance he would have of gaining entrance to a closed castle no matter his reasons.

He did not dismount, merely did he locate Rowena and hold out his hand to her. "I have decided to say I found you on the road, without escort, and as you would not tell me whence you came, I was forced to bring you with me. 'Tis my hope they will take you off my hands, as my business for the king is urgent and cannot be delayed even for so comely a lady." Then he grinned widely to ask her, "Think you they will relieve me of the burden of you?"

"Since they were liable to be dismissed or severely whipped for letting me escape to begin with, aye, I do not doubt the drawbridge will be lowered."

She made her voice as surly as possible, as if she despised the idea. It must have worked, for he laughed.

"Fret not, Rowena. You need endure that dungeon for only a few hours more, then never again. Is that not worth Fulkhurst's downfall, after what he has done to you?"

She would not answer that. What Warrick had done to her was get even for what Gilbert had done to her. The one man she had not blamed **too** much. He felt himself justified. The other she would blame forever.

"**If** you succeed in your plan, Gilbert, will be soon enough to see what my imprisonment is worth."

Since he had expected just such a response from her, he was not displeased. There was naught much that **could** displease him right now, with the taste of victory so close. But Rowena's surliness was not all feigned. She was glad that the doubts she had planted had borne fruit. She would be able to foil Gilbert's scheme and get him captured in the process, which **was** worth whatever it cost her. But she would have preferred her other strategy to have worked instead, so she would not end up back in Warrick's hands as she would now. The other would have left her with Gilbert, but before he could find a new use for her, she **would** have found a way to be rid of him and his threats.

But 'twas not to be. She looked once toward the deeper woods ere they rode off, but there was still no sign of his men coming to warn that he had lost his army. Thrice more she looked back. There was still time. But all was quiet behind them.

Then they were before the gates of Fulkhurst, and Gilbert was calling out his false name, his status as Stephen's messenger, his contrived tale of finding Rowena on the roadside. She did not listen to the story a second time, nor did she look up from her perch behind Gilbert so she might be recognized by the guards in the gatehouse. She did not feel like being any more helpful. She was there. She would do what she had to do. But more and more she was resenting that she had to.

She looked behind them one last time, and there . . . was that one of Gilbert's men racing toward them down the road? And slowing when he saw them before the castle? Had those Kirkburough knights waited until near dark, then, to pass on her tale? Smart men after all. In the dark, Gilbert would **not** give chase. He would be inside the castle, waiting for an army to appear that would not, and thanks to her embellishment on Warrick's ruthlessness, that army expected **that** to be the last they would ever see of Gilbert. But their strategy, fine for them, was too late to help her.

The man was already turning around, drawing

the same conclusion. He was too late to give Gilbert warning. But mayhap he felt it mattered not. Mayhap Gilbert still had enough men left to serve his purpose . . . but that would not serve hers.

Rowena started to tell Gilbert what she suspected when the guard called down, "Wait there. My lord himself will take the girl from you."

Rowena frowned, wondering what ruse they were perpetrating. But Gilbert looked off to the side and cursed. Then she heard it, the unmistakable sound of a great many horses approaching, and looked for herself. 'Twas indeed the dragon returned. In the last light of the day, his army was just barely discerned, but she had no doubt 'twas him. Neither did Gilbert.

He was still cursing, though not loud enough for the guards to hear. "Damn the man, he could not have reached Gilly Field and returned this soon. 'Tis impossible!"

"So he changed his mind."

Her voice recalled her to him, and some of his composure as well. "Worry not," he told her. "This merely alters my plan to a siege. Aye, my army is still larger than his, and I will return with it this very night. 'Tis fortunate I did not ask yet to spend the night, for now I will insist I must travel on."

He could not mean what that sounded like. "You intend to stay here and greet him?" she asked incredulously.

"Why not? He has never seen me close enough or without armor to know me." Gilbert was just short of laughing. " 'Tis a fine joke on him, which I will be sure to point out when I return."

'Twas more than Rowena could resist. It served her absolutely no purpose, except the pleasure of being the one to burst his confidence.

"I hate to mention this at such a time, Gilbert, but he **will** recognize you. He knows you only as my stepbrother, not as d'Ambray. But still you are another man he wants to kill, for you are the man who had him chained to a bed at Kirkburough. The joke, brother, was on you both."

"Damn you, you lie!" he exploded. "I could not have had him and not known! And he could not have come with an army if he was chained to a bed."

For her own sake, Rowena twisted the truth somewhat. " 'Twas his army, but he did not lead it. They came not for you, Gilbert, but for him. And the moment they released him, he sent me here to his dungeon. He intends to make me suffer for the rest of my days for what I did to him. You he simply wants dead. But take not my word for it. You will recognize him yourself do you stay and greet him, so by all means—"

"Enough!" he growled as he grabbed her arm and swung her off his mount.

"What are you doing?" she demanded, furious, because she knew.

"They know inside the castle 'tis you. Do I take you with me, they will give chase, which does not suit me. So tell them my business was too urgent to wait. And fear not. My first demand when I return will be your release."

He did not give her a chance to reply. He rode off, his men following, and 'twas dark enough now that they were gone from sight in moments. The approaching army could no longer be seen either, though the sound of it had grown louder.

It occurred to Rowena to wonder why she just stood there and waited. She could have easily slipped into the moat instead, with no one to see her do it. She could even hide under the drawbridge once it was lowered, then make her escape later, after all was quiet. 'Twould be assumed she had been carried off by Gilbert's party. But that would lead to a chase, with Warrick in the lead. And Gilbert was heading straight for his army—or what was left of it. And Warrick would not take his with him, not to track seven men. And she was a fool, because she was still standing there when the first horse appeared out of the blackness and was halted next to her.

Torches were thrust into the outer walls, casting not much light—except into the moat. So she would have been seen in the water after all. For some reason that made her want to laugh. She did not, for 'twas Warrick himself who sat there on his great destrier looking down at her.

✖ 37

"Is there a reason you await me out here, wench, instead of where you belong?"

"I escaped," Rowena replied baldly.

"Did you?"

The skepticism of that reply, as well as Warrick's smile, told her he did not believe her. Well and good. She would get more said if he thought her spinning improbable tales for his amusement—as long as she left out the key words that were sure to enrage him.

So she shrugged, sighing. "Alas, I am not noble enough to take blame here when blame is not mine. I **had** to leave, else I would have spent last eventide in your dungeon."

"Ah," he said, as if that explained all. "You dreaded a place that by your own words you found to be 'really quite comfortable.'"

Did he have to remember what she had told the Lady Isabella?

" 'Twould not have been so **this** time," she replied sourly, then quickly reverted to a nonchalant tone. "And I tell you true, I would not have returned, except I was found by the most dastardly lord who thought to use me to gain entry to Fulkhurst, which he came here to capture."

When that did not raise a brow, she was annoyed enough to lay on the insouciance even thicker. "As to that, it might behoove you to enter Fulkhurst and make ready for a siege. On the other hand, I might have dispersed the army that was waiting in yonder woods with a few simple truths. I cannot be sure, mind you. But I explained to one of the knights that I knew for a fact that the lord he and his fellows were following had no right to their service, and so they ought to return to their rightful lord. I am afraid I also painted a rather black picture of you, on the off chance that fear might work where logic fails."

"I gladly accept all embellishments to my reputation."

"You **would**," she grumbled.

He grinned at her. "Tell me now how you enacted this remarkable escape."

" 'Twas not easy," she assured him quickly, too quickly, for he laughed, still assuming he was being "amused."

"If I thought it was," he replied lightly, "I would install you back in the dungeon myself for safekeeping, though I wouldst visit you—often."

The likelihood that **he** was not joking put an end to Rowena's attempt to "amuse" him. "You are returned just in time to save your castle, as well as your family. I would have tried, but there is no guarantee that your men would have believed me when I told them that the 'king's' man who just fled here was no king's man at all, that he planned to open the gates to his army later this night. Had you returned any later, you might have found your daughters held hostage to his demands, and what he meant to demand was your life."

All amusement had left him ere she finished; in fact, his expression had grown quite dark. "Why do I feel you are no longer jesting?"

"Because I am not, nor have I been. 'Tis all true, Warrick. You will find evidence of that army in those woods east of here, if not the army itself—if they do not come to besiege you this very night. The dastardly lord? He—he is my stepbrother. He came here because he wants revenge against you— for destroying Kirkburough. You understand revenge, do you not?"

Without answering, Warrick leaned down and yanked her onto his horse. His hands, which held her in front of him, bit deeply into her flesh, as did the conclusion he came to. "And you would have helped him."

"I would have betrayed him!"

"You expect me to believe that?" he asked sharply. "Your own brother?"

"No blood relation, and despised so much that I would kill him, **will** kill him, if given the opportunity."

"Then let me do it for you," he suggested reasonably, though his tone was chilling. "Tell me where he can be found."

Was it time for the whole truth? Nay, he was too angry just now to hear that, too.

She shook her head in denial. "You have taken more than enough from me. Now you wouldst take my revenge, too? I think not."

He scowled at that answer. He even shook her for it. But she still would not volunteer the information he wanted. He finally growled low and released her. She had to grab for his chest to retain her perch. Then the drawbridge dropped, startling her, and the horse moved under her, and she realized she was running out of time to tell him the rest, which he would soon hear from others—but to her detriment.

"You have not asked why I would have been put in your dungeon, my lord."

"You have more confessions to make?"

She winced at that snarl. " 'Tis not a confession, but the truth as I know it. I was to be accused yestereve of stealing an item of great value from one of the castle ladies. 'Twas to be found in your solar, thereby proving my guilt. This would give an excuse to 'question' me about other supposed thefts. 'Twas hoped that there would not be much left of me to tempt you when you returned—and that the pain of my interrogation would cause me to lose the babe I carry. I was not willing to suffer that when I was innocent of the charge, so I left ere the accusation could be made."

"And if you are guilty, then you are making this confession to allay your guilt."

"Except I am not. 'Twas Mildred who overheard the plot and warned me. You can ask her—"

"Think you I do not know she would lie for you? Best you do better than that to prove your innocence."

"You see now why I had to leave," she said bitterly. "I cannot acquit myself with other than what I have just told you. 'Tis you who will have to do so by proving my accuser a liar—else will you have to punish me with the severity that this crime demands."

She felt him stiffen at those words. "Damn you, wench, what did you do to cause such enmity in this woman?"

Rowena took heart. The question said he believed her—or wanted to.

"I did naught," she said simply. " 'Tis not even me she wants to hurt, but you. And with me gone, she may not have accused me at all, or even reported the theft. 'Twould have served no purpose. With me returned, however, she may yet decide to do it, to force you to punish me."

They had stopped before the castle tower. They had been stopped there for some time according to all the activity around them, men dismounting, horses being led away, squires and stableboys jostling about. Rowena suddenly thought to ask, "Why **are** you returned so soon, Warrick?"

"Nay, you will not change this subject, wench. You will tell me who the lady is who thinks to hurt me through you, and you will tell me now."

She slid off the horse before he could stop her, but she turned to look back up at him. "Do not ask me that. If she changes her mind, deciding to do naught, then she redeems herself and should not be punished for what she plotted in the heat of anger. If not, you will know soon enough."

His scowl was blacker than ever, seen so easily now with so many torches lightning the inner bailey, then seen even easier as the sky cracked with thunder and flashed with lightning. A chill went down her back, for he looked like the very devil, sitting there passing judgment on her . . . then he sounded like it, too.

"I will decide what deserves punishment," he warned her. "So do not think you can keep this from me as you have your brother's name. I will have an answer or—"

"If you dare to threaten me after what I have been through," she cut in furiously, "I swear I will lose what little food I ate today—which was army fare and rancid—right . . . on . . . your . . . foot! You would be better served by preparing for a siege—just in case—or is that not more important than one worthless prisoner who is going nowhere now, thanks to her accursed brother? **Then** you will have ample time, I doubt it not, to deal with my escape, my theft—my audacity!"

She whirled around and left him sitting there, too angry to care if she had enraged him beyond reason with her tirade. So she did not see the slow grin that came to his lips, or hear the laughter that followed. But his men did. And more than one wondered what he found so amusing whilst he issued orders that saw to the castle's defenses.

✤ 38

The noise coming from the Great Hall predicted the evening meal was still in progress. Rowena could hear it as she mounted the stairs to the hall, and her step slowed. Her temper cooled as well with the reminder of what she was about to face.

She had intended to go straight to the kitchen to rectify the scant amount of food she had eaten that day, but now she changed her mind. Only there was no place **to** go that would not take her through that hall. Back outside, then? Nay, the first drops of the long-brewing storm had just started to fall as she had entered the tower. She had avoided being caught in it all day. She was not going back out in it now.

Warrick found her sitting dejectedly on the steps in the darkest shadows cast by the torches at both ends of the stairs. He waved on the few men who had entered with him, until only he stood over her. She would not look up at him, though he knew she was aware 'twas him. She was not forthcoming with an explanation for being there either.

He finally had to ask, "What do you here? I would have thought you would be replacing that **rancid** meal in your belly with more tempting viands from Master Blouet—that you will not be as likely to vomit."

She still did not look up, but she did shrug. "I would have thought so, too, but I have to enter the hall to get to the kitchen."

"So?"

"So I—I would like you with me if I am to be accused."

Rowena could not imagine why that statement would cause Warrick to draw her up into his arms and kiss her, but that was what he did. He was soaking wet, but she did not care. She clung to him, noting the lack of passion in that kiss, and welcoming what was there instead: warmth, safety, his strength—and tenderness. She almost cried, to be given something like that after what she had been through.

When he set her back, his hand still caressed her cheek, and his smile added warmth to his eyes. "Come," he said gently and led her up the stairs with an arm about her waist. "I will not have you blame me again if you feel the urge to empty your belly—or is it the babe?"

"Nay—leastwise I do not think so."

"Then go eat," he said, pushing her toward the kitchen stairs.

"What about you?"

"I am sure I can make do without your attendance this once, though when you have finished, you can bring me a bottle of my new wine—and order us a bath."

'Twas not a slip of the tongue, that "us," and Rowena was still blushing from it as she entered the kitchen moments later. Once she was there, everything seemed normal. Work did not come to a standstill at her appearance. Guards were not summoned. But Mary Blouet did notice her, and bore down on her like a war-horse in full charge.

"I ought to take a stick to ye, girl," were her first words as she pulled Rowena into the stores room, away from other ears. "Where the devil have ye been? The whole castle was searched. They even sent out patrols."

"Did—did aught happen yestereve that I should be concerned about?"

"Ah, so that be why ye hid," Mary replied, only to frown. "But ye were hiding long before then. I looked for ye all afternoon, as it happens, but—well, I told no one ye was missing. Ye earned the respite, was the way I saw it, as hard as Lord Warrick had been working ye. Then when Lady Beatrix made such a ruckus over her missing pearls—it be no wonder ye did not come out of hiding."

So that was why Beatrix had gone ahead with her plan. She had not known that Rowena had left the castle, because Mary felt she had needed a rest. 'Twas worth laughing over, but Rowena had turned cold with dread at Mary's confirmation that she had a good reason to hide.

"Were the pearls found?"

"Aye, in Lord Warrick's solar. It be strange, that. The guard Thomas said Lady Beatrix seemed to know right where those pearls would be, as if she had put them there herself. Yet Lady Beatrix claims ye be the one took them, since her sister says she saw you outside their chamber just before 'twas time to change for dinner."

Rowena gasped. "When?"

"Before dinner," Mary replied. "That was when they could not find the pearls, yet do they claim to have seen them just an hour earlier."

"That wouldst be late afternoon when last they saw them?" Rowena asked excitedly.

"Aye, so they say."

Rowena laughed. She almost hugged Mary Blouet; then her relief overcame her and she did hug her.

"Here now," Mary grumbled, though not really displeased. "What was that for?"

"For letting me have a lazy day and not telling anyone about it, which is going to prove me innocent of Beatrix's charge."

"I do not see how, but I am right glad to hear it, for the guards are still looking for ye, girl. It be a wonder ye made it down here without being stopped."

"Mayhap with Warrick at my side, they felt he would handle the matter now."

"He be back?"

"Aye." Rowena grinned. "And he has ordered me to eat, so I had best get to it. God's mercy, I think I have my appetite back. I also need to order a bath and a bottle of Tures wine."

"Go eat, then. I will see to the bath and get the wine for ye."

"Thank you, Mistress—"

"Mary," the older woman said, grinning herself. "Aye, I think **ye** can call me Mary now."

When Rowena entered the hall not long after, she cradled the bottle of wine in her arms like a babe. Her step was not the least hesitant, and she was grinning at Warrick by the time she reached him.

He did not look very pleased himself. He had heard the accusations. Verily, Beatrix had not even waited for him to come to the table, but had followed him into his solar to give him a full rendering of the facts whilst he changed his wet tunic and dried his hair.

Now his flaxen-haired wench looked as if she had a very pleasant secret to tell. He hoped so, for the case against her was damning.

He had moved to the hearth, the lord's table already being cleared of the meal. Beatrix sat in one of the chairs, Melisant beside her on a stool. Warrick nodded Rowena into the other chair.

Beatrix gasped at this, though she said naught a word. Her father had been frowning at her ever since she had charged his leman with theft. That delighted her. She hoped he was furious. She would have preferred he come back to find the wench scarred and no longer desirable, but mayhap he would scar her himself when he passed judgment. At any rate, he would not take her back to his bed after he adjudged her guilty. Beatrix had at least accomplished that.

"My **daughter**," Warrick began in disgust, addressing Rowena, "has made a serious charge against you, wench. How do you answer to the theft of a pearl necklace?"

"Did she say when it was taken?"

"When, Beatrix?"

"Just before the dinner hour," Beatrix supplied.

"Ask her, my lord, how she is certain of this," Rowena suggested.

"**How**, Beatrix?"

Beatrix just barely managed to keep a frown from her brow. She could not see what difference it made. The necklace was taken, then found in Warrick's solar. Surely the wench was not going to suggest **he** took it.

" 'Twas late afternoon when I last saw it and decided I would wear it to dinner. Not an hour later 'twas missing, and **she**"—she stabbed a finger toward Rowena—"was seen outside my chamber during that time. 'Twas Melisant who saw her."

Rowena grinned at Warrick. "Did I tell you, my lord," she asked casually, "what time I escaped yesterday?"

"Escaped?!" Beatrix exclaimed. "Do you mean to say you were not hiding in the castle since yestereve?"

"Nay, my lady. I could not trust a mere hiding place for what **you** had planned for me."

Hot color stole into Beatrix's cheeks before her eyes glittered with malice. "You admit you ran away? Do you know what the punishment is for a runaway serf?"

"Aye, Lady Beatrix. I have my own lands, my own serfs, and attended my father's court quite often ere he died. I should know—"

"Liar!" Beatrix hissed. "Are you going to stand there and let her lie like that, Father?"

"I doubt she lies," he replied. " 'Twas I who made her a serf, not her birth. But we digress. What time did you leave here, Rowena?"

" 'Twas noontide."

"Again she lies!" Beatrix fairly shrieked this time. "How can you listen—?"

"Not another word, Beatrix," Warrick warned, his tone pure ice.

"The time of my leaving **can** be verified, my lord," Rowena offered. "Mistress Blouet will tell you that she looked for me, but could not find me the entire afternoon. And the guard at your postern gate can tell you exactly what time Mildred engaged him in conversation so I could slip past him unnoticed. 'Tis my hope you will not reprimand him for his carelessness, for had he been more diligent, you would have found me not at your gates, but in your dungeon—at least, you would have found what was left of me," she ended, giving Beatrix a look of undisguised contempt.

"What say you, Beatrix?" Warrick asked.

"She lies," Beatrix said disdainfully. "Bring in those she claims will support her lies. Let them say so to my face."

"So you think to intimidate them into silence?" he replied, the smile on his lips that Rowena hated. "I think not. But answer me this. If she stole your pearls, why did she not take them with her when she escaped?"

"How should I know how a whore thinks?"

That remark brought his blackest scowl into place. Beatrix stared back at him stonily, too angry to be afraid. But when that scowl came to bear on Melisant, his youngest daughter promptly burst into tears.

"She made me say it!" Melisant wailed frantically. "I did not want to, but she slapped me and said that she would say **I** stole her necklace if I did not say your leman did it! I am sorry, Father! I did not want to hurt her, but Beatrix was so angry with you—"

"Aye, with me," Warrick growled low. "All this for **my** benefit. Well, what you have earned, Beatrix, is for **your** benefit, and long overdue."

❧ 39

Warrick whipped his daughter right there in the hall for all to see, and he used the thick leather of his sword belt. Rowena leaned back in the chair she had been allowed to use and closed her eyes to it, but she could not close out the sound. And it was a brutal walloping. Beatrix's screams became hoarse, her pleadings pitiful to listen to. Rowena had to bite her lip to keep from trying to end it sooner than Warrick deemed sufficient. But by the time he was through, his daughter was utterly repentant, and utterly cowed.

After she was assisted from the hall by her ladies, Warrick dropped into the chair next to Rowena. "That should have appeased my anger, but it did not."

"It certainly took care of **mine**," Rowena assured him dryly.

The sound he made was choked laughter. "Wench—"

"Nay, I am sorry," she said seriously. " 'Tis no time for levity. And your continued anger is certainly understandable. It can only be heart-sickening to know that your own child wouldst do you harm. But try to remember that she **is** still just a child, with childish reactions, which was what her attempt at revenge was."

He cocked a brow at her. "Are you trying to console me, wench?"

"God's mercy, I would not dream of it."

He could not choke back his laughter this time. "I am glad you are still here."

Rowena stopped breathing at those words. "Are you?" she asked softly.

"Aye. I would hate to have to go out to hunt you down in that rain."

She glared at him for that answer, until she noticed the slight curl of his lips. Was the feared dragon actually teasing her?

'Twas amazing how relaxed she felt with him now. Verily, he seemed no longer her captor, nor she his prisoner. Had that night of mutual passion they had shared really put an end to his need for vengeance against her? The thought was too tempting not to explore further.

"The question of my stealing," she began carefully. "Has it been settled to your satisfaction?"

"Aye—in this case."

Rowena almost stopped there, for that taunt did

not bode well for what she hoped to hear. But it had not brought annoyance to his expression, so she braved on.

"What of my—temporary sojourn in yonder woods?"

He snorted at her mild terms for what would have been a successful escape if her brother had not been in the area seeking vengeance. "What is it you ask, wench?"

"Am I to be punished for it?"

"Am I a monster that I would do so, when I am aware of the harm that could have been done you had you not left the castle when you did?"

She grinned. "Actually—"

"Do not say it," he warned.

"What?" she asked innocently.

His frown was not the least bit intimidating. "As we have dealt with your theft and your escape, would you now like to discuss your audacity?"

Rowena rolled her eyes, wishing he had not so fine a memory. "I would as soon that discussion be saved for some future time—some **far** future time. But there is another thing . . ."

Now that she had reached the point of asking, she was losing her nerve. His mood was mellow, despite the unpleasantness of dealing with his daughter. She hated to change that, to see again the cruel visage that bespoke his darkest rages. But she had to know if his new attitude toward her ran deeper than what she saw on the surface.

Finally she just blurted it out. "Do you still mean to take my child from me, Warrick?"

What she was afraid of happened—the cruel mask coming so quickly to the fore, the slant of his mouth, the narrowing of his eyes, and the icy menace in his tone. "What would make you think I no longer want it?"

"I—I did not think that—only—"

"So you would raise it as a serf?"

"I am not a serf!" she snapped. "I **do** have properties in my own right."

"You have no rights other than those I give you," he growled.

"What will you do with the babe?" she demanded. "Who will see to it whilst you are off fighting your damn wars? Another serf? Your wife?"

He did not seem to note the sneering tone she ended with. "Do you give me a son, I will see to him myself. I want a son. A daughter?" He shrugged. "Bastard daughters have their uses, I have only just learned."

She was so angry over that answer she could have screamed. But losing her temper, as she had just done, was not how to reason with a man, particularly this one.

So she schooled her features to express mere annoyance, and dropped her tone to a moderate level to ask, "What of nurturing and love and proper guidance?"

He cocked a brow. "Think you I am incapable of supplying those things?"

"Aye. Beatrix is a fine example."

That was a harsh blow, and one that struck true. His expression changed to that of a man in deepest pain.

Incredibly, Rowena felt it, too, a tightening in her chest that hurt for him and sent her from her chair to his. "I am sorry!" she cried as she wrapped her arms around his neck and squeezed in measure to her regret. "I did not mean that, I swear I did not! 'Tis not your fault that the land is run so rife with lawlessness that you must be forever gone to protect what is yours, instead of at home with your family. That damn Stephen is to blame for that. Because of him, my own father took off to fight again and again, and you can see how unruly that has made me, even though I had my mother to guide me. **You** can only be faulted for not frightening me anymore, so that my cursed tongue now runs away with—"

"Be . . . quiet."

He was shaking, and his arms were squeezing her. She tried to lean back to see his face, but he was holding her too tight. He was also making the most awful noise.

"Warrick?" she asked with dread. "You—you are not crying, are you?"

He shook harder. Rowena's brows narrowed

suspiciously. His head finally came up off her shoulder, but one look at her and his silent laughter turned to loud guffaws. Rowena screeched in exasperation and hit his chest. He clasped her face in both hands and kissed her, only he was still chuckling, so 'twas a ticklish kiss—at least at first. But she was annoyed enough at him for such a rotten trick that she slid her hands up into his hair and pressed her breasts tight into his chest. And **that** took care of his amusement. After a few moments, it took care of her annoyance, too.

They were both out of breath when they separated. Rowena was too comfortable to move, though she had not been invited to his lap and ought to make some effort to get up. He settled the matter by pressing her cheek to his chest and holding it there, whilst his other hand caressed her hip.

"You are so silly, wench. You cannot even have a good argument, because you worry too much that you will hurt your opponent's feelings."

They were not alone in the hall, but for the most part, they were being ignored. Rowena did not particularly care either way, and that surprised her. Just a few nights ago, she had been mortified to be held like this in front of everyone. And just a few nights ago, Warrick would not have said something like that to her.

She grinned to herself. "Most women do happen

to be burdened with compassion. Are you scolding me for being womanly, Warrick?"

He grunted. "I merely point out there is a time to be merciless and a time to be—womanly. Just now, however, I like you womanly."

She stretched, sensually, rubbing her body more closely into his. He sucked in his breath.

"Was that womanly enough for you?" she taunted with a seductive purr.

"More like merciless—or do you want me to carry you to my bed right now?"

Actually, she would not mind that, not at all, but she said instead, "Did you forget you ordered a bath?"

"If that was said to cool my ardor, **you** forget the last bath I had—with you in it."

"Nay, I do not forget, but 'tis like to be cold again," she warned him.

He bent to nuzzle her neck. "Do you mind?"

"Did I then?"

He chuckled as he stood up and set her on her feet. "Come, then, and bring the wine. I trust you will not choke on it this time?"

"Nay, I am sure I will not."

Rowena was not yet used to such verbal play. It had her cheeks glowing, but also her pulses racing. She was still a prisoner after all, 'twould seem—of her desires. But mayhap Warrick was, too.

❧ 40

"I had sent a man ahead to Gilly Field, to scout the area. By the time he returned to report that he could find no activity of any kind, I had already received other reports of a large army seen moving north toward Fulkhurst."

"Then you **knew** about the army in those woods?" Rowena exclaimed. "You let me go on and on about it, trying to convince you of the danger, whilst all along you—"

"What are you complaining about?" Warrick asked. "Did I not listen to your every word?"

"You were **amused** by my every word," she retorted indignantly.

"Not every word."

That curt reminder closed her mouth for the moment. He had asked her again her brother's name. Then he had thought to ask where the lands were located that she had claimed to possess, possibly thinking Gilbert might be there. He had become quite annoyed when she would not answer either query, and she could only guess how furious he was over what Gilbert had attempted to do here.

They had not left his chamber yet this morn, though Warrick had been up for several hours already. Gilbert's army, or what was left of it, had not come to besiege the castle during the night, and was not like to now. But Rowena had finally got around to asking again what had brought Warrick back so soon to Fulkhurst. 'Twas what he was now telling her—if she could keep from interrupting.

He did wait a moment, to see if she would say more, then finally continued. "Since we did not come upon this reported army by the end of the first day's march, I thought it prudent to return home. 'Twould have been what I might expect of d'Ambray, to lure me out so he could attack Fulkhurst whilst I was not there to defend it. Instead, your brother thought to take advantage of my absence. I wonder now if d'Ambray did not receive word of this other army and thought it mine, lying in wait to ambush the ambusher. If so, he must have been furious to think I had guessed his plan."

And Warrick was going to be more than furious if he ever found out that d'Ambray and her stepbrother were one and the same.

He could have guessed with this latest fiasco. Rowena was surprised he had not, since only the one army had been sighted in the area. But to draw the right conclusion, he would have to acknowledge that 'twas his worst enemy who had captured and abused him at Kirkburough, and he was like to accept any other possibility, no matter how outlandish, before he would accept that one.

She had kept silent on this subject for too long. As soon as she had concluded that he would not kill her for who she was, she should have told him the truth. Now he might see her silence as a plot against him, her seduction of him as a means to learn his plans so she could warn Gilbert. After all, why should he believe that she hated her stepbrother, when 'twas just as likely that the two of them were working together against Warrick? The truth now would not only bring his anger back to her, but 'twas like to have him wanting revenge again also. She could not bear that now, not when she was discovering she had strong feelings for the man.

'Twas stupid of her to let that happen, she knew. Mildred had warned her of the possibility. Though she had scoffed then, she did not see how she could actually have prevented it, since it had sneaked up on her when she was not looking. The culprit was likely those damn desires of hers that she had so little control over. 'Twas hard to dislike a man she so enjoyed in bed. 'Twas harder still to dislike one who kept showing her a more gentle side to his nature.

She finished combing her hair and started to braid it. She was wearing her yellow bliaut again, which had not drawn comments yesterday, nor yet today, even though she had the serf's gown that she had stuffed in the sack she had brought back with her. She supposed she was testing Warrick by not donning it instead, to see just how closely he meant to adhere to the original dictates he had set down for her, when his attitude toward her was no longer the same.

She turned now to ask, "Think you d'Ambray will try something else underhanded?"

Warrick dropped back on the bed, where he had been sitting and watching her. "I do not intend to give him the opportunity. I march on his castle in two days."

Rowena's fingers stilled in her hair, her breath in her throat. "Which—that is, has he more than one?"

"Aye, and others in his control that he has no right to. But 'tis his stronghold, Ambray Castle, I will take. Hopefully, this time he will be in it when I do."

If Gilbert was not, Rowena's mother still was. The Lady Anne could be freed, finally, from Gilbert's control—or she could be hurt if Ambray did not surrender, if the battle was taken inside its walls.

"Do you and your men—kill wantonly when you take a castle?" she asked hesitantly.

"Was anyone killed at Kirkburough?"

"Kirkburough was not defended," she reminded him. "Ambray will be."

"Men die indiscriminately in any battle, Rowena, but I have never killed wantonly." Then he sat up. "Why do you ask? And if you tell me you are worried for folk you do not even know, I will—"

"Do not start threatening me so early in the morn," she cut in crossly. "I was only thinking of the women and children. Does this lord have a family, a wife—a mother?"

"No one since his father died . . . nay, actually, there are his father's widow and her daughter, but they are no blood kin to him."

"Yet I have heard it said you destroy whole families when you go after an enemy."

He grinned at her. "They say a great many things about me, wench. Mayhap half is true."

He was not telling her what she needed to hear, and she was starting to feel sick in her apprehension, so she asked outright, "Then you would not kill those women, though they are related to the Lord of Ambray through marriage?"

He finally frowned at her. "Were I capable of killing women, Rowena, **you** would not be here to ask me such silly questions."

She turned her back on him, but not before he saw her stricken expression. He muttered a curse and moved to stand behind her, drawing her back against his chest.

"I did not mean that the way it sounded, but was merely making a point," he told her. "Think you I like these questions of yours when they paint me so vicious? I thought you were not frightened of me anymore."

"I am not."

"**Why** are you not?"

She turned around to look up at him, but color suddenly flooded her cheeks and she looked down again in embarrassment. In a small, repentant voice, she said, "Because you do not hurt women—even when you have reason to. I am sorry, Warrick. I should not have let my thoughts run hither and yon, but—but I like it not that you go to make war."

"I am a knight—"

"I know, and knights will ever have one battle or another to fight. Women do not have to **like** it. Will—will you be gone for long?"

His arms wrapped around her to draw her close. "Aye, mayhap months. Will you miss me, wench?"

"When half my duties go with you?"

He whacked her bottom. "That was not a proper answer for your lord."

"That answer was for the man who calls me his serf. I have another answer for the man who loved me through the night. Him I will dream of, and pray for, and count the days until he comes safely—"

His arms crushed her. His mouth devoured her. Before her thoughts scattered from the heat he aroused so quickly, she decided he must have liked that answer better. She just wished it were not all true.

❧ 41

Warrick looked up from his cold meal as the tent flap opened. He grinned slowly as he saw who had entered.

"Be damned, what do you here, Sheldon? And do not tell me you were just passing by."

"I come with your supply wains from Fulkhurst. You might want to put that slop aside and wait for some fresh pork. I counted a dozen fat pigs, one of which is even now being slaughtered."

"We were not doing so badly," Warrick replied. "The village had had a prosperous summer ere we arrived, and I made sure **none** of its stock was herded into the castle, though I let all of the villagers seek shelter there."

Sheldon laughed at that strategy. "More mouths for them to feed, but less food to feed them with. Usually besiegers are not so lucky."

Warrick shrugged. "I was fortunate in catching them unawares with an advance guard. But with the harvest just in, the castle was likely well stocked. It has been a month, but I doubt they are even rationing yet."

"Well, I have brought you a few trebuchets you might make use of."

"The devil you did!"

"As well as a small mountain of stones to fire from them. But I noticed you brought your mangonel down from Tures. I should have brought you boulders instead."

Warrick chuckled. "That would have been appreciated, since most of mine are sunk in the damn moat, with not much damage to their credit. Now tell me what you are doing here, my friend. This is not your war."

'Twas Sheldon's turn to shrug. "With my own harvest in, I was going mad with boredom. You have made our neighbors so law-abiding with your quick retaliations for any little trespass, naught exciting ever happens anymore in our shire. And since Eleanor died, I no longer have a wife to keep me content at home. 'Twas either do a little raiding across the border, go to court—which I abhor—or come and offer you my excellent advice for a fortnight or so, or at the very least, my company."

"You are most definitely welcome, though you are like to be as bored here as at home."

"Your company is never boring, Warrick, not

when it is so easy to rile you." Sheldon grinned. "But does that mean you plan to just sit them out?"

" 'Tis not my habit to be a passive besieger. We keep them busy and ever alert."

"How many towers have you employed?"

"Three have been burned, now rubble filling the moat. I am building two more."

"That should be demoralizing for those watching from the battlements, as was your supplies arriving. But have you cornered the illusive wolf this time, or did he get away?"

"As of last week he was still telling my heralds to go to hell, though he does not show himself on the walls to make my archers happy. However, there was a fire our first week here. I know not whether some brave yeoman climbed down from the castle walls to make mischief, or if 'twas carelessness in my own camp, but in the ensuing commotion, a whole troop could have escaped over the walls, or through the postern gate, which is so carefully concealed on the outside that we have yet to locate it. There is also the possibility that d'Ambray was not here at all and his constable answers in his name. I will not be at all pleased to learn if that is so."

" 'Twill not be the first time you thought you had him but he managed to escape."

"Aye, but does he do so this time, I swear I will take this castle down stone by stone and cart the debris away."

"Now **that** would be a waste. If you do not want it, why not give it to the Malduits as Beatrix's dower? Let **them** worry about keeping d'Ambray from getting it back—if you do not end him in this effort."

Warrick grinned at the notion. 'Twas subtle in the way of revenge, yet did it have amusing ramifications, especially after Lord Reinard had tried to dupe him with an unwilling bride, and had thus far been rewarded for it. He and d'Ambray did, in truth, deserve each other.

"Are you sure you would not like Emma to have it instead—to relieve the boredom you complained of?" Warrick teased.

Sheldon looked horrified. "God's blood, do not be so generous with us! A farm or a mill will do Richard nicely. He is the scholar in our family, after all. Barely did he earn his spurs, for truly do I think Lord John took pity on him when he knighted him this year."

Warrick laughed at those half-truths. Richard **was** scholarly, true enough, but all three of Sheldon's sons, though none yet twenty, took after their father in knightly skills.

"Best I see if I can capture Ambray ere I dispose of it," Warrick conceded.

"That is in little doubt considering the size of the army you have here. The hundred men I brought with me—"

"Will be welcome."

"But are not needed." Sheldon snorted. "Where **do** you come by so many?"

"Landless knights are plentiful these days. Those who come to me do not find outlawry to their liking, nor the political machinations at court. My wars are simple and straightforward, my army not beset with indecision or too many lords back stabbing for supremacy. For men who prefer fighting to peace . . ."

"But this is to be your last campaign, is it not? What will you do with such a large army when you are at peace?"

Warrick shrugged. "At least half I will keep. I have enough properties to support them. The rest, mayhap I will suggest they seek service with young Henry. 'Tis rumored he plans to come after the throne yet again."

Sheldon chuckled. "So you will no longer hold yourself neutral in the political arena?"

"I have fought for Stephen only when it suited me, paid scutage when it did not, and have even gone against him when one of his loyal followers has earned my enmity. But I would welcome a king who can give us peace again, so I will not have to be troubled in my old age to keep it myself. I believe the Angevin can do that."

Sheldon was in agreement, and they spoke of some of the great earls already in Henry's camp.

Chester had visited Sheldon to feel him out on the subject. Hereford had spoken in private to Warrick when he was last in London. 'Twas going to come to civil war again, and Henry's vassals wanted to know in advance who would stand by them, or at least continue neutral.

But that was for future debate. Sheldon got back to a subject of more immediate concern to him.

"I would have had Richard with me, but we stopped by Fulkhurst on the way here, and I could not drag him away from his hoped-for bride. You will not believe her transformation, Warrick. I am almost inclined to tell my son that you have changed your mind and decided to offer her to me instead, but I doubt not he would challenge me do I suggest it. He is more smitten than ever."

"But what of her manner?" Warrick asked. "Noticed you any improvement?"

"Your little lady-serf has worked wonders in so short a time. She has sewn for Emma a new wardrobe, and instructed her in every aspect of castle management and wifely duties. Verily, you can in no way tell Emma was raised in the village. She is gracious, softly spoken, and—"

"Enough, Sheldon! Richard can have her."

"Then I will be glad to accept her as a daughter-by-marriage instead of as a wife."

Warrick snorted. "That was never in doubt."

Then he asked nonchalantly, "And what of Emma's tutor? How does she fare?"

"Ah, that is right, you have not seen her this last month, have you?"

Warrick did not need reminding of that. He wanted to go home. For the first time since he was a boy, he had a **reason** to go home, and it was frustrating him that he could not.

"How are the camp whores?" Sheldon was saying. "Any worth trying?"

"I would not know," Warrick growled. "And you did not answer my question well? Is Rowena well? Is she eating properly? Emma is not tiring her, is she?"

Sheldon chuckled. "Nay, she thrives with you not there to intimidate her. She adds grace and beauty to your hall. Emma adores her. Your servants defer to her. Melisant prefers her company to that of her own tutor. Aye, even your youngest daughter has improved in manner since Beatrix was sent to abide with her future in-laws. Likely you can thank your little Rowena for that as well."

"Mayhap I should bring her here," Warrick said dryly. "She can single-handedly take Ambray for me."

"Was I singing her praises too highly?"

"A mite—and for naught. I have already decided on a new wife."

Sheldon's expression turned blank for several

seconds before he exploded. "You did not! Say you did not! Damn you, Warrick, I could have sworn you were developing a fondness for Lady Rowena. So she is landless. So she is without family. Have you not got enough that matters of the heart can now take precedence for you? Who is this other lady? What does she bring you that is so important you wouldst risk another Isabella?"

Warrick shrugged. "She claims to have some properties, but for some silly bit of stubbornness, she will not tell me where they are."

"**She** will not? Not tell you—?" Sheldon's peppered brows narrowed. "Have you just got one back at me, friend?"

Warrick grinned. "Aye, the little wench has bewitched me as you thought. And as long as she has already taken over my castle, I might as well make her lady of it in truth."

✽ 42

Rowena laughed as Emma's nose scrunched up when she smelled the rancid fat boiling. "Do I really need to know everything about everything? Even candle-making?"

"You will be fortunate if you have a candle-maker. If you do not, will you hire one at a cost to your husband, or will you be able to instruct one of your servants to do the task instead? If your soap-maker only knows how to make lye soap, will you never again have the sweet-scented one you prefer, because the merchants charge too much for it? Or will you be able to make your own?"

Emma blushed as she usually did when she had asked a silly question. "I hope Richard appreciates what I am going through for him."

"He will appreciate having his home run smoothly. He need not know about the fire in the kitchen, the cow that got loose in the laundry yard, or the merchant who tried to overcharge you for pepper, and whom you had thrown out on his arse. Richard will see the quickly prepared boiled fish and eggs on his table, smile at you, and tell you about his own day, which was as naught in comparison to yours. Thus he will brag to his friends that he has the most wonderful wife in the land. She never complains, she never worries him with matters that **he** knows naught about, and she rarely dips into his coffers."

Emma giggled. "Does she really have to be such a paragon of saintliness?"

"Certainly not," Rowena replied as she led them away from the noxious odor of the boiling fat. "Did I have the misfortune to still be wed to that old lecher, Lyons, I might have bought the overpriced pepper and stuffed his fish with it. I offer only general advice, my dear, that which my mother gave to me. You will find your own way with Richard, never fear. Now go and seek out Edith. There is no reason for **me** to take you through the step-by-step process of candlemaking, which I already know, when Edith can do it. And do not ask again why you cannot simply be told how to do it. Hearing is soon forgotten, whereas doing is not."

Rowena returned to the hall and the sewing she had left by the hearth. She was making Warrick a tunic in bright red samite, a lengthy task, as the thin silk required small, careful stitches. The light

would have been better to see by in his solar, but
she could not get used to treating that chamber as
her own, even though he had told her to do so the
day before he left, and even though she slept there
every night.

Her trunk of clothes had appeared in his chamber that day, too. Not one word did he say about it,
other than to remark on the prettiness of the royal
purple bliaut with gold trim that she wore that
evening. That her duties were to change completely with his going she did not find out until he
had gone.

First Emma told about her wedding, which
would come about only if she could master the duties of a lady wife, but she had her father's permission to ask Rowena to be her teacher in those
duties. Rowena had, perforce, put her foot in her
mouth to ask who Emma's father was. She had
been furious with Warrick for a sennight for not
giving her warning. But that same day, Mary
Blouet had informed her that if she had agreed to
instruct Emma, which she already had, then she
was to be excused from all of her other duties.

Helping Emma was a pleasure. Rowena had developed a fondness for the girl that was going to
make her miss her sorely when Emma married
young Richard. That would not be until after Warrick returned, however, and no one could guess
when that would be.

There had been other changes. Beatrix had been sent off to live with her new family the day after her punishment, and 'twas as if the whole castle breathed a little easier with her going. Once Warrick left, his youngest daughter had made shy overtures that Rowena encouraged, finding that Melisant was not as mean-natured as Mildred had thought, merely had she been wrongly influenced by her older sister.

Rowena's change in circumstance had its effect on others, though she was inclined to think that where she was sleeping had had the most effect. Mary now came to her with her problems, and Mary's husband saved the tenderest morsels of food for her. Even Warrick's steward consulted her ere he sent John Giffard to the nearest town for supplies. John, when he was not off on errands, joined her and Mildred for their meals. Though Melisant had invited Rowena to dine at the lord's table with her and Lady Roberta—who was the only one to still disdain Rowena—that was one presumption she would not make. Warrick might have made things easier for her ere he departed, but he had not said she was no longer to consider herself his serf. And a serf, even in the rich gowns of a lady, did not dine at the lord's table.

Though her days were full with Emma, she still found too much time to think of Warrick. And she knew those strong feelings of hers were getting out of hand when missing him actually hurt. But with him not there to look at her with desire blazing from his eyes, she lost the confidence she had gained in those last days she had spent with him. He had wanted her when he was there. He had made concessions that she would never have expected. But she was, after all, no more than what he had made her, his leman, his servant, his prisoner. She could not expect more than that. She could not even expect when he returned, for time dimmed all memories, and he might have already found someone else to interest him.

"Mistress, you are to come with me."

She looked up to see Sir Thomas, heavily stained from travel, standing in front of her. He had left the castle with Warrick over a month ago. She looked hopefully beyond him.

"Is Warrick returned?"

"Nay, Mistress, he is still at Ambray Castle."

"And you are to take me there?"

"In all haste."

The color drained from her face. "He is wounded?"

"Certainly not."

"Well, you need not say that as if 'twas a stupid question," she snapped. "What else was I to think when you say we must make haste?"

" 'Twas my lord's order," he explained. "But we will not travel so swiftly that you end up looking as begrimed and weary as I. I rode through the night, but I am allowed a day and a half to bring you safely to Ambray. If you would but make haste now to gather a few clothes and what you will need, we can ride at a more leisurely pace."

Rowena's brow knit curiously. "Do you know why I am summoned?"

"Nay, Mistress."

She suddenly gasped as one reason occurred to her. "Is Ambray taken?"

" 'Tis still under siege, though safe enough for you to venture there for a time."

Then this summons made no sense.

❧ 43

There was one other reason that Rowena could think of for being summoned to Warrick's presence. It had her beset with dread the entire journey, but 'twas definitely possible—nay, likely. Warrick could have seen Gilbert from the battlements and recognized him. She could be going to face his blackest rage, his cruelest visage. He could want revenge again, mayhap even to use her against Gilbert, torture her before the battlements, hang her—nay, nay, he would not do that. But she remembered the walloping Beatrix had got. She remembered the dungeon. She remembered being chained to his bed—well, that had not been so bad in retrospect—but that beating . . .

She was so afraid when they reached the camp that surrounded Ambray, she barely noticed the silent castle towering in its midst. She was taken straightaway to the tent set up for Warrick's use, but he was not in it. That did nothing to soothe her jumbled nerves. She was here. She wanted whatever she would have to deal with to be over.

But she had no time to even build up a bit of annoyance that she was to be kept waiting, for Warrick walked in less than a minute later. There was no time either to judge his mood, for she was yanked right into his arms. And that left no opportunity to get a single word out, for his mouth covered her gasp, the entreaties she would have made, the excuses.

For endless moments she was overwhelmed by sheer possessiveness, for that kiss said she was his and he wanted to consume her. Her anxieties did not return immediately when she was allowed to breathe again, did not get through her aroused senses at all until she was lowered to Warrick's pallet and saw him throw his sword belt aside just before he dropped to his knees to descend on her.

"Wait!" she cried, thrusting both hands up to hold him back from her. "What does this mean, Warrick? Why am I summoned here?"

"Because I missed you," he replied, defying the pressure she was exerting against him to lean down and say the words against her lips. "Because I felt I would go mad if I had to wait another day to see you."

"Is that all?"

"Is that not enough?"

Her relief was so great, she kissed him back with more passion than she had ever shown him. His hands came to her breasts, claiming them. Hers went to his hips, pressing him closer. But 'twas an unsatisfying embrace, hampered by clothes he would not stop kissing her to remove.

When he did finally get around to yanking off his tunic, it was with such haste he caused her to laugh. "You ruin more clothes that I must then repair."

"Do you mind?"

"Nay, you can rip mine, too, if you like." She grinned at him. "But I might be able to be rid of them quicker do you let me up."

"Nay, I like you just where you are. You cannot imagine how often I saw you just so in my mind."

She ran her hands up the chest he had bared for her touch, then leaned up to lick one nipple. "As often as I imagined doing that?"

"Rowena . . . do not," he said raggedly and tried to push her back down, but she held on tight and attacked his other nipple. "Desist, or I will come the very instant I get inside you."

"That is all right as long as it gives you pleasure, Warrick. Think you I will not make sure that you see to me after?"

He groaned, yanked her skirts up and her braies down, and plunged into her. And she did make sure he brought her to the same pleasure after.

❧ Warrick did not leave his tent that afternoon, nor that night. The next morning when Rowena awoke, she was told Sir Thomas was waiting to take her back to Fulkhurst Castle. 'Twas Warrick's squire who told her. Of Warrick there was no sign at all.

She was bemused, then annoyed. To be brought all this way just for one day of loving? She did not see why she could not stay longer.

She demanded to be taken to Warrick as soon as she dressed and stepped outside his tent, where Bernard was waiting to escort her to Sir Thomas. The boy shook his head but frowned, trying to remember the message he had been instructed to give her on such a request.

"He said to tell you, Mistress, that if he sees you again, he is likely to keep you here. Yet is this no place for you to be, so you are to go."

Rowena opened her mouth to argue with Bernard, but just as quickly closed it. God's mercy, how could she have forgotten **where** she was?

She turned to look at the castle and the tower rising above its fortifications. Her mother was in there somewhere, so close but impossible to reach—now. But soon Anne would be freed from the place that had been her prison these three years. Warrick would do it. He would not leave here until he did.

Some of the outer walls had suffered damage from a mangonel, though not enough to bring them down or open a small breach for entry. Rowena knew where the postern gate was located, though. She had been taken through it the first time she had left here, when she and her mother were separated. But to tell Warrick about it would tell him she knew Ambray, knew Gilbert, and she could not do that.

But did she dare risk trying to stay here so she could see her mother once the castle was opened? She could refuse to go. If she could just speak with Warrick, she knew she could convince him to let her stay or at least remain near. But how could she then get to her mother without Warrick being present to witness it? She could not, and Anne would not think to pretend she did not know Rowena.

'Twas best she did leave, though 'twas maddening to know that she could do naught to help her mother escape that place any sooner than Warrick could—at least not without detriment to herself. And as her help was in no wise guaranteed to work, 'twas best left unoffered.

But soon Anne **would** be freed. And Warrick would either send her to her dower lands, which she could hold closed to Gilbert—though he was unlikely to bother to try and get her back when he no longer needed her for a hold against Rowena or aught else—or Warrick would send Anne to Fulkhurst until this war was over. There Rowena would have a better opportunity to warn her mother not to know her—at least not in Warrick's presence. And they would be together again, finally.

❧ 44

Warrick castigated himself for the hundredth time for giving in to his needs and sending for Rowena. It did not make it better, his seeing her. It had been sweet, so sweet, but his craving was now worse, for now he wanted to be with her more than ever—and she had been gone only two days.

What the brief visit did, however, was make him determined to end this siege in a more aggressive manner. He increased the work on the two towers so they would be ready for the morn, and started work on two others. He sent out patrols to find him more boulders and heavy missiles for the mangonel. From the village were rounded up all large cauldrons to be packed with dirt and small stones for improvised boulders. He laid plans for a tunnel to be started if the attack on the morrow failed, though he had no miners in his ranks to oversee that last resort.

That evening he inspected the finished wooden

tower he would ride in himself. He meant to be on the top platform when it was pushed to the moat and tilted until it spanned the water and settled against the walls. 'Twould be on fire by then, for flamed arrows would be shot at it as soon as it was in range, so the whole process had to be accomplished with the greatest speed ere it became a fiery grave for those concealed within. But in being a shielded ladder, it still offered the most protection for those men he had picked to take the walls, then fight their way down to open the gates for the rest of the army. And he meant to be one of them, in on the first fighting, not the last.

He was giving orders to have the two towers doused again with water when Sheldon found him. "This ought to amuse you, Warrick," he said as he dragged forth a very frightened, very wet woman. "She claims she and her lady have caused half the castle garrison to sicken. This was done so that we can take the castle this very night, with little to no effort."

"Is that so?" Warrick's tone matched Sheldon's for dryness. "And when we leap on this unexpected though naturally welcome aid, I am certain to lose half **my** army in the trap." His voice had turned to a growl ere he finished, and continued so. "Do they think me a lackwit, to fall for such a common trick? And to use a woman! Get the truth from her, I care not how."

The woman burst into tears upon hearing that. "Nay, please! 'Tis true what I claim. My lady bears no love for the new lord, and did despise his father. Ambray has been a prison to us. We want only to leave!"

"**You** found your way out, wench," Sheldon pointed out. "So could your lady. Why did you both not just go, instead of concocting—"

"Because I need an escort to my dower property if I am to arrive there safely," Anne said as she was brought up behind Sheldon. "I thought to assist you in getting what you want, which appears to be Ambray, in exchange for that escort."

"My lady, ye should have waited!" the servant wailed. "Ye should not—"

"Be quiet, Helvise!" the lady snapped. "I had no patience to wait when that gate stood unguarded. And I would rather be here than in there, whether we are believed or not."

She was as soaked as her servant from having crossed the moat without the aid of a bridge, but she held herself regally despite the guard, who still clasped her arm in his rough grip. Sheldon stared at her in bemused attraction, for she was a comely woman, apparent even in her bedraggled state. Warrick stared at her just as bemused, for she seemed familiar to him, though he had never met her.

"So we are to believe you, lady, merely because you say 'tis so?" Warrick asked skeptically.

Then Sheldon inquired, "Who are you, lady?"

"Anne Belleme."

Warrick snorted. "Belleme now d'Ambray."

"Nay, I do not recognize that name as mine, since the priest did not hear a yea from me to consent to that forced marriage. 'Twas a farce that has kept me prisoner here for three years."

"Then if you had the means to aid us to put an end to your imprisonment, why did you wait this long?" Warrick demanded. "We did not only just come, lady. We have been camped here for thirty-three days."

That Warrick was counting the days to know them exactly elicited a chuckle from Sheldon, which brought Anne's eyes to him. She blinked to see that he was not as old as he had seemed at first glance. When he smiled at her, she blushed, for she did not find him unattractive. Nay, just the opposite.

Warrick scowled at both of them for their sudden distraction with each other that was not getting him answers. "Do you **mind**, Sheldon?"

"Actually, I think the Lady Anne should be made dry ere you continue—"

"There is no time for that," Anne interrupted. "The malaise that has struck so many of the garrison will not last beyond the emptying of their bellies. We did but add fouled meat to their dinner, which all have not eaten yet."

"You still have not said why you would do this now," Warrick pointed out.

"If you are Lord of Fulkhurst . . . ?" She waited for him to confirm it, which he did with a curt nod, then she explained. "I was told horrible tales about you, so that I would add my prayers to others that you would not be successful here. But when I saw you had my daughter in your camp, and she appeared well and healthy, I realized I had been lied to."

"Daughter?" He snorted. "You think you have a daughter in **my** camp, lady? Well, you are welcome to look for her, but 'tis doubtful my men will want to give her up if you think to take her away."

What he was implying had her blushing furiously. "My daughter is **not** one of your camp followers. I know not how she came to be no longer in Gilbert's foul care and with you instead, for he made no mention that he had lost her. Nay, he took pleasure in telling me she had done everything that he—"

"Is d'Ambray in the castle, then?" Warrick cut in impatiently, not interested in her family woes.

She shook her head, bringing a foul curse from him and the gentle query from Sheldon: "Did he escape?"

"Nay. He had come here in the most horrid rage. I thought surely he must have lost another castle, to put him in so dark a mood. But he stayed here less than a sennight, and in fact, left the day before you arrived."

That brought another foul curse from Warrick. "Know you where he has gone?"

"To court. His resources are so depleted, he cannot continue this war with you without aid from Stephen. But that has been tried before and is not like to do him any more good now than then, for the d'Ambrays have not been on the king's list of favorites since Hugh sided against Stephen on some matter several years ago. Verily, in rescuing my daughter from Gilbert's clutches, you have wrested her remaining properties from his control. Do you take Ambray, all Gilbert will have left is one small keep in—"

"Lady, I do **not** have your daughter," Warrick interrupted in exasperation. "Think you I would not make good use of Lord Belleme's only heir if I had gained such a prize? As you say, control of her would deplete d'Ambray's last resources."

"I do not know why you insist—" Anne began, only to frown. "Can it be you do not know who she is?"

"God's blood, I have heard enough of this!" Warrick exploded. "Sheldon, **you** deal with her."

"That will be my pleasure," Sheldon said, starting to laugh. "But before you stomp away, why do you not ask her for her daughter's name—or has it not occurred to you yet who this lady so closely resembles?"

Warrick looked hard at his friend, then at the

lady. Then he became very still. He did not curse again as he saw why she was familiar to him, but his voice was as coldly chilling as it could get.

"So tell me, Lady Anne, what is your daughter's name?"

She was not at all sure she wanted to answer him now. She had never seen anyone change so suddenly in appearance, to where he now looked—cruel. She took a step back. Sheldon put his arm around her shoulder, which was a great comfort, but still . . .

"Mayhap I am mistaken—"

"Nay, you were not, but I was, to think I could trust that deceitful witch!"

"Why is he so angry?" Anne asked Sheldon as Warrick walked away from them. "It **was** Rowena I saw, was it not?"

"Aye, and you were correct also in thinking she did not tell him who she was."

"If she did not, she must have had good reason."

"I doubt my friend will think so," Sheldon replied, but when he saw Anne's anxious expression, he assured her, "He will not harm her. And he is sure to rid himself of his anger he is like to get rid of immediately by entering the castle now, whether he still thinks a trap is waiting for him or not. He is that angry."

"But I did not lie. The postern gate is open and unguarded."

"Then come, I will take you to my tent, where you can wait until this is over."

✤ 45

Rowena saw the two guards walking so deter-
minedly toward her that she knew. Before they
opened their mouths, she knew. They did not have
to tell her. But they did.

"We have a message from Lord Warrick, Mistress. You are to abide in the dungeon henceforth."

She had known they would say exactly that; still
she turned ashen to have it confirmed. "Did he—
say for how long?"

"Henceforth," was repeated.

That, of course, was indefinitely—or forever.
"Did he say why?"

Stupid question. Why was she torturing herself?

She had known this would happen if Warrick
found out Gilbert d'Ambray was her stepbrother.
She should have taken her courage in hand and
told him herself when she'd had the opportunity.
She would have faced his anger, true, but she
would have been there to try and soothe it, at least
to tell him why she had kept silent. Alone, he had

concluded the worst, and now wanted naught more to do with her, wanted revenge—nay, this was not that. This was pure fury, and final.

The guards had merely shaken their heads to her question, then directed her to come with them. She did. What choice did she have? At least she had been alone in the hall when they had come for her. Emma had not been there to protest, nor Mildred, which would likely have brought Rowena to tears. It was all she could do now to hold them back in front of the two guards.

Aye, she had known Warrick would do this to her—but deep down she had not thought he really would.

When the jailer she dreaded showed up with his leering grin to gloat that she was to be in his care again, Rowena turned her back on him ere she was sick. 'Twas not the babe making her feel so. 'Twas the tightness in her chest that was turning hollow. Now she wished the tears would come, but they would not.

When John Giffard arrived not an hour later to tell her he had had to clout the other one this time to get him to leave, she had only one question for him. "Are you here at Warrick's behest?"

"Nay, my lady. The word has spread fast that you were brought here again. I came as soon as I heard."

At that point she cried. Why John had been given to her the last time she did not know. She had never asked. But that he was not this time was self-explanatory. Warrick did not care what happened to her now, as long as she was locked away where he would never have to lay eyes on her again.

A while later she heard an argument out in the guardroom. She recognized Mildred's voice. She and John had become very friendly of late. Just now they were not. When silence returned, Rowena knew John had won, knew also what the argument had likely been about. Mildred was not to be allowed to see her, nor would John go against his lord to let Rowena out.

Two more hours passed, then John came again to open her door. "He has changed his mind, my lady. I knew he would, but—You are to be locked in his solar instead of here, with a guard at the door."

"What if I prefer it here?" she wanted to know.

"You do not mean that."

"Aye, I do."

John sighed. "The guard has his orders. He will drag you from here do you not go on your own."

"Then by all means, I shall walk."

"Take heart—"

"Nay, John," she cut him off curtly. "Mine is dead now, for it hurts no longer."

God's mercy, why could that not be true? She prayed for blessed numbness, yet it would not come with this much pain. But no one was going to know that, not John, and especially not Warrick.

No hope came to her from the change in prisons. Warrick must have merely recalled that she was carrying his child. Obviously he had forgotten that in his first rage, and it must have enraged him more when he remembered and thus had to make allowances for her just to protect the child. She did not think for a moment that he had any other reason for moving her to a more comfortable prison.

She was allowed to see no one except the guard, who handed her food to her each day. Every time she had tried to speak to him, she had gotten grunts or mutters in answer, so she did not try anymore. Verily, she **would** have preferred to stay in the dungeon with John.

She sat often in the window embrasure, from where she could look out on the side yard. Not much activity ever happened down there, but 'twas a better view than none at all. She sewed a lot, too, for the child that was nigh three months along, soft chemises for Emma—naught at all for Warrick. What she had made for Warrick ere he left for Ambray she now ripped apart to make tiny tunics for the babe.

No one had told her aught about the siege at Ambray. For Warrick to have learned the truth of who she was, he had to have taken the castle. Had Gilbert been there? Was he captured or dead? Was her mother all right? Free? In a new prison as a result of Warrick's fury?

She counted the days. For each one that passed, she stabbed a hole as deeply as she could with her small eating knife in one of the carved bedposts. They had been fine bedposts, richly detailed. Now there were twenty-five unsightly holes that she took to admiring. Before the twenty-sixth could be added, Warrick returned.

Rowena had had no warning. He was just there, walking into the room, stopping before the window embrasure, where she sat with her feet propped up on the opposite seat, her hands on her belly, which was thickened, but not yet rounded. She had been trying to determine if the fluttering she had felt was the child or indigestion. Her first look at Warrick, and she decided 'twas **going** to be indigestion.

"So the mighty warlord returns," she said, not caring whether he liked her sneering tone or not. "Did you kill Gilbert?"

"I have not found him yet, though not for lack of hunting him these weeks past."

"So that is why you did not return here? But there was no hurry to return here, was there? You sent your orders. That was sufficient."

"God's blood, do you dare—!"

He stopped when she looked away from him to stare out the window, deliberately ignoring him.

She was not frightened or contrite. Her expression was calmness itself. He had not expected that, but then, he had not given what he did expect much thought, for he had forced her from his mind to concentrate solely on finding d'Ambray. But he found now that he did **not** like her undertone of resentment. And the anger he had felt that night he met her mother was starting to rekindle.

He sat down on the opposite bench to face her. "Such an innocent demeanor to hide such deceit," he remarked coldly.

She glanced at him with raised brows to ask quietly, "When was I deceitful? At Kirkburough when I knew not who you were? Or at Kirkburough when you came with your army to kill my stepbrother, knowing not who he really was? But I thought you were there for Gilbert d'Ambray, your avowed enemy, so aye, I should have told you then, when I was sure you would kill me as well if you knew he was my stepbrother. Or mayhap I should have told you when you took me out of your dungeon the first time to explain to me how you were going to have your revenge. Was I to tell you then, Warrick, to add to what you had already planned for me?"

"You **knew** I would not kill you!"

"Not **then** I did not!"

They glared at each other. Rowena was in no wise calm now. There were twenty-five days of repressed anger glittering in her eyes. His had turned to silver ice.

"What excuse do you offer for your later silence, wench, when you escaped, only to have d'Ambray return you? Did he send you back to spy on me?"

"I am sure he would have asked me to if he had thought of it. But until you arrived, he thought he had won the day, that he would have the means to bring you to your knees. When you did arrive, he had no time to think of aught but escaping himself. But I did not tell you then that he was d'Ambray, for the same reason I did not tell you when you summoned me to his castle. I did not want to face your anger again—or **this**." She waved a hand to indicate her imprisonment.

"And I am to believe that, when 'tis more likely that you and d'Ambray go hand in hand in this deceit? He left you at Kirkburough for me to find," he reminded her harshly. "Was I to become smitten with you and tell you all my plans?"

"He assumed you would make terms with me. But I was left there because he panicked. You were approaching with five hundred men, while he had only a handful remaining. He intended to come back with Lyons' army, which had been sent to retake Tures from you. Possibly he hoped I would distract you long enough for him to get away. More like he thought I would slow him down if he took me along. Whatever ran through his mind that day besides fear and rage, I know not. But I do know 'twas not his intention to leave me with you any longer than it would take him to return. And he did return. When he found me that day in the woods, he told me he thought you had killed me."

Warrick snorted. "Very cleverly said, wench, but I do not believe a word of it."

"Think you I care anymore what you believe? Last month I would have, but now I do not."

"Your circumstance depends on what I believe, wench," he reminded her.

"My **circumstance** cannot be any more wretched."

"Can it not?" he replied with quiet menace. "I ought to punish you properly, not just curtail your freedom."

That brought her to her feet in a burst of wrath. "Go ahead, damn you! Do it! It will not make me despise you more than I do now."

"Sit down," he growled low.

She did not, not by him. She stalked around the fireplace to the other window and took a bench there, her stiff back half turned away from the room. She stared blindly out the window, seething so much her hands trembled in her lap. She hated him. Despised him. She wished he . . . she hated him!

She heard him behind her, come to block the opening of the other window embrasure so she could not leave it without pushing him out of the way. As if she could, and she resented that fact, too.

"You have not acquitted yourself, wench. Verily, I am not like to believe aught you say ever again. What you did was akin to betrayal. Had you told me it was d'Ambray on my land, I would have run him to ground despite the blackness of the night. Had you told me you were Rowena of Tures, I could have secured your remaining properties the sooner, thereby—"

"The sooner?" she cut in scathingly. "You do not think I will help you to secure them now, do you? I would not help you were you—"

"Be quiet!" he snapped. "Your resentment is misplaced, wench. I could not leave you free to communicate with that devil's spawn, and I doubt it not that he has secreted someone here to carry your messages to him. I needs now interrogate my own people to be rid of any who were not here ere you came, be they innocent or not. Be grateful I did not leave you in the dungeon."

"Grateful for this tomb, where I have had no one to speak to since I was shut in here? Aye, I am grateful," she sneered derisively.

Silence greeted that. She did not turn to see if he showed any contrition, if he had even realized what he was sentencing her to when he had ordered her confined. In his rage he had condemned her without trial, without even asking if she was guilty. That damn pain she had thought would have gone numb by now was becoming more acute, twisting in her chest, tightening in her throat.

Finally she heard him sigh. "You will return to your duties, those first given to you. But you will be watched, doubt it not. And never again will you be trusted."

"When was I ever trusted?" she asked in a small, bitter voice, the pain nigh choking her.

"When you shared my bed, wench, I trusted you not to betray me."

"Nor did I. What I did is called self-preservation."

"Your pretense of wanting me?"

She would have liked to say, "Aye, that, too," but she would not lie to hurt him as he was hurting her. "Nay, my silence. But you need not worry that my unseemly behavior of the past will bother you again. Whatever I felt for you is no longer there."

"Damn you, Rowena, you will **not** make me regret my actions! 'Tis you—"

"Spare me any more recriminations. There is naught else I want to hear from you, except—tell me what you did with my mother."

He was silent for so long, she did not think he would answer her. He was cruel enough to leave her wondering—nay, not that cruel.

"I gave her into the care of my friend, Sheldon

de Vere. She assisted me in taking Ambray Castle. For that she has my gratitude. She also assisted in opening your remaining properties, which **you** should have done. D'Ambray's men were ousted with little bloodshed. He no longer has control of aught that is yours."

She did not thank him for that. **He** now had control of all that was hers, as well as herself, and he was not like to ever relinquish it.

Quietly, without looking back at him, with despair about to crush her, she said, "That day you came triumphant to Kirkburough, I had intended to offer you my wardship—despite all the horrible tales I had heard of you—if you had proved to be just a little less despicable than Gilbert . . . but you did not. You sent me straightaway to your dungeon. Small wonder I never got around to telling you who I was."

He walked out ere her tears betrayed her.

❧ 46

The resumption of Rowena's previous duties did not lift the gloom that had come to Fulkhurst. Mary Blouet was not happy to have charge of her again. Melisant cried frequently. Mildred grumbled constantly. Emma gave her father such baleful looks that he ought to have reprimanded her for them, but he did not. And the hall was so subdued at meals that even a cough was embarrassing.

Rowena refused to speak of it to anyone, including Mildred, whom she was annoyed with for instigating a plan that had so horribly backfired on her. Warrick had not been caught by it, **she** had, and so she listened to Mildred now with a closed ear and few, if any, comments.

The weeks that followed were much like her first days serving Warrick, with a few notable exceptions. She was not called to assist him at his bath now, or in his bed. Nor did she receive any of those humorless smiles she had hated. He barely looked at her at all, but when he did, his face was devoid of expression. She was no more than what he had first intended her to be, a servant beneath his notice. Perversely, she stopped wearing her own clothes, though he had not insisted on that. But if she would be no more than a servant, then she would look like no more than a servant.

She still instructed Emma when she had time to spare. That she enjoyed doing, and so tried to keep her own feelings from the girl; these waxed between depression and bitterness, then just bitterness. She took even more pains, however, to keep her emotions from Warrick's notice.

But then the day came that Emma was taken from her, sent to Sheldon's home for her wedding to young Richard. Rowena was not allowed to witness it. She had sewn the gown Emma would be married in, but she was not there to see her wear it.

That was the day she stopped keeping her resentment to herself.

Warrick noticed the change immediately. Twice in one day food was dumped in his lap. Both times could not be accidents. He could no longer find clothes in his coffer that were not in need of some kind of repair. By week's end his chamber was filthy. The linens on his bed had not been rinsed properly, which caused him a rash. His wine became more and more sour, his ale more and more warm, the food she now slammed down in front of him more and more salty.

He said naught to her about any of it. He did not trust himself to speak to her at all without dragging her off to his bed. He wanted her so badly it took his every effort not to touch her. But he would not. She had deceived him. She had plotted with his enemy against him. Her laughter, her teasing, her desire for him—all lies. Yet he could not hate her. He would never forgive her, never touch her again, never let her know how vulnerable she had made him, but he could not hate her—or stop wanting her.

He knew not why he stayed there to torture himself. He ought to go and hunt for d'Ambray himself, instead of sending others to do it. Or visit Sheldon and his new wife. Had he told someone to mention the marriage to Rowena? He must not have, for surely that would have put a halt, at least temporarily, to whatever maggoty bit of resentment she was indulging. As if she had reason to be resentful. **He** did, but she did not.

Though he should leave, he did not. So he was there two days later when Sheldon showed up with his new wife.

Warrick met them on the stairs to the keep. Sheldon merely grinned in greeting and told him to "brace himself," before he went on into the hall, leaving Warrick alone with the Lady Anne. Her tight-lipped expression gave him warning of what was to come. It came without preamble.

"I am here to see my daughter, and do not think to deny me, sirrah. Your own daughter has just confided to me the atrocious treatment Rowena has had at your hands. I am not sure I can forgive Sheldon for not telling me himself. Had I known before, I **would** have set a trap for you at Ambray, instead of handing the castle over to you. That any man could be so—"

"Enough, lady! You know naught of what has transpired between Rowena and me. You know naught of what your daughter has done to **me**. She is my prisoner and so she will stay. You may see her, but you may not take her from here. Is that clear to you?"

Anne opened her mouth to argue that point, then closed it. She glared at him for a moment more before she nodded curtly and started to pass him. But she took no more than two steps ere she whirled back around.

"I will **not** be intimidated by you, Lord Warrick. My husband assures me that you have good reason to be the way you are. I doubt that, but he has also told me that you might think Rowena was a willing pawn in Gilbert's schemes."

"I do not think it, I know it," Warrick replied coldly.

"Then you are misinformed," Anne persisted,

but added in a more reasonable tone, "My daughter loves me. Think you she would aid Gilbert in any way after she saw him viciously beat me to get her cooperation?"

Warrick stiffened. "Cooperation for what?"

"Gilbert had made contract with Godwine Lyons for her. She refused. I also disdained the match. He was an old lecher with scandal attached to his name, in no wise her equal. But Lyons had promised Gilbert his army, which he needed to fight you. So he brought her to Ambray and had her restrained to watch while he beat me."

"Why you? Why not her?"

"Because in a twisted way, I think he cares for her. He would not want to mar her beauty, at any rate, when the wedding was to take place as soon as they reached Kirkburough. But he had no difficulty beating me, nor would he have stopped until he had her agreement to marry Lyons. But I thought surely she would balk again once they were away from me. She is stubborn, after all, and not above wanting to ruin Gilbert's plans after what he did to me. But he bragged to me, when he came to Ambray for those few days, that he had completely cowed her, that she would do whatever he required, because he had warned her he would kill me if she did not. I am not sure he would have. He is not as inherently cruel as his father was. Yet would she have believed him. And she would have hated him for—what is wrong?" she gasped when he turned so ashen.

Warrick shook his head, but a groan escaped him as other words came at him from memory, when Rowena had stood over his chained body and explained what she would do. **"I like this no better than you, but I have no choice—and neither do you."** No choice. She had been trying to save her mother's life. She had not wanted to rape him. And she had been so sorry for it that she had accepted his revenge as her due.

"Ahhh!" he roared in anguish, the pain ripping at his chest unbearable.

Anne became alarmed. "Wait, I will get—"

"Nay . . . there is naught wrong with me that a whip would not cure," Warrick said with self-loathing. "You were right to revile me, lady. I am the veriest . . . ah, God, what have I done!"

He ran past her and into the hall. When he passed Sheldon, he told him only, "Keep your wife here," then was running up the stairs.

Rowena was not alone when he found her in the sewing room. Mildred was with her, and three others. They took one look at him and hurried out. Mildred was slower to go. She gave him one of the frigid looks she had been giving him for weeks that he had not noticed. He did not notice now, either, for he was staring only at Rowena.

She stood up and tossed aside the cloth from her

lap, her demeanor what it had been for several weeks, sheer disgruntlement. "Now that you have interrupted our work," she said crossly, "what do you want?"

"I have just spoken with your mother."

Rowena's expression changed to surprised delight. "She is here?"

"Aye, and you can see her anon, but I needs speak with you first."

"Not **now**, Warrick!" she said impatiently. "I have not been with my mother for three years. I saw her only once some months ago, when . . ."

Her words trailed off with a frown, causing him to prompt her. "When what?"

"It does not matter."

"It does. When d'Ambray beat her?"

"She **told** you that?"

"Aye—and more. Why did **you** never tell me he had threatened her life?"

Her eyes flared wide, then lit with a glittering blue fire. "You dare to ask me that? You would not listen to reasons! 'Never mention to me again an excuse for what you did.' **Those** were your words, my lord."

He winced. "I know. At that time, 'tis like to have made no difference if I knew. I was that angry. But **now** it matters." He hesitated then, but he had to know. "Did he also force you to spy on me?"

"I told you, he never thought of that. He was too

busy thinking of how he could use against you the army he had just gained."

Warrick leaned back against the closed door, his expression bleak. "Then I erred even more than I had first thought? My God, you were innocent of it all, even the deceit I most recently accused you of."

Rowena stared at him incredulously. "Innocent of it all? I **raped** you. Are you forgetting that?"

"Nay, I forgave you that. But—"

"**When** did you forgive me?" she demanded. "I heard no words to that effect."

He scowled at the interruption, **and** at her obtuseness. "You know exactly when, wench. 'Twas the day you asked me for a boon—the night you had no sleep."

Color came hotly to her cheeks. "You could have mentioned it," she grumbled, only to add as she recalled these past weeks, "Not that it matters now."

"You are correct. That matters not at all when there was naught for me to forgive. But there is everything for **you** to forgive. Can you?"

She stared hard at him for a long moment, then shrugged indifferently. "Certainly. You are forgiven. Now may I see my mother?"

Warrick frowned. "You cannot absolve me of my guilt that easily."

"Can I not? Why not? Or has it not occurred to you that I simply do not care if you are sorry?"

"You are still angry," he guessed, nodding, as if

that explained her strange behavior. "I cannot blame you. But I will make it up to you. We will be married, and when—"

"I will not marry you," she interrupted quietly—too quietly.

'Twas his turn to stare hard, then to explode. "You must marry me!"

"Why? So you can atone for your guilt?" She shook her head slowly. "Were you not listening the day I told you that whatever I felt for you is no longer there? Why would I want to marry you, Warrick?" And then her composure slipped. "Give me **one good reason!**"

"So our child will not be a bastard!"

She closed her eyes to hide her regret. What had she expected? **Because I love you?**

Rowena sighed. When she looked at him again, she was without expression—just barely.

"Well, there is that," she allowed tonelessly. "But that is not reason enough—"

"Damn it, Rowena, you—!"

"I will **not** marry you!" she shouted back at him, her endurance gone and every bit of her resentment released. "Do you try to force me to do it, I will poison you! I will castrate you whilst you sleep! I will—"

"You need not go further."

He wore the same expression he had duped her with once before, that of a man racked with pain. She did not fall for it this time.

"If you want to atone for your guilt, Warrick, set me free. Relinquish claim to my child and let me go home."

After endless moments Warrick's shoulders drooped—but he nodded.

❧ 47

He did not come. She was to give birth to his daughter any day, nay, any moment now, but he did not come. And it **would** be a daughter, her child. That was a fine little revenge on her part, not to give Warrick the son he so wanted. She had decreed it so, willed it so, so it would be a girl-child. Luck did finally have to come her way **some**time.

But Warrick did not come. Why had she thought he would, just because he had ridden to Tures once a month, every month, since she had left Fulkhurst?

He still wanted to marry her. She still would not. She was rude to him. Twice she had refused to see him at all. But he kept coming back. He kept trying to convince her that she belonged with him.

So he was contrite. What did she care? 'Twas too late.

But he was ruthless about it. He got her mother

on his side, and Anne was very good at badgering. She had been saving it up for three years.

"His wanting to marry you has naught to do with his guilt," Anne had assured her on one of her many visits. "He was going to marry you before he knew he had aught to be guilty about. He made the decision when he brought you to Ambray Castle. Sheldon told me so."

Sheldon was another sore subject. As far as Rowena was concerned, he had stolen her mother from her. He had taken advantage of Anne's vulnerability, seduced her affections, then married her before she could catch her breath. Now he had her convinced that she adored him, when she could not possibly—not a friend of **Warrick**'s.

And then last month, when Rowena's spirits had been particularly low, Anne showed up with another revelation. "He loves you. He told me so himself when I asked if he did."

"Mother!" Rowena had complained, horrified. "How could you ask him that?"

"Because I wanted to know. **You** certainly never bothered to ask."

"Of course I would not," Rowena replied huffily. "If a man cannot say it on his own, without having it pried out of him—"

"That's just it, my dear. When I then asked if he had told you, he said he did not know how."

Her mother would not lie about that—but Warrick would. Tell a mother exactly what she wants to hear. How underhandedly clever of him.

But it meant naught to her. She was not going to break down and marry the man, even if he **was** proving to her that she was not as dead inside as she had thought, that her heart could still race when he was near her—that she could still crave his body, **even in her condition!** But her awakened desires made no difference. She was not going to play the fool again and open her heart to another rending.

Today she sat in the window embrasure of her room. She might be Lady of Tures now, but she had wanted the familiarity of her old chamber when she arrived here, rather than the much larger solar.

She patted the cushioned seat under her, smiling smugly because it was so much nicer than Warrick's hard benches in his window alcoves. Of course, he had two windows, while she had only the one, and his had costly glass, whereas hers had been broken during one of the recent sieges. It now had just a thin oilcloth covering that she could barely see through ordinarily, but it had come loose and was flapping in the April wind, giving her clear glimpses of the road that snaked around to the gatehouse. 'Twas still empty, that road, except for a traveling merchant and his baggage wain that could not hold her interest.

'Twas not the first time the window had been broken. She had broken it herself when she was nine, an accident, but it had not been replaced for nearly two years. The window overlooked the forebuilding, which was one story lower than the tower. Its top floor housed the chapel, and 'twas the roof of this that she looked down on just six feet below her window, though a little to the left of it, for the front wall of the forebuilding was actually directly below it.

Rowena had jumped out that window once before it was repaired, landing right on the foot-wide battlements, then hopping down the other three feet to the chapel roof. She had done it on a dare to frighten another maid.

She had frightened the other girl, all right, who had run straight to Anne screaming that Rowena was dead, fallen out the window straight down to the forebuilding stairs, which **did** happen to be under the left half of her window, and two stories down. Rowena had wished she **were** dead after the tongue-lashing she had received, as well as confinement in her room for . . . she could not remember how long now.

She smiled with the memory as she patted the huge girth of her belly. Her own daughter would never do anything so foolish, not with the iron bars Rowena would have installed over her windows. But she could now understand her mother's frightened rage. She **could** have killed herself. One slight misstep and she would have tumbled . . .

"Daydreaming, my lady?"

Rowena went deathly still. It could not be. But she turned, and it was Gilbert inside her door, closing her door, walking toward her.

"How did you get through the gates?"

He laughed. "That was the easy part. Today is merchants' day, when they come up from the town to tempt your ladies to part with a few coins. So today I am a merchant. 'Tis getting an army inside that is difficult, not one man."

"Do you still have an army to speak of?"

That got rid of his good-humored boasting. "Nay, but—Mary be praised!" he exclaimed when he was close enough to see her rounded form. "So it worked."

That calculating look came over him, where she could almost hear the exact bent of his greedy thoughts. "You will **not** claim this is Lyons' child. I will deny it—and Warrick de Chaville knows better."

"That is right," he snarled. "**He** had you!"

"**You** gave me to him!" she shouted back. "Or do you forget that it was your idea, **your** greed—?"

"Be quiet!" he hissed, looking back nervously at the door. "It matters not whom the child belongs to, as long as I can make use of it."

She stared at him wide-eyed. "You **do** still think to claim Kirkburough? How can you?"

"I have to. I have naught else. Even now that bastard has besieged my last keep. I cannot go there. I have nowhere to go, Rowena."

She realized he wanted her to understand and mayhap feel sympathy for him. She wondered if Warrick had driven him a little crazy in his relentless hounding of him. Or was this what desperation did to a man?

Her brows narrowed suspiciously. "That cannot be why you came here, for you knew naught about the child. What did you come here for, Gilbert?"

"To marry you."

"You **are** mad!"

"Nay, you have back all of your properties, all in your control," he said, explaining his reasoning. " 'Tis profitable to wed you now, for as your husband—"

"I swore fealty to Warrick," she lied. "He will not let you have me."

"He cannot stop me. Let him try. He will have to retake those castles he gave back to you, as well as your others. He will deplete his own resources this time, and then I will have him at last."

"Gilbert, **why** can you not give this up? You have lost. Why do you not leave the country while you still can? Go to Louis's court, or Henry's. Start anew."

"I have not lost, now that I have you."

"But you do not have me," she told him calmly. "If I would not marry Warrick, whom I love,

God knows I would not marry you, whom I detest. I would as soon jump out this window. Shall I prove it?"

"Do not speak foolishness!" he snapped, furious at her threat **and** her revelation of her love for his enemy. But at the moment, he was more concerned with the threat, for she sat too close to that window. "If—if you do not want me to bed you, then I will not, but I have to marry you, Rowena. I have no choice now."

"Nay, you do have a choice," Warrick said from the doorway. "Draw your sword and I will show you."

Rowena was so startled by his appearance, she did not have a chance to react when Gilbert leaped toward her and placed a dagger at her throat.

"Drop your own sword, Fulkhurst, or she dies," Gilbert ordered, his voice almost exultant with triumph.

"Warrick, do not!" Rowena cried, assuring him, "He will not kill me."

But Warrick was not listening to her. He was already throwing his sword down. That easily would he give away his life? Why, unless . . . ?

"Come here now," Gilbert ordered him.

Rowena's eyes flared incredulously when Warrick took a step forward without the least hesitation. He was actually going to walk to Gilbert and just let him kill him. Nay, not while she still had her wits about her.

Gilbert stood near her, but closer to the entrance to the alcove than across from her. His dagger was not even touching the skin at her throat, and his eyes were only on Warrick.

Rowena drew her knees up and kicked him toward Warrick, then immediately swung her legs over the window ledge and slipped outside. She heard both men shout her name as her feet touched on the flat square of the battlements with a jarring impact. God's mercy, it had been so easy when she was younger—and not so encumbered. Jumping the last three feet to the roof of the chapel was out of the question. She was carefully sitting down on the edge of the wall to ease herself the rest of the way down when Gilbert stuck his head out the window and saw her.

"Damn you, Rowena, you frightened me half to death!" he roared at her.

Only half? God's mercy, **when** was she going to get lucky?

But he did not stay there to berate her further. The sound of swords meeting in deadly combat came clearly through the window to tell her what had distracted him. So the two of them had finally got their wish to kill each other? Never mind that she was out here sitting on the edge of the battlements wall with a hundred-foot drop to the bailey at her back—well, seventy-five feet mayhap, since the forebuilding was not as high as the tower.

The cramp caught her unawares, making her

sway, then gasp as she nearly lost her balance. Heart racing, she no longer took her time getting to the roof, but jumped the remaining distance. 'Twas another jarring landing, and another cramp protested it. She bent over this time, holding her breath until it eased, but then a cold chill passed over her. Nay, not now. Her daughter could not want to be born **now**.

She glanced back at her window as she got a firm footing on the two-foot-wide stone wall-walk that surrounded the flat wooden roof of the chapel. Though she was compelled to get back up there to watch what was happening in her room, she doubted she could manage it without help. Getting down off the three-foot-high battlements was one thing, climbing back onto the narrow, crenellated edge of it quite another. She **could** do it, but she was too unwieldy in shape just now to make it a safe undertaking.

There was the large trapdoor in the chapel roof, however, near her feet. It allowed men up here during an attack, to shoot arrows from the cover of the crenellations. It dropped down about twenty feet to the chapel, but required a ladder to be used. 'Twas the only entry to these battlements aside from her window.

No ladder would be there now, she knew, but she threw open the door anyway and leaned over to look down. Father Paul was not likely to be there either this late of the morn, but she called his name anyway. As expected, there was no response, so she merely shouted "Help!" instead.

That got her more response than she wanted. A servant came running into the chapel, but he was no more than a boy, and all he did was stare up at her in amazement. And before she could tell him to fetch a ladder, Gilbert was climbing out on the window ledge with sword in hand.

"Move back!" he shouted at her just before he jumped straight to the wall-walk.

But Rowena did not move, too paralyzed with fear that his appearance meant Warrick was dead. He bumped into her when he landed, not hard, but enough to send her back a few feet. He was already weary from fighting Warrick. One of his legs buckled as he landed on the stone walk, and he fell toward the roof. But his knee came down right into the opening of the trapdoor. That threw him even more off balance, and he would have fallen right through the hole, but his belly struck hard against the edge of the trap, holding his body there. He had been hurt, the breath knocked out of him, his sword skidding across the roof, yet he was able to climb out of the hole easily enough.

And Rowena just stood there, numb with the thought that Warrick was dead. She made no move to push Gilbert through the hole while she had the chance, no move to get his sword and toss it over the wall. She just stood there, spellbound with horror . . . until Warrick landed right in front of her.

She shrieked in startlement, moved back yet again, coming up against the low wall behind her. He just grinned at her in reassurance, then went right after Gilbert, who had already retrieved his sword.

Her relief was cut short by another pain, not as sharp as the others, but deeper, and worse for that. She ignored it, however, watching the two men hacking away at each other.

They moved back and forth across the small area. Rowena moved out of the way when necessary, careful to avoid the trapdoor, which was still open, as well as the swinging swords. More pains came that she continued to ignore. But finally the fight was confined to the area opposite the trapdoor, so she was able to move to it to find out what was keeping help from arriving. Help had come. More servants were below, grouped around the altar cloth they were holding, and one shouted up for her to jump.

Idiots! She was not a lightweight to go bouncing on altar cloths. She would rip that thin cloth in twain, if it did not rip out of their hands with her landing. Either way, she would end up flat on the stone floor, most likely dead.

But suddenly the choice was taken out of her hands as the fight came back her way. Gilbert backed into her unawares, shoving her right into the hole. She screamed as she felt naught but air beneath her feet. He turned and grabbed her with his free arm, but her extra weight caught him off guard, and he had to drop his sword to use two arms to keep her from disappearing through the hole. He turned his back on Warrick to do this, with no thought other than of saving Rowena.

She held on to him for dear life, and was too shaken to release him even after she was yanked away from the hole and had purchase for her feet again.

Warrick, forgotten for the while, brought himself back to mind. "Step away from her, d'Ambray."

The inherent threat in those words, as well as the sword point that came across Rowena's shoulder to press against Gilbert's chest, was incentive to do as told. But Gilbert did not release her, his hands tightened on her instead, and Rowena knew him well enough to know where his thoughts were going.

"He will not believe a threat to my life after you have just saved it," she told him.

The expression those words brought to Warrick's face was almost comical in its frustration. Rowena turned in time to see it and was disgusted in reading it correctly. He truly did not want to let Gilbert go now that he had him, but to kill him now would not be part of their knightly code of fair exchanges. A saved life was **always** worth a just reward. But this life in particular Rowena still found despicable. If Warrick had to turn forgiving, could he not have waited a few more— Forgiving? Warrick? Had the vengeful dragon of the north really changed that much?

He had, but he was not exactly happy about it himself. His snarl was less than gracious as he lowered his sword. "I give you your life do you trouble me no more."

Gilbert had never been one to thumb his nose at a golden opportunity. "Give me back Ambray as well."

Rowena gasped at Gilbert's audacity. "Nay, Warrick, do not! He does not deserve—"

"**I** will decide what your life is worth, Rowena," Warrick cut in. "As it happens, a castle—nay, a hundred castles—cannot compare with what you mean to me."

Not very romantically put, to be compared to stone edifices, but 'twas the meaning behind the words that counted and rendered her speechless, long enough for Warrick to tell Gilbert, "You would have to swear vassalage to me."

Gilbert did not hesitate, amused at the irony of having Warrick sworn to protect **him**. "Done. And Rowena—"

The sword came back up, and Warrick's expression was now dangerous rather than just chagrined. "Rowena will be my wife once she agrees. In either case, she will never be in your care again. Tempt me not to change my mind, d'Ambray. Take what I offer and count yourself fortunate that I no longer require absolute vengeance."

That got Rowena released, and she was snatched immediately into Warrick's arms. The hard contact brought along another pain, however, to remind her that she had no more time for their squabbles.

"If you two are finished, my daughter would like to be born now, Warrick, and not out here on the battlements." Both men just stared at her in bemusement, so she added with a lot more volume, "**Now**, Warrick!" and got better results. Panic, actually. Verily, men were ofttimes useless. . . .

❧ 48

"And what was that swearing about after 'twas over?" Mildred wanted to know as she laid the baby in Rowena's arms. "You did good, my sweet one. He is the veriest angel, the veriest—"

"**He** should have been a she," Rowena grumbled, though she could not hold her sour expression once she looked down at her precious, golden-haired baby.

Mildred was chuckling. "You cannot still be holding that grudge. Look how many months you made the man suffer. I felt so sorry for him."

"You did not," Rowena countered. "You were the only one who did not try to get me to change my mind."

"Only because I knew your stubbornness would dig in its heels even deeper with any more pushing. There was no reasoning with you on the subject. You had to figure out for yourself that the man loves you. But did you have to make him wait until the last minute to wed him?"

"Wait?" Rowena said incredulously. "He did not fetch the midwife, he fetched the priest! And none of them would leave until they had an 'aye' from me. That was blackmail. That was—"

"Pure stubbornness on your part. You knew you were going to wed him. You just had to make him suffer right to the end."

Rowena snapped her mouth shut. Arguing with Mildred these days was like pulling hairs. She lost a lot of hair.

Of course, she **was** just being stubborn. The man had been willing to die for her. No grudge could hold up against that.

"Where is my—husband?"

"Waiting without to see his son. Do I show him, or will you?"

Not waiting for an answer, Mildred was already walking to the door to bring Warrick in. Then he was there, looking down at her with such warmth and pride in his eyes that the last of her animosity fled. She did love him, after all. That had been made clear to her in so many ways long before she'd left him that it was useless to deny it any longer.

She smiled shyly up at him. "What do you think of him?"

Warrick had not even looked at the baby yet. He did now, but his eyes came right back to hers, and there was humor in them. "I trust his looks will improve with time?"

She looked down at her son in alarm, but was soon chuckling. "There is naught wrong with the way he looks. He is supposed to be red and wrinkly."

"What happened to the daughter you hoped to give me?"

She flushed, then grinned. "I believe I finally got lucky, my lord—not to get that particular wish."

He sat down on the bed to surprise her with a kiss. "Thank you."

" 'Twas not so difficult—well, mayhap a little."

"Nay, I thank you for marrying me."

"Oh," she said, filling with such warm feelings she felt like laughing. "That was actually . . . my pleasure."

That got her another kiss, one not so tender. "You are no longer angry with me?"

"Nay, but if you ever send me to your dungeon again—"

"I no longer have one. 'Twas torn down after you came here to Tures."

"Why did you do that?" she asked in surprise.

" 'Twas an unbearable reminder of what I had done."

"But you had reason, Warrick. Even I can—"

"Do not make excuses for me, wench—or have you so soon forgotten the words you threw back at me?"

He was serious, but there was self-mockery

there, too. "Very well, suffer a little longer if you must. But 'twas a waste of a good dungeon do you ask me."

Her sigh made him chuckle. "Mayhap I did act too hastily. I can always have it excavated again."

"You had better not, my lord," she warned with mock fierceness.

"Then if I ever find the need to lock you in my solar again—I will be sure to be locked in with you."

"Now **that** I will not object to."

"So you are still a brazen wench?"

"You do not mind my brazenness."

"Nay, I do not."

"And you love me."

"All right, I love you."

"Do not say it as if you are indulging me. You do love me, Warrick. How can you not when I—"

"I **do** love you, wench."

That sounded much better, so much better she drew him down for another kiss, then the soft whisper, "I am glad 'twas you, Warrick. So glad."

He remembered those words, spoken so long ago, and admitted finally, "So am I, my lady. So, too, am I."

M. Walker 2010